Sustaining Faith

Books by Janette Oke and Laurel Oke Logan

WHEN HOPE CALLS

Unyielding Hope • *Sustaining Faith*

RETURN TO THE CANADIAN WEST

Where Courage Calls • *Where Trust Lies* • *Where Hope Prevails*

Dana's Valley

Also look for *Janette Oke: A Heart for the Prairie* by Laurel Oke Logan

Books by Janette Oke

*Return to Harmony** • *Another Homecoming** • *Tomorrow's Dream**

ACTS OF FAITH*

The Centurion's Wife • *The Hidden Flame* • *The Damascus Way*

CANADIAN WEST

When Calls the Heart • *When Comes the Spring* •*When Breaks the Dawn*
When Hope Springs New • *Beyond the Gathering Storm* • *When Tomorrow Comes*

LOVE COMES SOFTLY

Love Comes Softly • *Love's Enduring Promise* • *Love's Long Journey*
Love's Abiding Joy • *Love's Unending Legacy* • *Love's Unfolding Dream*
Love Takes Wing • *Love Finds a Home*

A PRAIRIE LEGACY

The Tender Years • *A Searching Heart* •*A Quiet Strength* • *Like Gold Refined*

SEASONS OF THE HEART

Once Upon a Summer • *The Winds of Autumn*
Winter Is Not Forever • *Spring's Gentle Promise*

SONG OF ACADIA*

The Meeting Place • *The Sacred Shore* • *The Birthright*
The Distant Beacon • *The Beloved Land*

WOMEN OF THE WEST

The Calling of Emily Evans • *Julia's Last Hope* • *Roses for Mama*
A Woman Named Damaris • *They Called Her Mrs. Doc*
The Measure of a Heart • *A Bride for Donnigan* • *Heart of the Wilderness*
Too Long a Stranger • *The Bluebird and the Sparrow*
A Gown of Spanish Lace • *Drums of Change*

* with Davis Bunn

WHEN HOPE CALLS

BOOK TWO

Sustaining Faith

JANETTE OKE

LAUREL OKE LOGAN

BETHANYHOUSE

a division of Baker Publishing Group

Minneapolis, Minnesota

Published by Bethany House Publishers
11400 Hampshire Avenue South
Bloomington, Minnesota 55438
www.bethanyhouse.com

Bethany House Publishers is a division of
Baker Publishing Group, Grand Rapids, Michigan

Printed in the United States of America

Library of Congress Cataloging-in-Publication Data
Names: Oke, Janette, author. | Logan, Laurel Oke, author.
Title: Sustaining faith / Janette Oke, Laurel Oke Logan.
Description: Minneapolis, Minnesota : Bethany House, [2021] | Series: When hope calls ; book 2
Identifiers: LCCN 2020053965 | ISBN 9780764235122 (trade paperback) | ISBN 9780764235139 (cloth) | ISBN 9780764235146 (large print) | ISBN 9781493431700 (ebook)
Subjects: GSAFD: Christian fiction.
Classification: LCC PR9199.3.O38 S87 2021 | DDC 813/.54—dc23
LC record available at https://lccn.loc.gov/2020053965

Scripture quotations are from the King James Version of the Bible.

This is a work of fiction. Names, characters, incidents, and dialogues are products of the authors' imaginations and are not to be construed as real. Any resemblance to actual events or persons, living or dead, is entirely coincidental.

Cover design by LOOK Design Studio
Cover photography by Aimee Christenson

21 22 23 24 25 26 27 7 6 5 4 3 2 1

To David Horton, Jim Parrish, and Steve Oates
of Bethany House Publishers,
who for many years
through their dedication and diligence
have had such a big part in getting our stories
to readers.

With deep appreciation we say
THANK YOU.

God bless!

We will miss you.

Janette & Laurel

Contents

Chapter 1

New Year's Eve

Lillian reached for the little wine-colored sweater and touched its pearl-shaped buttons. Miss Tilly, their dear housekeeper, had knitted it especially for Hazel. Lillian held it up against her face and squeezed her eyes shut for a moment before folding it and adding it to the suitcase that held Hazel's belongings.

Parting was always difficult, even when it was clear that a good family had been found for one of their precious little charges. There had been a doleful period of mourning for each child who'd left their home—more correctly had left Father's house, which had been turned into a makeshift children's home last September while he was traveling on business so far away in Wales. Both Lillian and her sister, Grace, felt the sting of loss mixed with gratitude. After all, they weren't trying to be mothers. They were merely the best temporary guardians they were able to be, investing wholeheartedly in the lives of these precious children for a short interval of time. But the children needed real mothers, and fathers, and siblings—permanent families.

Lillian gathered Hazel's long wool stockings and rolled them into little bundles before packing them away too. She closed the suitcase lid carefully, pressing down hard to snap its clasps shut. *Poor little battered luggage. It speaks of the long, hard journey Hazel has endured already, our tough little "Hazelnut." At least now it holds far more possessions than it did when she first came to live with Grace.*

The suitcase had come all the way from England the previous winter, toted along by Hazel, who was eight years old at the time. Her mother had died, but Hazel wasn't truly an orphan. Her father had been left with five children to raise and little opportunity to provide for them. They'd been passed among relatives and finally surrendered to the government. Then the state had transferred the burden of their care to a large children's aid society, one of many approved by the government to emigrate "Home Children" from England to various lands within the British Empire. Here in Canada, as they stepped off an immense steamship, they were received by the Viney Boggs Mercy Society, a much smaller organization named for a wealthy eastern Canadian woman who had donated funds for its establishment. Because of the work of that humble charity, Hazel and her brother George had rather miraculously remained together when they arrived by train to the vast prairie province of Alberta, Canada. But after their first placement into a family had been a disaster and the siblings had run away together, they had come to live with Grace in a broken-down little house in Lethbridge.

Lillian shook her head even now as she remembered the events of the past year. First, she and this long-lost sister had been reunited. And then shortly afterward she'd been introduced to four sweet children who lived under Grace's protection—an overwhelming responsibility for a single woman in her mid-twenties, let alone a person who'd had no family to support her up until then.

The resulting offer had been so obvious to make, bringing

all of them to live in the home of Lillian's adoptive father until proper families could be arranged for the children. So Hazel's suitcase had been packed again for a move here to the edge of the little town of Brookfield, where Lillian had grown up under the shadow of the Rocky Mountains. And now, after just a few months, Hazel and her brother George would travel a little farther to the coal-mining town of Hope Valley to join their new family.

Lillian opened each drawer of the dresser once more to check that nothing had been overlooked. The bureau was completely empty now. She turned and scanned the bedroom, one of six on the second floor of the large house. There was a pair of shoes left under the corner of the bed, Hazel's best shoes for school and church. Lillian picked them up and held them against her heart. Her childhood bedroom would sit empty again now. Clean and quiet and abandoned.

First to leave their care had been Hazel's little roommate, Bryony, their darling eight-year-old, so guarded and withdrawn. But Bryony was now settled in well with the Mooreland family. Lillian and Grace crossed paths with the youngster often at church, sharing hugs and listening to stories from her new life. Bryony seemed content and at ease now with her new parents and two doting older brothers. The sisters knew Bryony was receiving the piano lessons she loved and that school was going well. Still, they missed her—felt the absence of her shy spirit around their kitchen table. It helped that Roxie Mooreland encouraged Bryony to refer to the sisters as Auntie Lillian and Auntie Grace. Lillian truly did feel that the child was family still.

Next to leave their home were Lemuel and Harrison. The boys had been adopted by Mr. and Mrs. Thompson shortly after all the chaos of late November, both of them anxious to serve in any capacity to nurse Arthur Thompson's filly back to health. And the young horse had recovered well, much to everyone's relief. Harrison had become rather a stranger in the weeks that followed, reveling in his newfound family. But Lemuel continued to stop by often, walking the snowy mile that separated their homes in order to ask if there were any ways he could help. *Still a servant at heart*, Lillian thought as she wiped Hazel's school shoes carefully and wrapped them in a cloth. Having gathered up all the girl's possessions, including Nellie, the rag doll that had been sent from Hope Valley, Lillian moved out to the second-floor landing and paused, looking across to the doorway of a smaller room.

From time to time Lillian would stand at the entrance to Lemuel's bedroom. If she were completely honest, she would have admitted that she dearly wished he were still living with them. Oh, she was grateful that Lemuel was with the Thompsons now, overjoyed that he could live with parents who devoted themselves to helping him finish high school and perhaps could even offer him the college education that he'd meekly admitted he'd set his heart on. And yet privately Lillian cherished Lemuel as the nearest she'd ever come to having a brother of her own. She suspected Grace felt the same way about him, and hoped that he would always visit often.

And then, just before Christmas, arrangements were settled with the Akerlunds, the family from Hope Valley who'd pursued the chance to adopt George and Hazel. Miss Tilly had been the one to communicate their wishes first, and then Grace had made the journey into the mountains to meet the young family. Grace and Lillian had discussed their situation thoroughly. They knew that the couple had three younger children and that Estelle Akerlund, who took in mending and sewing, was anxious for the older children to help around the house. Hazel was only nine and yet Lillian fully expected her to be a competent assistant to her new mother. George, at age thirteen, would be very useful too. He'd become well acquainted with the husband, Ralph Akerlund, during trips with Miss Tilly while George was suspended from school in Brookfield. He seemed enthusiastic about having this new father.

But what about what's best for Hazel—and George? How do I know that they'll be loved and cared for and—well, nurtured? Despite the assurances of Miss Tilly and Grace, it made their parting so much more difficult for Lillian to wonder if the youngsters would be seen as family members or as live-in help. She understood the logic. Running a home was constant work, hauling buckets of water or coal, chopping wood, and keeping the fire stoked. Her own workload had increased as each of their little charges had moved away. Now she and Grace took extra turns at every task in endless succession, in addition to baking and cleaning and laundry and sewing. *But there's more to parenting than feeding and clothing. Will Mr. and Mrs. Akerlund understand how much Hazel and George will need someone to listen and shepherd them—especially since they've already been wounded by the trials of life?* Lillian wished once again she'd been able to meet the couple for herself.

This fear caused the brooding thoughts that held Lillian captive on this gray winter afternoon. It had always seemed that Hazel wore a little shell of protection in order to keep the difficulties of her life experiences at bay. But surely, underneath it all, the most tender parts of her spirit still waited for healing and restoration. Lillian prayed again that the Akerlunds would be able and willing to invest in the children's overall well-being, that they would be sensitive and trustworthy. Perhaps even Elizabeth Thornton, their schoolteacher in Hope Valley, would be able to minister to George and Hazel's hearts as well as to their minds.

Sighing deeply, Lillian moved toward the stairs. Miss Tilly would travel tomorrow to Hope Valley with the children. Pastor Bukowski, or Bucky as he was often called, would drive them all in his automobile. And they were to leave in the morning, on New Year's Day. By tomorrow there would be only two children left in the house—Matty and Milton, the six-year-old twins. As always, picturing the silly little boys brought a smile to Lillian's face.

Sounds echoed below. The front door clicked open and a whoosh of winter winds pushed inside. *Grace must be home.* The door closed with a thud, and footfalls stamped snow off boots. Lillian made her way downstairs but turned toward the kitchen instead of the front door.

Soon Grace's voice called from the foyer. "Sis? Are you around?"

"In the kitchen."

Grace made her way up the hall and into the kitchen, still wearing her heavy winter coat, house slippers now warming her feet. She set down her shopping basket and paused in front of the stove to cup cold hands over its radiating heat, then nodded toward the two suitcases now waiting beside the back door. "I see you've packed their things for them."

Lillian nodded sadly.

Leaving the pool of warmth around the stove, Grace crossed the room to give Lillian a hug. "I know how you feel. I can't believe they'll be gone tomorrow—so soon after Christmas. We'll have to do something special with them tonight to make the evening memorable."

"I suppose. Yes, that *would* be nice."

"I brought the mail."

"Any word from Father? I was hoping he'd write something about his latest round of speaking engagements. He traveled all the way to Scotland this time, you know. He and a distant relative. Dell-something. It's a Welsh name. I'm so glad Father made a friend there. I can just see those two men hiking around the countryside. He loves to explore."

"I didn't look through the mail. I just wanted to hurry home before it got too dark. Sorry."

Lillian pulled the cloth away from the straw shopping basket. She began pulling out the supplies Grace had just purchased, preparing to move them to the shelves in Miss Tilly's room. Grace slipped out of her coat in order to help. At last Lillian came to the mail that was tucked down along the side. *A bill from the grocer. A letter from Lethbridge. That's all there is.*

Lillian tugged at the corner of the envelope until she could slip a finger in, then ripped one side open rather impatiently. The carefully penned letter was short and to the point.

Dear Miss Bennett and Miss Walsh,

We regret to inform you that permission for you to operate as a children's home under the auspices of Brayton House in Lethbridge, Alberta, has been withdrawn. Charges have been filed against you by Mr. and Mrs. Jack Szweda of Kedderton, Alberta. Until the complaint has been thoroughly investigated, we must ask you to suspend all activity as a temporary residence for children. You are to surrender any orphans still in your charge to the management of Brayton House as soon as you are able. We hope to receive your full cooperation in this investigation.

Sincerely,
Quinley Sinclair

"It's from the society," Lillian gasped. "Grace, look!" Her hand trembled as she passed the page to her sister. "We're being accused."

Grace's eyes widened as she surveyed the letter. Her words came slowly and on a whisper. "Oh dear. And we're probably guilty."

• • • • • • •

Ben Waldin shoved his hands deep into his pockets and stepped outside the company office door into the chill afternoon air of the Liverpool docks. One more voyage completed, his pay pocketed, and his next steamship to set sail shortly after the new year. He should feel grateful for a job well done and almost a week of shore leave. But his mood was as dreary as the low-hanging sky. He scratched at the stubble on his cheeks and wished he'd bothered to shave before debarking. Sheltered for a moment beneath the awning of the ship offices, he watched the crowd surging around him. And he procrastinated.

He loved the sea. He enjoyed life aboard ship more than anything he'd known here on land. It was all he'd ever wanted to do. In fact, he still refused to regret that he'd run away from home at the age of fourteen to become a seaman. True, he'd started as little more than a ship rat, climbing inside the narrowest recesses of the heavy metal skeleton between the massive double hulls of a very modern steamship in order to clean and scrape and repaint all the places where grown men could never reach, but even with such laborious work Ben had somehow thrived as each year passed.

The great steamers plying the vast oceans were his pride and joy. He was glad to do his part. On his off hours he had the run of the hidden corridors, could quietly observe what none of the passengers knew of the frenzied activity below. And whenever he preferred solitude, he could dangle his legs from a narrow ledge far above the waters, arms draped around deck rails, apple in hand, listening to the steady sloshing of waves below and watching the slow progress of the moon across the night sky. By the end of his very first voyage Ben had become intimately familiar with the moon. And this same faithful moon hung above each subsequent expedition, waiting for the moments of solitude they shared. All through his twenties this secret, boyish practice made him feel most alive, most satisfied with his place in the world.

He snickered as he thought of it. Now in his early thirties, he realized it had been some time since he'd stolen away alone and spent a night just watching the sky. *Goin' to have to get back there soon, I s'pose.* But first, there was this visit home to manage, not to mention the obstacles of his unwelcome assignment to be confronted. Tipping his face up to find a hazy patch of sunshine filtering through moist gray clouds, Ben drew the coarse wool collar tighter around his neck and flipped his worn flat cap back onto his head, then reached down a hand to heft his kit from the ground. All that he owned in the world was inside this duffel bag. He began the slow push through the crowded maze of people and cargo, past the swarming wagons and carts. He pressed forward toward the massive stone buildings of the grand city of Liverpool looming beyond.

Even as he trudged along, Ben sighed. It wasn't as if seafaring life had been easy. Gradually he'd worked his way up through various jobs: wiper, oiler, water tender, assistant to engineers, personal assistant to the officers . . . But this new job? This was the most distasteful kind of task he'd ever been assigned in his nearly two decades of seafaring, and he feared there'd be more voyages like it.

Now that he'd made the journey from Liverpool to Canada a couple times, his new captain seemed to think that his temperament made him the ideal person to handle the peculiarities of *this* new job. However, if there were any task he'd faced that he detested with all his being—this was it. All these young passengers—orphans, they called them.

Cast-offs from society, more like. I've seen 'em oft enough in the slums ashore. Ain't that just the kinda thing I wanna leave behind? The crowded trash heap'a mankind pressin' in all 'round? Children, no less.

And the worst part of it all was that they were already undernourished, sickly. He knew from personal experience that some of them would never survive the trip. He loathed every memory of his own involvement. Those staring eyes. That row of grim little faces pushed against the metal gates that kept them below, in their place, in steerage.

There were always caregivers with them. He didn't doubt that the requisite adults were doing the best they could under the circumstances. Ben's job was not to work directly with the children, but to see that their group had every available resource provided for them by the ship company. While aboard, they were his responsibility. He delivered pushcarts of meals and towels and bedding, wheeled away soiled clothing, empty dishes, and slop buckets. He tried to avoid the ever-inquisitive eyes but, despite his best intentions, found himself carving whistles and tops in his spare time, pilfering the occasional item that the upper classes had thrown away, and constantly wrestling between wanting to be kind yet still keeping a detached distance. In his opinion, this interaction with children was not what a sailor's life was meant to be.

Yet there were really only two choices available to him. Take it or leave it. His value to the shipping company wasn't high enough to allow him to make special demands. And clearly those in charge saw this change of duties as a promotion—to be trusted enough to interact with actual passengers. He was aware that few of his fellow seamen were up to that particular Gordian challenge.

"I'd rather stay below," he grumbled into his wool collar as he struck off on his own at last. Raising one shoulder as a shield, he turned sideways and pressed through a row of vendors hawking their wares, dragging his heavy kit behind in the space left by his wake. He thrust his free hand deeper into the coat pocket where his money was hidden, didn't bother with an answer as the vendors called out to him to make a purchase, ignored them as they grasped at his coat sleeve.

He could try to hire on elsewhere, but times were hard and there was no guarantee of alternatives. Indeed, unless he was ready to give up the sea, prudence dictated that he'd simply have to surrender to the tasks assigned to him—whatever they involved.

Emerging at last onto quieter streets, he determined to close the distance between himself and the inevitable. It was time to face yet another unpleasant part of his life—a short visit with his family. Jane would be there, his darling younger sister, innocent and sweet. But also his parents—the ones he'd disappointed most with his life choices, the ones whose constant criticism made it difficult to return to them each time he was in port. They'd insist again that at past thirty he should seek a new profession. The arguing was exhausting and more difficult to bear now with the weight of his next voyage already pressing down upon him. But they'd be all too ready to receive a portion of his earnings from him just the same. Every little bit helped. His dada's work was intermittent and his wages low.

Ben's feet took him dutifully through town, down the familiar streets, and at last up to the worn stone steps of his family home. But something was amiss. He knew it immediately. The door refused to open. His gloved hand thumped against the rough wood, but there was no answer and a strange echoing emptiness inside. Stepping back to survey the façade of their row house, he noticed a bill posted in the home's front window just above the long crack in the glass that had been there since he was a boy.

For Rent.

"What?" he breathed aloud. "Where've they gone?" For a moment he floundered in confusion, glancing up and down the line of houses for some clue, scratching again at the stubble on his face.

And then a shrill voice cried out from an open window not far above him. "Ebenezer Waldin? That you? Yer folks 'spected ya weeks ago."

Mrs. Gillery, the neighbor, had already noticed his presence. No doubt she'd heard the sound of his knock through the thin wall between their homes. The window not far above him had opened so that she could peer out and call below from her favorite perch.

"Aye, ma'am. It's Ben come home fer a visit. D'ya know where me parents are, Missus Gill'ry?"

"Ben—pah! You're Ebenezer Waldin, son of William and Viola, y'are. Can't fool those what know ya. And I know what become'a yer kin too. Gone with nowt left behind 'em."

"Gone?"

"Yes, gone, I said, and gone they be. Off ta Canada."

Ben's mind refused to make sense of her claim. "I'm sorry, ta where?"

"Canada—by ship. You of all folk should savvy that. So, since ya wouldn't abide with yer parents, they up and set out without ya."

All of 'em? Even Jane? He managed to answer aloud, "But when?"

"Three weeks now."

He turned back toward his own door, paused. Slowly his eyes swept farther down the street in one direction and then up the other in search of some additional witness from whom to inquire. Finally he rotated back to face Mrs. Gillery's open window, completing a full circle in place while just trying to clear his head. He was ready to follow them, but how? Ready to surrender and obediently join them at last, but where? "Did they say anythin' more?"

"Left ya a letter. Come here an' I'll give it t'ya."

Ben trudged the few steps along the cobbled street to the neighboring stoop. The door opened before him, releasing the moist air of a boiling vat of dank laundry, the widow's source of income.

"Come in," she ordered.

"I'll wait here, ma'am."

"Do's ya like. Ya always did." Mrs. Gillery hobbled away into the dimness and returned with a sealed envelope. "See, I kep' it fer ya as promised. Figured ya'd be back—by and by."

"Aye, ma'am. Thank ya."

"S'pose that's the last of ya, then, Ebenezer Waldin. Wish't ya had not'a broke yer mum's heart." Pressing the letter into his gloved hand unceremoniously, she closed the door on him.

Ben called after her, "Thank ya, Missus Gill'ry." *Now what? The docks, o'course. There's surely nothin' fer me here.*

• • • • • • •

Despite her efforts to participate in a lovely farewell supper for Hazel and George, Lillian could focus on nothing other than the Szwedas' legal actions. Swirling through her mind were the same truths over and over. *We lied to them when we said the boys couldn't be separated, that Grace and I could only take them if the twins stayed together. By now, authorities on the matter have no doubt informed the Szwedas that this was false. In truth, we didn't have any authority to accept Matty, let alone to make demands regarding Milton, the healthy one.* Then the internal arguments would follow. *But we couldn't let them separate Matty and Milton. They're twins! It would have been an outrage. And with Matty's health issues, with his tongue-tie, his inability to speak well, how would he have survived a separation from his twin, on whom he depends so strongly?*

With a great deal of sorrow, Lillian had spent time alone in the afternoon writing a letter to Father. His trip to Wales not long after Mother's death had been a constant drain on Lillian emotionally. She needed him, needed his guidance far more than a letter could give. And though she'd tried to be honest and candid in her letters, she'd failed to tell him the whole truth about the twins' arrival to their home. Oh, she'd told about the dreadful Szwedas. She'd made a solid argument that the boys should remain together. What she'd failed to mention was the lie. The dreadful lie. Many tears were shed as Lillian transcribed the event more fully in this letter, explaining how she and Grace had brought the current trouble on themselves.

While cooking for the supper celebration, they'd made arrangements by telephone to pack up the little boys the very next morning after George and Hazel's departure, and in the afternoon they would drive out across the prairie to Lethbridge in Walter's automobile. Lillian worried again that they were all asking too much of her long-standing friendship with Walter, though he'd brushed aside her uneasy comments as usual.

Walter was so steady and gracious and helpful. With his unhurried words accentuated by the complexity of his quiet smile, the flecks of gold highlighting his brown eyes half hidden by the ever-present Stetson, there was much more to Walter than what some might expect of a cowboy, a cattle ranch foreman. But Lillian had known him long before that, when he was still a high school baseball star and considered quite a catch by many of the girls she'd grown up with. At the time, to Lillian, he was just Maeve Norberg's one-year-younger brother—the boy she'd tutored a little when he was in high school.

But that had all changed last fall when they'd been reacquainted. Lillian couldn't deny how much her feelings had stirred toward him. More amazing still, Walter had declared outright his intention to court her, asserting his patience with his long-standing interest in Lillian as she struggled with adjusting to so much change around her. She hoped she'd communicated her feelings to him well in return—demurely, yet earnestly. She feared sometimes that her reserved nature might give him less encouragement than a man might need. Yet, here he was again, rising to their aid during another crisis without reservation, empathetic and kind.

When Grace had shown the letter from the Mercy Society to their housekeeper, Mrs. Tillendynd, the older woman had reasoned that if such problems must be faced, they may as well be faced immediately. Dear Miss Tilly, always practical and direct. So just as Hazel and George were heading deeper into the Rockies to join their new family, Grace and Lillian would be escorting Matty and Milton out onto the prairie, toward adoptive parents who had already failed them once. Lillian shuddered at the thought.

Seated in the dining room for the going-away party, she looked across the table to where the six-year-olds were enjoying the festivities, giggling and leaning against each other. They shared that special bond reserved for twins. O *Heavenly Father, what would have become of either boy if we hadn't intervened? Surely that makes it right—what we did, doesn't it?* But one vexing question remained unanswered despite her persistent internal debate. *What will happen to them now because of what we did, because of us? Will they go back to the Szwedas? Could they be separated even now? Heaven help them! Heaven help us all.*

During supper, Lillian found herself frequently jolted out of her internal dialogue and back into engagement with the activity around her. Miss Tilly and Grace were managing to hostess well. Their precious children—George and Hazel, the twins, and even Lemuel and Harrison were gathered together at the table. But Lillian was certain the unexpected tidings hung heavily over every adult's heart.

"These are for you." Lemuel slid two brown-paper-wrapped packages across the table toward George and Hazel. "They're from all the kids at school." The shapes were easily recognizable as rather slender books, about the size of a postcard.

Hazel beamed and ripped away her paper wrapping. George seemed a little more reluctant.

"Oh, it's an *autograph* book. Lucy Schiller and Willa Blanding each have one. They're lovely." She allowed the signed pages to flip past her fingers, stopping on one of the entries surrounded by pink printed roses, then read aloud, "'I ought to smile, I ought to laugh, but in this book I autograph. With love, Rose Friar.'" She snickered and showed the page to Grace.

George seemed reluctant even now that he knew the book wasn't something for school. "Thanks."

"Oh, read it, Georgie. Read us one."

"Fine, then." He turned to the first entry apathetically. "'As blue sky follows the ship at sea, so may my good wishes follow thee.

Your friend, Hugh Grenville.'" He nodded and looked around the table to see if it would be enough, closing the book slowly. "It's nice. Thank you."

"Mr. Thompson bought 'em," Harrison announced. "An' me and Lemmie got everyone to sign." It seemed that referring to the man who was both school principal and adopted father as "Dad" was going to take some time.

"Thank you," Hazel repeated. "It's so pretty. An' not many of the girls have one yet."

A chuckle from Miss Tilly. "Not in Hope Valley, a'that ya can be sure."

Grace accepted the book from Hazel and turned a few pages slowly. "It's lovely, dear. And when you're older you can recall the friends you had at various seasons of your life. See, there are plenty of blank pages still. It'll be a sweet remembrance for you." Grace passed the book to Miss Tilly for inspection.

The work-worn hands slid across its fresh pages gently, pensively. "Comin' and goin'," Miss Tilly said quietly. "That's what life is—jest so much comin' and goin'. If I had a book'a remembrances, oh the pages I'd fill up with the ones I loved. But more, much more, think'a the people I missed who I might'a knowed. Only the Good Lord sees the workin's of it all—knows the ways'a all His children everywhere."

• • • • • • •

Ben walked slowly, uncertain as to his destination. There were cheap rooms near the docks, but what went on inside them were things that he had always guarded himself against, avoided at all costs. For one thing, he wanted to consider himself a moral man—but even more, he'd seen the consequences of poor judgment in those around him, the poverty of soul and pocketbook that bad decisions wrought. These were things he'd grown to fear lest any would take root in his own life.

He purchased a meat pasty for his dinner and ducked into a corner between shops to eat the steamy morsel in peace. At last, having nowhere else to go, he decided to fall in with the other deckhands who were loading cargo inside the steamer from which he'd just debarked. He wouldn't have an assigned berth, but there were plenty of hiding places where he could spend a couple nights before it set sail for its destination. A few treks in and out assisting with cargo would assuage his conscience about the unauthorized lodgings. Not one shipmate cast a questioning glance toward him since he was familiar enough to be recognized among the swarming crew. After establishing himself, he could find somewhere to rest. *Perhaps at long last I'll have another parley with the moon.*

He settled near an isolated porthole just in time to watch a winter storm roll in from the Irish Sea and up the River Mersey. Stuffing his kit bag into a corner, he lowered himself against it. It wouldn't be as comfortable as the feather mattress at his dada's house would have been, but it would do.

At last he drew the letter from inside his coat. What would his parents have to say to him now? How angry had they been while leaving him behind? However, the letter was in Jane's feathery hand. He recognized it immediately.

My Beloved Brother,

I'm afraid we shall miss you, departing before you return. Dada is taking us to Canada, as he believes there is better opportunity in such a young land. I wish I knew how to instruct you to find us, but we don't know where we shall settle. My sole prayer is that you will follow.

And yet my heart is torn in two. With all of my being I want to see you again, and at the same time I wish you to live in the manner for which you were created, to be free. Why can't it be both? I don't understand. If only I'd been born a man so I could work alongside you wherever you are.

I shall attempt to leave messages for you upon our arrival. I don't know how. But I trust that the God who bound us to one another as family will perform some miracle to bring us together again someday.

I love you, as always.
Your devoted sister,
Jane

Ben rocked forward, hung his head between his knees, and wept.

Chapter 2

Edgar

Pelting, icy rain on the tin roof woke Edgar from sleep. He shifted his position in bed slowly, one small body part lifted and relocated at a time, moving as gently as possible. At seven, he was the smallest of the boys taken in by the parish vicar. The space they shared was little more than a lean-to shed attached to his residence by a short door and crammed tight with two beds. But still, it was so much better than sleeping under the bridge down on Willow Lane, where they'd all lived together before—especially now that it was winter. And here there was a steady supply of simple food.

For now, as much as he feared waking the older boys, Edgar reasoned that the adjustment of position was necessary—that without it he wouldn't sleep at all due to the persistent dribble of freezing rainwater down the back of his neck. He pressed closer against Jonah. At least Jonah was kind. Of course, the older boy jolted a little and grumbled, but he allowed the encroachment into his personal indentation in the straw mattress. There'd be no consequences to pay in the morning from him, something that surely would have occurred with any of the others. Had he been next to Freddie, for instance, such an intrusion would never have been tolerated. More than once the fourteen-year-old had boxed Edgar across the ears for merely asking a question. Making the older boy even more frightening, Freddie's palms had cruel scars from unexplained burns. None of the boys was brave enough to ask about the patches of pale, puckered flesh.

Cholera had swept their village, taking Edgar's parents and siblings—though he wasn't exactly sure where that phrase meant they'd been taken to. Over the course of a single year, five rough wooden coffins had been lowered into the ground not far from where he now lay. At the very least, Edgar determined that they hadn't been taken very far. Oddly, the sorrowful thought actually brought him comfort. To ward off his frequent loneliness he could visit the mounds whenever he liked. The vicar had spoken kind words about heaven over each grave, though the general idea of it made no sense to Edgar. He knew exactly where his family lay. So how could they also be somewhere else?

Still, the vicar was a gentle man. His dark cassock matched his graying black hair and thick beard. His narrow brown eyes seemed always to be hiding, either beneath heavy, troubled eyebrows or squeezed into narrow slits by the creases of his broad smile. Chatting with the boys was a sure way to coax out a squinting grin from him. But Edgar had noticed that the heavy brows quickly returned, weighted down by something far beyond the young boy's grasp. Snug against Jonah's bony shoulder, sleep claimed Edgar again before any new conclusions had been drawn.

• • • ● • • •

"Jamie—late ta breakfast? He ain't ne'er late to table."

"Naw, ate early 'cause Vicar sent him off while it was still dark to fetch a letter from the post."

Edgar dipped a spoon back into his mash, lifting it to his

mouth still steaming. An arm shot across his bowl as Rowley reached for the last boiled egg. With a glance from side to side, Edgar pulled his porridge bowl closer and dipped his spoon in again, listening to the chatter around him.

"Vicar's been writing ta the lady again—the one what takes kids and sends 'em away."

"Away? Away where?"

"All over—Africa, an' Australia, an' Canada."

"Africa? What for? Who wants 'em there?"

"Fam'lies what ain't got no kids—English folk—who need help on farms an' all."

Silence swept around the table. Jonah was the first to break it. "He won't do it. Wouldn't send us away."

"Can't keep us all, though, can he?"

Something in Edgar's throat began to tighten, making it difficult to swallow. He glanced across to Freddie and dropped his eyes again. No sense risking a comment.

Rowley suggested, "May be fer the best. Better ta be in a fam'ly—any fam'ly—than here. We knew it wouldn't last. Can't afford to keep us all, then, can he?"

"Should send away Jamie. He eats the most," Jonah said. Forced laughter from the older boys followed.

Edgar looked down at his remaining mash. If he ate less, perhaps he might be allowed to stay. After all, he was the smallest. And Vicar was always kind. Even while teaching them their short daily lessons, there were no raps with a ruler or scolding words. It wouldn't be so bad to remain here at the vicarage close to his family's graves.

• • • • • • •

New Year's Day dawned with a bright, clear Alberta sky. Through Lillian's window the Rocky Mountains stood like chiseled sentinels in the frigid winter air. She breathed a silent prayer of gratitude that it wasn't snowing and hustled to dress for the unwelcome morning.

All three women shed tears, even Miss Tilly, as just after breakfast the sisters watched Pastor Bukowski drive away with Miss Tilly, Hazel, and George. Immediately afterward, Grace walked into town to place a call to Brayton House informing them of the sisters' intended trip. She was told that Mr. Sinclair, who had sent the frightening letter to them, planned to leave soon. If they wished to meet with him before he traveled to see the Szwedas, it would need to happen immediately.

At home and packing for a second day in a row, Lillian labored to sound comforting while explaining for the umpteenth time to little Milton why they, too, were making a sudden trip by car. Her frustration only grew with the effort. But even more so, she felt tired. Inexplicably, irrationally tired.

"Miss Grace and I are needed in Lethbridge. There are some people with whom we must speak."

Milton hovered at her elbow, kicking his toe against the leg of his bed, a frown on his face. It was the most defiance Lillian had observed from him. "But we wanna stay here," he whined.

"I understand, dear. But you'll have to come along with us anyway. You and Matty will share a room with some other children in the home where Miss Grace used to live. I expect you'll make some new friends." She doubted her attempt at a positive spin would be successful. "Anyway, that's just what needs to happen for now."

"I don't wanna go. An' Matty, he don't wanna go neither." Milton's eyes implored Lillian to understand how strongly he felt—he and his much quieter brother.

He knows. Fear prickled at the back of Lillian's neck. *Intuition is telling Milton not to leave the home where the two of them finally feel safe. I can't blame him at all.* She lowered one knee to the floor and reached out her arms to draw him close for a moment. "I'm sorry I can't say yes to you. Sometimes we all have to do things we don't want to do. And when that happens, it makes everything much more difficult if we fight against it. Can you see that?" Her hand rubbed against his flannelled back in hopes of bringing comfort and eliciting trust. But her words brought meager comfort even for her own stubborn worries.

"When're we gonna come back?"

Oh dear. "I'm not sure. Miss Grace and I don't know. This will have to be a—an adventure. That's all." *Oh my! Now if it turns out poorly for him, will my careless choice of words cause Milton to despise forevermore the idea of adventure?*

• • • • • • •

The city of Lethbridge was just as Lillian remembered it, tucked away in the deep folds of winter-barren prairie as if a giant had discarded a fawn-colored towel and a town had sprung up on it. Their approach animated Grace, who watched through the foggy windows of Walter's motorcar for people she recognized. This small city had been Grace's home for many years after Mama and Papa had died and Lillian had been adopted without her. It amazed Lillian again that Grace showed no bitterness that she'd been remanded to children's homes rather than the sisters being adopted together.

In the back seat, Lillian reached for Milton's hand. It felt cold and clammy. The first thing to occur would be to surrender the boys to the staff of Brayton House. *However, can it be accomplished without additional trauma to the twins?* She breathed a quick prayer that the staff would be gracious to the boys during their stay.

The vehicle slowed, then drew to a stop along a side street beside a bank of snow. A voice called, "Grace. Grace!"

Lillian stepped out of the vehicle, turning in the direction of the sound just as Roland Scott approached, still pushing his arms into the sleeves of his heavy jacket.

"Welcome back, Grace. It's so good to see you."

"Hi, Rolly."

Lillian helped Milton step from the car. Matty was right on his heels. She took each boy by the hand and moved gingerly across the trampled path in the snow toward the looming children's home. "Hello, Roland." She attempted a smile, but her teeth were already chattering.

"Hi, Lillian."

Walter scooped up Matty for the short walk. His slow, deliberate words of greeting followed. "Good to see ya, Rolly. Keepin' warm? I think it's even colder here than back home."

"Come on inside. Coffeepot's already on." Roland had taken Grace by the elbow to help her up the broad steps.

Lillian followed the cluster of people into the sandstone building. She'd been here often with Grace as they set their plans in motion to bring Grace's charges out to Brookfield in the first place. For Lillian, the building felt austere. *A children's home bears so little resemblance to a real home, regardless of its name. And now Matty and Milton are going to be housed here, despite Grace's strong objections.*

Lillian recalled how ashen Grace had looked when she'd returned from town the previous day and reported that Sid would be prepared to officially receive the boys. And here they were on the threshold of losing them.

Lillian let her coat slip from her shoulders, and Walter hung it in the entryway, dropping his hat on the hook beside it.

Sid Brown, director of the orphanage, met them in the foyer. "Good afternoon, ladies. We were worried about you coming by car in such cold weather. It's good to see you arrived safely."

Lillian held her tongue. *It certainly wasn't our idea.*

"And these must be the twins—Matty and Milton. Welcome, boys. We're glad to have you here for a visit."

Visit? Well, that's an encouraging description, isn't it?

Sid continued, "Boys, this young lady is Ruth. She's been a resident here for quite some time. She's going to show you around and help you get settled in your room. Then she'll introduce you to some of the other children, who are just about ready to have their afternoon tea. Maybe you'd like to have cookies with the others?"

At the mention of food, both boys raised their faces. Milton answered, "Yes, please. We're pretty hungry."

Matty nodded vigorously in agreement.

Grace smiled warmly and stepped closer to the round-faced girl with a thick dark braid hanging down the center of her back. "Hi, Ruth. It's so good to see you."

But Lillian's mind was focused on the boys as they greeted the teenager shyly and allowed themselves to be led away from the adults. Lillian fought the urge to follow, breathed deeply, and straightened her sweater instead, the one Miss Tilly had made for her, pleasantly thick and warm and homey—comforting. Lillian knew she could help the boys best with her words now, rather than her presence. She had prepared her defense—their defense. But even more painfully, she had prepared her apology for the deceptive words she and Grace had spoken. Her heart had sputtered in fits whenever she'd pictured this moment. She willed her hands not to tremble.

"Let's go into the office. We'll have our afternoon tea brought to us there. As I told Grace on the telephone, we rushed your meeting with the society rep because he's set to be on the road again in the morning." Sid motioned up the stairs and Roland led the way.

Walter, walking at Lillian's elbow, was a comfort and a source of courage. She eased just a little nearer, grateful for his company.

However, as they entered the room, there was a man already seated at Sid's large desk with his things spread out across it as if it were his own. His head was lowered over paperwork, but his broad shoulders and straight posture evoked an air of intimidation. Lillian swallowed hard, certain at once this must be the dreaded Quinley Sinclair, who had written the foreboding letter to them.

Then his eyes lifted and he glanced from Lillian and Walter to Grace. He paused as if studying Grace for a moment. Lillian watched Grace blush under his strong gaze, dropping her soft brown eyes toward the carpet and tucking a strand of hair behind her ear self-consciously. The corner of Quinley's mouth twitched upward into a slight smile.

He stood to his feet, the look of formality on his face softening. He cleared his throat, straightened the knot on his narrow silk necktie, and buttoned his jacket before ambling across the room to greet them with an extended hand. His suit was fashionable, his trousers neatly creased. His wavy hair and charming smile were sculpted and perfect.

Lillian froze in place, her mind working furiously. *I expected him to be remote and stern—like his letter. What could have prompted such an alteration of demeanor?*

"May I introduce Mr. Quinley Sinclair?" Sid began. "Quin is the western representative for the Viney Boggs Mercy Society, which brought Matty and Milton, as well as quite a few other children, to the West in the last several years. He works as a representative and an inspector of post-placements for them here. Quin, this is Miss Grace Bennett."

All the man's attention was focused on Grace. "Good afternoon. I'm pleased to meet you, Miss Bennett." He grasped her small hand in both of his. "I've heard so much about you since writing my letter, Grace—may I call you Grace?" Without pausing for a reply, he continued, "All good things, of course! The staff here has raved about your volunteer service to them—and your devotion to the children. I assure you, your role is quite unique. I'll admit that I didn't understand at first what sort of arrangement you had with Sid's orphanage here—when I first heard of you and—I wrote to you."

Was that a look of regret? Of apology even? Lillian stared at

Quinley Sinclair, uncertain quite how to interpret his words. She wanted to let out a sigh of relief but held her breath instead. *So much is riding on the decision of this stranger.*

Sid continued, "And this is her sister, Lillian Walsh."

At last Quinley's eyes turned to her. "Miss Walsh." Lillian felt her fingers enclosed and pressed tightly by soft hands. She noted that he wore no wedding ring, though she guessed he was a little older than she was. Her lips parted, but words failed to form.

Curious brows rose slightly but his smile remained as Quinley dropped back a step, motioning them forward as if hosting a dinner party instead of a legal meeting. "Please, ladies, won't you take seats at the table? I thought we'd be comfortable gathering here to talk—less formally."

Roland sat next to Grace, while Walter, unintroduced, drew back a chair for Lillian and seated himself next to her. Lillian let her eyes pass over their side of the table. They made a rough little crew lined up against Sid Brown and Quinley Sinclair. Between her chunky homemade sweater and Walter's simple plaid shirt and jeans, Grace's poise would have to carry the day if they were to hold their own at all. *How did I ever walk into something so important with no thought to the impression we were making? Mother taught me better than that, and Father would be appalled. Though, to be fair, most of my wardrobe went on without me to Wales with Father.*

Coffee was served with the requisite small talk. How were the roads? Was there as much snow in Brookfield? Was Grace glad to be back in Lethbridge? Lillian lowered her eyes, hoping to keep her cup from rattling against its saucer as she set it down with unsteady hands. It was a relief that Grace was managing so much of the discourse, seemingly unaffected by the gravity of this moment. Indeed, it seemed Quinley showed little interest in anyone else.

As the conversation spiraled ever closer to its intended target, Lillian waited through each stage of distraction, nodding and smiling with what she hoped was a relaxed expression. Their host seemed in no hurry to address the real issue at hand.

"How long have you been with the Mercy Society, Mr. Sinclair?" Grace directed them closer to the purpose of their meeting.

"Oh, not long at all. I was educated as a solicitor first—more my father's choice than my own. The practice of law turned out to be a little mundane to me, but I've found it useful to have a legal background." Quinley retreated again to other topics. "Once I graduated, I did a little teaching too. I discovered that I have a strong interest in children and education. I've traveled rather extensively and am pleased to finally come out West."

Sid added, "Quin was hired a little over a year ago by the Mercy Society to oversee their western placements, which had been running into some trouble. We at Brayton House haven't been associated with the society for much longer than that. It wasn't until there were difficulties with some of their placements and some of their children showed up on our doorstep—more specifically, children like George and Hazel, Bryony and Harrison. As Grace is well aware, before that we each just operated independently."

"And we still do. Operate independently, that is," Quinley pointed out bluntly, his tone suddenly sounding as if he were back in a courtroom. "Any child we place remains in our purview legally until they're eighteen. None of them is registered with Brayton House in any way. Although, we're grateful to have partnered with you regarding these exceptions."

Lillian cringed.

"Exceptions?" Grace pounced on the word. "They're not exceptions, Mr. Sinclair. They're children. And children in desperate situations, at that."

"Oh yes. Of course. Forgive me, Grace—please." His hand reached across the table toward her, open and conciliatory. "I misspoke. I should have said *dilemmas* or *debacles*. No one who represents Mrs. Boggs in any way has a lack of respect for the gravity of such situations. It's our primary goal—our very reason for existence—to serve the children to the best of our ability. Frankly, we've been shamed by the way we failed in these few cases. And it's my top priority to be certain such things don't occur again. Please, Grace. I meant no offense by my poorly chosen comment."

"But once they came to Brayton House, weren't they *our* responsibility, Sid?" asked Grace.

All eyes turned toward Sid's familiar face. He hedged. "It's complicated, Grace. There's been a bit of a gray area legally."

"And we're working hard to button up anything that's unclear," Quinley continued confidently, without a pause to allow any more comments. "We're grateful, Sid, to be working with you—that you've stepped in so graciously to help and even given us a point of contact locally when it's convenient. That's proven to be a welcome benefit for a society that's based in the East. I'm looking forward to working closely with you here." He nodded toward Sid as if offering his thanks. "You see, Grace, Lillian, this was a large part of the reason I was hired, actually." Behind the table, Quinley unbuttoned his jacket, then stretched out his elbows and settled himself more comfortably on his seat. "We can't have any of the children unaccounted for, can we? That'll never do." He winked at Grace.

A polite chuckle came from Sid and Roland on the opposing side of the table. Without looking toward Grace, Lillian was certain her sister had not shared in the courtesy.

"As I understand it," Sid continued, "Quin's done little other than travel since he was hired. This is the first we've had the opportunity to meet with him directly—though we've spoken over the telephone. He seems to stay very busy."

A well-governed smile answered Sid's explanation. "It's far too big a task for one man, unfortunately. I've been promised more staff at some point. Be that as it may, I'm responsible for a great many children." The conversation drew closer to the topic at hand. "Too many to inspect yearly, for certain. It's the bane of my occupation, I suppose—to be desperately overworked."

He doesn't seem to be suffering too much. Lillian attempted to shake off her darkening thoughts. She set down her cup and rose a little straighter in her chair before speaking. She'd had enough. "Yes, it is difficult, isn't it? To manage without support, make decisions without guidance. I feel that's rather what happened with Grace and me. We were thrust into a situation with the Szwedas where we weren't certain what to do and had no one immediately at hand to ask for help."

Quinley began to speak but Lillian rushed on. "We were wrong, Mr. Sinclair, to make statements that were misleading and false. I feel the sting of that error to the core of my being, I assure you. And I will own the wrong of it entirely. But if you'd been there, if you'd seen the way this couple was speaking to us and treating the boys . . . I'm sure there must have been a way—a correct way—to have managed the situation without resorting to lying, but even after weeks of regret, I can't think of what that would have been."

Silence followed. Sitting beside Quinley, Sid dropped his head to scratch at the loose skin of his wide forehead.

With a glance toward Grace, Quinley answered evenly at last, his voice calm yet firm. "Miss Walsh, please don't think that I'm here to stand *against* you. I make no judgments concerning the morality of your words or actions. My only purpose is to sort through what's been done and what should be done next—for the benefit of the boys and to meet the requirements of the law. I'm not your judge and certainly not your priest. You needn't apologize to me for anything."

Lillian studied his self-assured expression.

"The law, Miss Walsh, is a steady plow horse, dependable and sturdy, ever moving forward. Please allow me to guide us through this—this rough patch of ground. I assure you that I'll find a way to maneuver the legal process to protect those in need, to keep everyone involved from being—from *feeling* dragged along behind it or, worse, trampled beneath it. I'm asking you to trust me, Lillian. Can you do that?"

For a moment there was no one else in the room. She scanned his eyes, his composed expression, and allowed herself to feel a glimmer of hope. "I'll try. I'll certainly try."

• • • ● • • •

Thrusting his small hand into the large wooden bin, Edgar reached for another softening, wrinkled potato. He tore off two small white shoots from its eyes and inspected it in the flickering lamplight, as he'd been taught, for signs of rot. Seeing none, he dropped it into the new crate with the others. However, the pile on the dirt floor between them of unsatisfactory product was growing too quickly. Each of the boys was aware of the implications. Vicar would salvage any portion of the discarded potatoes that could be used soon for soup, but the store of food in the cold cellar was dwindling too quickly, even with their combined efforts. This supply was Vicar's own stockpile, given to him by the poor parishioners he served. It was meant to feed the man himself until spring.

Edgar cast a glance at the big boys around him. Wiping the back of his hand across his cheek left a cold smudge of dirt from his brown fingers. Jamie would be back again soon with some form of answer. Though not one boy scattered around the cellar spoke the thought aloud, all were wondering what this return trip would yield.

It had been several days since the vicar's letter had been sent. In that time, Jamie had overheard a number of conversations between Vicar and men who visited concerning the looming decision. The boy had shared every detail with the others while they huddled under their blankets at night, listening to cold rain drumming on the roof.

"Where's Africa? Ain't it on t'other end of the world?" Rowley asked.

"Shut up." Edgar could hear the snap of Freddie's backhand against Rowley's chest cutting through the darkness. "It don't matter. They ain't decided nothin' yet."

Jonah rolled to his back. "Thet we know'a."

"Yeah, thet we know'a," someone else said.

A trickle of sorrow forced its way onto Edgar's cheek. It was terrible enough to have shed a tear in the darkness where no one could see, but the question inside him refused to quiet. He breathed deeply first, then uttered timidly into the cold air, "If we get sent away, I'll ne'er see me mum and dad again? I mean, where they be now."

Freddie inhaled as if to reply, but Jonah spoke quickly and decisively. "We all got kin in the ground here. But it don't matter where they send us, we can't really leave 'em. 'Cause they're part'a us. Always. They still kinda live in our memories, yeah?"

"Yeah," they all agreed.

But Edgar wrinkled up his forehead and frowned. That made no more sense than Vicar's talk of heaven. "God," he prayed softly, "wherever they are—an' wherever *You* are—can I just stay with Vicar, please?"

• • • • • • •

The day of the boys' departure from their little village arrived. Vicar cleared his throat again and again as they slogged along beside the fence between fields bordering the path to town. His wide collar was drawn up around the back of his head, and the broad-brimmed hat he used to shield himself from the drizzling sky kept his face from view. On other rare excursions he'd whistled as they marched along behind him, sometimes stopping to point out wildlife or plants of interest. Today there was only the hunch of his shoulders to direct them forward.

With all his heart Edgar wanted to reach out and grasp Jonah's hand. But he was seven now, and far too old for such childishness. What would Freddie say? Clutching his small bundle, he hurried to match the strides of the older boys.

His free hand ferreted into his pocket for the small bit of stone hidden there, grasping it firmly. Last night Jonah had led him to the graveyard as evening shadows lengthened and then had produced a hammer. Walking with Edgar to the simple fieldstone grave marker of Edgar's mum and dad, Jonah brought the tool down with a sharp crack against the roughly engraved rock, breaking off a small corner.

At first it had seemed all desecration. The sound of hammer against stone shattering the stillness of the solemn place almost made the little boy flee. But the moment the chip was placed on Edgar's palm, he understood. Whatever the brashness of the boy who had pilfered it for him, he cherished the nugget of grave marker more than anything else that he carried away from his village. It was his private reminder of his former place in the world, where he had once been loved and secure within a family.

Standing with Jonah in the failing light for a moment of solemn respect, Edgar had been shocked as Freddie appeared suddenly from behind nearby bushes, wrenching the hammer from Jonah's hand. Without a word the older boy had sauntered to the far side of the yard until he towered over another gravestone resting there. Over and over the youth swung the tool with all his strength, dark tufts of thick hair lashing wildly about his head, chips of stone flying out in all directions from the grave marker of his own father. Jonah had placed a hand on Edgar's shoulder and ushered him away quickly, leaving Freddie to his frenzied labor.

Now, trudging through town toward the train station in silence, each of the boys seemed aware of the expressions of remorse on the faces of villagers nearby, faces familiar to them all. These were adults who had known their parents, children whom they'd grown up alongside. Activity around them paused somberly as they marched past. Not one of their meager homes had been offered as shelter.

The boys made a short row on the edge of the platform. Edgar squeezed between Jonah and Jamie, taking shelter from the lightly sprinkling rain by tucking himself under Jonah's umbrella. At one point Vicar began a speech. "Boys, I wanted . . . I had hoped . . . That is, we all . . ." Helpless, he turned quickly and strode back toward the little station, disappearing for a short time around the far corner.

"Coward!" Freddie accused under his breath.

"Leave off, you. Only doing what he must."

"But he don't even know where he's sendin' us." Jamie's voice sounded frightened. "An' he said we ain't all gonna end up t'gether. I heard Mister Grabel sayin' we'll go to the four corners. Jonah, I don't even know where that is!"

"It ain't a place, it's . . ."

As if immune to their words Rowley blurted, "What's it like in Africa?"

Three scowling faces turned toward him in unison, high above Edgar's searching eyes.

At last Freddie muttered, "Dunno, but I guess it ain't rainin'."

Chapter 3

Ambages

Reaching for another battered train car from the box of toys, Lillian carefully lined it up after the others. The magnets holding them together were rather weak. And though the hardwood floor was a nice place to play, it was somewhat uncomfortable for her to kneel on. Furthermore, while Milton was actively scampering throughout the room, Matty was quiet on the floor next to her. Too quiet.

Lillian leaned back to rest on one arm, allowing her legs to unfold beside her as she shifted her weight, trying to sit more comfortably. "My father works with railway cars. Do you remember that?"

Little Matty shook his head without lifting his eyes.

"He figured out a better way to keep the cars cold on the inside—so that fresh meat could be shipped farther away—to the biggest cities. So whenever I see trains it makes me think of my father." Lillian allowed herself to smile a little. "I think we told you that he left on a trip last summer in a big ship all the way across the ocean to Wales, before Miss Grace and the others came to Brookfield. That's why he doesn't live at our house with us. Do you remember seeing his picture on top of my piano?"

No response.

"Matty? Matty, can you look at me?"

Blue eyes lifted. He needed a wash, for smudges of dinner still showed around the corners of his mouth.

"Matty, what are you thinking about? You're so quiet." Lillian reached out a hand to brush the fringe of hair away from his eyes.

He frowned mildly. So many years lacking a proper ability to speak had made him a master of avoidance. Instead of giving an answer, the little boy pushed the line of cars forward until they crumpled against one another in a zigzag pattern.

Milton crawled closer, dropping down on his belly beside them. "Not that way, Matty. Ya gotta keep 'em in a row." He began working to straighten out the line again. "If we had tracks, then we could push 'em. 'Member the ones at our house? It was the tracks kep' 'em straight, right, Miss Lillian?"

Lillian nodded with a smile and waited.

Slowly the train became a gentle curve again as two pairs of hands assembled it. "It's ready. You can push it now. But I get ta make the sounds."

Matty's eyes darted to his brother and then back to the train. His hand reached out.

"Chug, chug, chug."

A faint grin. The pudgy hand pushed a little harder, and the toy began to creep forward.

"Chug, chug, chug. Toot! Toot!" Suddenly Milton produced a stuffed dog, much larger than the train in scale. "Oh no, it's a bad wolf. He's gonna get 'em, Matty."

A spreading smile.

The expressionless dog thumped closer. "Hurry, Matty. Ya gotta get away!"

One by one the magnets failed. The line collapsed and folded against itself.

"Crash!" Milton hollered. "Bang, crash, smash!"

Matty began to giggle, falling over onto his side. Milton piled on top, making the dog trample harmlessly across his brother's shoulder. "He's gonna get ya. Get away! Get away!" They rolled across the floor together.

Lillian pushed up from the hardwood to take a seat on a nearby rocking chair, allowing the boys to continue with their own amusements. The playroom was surprisingly sparse for the number of occupants it served, not that she'd ever seen it crowded. The resident children were older, and they spent very little of their time here. They had more important things to do elsewhere—studying and learning skills for future employment. This room was used primarily whenever there was a younger child staying for a short time.

For three long days the sisters had waited aimlessly. Only a letter from Father, delivered by Walter on a return visit, had buoyed Lillian's heart. Father wouldn't have read yet about the trouble, but he wrote that his time in Scotland had been quite successful. And it seemed that Delyth, his friend who'd gone along, had been quite entertaining. When not otherwise occupied with speeches or sharing time at their host's home, it appeared that the two men had spent quite a few days sightseeing. Lillian was grateful that Father had discovered a true friend within his large clan. Still, she knew he'd intended that Lillian would be the one sharing his days, his travels. All she could share with him now was his disappointment that plans had changed—though she couldn't bring herself to regret much of what had happened to her instead.

Her mind turned to Quinley Sinclair, who was investigating the Szwedas' claim. Lillian made a mental note to write about their encouraging first meeting in her next letter to Father. However, she was still uncertain what the outcome might be. Mr. Sinclair was traveling now to a small town in central Alberta to meet with the Szwedas in order to take their statement. If she and Grace were found to have overstepped their authority, which of course they had, the boys might be returned to the Szwedas and the sisters' little makeshift children's home in Brookfield might be brought to an untimely end. It would be a dreadful shame.

After that initial meeting with Quinley, Grace and Lillian could have easily returned to Brookfield with Walter. But in a hushed voice Grace had pressed her opinion persuasively that "*there is always risk when housing children within a group setting.*" Lillian tried not to allow her imagination to draw too many assumptions as to what Grace had meant. The other children here were older than the twins. They might tease Matty and Milton. They might take advantage of them regarding chores or meals. And, at any rate, it was still necessary for someone to supervise their play and schooling. The classes provided at Brayton House were far beyond the little ones' abilities. If the boys were to continue gaining skills in reading, writing, mathematics, and Bible—and even help with speaking—Matty and Milton would need individual attention. So since there was no other pressing need for the sisters to return, Grace and Lillian lingered in Lethbridge in hopes of serving the little boys best.

Pulling her out of such dark thoughts, Milton climbed up onto Lillian's lap. "He's gonna hide now an' I'm gonna find him."

Lillian chuckled. Matty was clearly visible where he was burrowing down into the toy box in order to make room to close the lid over himself.

"Thank you, Milton," she whispered against his hair.

"Fer what?"

"For being such a good brother to Matty."

"I am? A good brother?"

"Of course. You're kind and gentle and thoughtful."

He leaned his head against her shoulder. "Naw. I jus' like ta wrestle 'im. 'Cause that's funner than bein' kind."

"Well, I can't argue with that, I suppose. But I'm glad you have each other. He's a very important person to you."

Her words seemed to make an impression, and Milton grew more pensive. "Miss Lillian?"

"Yes?"

"I wonder what it's like ta be—ta be just *one* person."

Goosebumps rose on Lillian's arms. She gathered the little boy tighter. "Is that how you feel about Matty?"

"'Course. 'Cause we're the same one, 'cept there's two'a us." Then he was gone again, slipping off her lap in order to feign a search around the room as if he had no idea where the muffled snickers were coming from.

He feels like he's two people? Can that be true? And if it is, how would he feel if they'd been separated—having lost half of his own identity? Such strange math the boy is using to describe their special bond! Lillian felt tears rising up at the idea. *And if Milton feels this way, how on earth does Matty feel about it? At times Matty still seems just a shadow of his twin, completely reliant upon Milton.*

She and Grace were sisters, but it was different. In all the years that they were apart Lillian had grieved and missed her younger sibling, but she'd never felt like less than a complete person. This fraternity went deeper. It went well beyond losing family. It threatened to alter each boy's sense of self.

"Father," she prayed silently, "I confessed already that it was wrong to lie, but I can't—I just can't feel sorry that we did *something* to keep these boys together. It would have been such a terrible sin to have let them suffer so much at the hands of hateful people."

• • • • • • •

Having loaded the steamship and watched it cast off from the wharf with a trail of thick gray smoke rising into the winter sky, Ben spent his days in port assisting with activity aboard another company ship or reading in solitary places, waiting for his next assigned ship to dock. He currently owned two books: a volume of the works of William Shakespeare and an English translation of *The Aeneid*. Years ago it had become his habit to trade his reading materials at used bookshops while he was in port. The practice saved money and also precious space in his kit. However, he had acquired these two volumes months before and had procrastinated about exchanging them. Instead, he read them over and over, feeling he drew more from the texts with each read.

Picking up where he had left off with *The Two Gentlemen of Verona*, Ben settled in for another comfortable night. He mumbled his favorite phrases aloud, enjoying the sound of them as they passed over his lips in whispers. Just as he was ready to blow out his candle, he reread Jane's letter, folded it neatly, and tucked it inside the back cover. Only the initial reading had brought tears. His sensible emotions had returned, and his mind had taken charge over his heart again. Here in the darkness he rationally reaffirmed his decision to find his family, whatever the cost.

He rarely left the shipyard except for meals, when he was forced to frequent the vendors along the docks, pushing himself back out into the swells of people crowding nearby. Head down, Ben avoided eye contact and conversation, keeping to his own purposes.

On Saturday he overheard a ruckus between a man with a clipboard and an angry woman dragging along a scrawny little urchin. It wasn't the woman who got his attention. It was the little waif she held by the hand. Never in his life had he seen such a sad little bundle. Suddenly the little girl turned and looked directly at him from across the wharf. Her intense blue eyes were too large for the sallow little face. He saw nothing but misery reflected there. His chest tightened. He couldn't remember feeling such intense compassion for another human being.

The man with the clipboard shouted a few more fierce words and turned away, waving off the woman with a firm hand. It was obvious he was demanding that the woman and child leave the premises. They turned to go, the woman still spewing words of anger, the child meekly falling into step behind. Ben knew exactly who the man with the clipboard was, a recorder hired to manage the passenger list for one of the organizations booked on an upcoming voyage. Was the woman hoping to purchase a ticket from him? Was she a member of his group, or trying to force her own inclusion? Would the child be a passenger? Surely not! She was far too frail.

Forsaking the angry man, the pair neared and stopped. The woman dropped the hand of the child, then rummaged through her handbag. "I know I put that paper in here. If only I could find the correct person with whom to speak."

The child's eyes lifted from the ground. A shiver ran through Ben as their gazes met. Before he realized what he was doing he smiled back, nodded a silent greeting. The little face flickered with a mild expression of hope that pierced Ben's heart even more deeply. *What is it 'bout this little girl?*

"Here it is. Here it is and I'm going right back to speak with that man again. I was told there was still time to get you aboard, and I won't be deterred by some little dictator with a printed list and a cocky attitude." The woman spun on her heel. "I won't take no for an answer. Come along, Jane."

Jane? Her name's Jane? Dumbstruck, Ben watched as the pair moved away again. Had he heard the girl's name earlier? Was that why he'd been so drawn to her? He rose to his feet, but they were gone again. He hoped the woman would find the help she was seeking for the sake of this poor little Jane.

• • • • • • •

Lillian set her book on the nightstand, at last giving up on trying to read. She drew up the edge of her covers and settled into the pillow. The room she shared with Grace was at the house of a friend, Mrs. O'Shea, a kind and generous widow from her sister's previous church. But it was awkward to stay without knowing exactly how long their imposition might last. Lillian yawned and rolled onto her side.

Grace opened the door quietly. She seemed uncertain if Lillian was asleep yet. "Oh good. I noticed the lamp was still lit, but I didn't want to wake you. Sorry I'm so late tonight."

"Don't worry, I've been reading. And I doubt I'll fall asleep soon anyway. I keep thinking about the boys, wishing they were here with us instead of in a room with strangers."

"I think they've settled in well. They seem to be adjusting. I've asked them repeatedly how things are going, and they seem to be coping well. Plus, they have a woman who sits outside their door on the landing all night long to supervise the children. I feel much better knowing that."

"Sure, but what happens next? I see the questions in their eyes, and it's certainly all I can think about. Every day that passes makes it harder to be patient."

Grace dropped her robe across the foot of the bed and leaned over to blow out the light. As she settled under the covers next to Lillian she whispered, "I know what you mean. We'll just have to keep praying."

"But the boys, they've already suffered enough for a lifetime. They need stability and love."

"You're right, Lillian, but we can't change what's happening, and we're staying as close to them as we're allowed. They light up every morning when they see us. . . ."

"Yes—even though they know we're going to sit with them over schoolwork."

"Yes, even with that. I just have to believe God's promise that He hasn't forgotten them, that He's still working a plan for their good."

Lillian sighed in frustration. Halfheartedly she muttered, "*Longa est injuria, longae ambages.*"

Grace's head rose up from her pillow. "I'm sorry—what? What did you say?"

"Oh, it's from *The Aeneid.* In context it means, 'Great is the injury and long the tale.' It's a saying that Mother used to quote from time to time." She frowned into the darkness hanging above them.

"Is it what you were reading?"

"No, it's from one of the books I studied years ago with a tutor Mother hired."

Grace muttered, "It's not a very encouraging thought, though, is it?"

Rolling to her back, Lillian stared up at the shadowed ceiling above them. "But it's true, isn't it? Life is often pretty discouraging. It's just plain hard, Grace. And so often there are ambages—unexpected detours—where the road ahead seems twisted and difficult to follow."

She heard Grace groan a little in the darkness. "Maybe it's even worse when the twisty road belongs to somebody you love, like the twins, eh?"

"Yes, exactly."

"Your quote makes me think of Psalm twenty-three and the line about walking through the valley. It's frightening to walk through life sometimes. I know what you mean. I do."

"Grace?"

"Uh-huh?"

"I hate to feel like the naysayer all the time, but Mother had me memorize that psalm too. 'Yea, though I walk through the valley of the shadow of death, I will fear no evil. . . .' I have to admit that I *do* fear evil—right now I worry about the evil that might fall into Matty and Milton's lives. I'm sorry, but I do."

"Well, sis, I've always felt it's much better to be honest about how you feel than to pretend. I think that's actually a kind of courage too."

Courage? If only that were true! It'd be nice to feel I have a little bit of courage. Shaking her head, Lillian continued, "Do you know what little Milton said to me today? He said he wondered what it would be like to be *just one person.*" She let the words hang in the air as Grace processed them.

"Oh," came a breathy reply. "He's *two* people. I think that's quite profound."

"Me too. And it makes me want to fight even harder for them. I just wish I knew how."

"We'll keep doing everything we can. And we'll keep trusting God to do everything else."

Lillian didn't say the words aloud. Instead, she let the house remain quiet and still, but she was thinking that it was very hard to trust God. Then the memory came to mind of how He'd worked to resolve the issue with the stolen foal, and also how He'd led her to find Grace. Silently she prayed, *God, I don't know how You can fix this. It's even worse that I feel so guilty about causing this problem. But will You please lead the twins to someplace safe at the end of these ambages? I know You love them too.* She lifted an arm to press over her eyes. *I don't know why it's so hard to trust You when I'm certain I've seen You work in the past. So I'm going to choose to hope You're in charge of this too. I'm certainly going to try.*

In the morning Lillian woke to an empty bedroom. She hated to sleep longer than Grace and worried that she'd made breakfast wait. Rolling over, she noticed a slip of paper laid on top of her book. It was a verse written out in Grace's hand. *For God hath not given us the spirit of fear; but of power, and of love, and of a sound mind. 2 Timothy 1:7.*

• • • • • • •

"I think it's time that I asked if I can put in a few hours at the diner again." Grace made the announcement as the sisters sat with the boys for lunch.

Lillian thought about the little restaurant where they'd met for the very first time as adults—the job that Grace had been working in order to provide for the little children she housed in

Lethbridge. The diner would always hold a warm place in Lillian's heart—but why would Grace return there now? "Do you truly think we'll be here long enough to benefit from you working?"

"I might as well. I don't see any reason to delay, and I just can't abide having so little to do, even if it's only been four days. I heard this morning when I went for a walk into downtown that Marta is away for a bit visiting her mother. Do you remember her? The other waitress I shared the morning shift with. So I think Murray Sands, who owns the place, will let me pick up a few hours, at least until Marta comes back."

Lillian looked down at her shoes. "What about me? Do you suppose he would let me work too—even for a day or two?"

"It wouldn't hurt to ask if you're interested."

Three children who'd been sharing their table gathered their empty dishes. The movements drew Lillian's attention. Grace smiled at them warmly, spoke to them a little. The teen named Ruth who had welcomed the twins was among them, the tallest. She seemed to be in charge of the other girls. But Lillian's mind was elsewhere as they walked away. She was thinking about her parents.

Oh, Father, what would you say if you heard I had taken up a paying job? She knew, though, without a doubt what her tradition-embracing father would say. He'd be against the very idea. Aloud she sighed. "I'd better not, Grace. I mean, I want to help as best I can, but I doubt my father would approve. He was always so clear that he was the provider for our family—and he's done a wonderful job of it. Even now, when he's so far away, I know he's still taking care of me."

Grace laid a hand on Lillian's arm. "It's okay. One of us should be near at hand for the boys as much as possible. Sid told me that Quinley Sinclair is expected back soon from his interview with the Szwedas."

"Then maybe you won't need to work either. Maybe we can head home again before long."

"I hope so. But even if I only help out for a few hours, it's probably worth it for me."

Lillian cringed. *Grace doesn't feel the safety of a father to provide for her. That's what she's thinking.* Aloud Lillian added what she hoped was encouraging. "I would never discourage you from doing what you feel is right, Grace. But please remember that you're family. And Father thinks of you that way already. I know he does."

A measured smile answered.

A group of children passed close by, speaking loudly. The sound of a heavy door closing echoed from the stairwell. "Could that be him—Mr. Sinclair?" With a glance at Grace, Lillian rose and moved toward the entry, then stood at the bottom of the landing. It was Walter, stamping the snow from his boots and hanging his coat and Stetson on a hook.

She called up at him, "Well, hello. I didn't expect you again today."

His face turned to find Lillian. A broad smile lit his eyes. "Hello. I wondered how quickly I'd cross paths with you here."

"I thought you were going to attend to business for the ranch."

Walter descended the stairs to join Lillian. His intense eyes studied her face as he answered slowly in his purposeful way of speaking. "I am—or, I will be. I've got some registry papers to pick up for the boss later."

"About his new bulls?" Lillian sincerely wished to sound as if she understood his work, reaching for the only bit of information she could remember. Tommy had recently imported new bulls.

"Well, it's about his herd, anyway." Walter laughed. "I know it's winter, but calvin' work will start again soon enough, and you'd be surprised how much paperwork is involved if you want the kind of reputation Tommy is shootin' for."

"Oh, I'd like to come out to see the calves in the spring. Maybe the boys would . . ." Lillian stopped as she remembered that the twins might no longer be around.

He placed a comforting hand behind her arm, slid it down toward her elbow gently. "I think it'll work out. I really do. I'm just certain you'll be able to bring those boys to see Tommy's calves after all the dust settles."

"I hope so," Lillian murmured gratefully.

He cleared his throat, and his expression became more serious. "But I'm not sure if I . . ."

"Good morning, Walter." Grace appeared beside them.

"Hi, Grace. I didn't see you there."

She seemed to sense the conversation had turned rather private. "I don't mean to interrupt. We were just finishing lunch."

"It's all right. It might be best to speak to both of you together. I was just tellin' Lillian that I might be gone north for a while."

It was Lillian who reacted. "North? To where?"

"I plan on applyin' for a job with an oil company. I'm gonna—"

"You're leaving Tommy's ranch?" The sound of Lillian's voice in her own ears betrayed a stronger reaction than she'd intended.

Grace's answer was far more guarded. "I'm sorry to hear that, Walter. I certainly wish you well. We'll talk later, I'm sure." Then she dismissed herself and nudged the twins away, back toward the dining room.

Walter took a step closer, ducked his head so he could speak quietly. "I'm sorry, Lillian. Maybe I should have told you while I was still thinkin' about it. Even now I'm not sure if it'll be worth the change, but I figured it didn't hurt to apply."

"I see." Her eyes studied the nearby wall.

"Are you disappointed?"

"No, of course not. I . . . You have every right to . . . I just hadn't considered . . ." For a moment she bit her lip. She wanted desperately to simply ask him *why*. But the word sounded too impertinent, too disparaging, too familiar—even between them. "May I ask what it is you wish to accomplish by this—this change?"

"Sure," he said softly, quietly. "Honestly, I just hope to make some good money. See, Lillian, the demand for gasoline keeps risin'—more and more people drive cars. I hear that some folk are makin' a small fortune and the rigs keep gettin' closer and closer. They need more men to keep up with demand. I feel like it'd be kinda foolish to stay on with Tommy and not take advantage of this opportunity when I want to . . . when I'd like to . . ."

This was a side of Walter that Lillian had never seen, this materialistic ambition. It made her feel uncomfortable. "Are you giving up the idea of ranching on your own someday? I thought . . ." She struggled to find the correct phrasing for her assumptions.

His brown eyes squinted back. "Oh no, just hopin' to make it easier to get started with that. Tommy has financial backin' from investors in the States, but I've always said I'd like to avoid goin' that route. If I can make enough in a year or two to purchase some land, I'd be ready sooner." He cleared his throat and glanced around them. "I'd sure like to be on my own—and out of the bunkhouse. I want to have the freedom to . . ."

He'll be gone for a year or two? Lillian's mind had frozen on the phrase. Eyes lifting to answer Walter, Lillian noticed instead that Roland was descending the stairs. She laid a hand on Walter's flannel-covered arm. "I'm not sure what to say, Walter. I think you know how much I'd miss you. I hope you know. But I wouldn't ever want to discourage you from trying to follow your dreams."

CHAPTER 4

Eavesdropping

The next day dawned clear and dry over the shipyards of Liverpool. Knowing how hard others would be working before the rainy weather returned, Ben joined the crew on the docks. Loading and pushing carts in and out of the holds for an entire morning was harder work than he'd done for some time. Soon he set his dark greatcoat aside and allowed the labor to warm his body, oddly grateful for the reminder of how much he could still demand from himself now that he was no longer in his twenties.

By noon the drizzling gray sky had returned. He contemplated the purchase of his meal. He could head toward the vendor carts as usual, or he could choose one of the nearby restaurants, where he could sit in warmth and watch the passersby through the detachment of a glass window. It would be a rare luxury, a way of rewarding himself for hard work done. As he strode across the docks toward the restaurants, he began to calculate how many crates he'd loaded, estimated how much longer it would take the men to finish this next ship, considering the stacks that remained. Still, he hadn't quite decided what to do for his meal yet.

A coat flashed past him. Above it perched a straw hat wrapped by a green ribbon that covered dull gray hair. It drew his attention. He'd seen that hat before. It belonged to the lady on the wharf with the little girl. Poor little Jane.

The woman strode into a restaurant off to his right. He was near enough to overhear her request a table at the door and explain that she was meeting a friend. It piqued his curiosity and made his own decision clear. Ben followed her inside and was seated in a corner near the window not far from her table. He smiled to himself at his good fortune. *Maybe I'll learn what this woman's plans are fer little Jane.*

She'd shed her coat and draped it over the chair beside her. With her stiff white collar, rows of starched ruffles down the front of her blouse, and the narrowness of her skirt, Ben could tell that she was in a class above his own, though not especially wealthy. The shirtwaist bore signs of wear, the skirt fit a little too loosely to be new. But the woman's posture and demeanor more than anything else broadcast to those around her that she considered herself superior. He wondered if her family had seen better days, had been reduced like so many others during the country's recent round of hardships.

As he speculated on the woman's past, a second lady entered. She seemed equally pretentious, quite out of place among the laborers and merchants who filled the seaside eatery.

"Matilda," she greeted her friend, laying her gloves on the table and positioning herself so the waiter could help her from her coat. Dutifully, he also drew back her chair so she could be seated. Ben caught a faint roll of the man's eyes.

"Hattie, I'm glad you've come. It's been so long, and so much has happened that—"

"My dear, I must tell you that my driver was reluctant to let me out of the car here. Honestly, whatever possessed you to ask me to meet you in a place like this?" She accepted a menu from the waiter but disdainfully set it aside without a second glance.

"I have business in the area and was hoping you might join me. I thought an extra person—a person of your stature—might tip the scales in my favor."

They ordered tea and Welsh bakestones made with currants, the only item on the dockside eatery's menu that was sweet.

Though she sat stiffly erect on her chair, Matilda's shoulders wavered with anticipation as she announced, "I was almost delayed today, as I was kept on the telephone for some time with some society people."

Hattie looked back sharply. "Society? Who from society was calling you?"

Matilda ignored the terse slight. She admitted, "Well, I don't mean *high society*. It was from *a* society." The self-satisfied expression on her face exposed how much she enjoyed the suspense of baiting her friend.

"Which society?"

"I didn't catch the name, but it was in regard to my kin."

"Kin?" Matilda seemed to have Hattie's full attention now. "I didn't realize you had any kin."

"Well, I do. My brother's—"

"You said your only brother died at sea as a young man, on one of your father's ships." Hattie stirred cream into her tea, ready to dismiss the topic out of hand.

"And so he did," Matilda replied with a bit of a huff. "Back when I was still a young woman, barely turned twenty."

"So?"

"He had an infant son at the time of his—departure."

"Ohhhh." The word was drawn out long with a mixture of accusation and acute interest.

Matilda took a sip of her tea. She seemed to linger over the coaxing expression on her friend's face. Ben's food arrived. He ate slowly.

"So—the son is—where?"

"Sorry to say, the son also passed."

"At sea?"

A contemptuous look. "Of course not at sea. He died of some illness—I don't know the particulars."

Hattie seemed to grow tired of Matilda's cat-and-mouse conversation. "So, I gather there are no kin," she proclaimed carelessly and helped herself to a round bakestone from the plate.

Matilda watched her friend break the little grilled cake in half with great ceremony, as if the dusting of fine sugar was somehow risky to touch. "Oh—indeed there are," announced Matilda at last. "And if you hadn't been on holiday, you'd have met my kin by now."

Hattie lifted an eyebrow. It seemed she now accepted that there might be a story here worthy of her attention after all. In Ben's estimation, clearly this was a woman who enjoyed a good session of gossip. "A wife?"

"No, she's gone, too, I'm afraid. Unfortunate accident."

Hattie shook her head. "What a family of continuous disaster! No wonder your father lost his fortune and you've never married."

The comment brought Matilda leaning in closer to the table, her voice lowering earnestly. She became more direct. "Two remain. Two girls. Ages twelve and six."

Hattie seemed to summon the grace to show concern. "So, they are alone? Where are . . . ?"

Her question was cut short. It appeared Matilda had reached the point of the story that was most exciting to her. "They were brought to me two weeks ago from my nephew's estate. Staff had been caring for them."

"Estate? Do you suggest he was a man of means? Did he marry well?"

Matilda seemed uncertain for a moment. "Well, I'm told there is an estate and that it's being sold. The staff was dismissed. But, as I am already in possession of the girls, well . . ." She paused dramatically before speaking again. "There will be remuneration, of course."

Hattie set the remainder of her dessert on her plate and leaned forward. "Are you saying that you intend to *keep* the girls? Why, you're totally unprepared for such a task. You do not even enjoy children. And haven't you always declared that your own mother was cold and distant?"

"I never said I don't enjoy children."

Ben thought about the manner in which the woman had dragged poor little Jane by the hand as they'd crossed the wharf. He was quick to agree with Hattie. This was not a woman who was likely to care well for children. He wiped at his mouth with a sleeve and reached for another swallow of his drink.

"You may not have voiced it—but you shoo them away whenever they dare approach your gate."

"Well, those aren't my kin. There's a difference, you know."

"Where will you put them? You've only one bedchamber in your suite of rooms."

The remark caused Matilda to lean away, turning her face to the far corner of the room. "I'm well aware of that. I've let out so many of the other rooms in my father's house that I feel more a renter than a resident myself. It's been such a hardship, Hattie, dividing the manor house up into so many parts. I can hardly describe the weight pressing down upon me. So unfair, as if I were fated for—"

"But if you keep the girls, then won't it be—"

"Of course I'm not keeping the girls!" she snapped tersely. "I don't even know them. But I can't quite make up my mind what *to do* with them. That's the whole reason I was on the telephone with the society before meeting you today."

"I see."

"The older one, Margaret, is easily managed. I've already contacted a boarding school for her. My guardianship of Maggie secures me to the estate. But the younger child, Jane, is much more difficult. She's only six, a little scrap of a thing. At first I wondered . . ." The words hung in the air, heavy with tension. "No, I *will* suggest it. Would you, by any chance, wish to keep the other? You have more room than . . ."

Hattie looked on in utter shock. "Me? Whatever for? I certainly have no need of a youngster underfoot. I wouldn't even consider such a thing. And if you were to ask my advice, I would tell you to think carefully before you accept such an arrangement. Remuneration or no, it's a foolish scheme in my opinion. Foolhardy. Get yourself a cat if you need company. Children are nothing but trouble."

The sudden eruption of vindictive words seemed to burst Matilda's inflated sense of self for a moment. Then her back stiffened again as she looked her friend fully in the eye. "It falls on me, Harriet Branch. These are my grandnieces—or nieces once removed—I'm not quite certain what to call them. But they're kin, as I've explained. And, like it or not, I am responsible for decisions regarding their well-being, for now. Not to mention that their estate—whatever its size—would be a source of assistance with my own debts."

Hattie set her teacup back on its saucer, rested her elbows on the edge of the table, and demanded, "Then what in the world are we doing here, Matilda? What on earth does your prolonged explanation have to do with the shipyards? Because you haven't explained that yet, have you?"

Matilda blushed. "It was an idea I had. I'd heard of—of ships that carry children to Canada. They're given a new life, with families who desperately want children. I've tried in vain to secure a place for Jane on the next ship. I wondered if you, if you might—well, exert your influence, use your family name, to make these people more attentive to my plight." Her voice broke. "You're right that I can't keep the young child. My health and resources aren't what they once were. I can manage the older, who'll be in school for most of the year, but the younger, I simply can't . . ."

A knobby old hand with thin blue skin crossed the table and enveloped the fingers of her friend, her demeanor suddenly affirming. "I don't mean to sound heartless, dear. But for the first time I agree with you. And I'm certain it's for the best. I'll do whatever I can to help secure her passage."

"Thank you, Hattie. I was certain you wouldn't leave me on my own. But I've had such a series of personal calamities. My only other alternative seemed to be to surrender her to the government, but I hate to think of her at a workhouse. She's so small and fragile. . . ."

Unable to restrain himself, Ben leapt from his chair. It struck hard against the wall behind him. Eyes lifted toward him from all around the room. The women, too, turned to face him. He stared them down. It was enough. The pair was conspiring to abandon that poor little waif, whose large blue eyes refused to leave Ben's mind, this woman's *kin*. He marched across the room, paid his bill at the desk, and turned his back on the entire scene. *Well, now I wish I'd ne'er listened ta 'em! No one, most 'specially a child, should e'er know the sight of such a God-forsaken place as a workhouse! How dare they consider such a thing, the pitiless old crones!*

• • • • • • •

Grace's offer to return to work at her old job was hastily accepted by Mr. Sands. Lillian found herself alone at the orphanage, helping out wherever she could create a useful purpose, sitting with the boys through their lessons, playing with them, reading aloud, and going for long walks when the weather allowed. The sisters had laughed when they referred to this time of "ambages," but neither was genuinely amused. It was a strain to simply wait, a difficulty not to know where the path ahead led.

And then on their sixth day in town, Quinley Sinclair suddenly returned. Meetings were held, meetings that did not include

Lillian or Grace. Lillian observed the faces passing by her in the hallways and held her breath. She tried not to imagine what they discussed—how her own words and actions were being judged. Instead, she stayed busy.

Tugging at a bedsheet corner and pulling it taut, Lillian smoothed it out and tucked it under with quick hands before lifting the coverlet into place. Milton worked across the bed from her, punching at a pillow to fluff it before setting it into place. He leaned a well-worn stuffed dog against the pillow. Then they moved on to the next bed in the short row.

"Miss Lillian?"

"Yes, Milt."

"Is Mister Norberg goin' away?"

Freezing in place, Lillian closed her eyes for a moment. *Has Milton overheard something about Walter?* "What makes you ask that, dear?" Once again Lillian's hands glided across the surface, working out wrinkles.

"He was talkin' to Miss Grace. He told her 'bout a job fer him—gettin' gas outta the ground—fer cars and things."

"Oh?"

"Yeah, she said it sounded scary. A'cause the gas gets on fire sometimes."

Oh, Milton. You are not helping. With a strained smile, Lillian drew up another coverlet and waited for the boy to complete his tasks. A soft rabbit nestled against this pillow.

"But Miss Grace talked about you too. She tol' Mister Norberg ta settle up with you first."

"What?"

"She tol' him—aw, I don't 'member what she said. But it was kinda like she wanted him ta talk ta ya first, 'fore goin' away. Guess he wants to tell ya 'bout the gas and fires and stuff."

An inner turmoil had begun. Lillian wanted to know more, and yet she knew the risks of listening to gossip—particularly words from a child so young he'd clearly understood very little of the conversation. Yet it was almost impossible not to succumb. "Milton, what did Mr. Norberg say in answer?"

He paused. "Ummmm, oh yeah! I 'member. He said he wants ta get married to ya, an' he wants ta buy a farm too. So he wants ta get the money first. Yeah, that was it." The boy seemed pleased to have recalled a large portion of the conversation so well. "Oh, an' then Miss Grace said he better say somethin' to ya 'fore he leaves. That's what she meant. He better tell ya his plans a'fore he leaves fer the job." He juggled another pillow in an attempt to fluff it before adding, "But I told ya. So now it's okay if he fergets. Right, Miss Lillian?"

Lillian lowered herself to a seat on the bed. Her head was spinning, but she forced the questions away for the moment. "Milton, I want to tell you that I'm sorry. It's my own fault, but I should not have asked you to tell me about a conversation you overheard. We call that gossiping. And it's something the Bible tells us not to do."

"You didn't wanna know?"

"Come here, please, Milt." She stretched out a hand toward him.

He hopped onto the bed and snuggled down close against Lillian's side.

"I should have gone to Miss Grace and Mr. Norberg instead. I should have asked them directly what I wanted to know. And in the future, I hope you can understand how speaking to people directly is better too. It makes God pleased when we don't talk *about* other people when they're not around. It helps avoid confusion and misunderstandings."

"I shouldn'ta told ya?"

"No, dear. It would be best not to share with others words that you overheard."

"Huh." He seemed to be mulling over this new information.

"You didn't know, Milton. But I did. And I should not have asked you to continue. I'm sorry. Can you please forgive me?"

"'Course, Miss Lillian. That's easy."

His childish words tumbled around in her mind for the rest of the day. *It's my own fault. I have no one but myself to blame! But what do I do now? How can I possibly begin a conversation with Walter? And why do I feel so annoyed with Grace? I know her intentions were kind, but it's hard not to be perturbed that she interfered. And, on top of it all, isn't Grace just as guilty of gossiping with Walter—talking about me when I wasn't around? These are all things he should have said directly to me.*

Chapter 5

Schemes

At last a meeting was scheduled with Quinley Sinclair that the sisters were invited to attend. As they walked the short hallway to Sid's office together, Lillian felt gentle fingers close around her hand. She smiled at Grace and squeezed back in response, certain that both of them were struggling with dry mouths and pounding hearts.

They took seats at one end of the table and waited for all of the other chairs to fill. Sid and Roland Scott provided small talk as they waited. Grace even managed to banter with them a little.

Two gentlemen in dark suits whom Lillian had not met previously entered the room next. Sid introduced them as members of the governing board for Brayton House. And finally, Mr. Sinclair arrived and took a seat at the head of the table. Once again, confidence seemed to glow like an aura around him.

"I'm so pleased to see you again, ladies. I hope your stay in town has been enjoyable. You've had almost a week of leisure."

Lillian rolled her eyes toward Grace, who was smiling back at him politely.

"Well, let's just begin. We're all busy people and this has been a long process already. As you all know, I've spoken to Jack and Katrin Szweda. I feel I was able to hear their complaints and truly understand how they perceive they were slighted. They maintain that they acted in what they thought was good faith. . . ." Here he hesitated, then added dryly, "In their own way. I was able to clarify the agreement they'd signed regarding the twin boys, and I explained to them how each side had failed to live up to the contract."

Lillian's mind was spinning, trying to follow the implications of his rapid flow of words, trying not to get bogged down with arguing and correcting in her own mind—but just to listen instead.

Quinley Sinclair's gaze moved around the room as he said, "The Szwedas now understand that they had contracted for two children and had agreed to provide for Milton and Matthew Baines until they reached their majority at the age of eighteen. Despite their own assessment that one of the boys was impaired, their contract with the Viney Boggs Mercy Society legally remained in force. To surrender Matthew was a breach of the contract." He turned over a paper that lay in front of him, pausing for only a moment before launching into his speech again. "However, there was also a failure on the part of Miss Bennett and Miss Walsh—a misrepresentation of their authority in the matter and an overreach of their responsibility in the situation, acting as a subsidiary of Brayton House and not, legally, for the Mercy Society."

Another pause. The room remained quiet. Lillian swallowed her own response.

"Complicating the matter, at no time was Brayton House responsible for the care of these children prior to their surrender to Miss Bennett and Miss Walsh. The Viney Boggs Mercy Society, who originally received them in Canada and assigned them to the Szweda family, was the only other legal custodian who had jurisdiction over the boys. And it was to this society that Mr. and Mrs. Szweda were entitled to appeal once they felt they'd been misled. It was their own error to involve Miss Bennett and Miss Walsh in the first place."

He paused. "Are there any questions?"

Lillian's mind was awash with questions, but she opted to hold back the flood. If no one else sought additional information, she didn't dare to speak. Instead, she struggled against the urge to hold her breath, forcing herself to exhale slowly.

"Well then, unless there is some comment concerning what I've already covered, I'll move on to the decision." With little hesitation Quinley continued. "I've recommended to my colleagues that the boys *not* be returned to Mr. and Mrs. Jack Szweda, on the grounds that the adoptive parents broke the contract between themselves and the Viney Boggs Mercy Society by surrendering the boys in an improper manner and to unapproved custodians."

A thrill of cool air rushed into Lillian's lungs. She closed her eyes. *Thank You, God, for that.*

"Furthermore, I am recommending to our board of directors that Miss Bennett and Miss Walsh be considered as legal *temporary* caregivers for future children placed by the Mercy Society, under the auspices of Brayton House, so that they may once again legally shelter children placed by said society should the need arise."

That's it. We've been exonerated!

Quinley set down his papers and shook his head emphatically, looking across the table at Lillian and Grace. "May I add, on a personal note off the record, that I wish we had homes like yours all across the country to take in these children when their placements don't work out. It would be such a benefit to all."

At last Lillian ventured a smile.

The gentlemen at the head of the table were first to stand, reaching to shake Quinley's hand. Lillian kept her seat, observing them all closely. His familiar charming smile once again on his face, Quinley leaned closer to speak into the ear of one of the suited men. The man laughed and whispered something back—no doubt some private joke between them.

For some reason, Lillian felt her back stiffen. *That's an odd ending to this meeting. They don't seem surprised at all. They seem to have known what Quinley was going to say, as if they had it all worked out before we ever sat down.* And then she countered her own concerns. *But why wouldn't they? It's not as if he should have kept it a secret. He's been investigating. He'll have spoken with everyone involved. So why does something seem to be a little off?*

Rising slowly, Lillian accepted Grace's exuberant embrace, then turned to Walter next. She tipped her head up, expecting to see him smiling in relief.

But Walter was watching Quinley closely too, contemplating thoughts of his own that were furrowing his brow. When his eyes turned down to meet Lillian's, the concern on his face dissolved instantly. "That couldn't have gone much better," he said with a grin, reaching his arm around her shoulders. "I never really doubted this outcome at all."

• • • • • • •

Memory of the women's restaurant conversation haunted Ben. This child's future was in desperate jeopardy and would be decided by two selfish spinsters. Yet he could think of nothing he could do to assist the little girl, no help to summon and bring to her aid. Who would bother to notice one more little orphan in need of a home among Liverpool's overtaxed charities? Still, he decided to watch for Matilda as he worked beside another ship, laboring now in full days so as not to miss her eventual visit.

At last the steamer on which he was to officially serve arrived in port. Ben was grateful to finally receive a berth assignment, tossing his kit bag under the bed and, after days of sleeping in dark corners, stretching out across a fresh straw mattress. For the first time he'd been given a small private room, evidence of his rising position in the company.

It wasn't until the ship was almost ready to depart that Ben noted the familiar hat bobbing through the crowd. Leaving his labors, he fell in step quickly behind the elderly woman in order to watch her closely. The child was again in tow. As Matilda disappeared into an office, Ben waited across from the door. Soon she exited, and there was no doubt she'd been declined again. Her eyes were blazing with rage.

A plan had formed during the time he'd been waiting for her to return. Ben chased after them. Just as he'd expected, they seemed to be heading directly for the train. He had to say his piece before she reached the station. All the way along the narrow streets he argued with himself. It was a crazy idea. It could get him fired. Even jailed. But those soulful eyes haunted him as no child's had before. With his heart in his throat, he hurried his step and approached the older woman.

"'Scuse me, ma'am. A minute, please. I saw what happened back there," he began, noticing the anger return instantly to her face, then be replaced by rising alarm. He hurried on. "No, please. Ya see, I–I work on that ship. I could get the girl aboard."

Now, the anger spiked. "Look," she said with a great deal of vehemence, "I have no money if that's your game."

"No," he quickly cut in. "I'm not askin' fer money. Just concerned fer the child. I could get little Jane to Canada."

Her eyes narrowed as she studied him. "Young man, are you on the level?" Her inflection told him how much she doubted his story.

He said the only thing he could think of to convince her. "I swear on me mother's Bible."

She stepped back, pulling the girl away with her. "How?"

"I could get the child on the ship. She needs a chance, much as the rest'a the lot. Lord knows, there's nothin' fer her here."

A shadow crossed the wrinkled face. Ben knew the comment

had come too close to accusing the woman, but he hurried on with renewed certainty in his voice. "An' I been ta Canada. I seen 'em—the people what care fer the kiddos. They got more fam'lies there what want a child, an' they can help. Good people, I hear. God-fearin' folk."

"How?" she repeated.

"I'd—I'd have ta smuggle her on, ma'am."

"Smuggle her? You could do that?"

He nodded.

"And you won't ask payment?"

"No, ma'am."

Slowly her expression softened, but her eyes revealed how quickly she was calculating the risks. "How do I know you are an honest man?" she dared ask.

He pointed to his shipboard identification tag.

"So." She still hesitated. "I see that you are from the ship, but that doesn't say—"

"My duty's ta look after the orphans, ma'am," he cut in. "To steward their journey where me ship's concerned—make sure they get proper food an' beddin' an' care—make certain there's a doc nigh if need be." He pointed behind him toward the harbor. "I've made the trip ta Canada more 'an once. I know how it works."

She studied him, frowning. There was doubt in her eyes as she puzzled over his words. "You'll look after her, a small child? You?"

Though his throat had tightened, he nodded firmly. "Aye, ma'am. As I say, that's me job."

With a slight shrug of her shoulders, she gave the girl a little push toward him. "Take her, then. But if you're lying, may God . . ."

He stopped her, lifting his hand slightly to halt her words. "No, ma'am. I can't take her now. Ya need ta bring the wee 'un back to the wharf. We're done loadin' at about six. There's a shed to the right side'a the ramp. I'll be close by then. Bring the girl ta me—

but make sure no one sees ya. Walk along with the crowd. Slip off ta the side an' leave her within. I'll—I'll take it from there."

She merely nodded at him warily. Then demanded, "What's your name? I need, at the very least, to know your name."

It was a risk. She could turn him over to the police for suggesting such a thing. "Ben Waldin," he answered, then corrected himself. "Ebenezer Waldin, rather. That's me full name." He turned away from the unlikely pair. There were things needing to be done before six o'clock. He wasn't certain he would see either of them ever again, but he'd be prepared.

• • • • • • •

Walter had waited patiently while congratulations were passed among the other people in the room. Lillian reached out a hand to squeeze his arm. "We can go home now—*with the twins.* Isn't that wonderful?"

"It is, truly."

Hesitating, Lillian studied his expression for a moment, then led him quietly out the door in order to speak with him more privately. "What is it?" she whispered. "What's wrong? What are you concerned about?"

Walter's eyes dropped to the floor and he shook his head. "Nothin'. I'm—just very glad for you."

His reluctance heightened Lillian's attention. Her heart fluttered a little. She hoped she already knew what other pressing issue he might want to discuss with her. Still, his face revealed nothing further.

His smile gradually returned, a little forced. "Let's find a way to celebrate. Where's Grace? We should all celebrate together."

Lillian hesitated, stepped closer rather than away. Her words softened. "You know you can tell me anything—ask me anything."

For a fleeting moment his eyes held again the look that she'd seen when they'd stood on Father's porch as Walter said good night to her and they'd shared their deepest conversation. *His trips back and forth to the ranch, my focus on the boys—it's all been too much of a strain on poor Walter. I've missed just spending time alone with him.*

He brushed a hand over his eyes as if to refocus himself. "I think for now we should probably find Grace."

"All right. Another time. Well, Grace was speaking with Sid and Quinley when I last saw her. I think they're working out the details."

"Can we take the boys too? We could go to Grace's restaurant for a treat. I can drive everyone."

"That would be lovely. I'll speak to Grace." Lillian motioned him forward. "Won't you come back inside the office with me?"

He fell in step behind Lillian, and they entered the room together, scanning around it to discover Grace absent already. Sid, too, had disappeared out the back door. Quinley was standing in the far corner with the two gentlemen from the orphanage's governing board. Lillian waited silently for their conversation to conclude in order to ask where Grace and Sid had gone.

His back to the door where Lillian waited with Walter, Quinley stood like a proud peacock as the taller of the two suited men seemed to bring their conversation to its conclusion, a rather earnest look on his face. "Yes, I believe that will suffice, Mr. Sinclair."

Quinley's confident voice carried across the room. "Then, you agree to the terms?"

"How soon do you think you'll be able to make arrangements?"

A longer pause. "I'll do my best, Leo. It'll require that I make contact with the office in Winnipeg. I'm sure they'll accommodate this request, but, well, you understand how slowly the wheels can turn at times like this."

The portlier gentleman cleared his throat. "But, sir, will that settle the matter, do you think? We're quite anxious to put all of this unpleasantness behind us."

Just then, the taller man nudged his partner. He seemed to have noticed Lillian and Walter's return.

Quinley's attention followed the man's eyes. He nodded in Lillian's direction before fastening a button on his suit jacket and answering in a confident voice. "It's a satisfactory resolution. I believe it's the best solution for all concerned."

"Yes, yes, I'm sure you're right."

Firmly patting the shoulder of the tall man, Quinley took a step away from them. "Pardon me, gentlemen. May I excuse myself, please? I believe I'm needed elsewhere."

"Of course. Thank you for your time, Mr. Sinclair."

"Certainly. Always glad to help. I'm sure we'll speak again soon."

Instantly Lillian felt oddly shy. Quinley Sinclair had the bearing of an important and powerful man, charming in an unfamiliar way. Father came the closest to him in her reckoning, and yet this young man seemed to carry himself with more self-assurance than even Father did. In fact, Quinley seemed to rise above all of the men she'd known. In some strange way he made her feel smaller.

"Miss Walsh, I thought you'd gone."

"I had—I did. But I'm looking for Grace. Do you know where she went?"

"I believe Sid took her back to see the boys."

Turning quickly toward Walter, Lillian hastened, "Oh, we need to catch up to them. I want to be there when she tells them." She began to move away, then paused. "Mr. Sinclair, we plan to go out for a little celebration. Would you care to join us? It won't be much, but you'd be welcome to come. We're so grateful for what you've done to help."

He smiled benevolently. "I'm sorry. Another time. But I'm certainly glad I could be of assistance."

Walter reached out to shake his hand. "Thanks for working this out in the boys' favor."

"Of course."

And Lillian added, "We'll hold you to that—to joining us another time."

Quinley smiled again and nodded.

• • • • • • •

The old woman came stealthily, pushing her way amid the multitude of passengers who walked toward the loading area. From his perch on a ramp above, Ben could see her eyes dart this way and that as she hurried forward. At the last minute she dragged the small one through the half-open door of the shed, then faded into the crowd and eventually turned back toward the street again.

Scanning around carefully, Ben moved closer and slipped through the shed's door, half closing it behind him. He saw the small body trembling in the shadows. He knew the child was consumed by fear and dropped to his knees in front of her. "I'm Ben Waldin," he said, tapping his chest. "I'm goin' ta help ya. I work aboard ship—takin' care'a other wee 'uns."

The wide eyes studied his face closely, but the child remained motionless in the dark corner where she stood.

"Yer name's Jane, ain't it? I've a sister named Jane. She's very sweet an' very kind. I'm goin' ta see her in Canada too. Maybe you can meet her."

Still no audible response. However, there was no time to allow the child a more guarded approach.

"Now, it may be a wee bit scary, but we'll—we'll pr'tend we're on the stage. Ya e'er been to a play? That's where people act out . . . adventures. All sorts'a adventures. We're goin' ta play a bit'a story too. I'm goin' ta put ya in this nice big box on me cart. See?" He lifted the wooden lid of the crate he'd prepared. "It has a nice soft blankie in it. You'll need ta curl up a bit ta fit. Then I'm goin' ta give ya a ride up that ramp an' onto the ship. When we get there I'll take ya outta the box, and we'll have tea and biscuits. How's that, then? Think ya can do it?"

She solemnly nodded, her big blue eyes clearly filled with questions and concerns.

"Good lass. You'll need ta be very quiet."

She nodded again.

"In ya go, then." He held the lid. To his surprise she didn't hesitate but trustingly climbed inside.

"Now I'm goin' ta put all the things from yer case in the box beside ya—yer clothes and such, yeah? I'll tuck 'em all 'round ya so that ya have 'em on ship." He worked quickly as he explained. Little Jane, though she had once lived on some type of estate, had few belongings. The job was easily done. However, among the child's possessions he found a strange envelope. He peered inside quickly. It seemed an official document of some kind—perhaps for the benefit of the child. He noted her full name, *Jane Henry*.

Stuffing the letter inside the crate, Ben drew the lid closed as softly as could be done. Then, leaving Jane's discarded suitcase in a dark corner of the shed and pushing against the cart on which the crate sat, he launched their perilous journey. No one seemed to pay him any mind as he walked along with other deckhands up the cargo loading ramp and onto the waiting ship, his shipboard identity card obvious for all to see. The cart rattled off the ridged steel ramp and onto the smooth wooden deck just as an officer called out to him. Ben froze.

"Hey, Waldin, as soon's ya get rid'a that cartage, go to the boardin' deck. Ya need ta check yer passengers off 'gainst the society's list. Don't want no stowaways slippin' aboard."

Ben nodded and rushed, wide-eyed, into the first narrow hallway, an artery that led to the heart of the ship. Against orders, his first stop would be his own berth.

Chapter 6

Departures

Before he even reached his narrow door, Ben realized that the first priority must be to win Jane Henry's trust. She had to be certain he intended her no harm. *Poor little thing must be scared outta her wits.* He managed the key in the lock, then pushed the door open with a foot. Maneuvering slowly so as not to bang the crate, he wheeled it inside. It barely fit within the berth and filled most of the available floor space. Carefully he shut them in and clicked the lock tight before breathing out slowly, wiping a clammy hand across his face.

When he lifted the lid, little Jane was still trembling, her big eyes filled with fright. He tried hard to make his voice light and cheery yet keep a hushed tone. All of the crew knew he lived alone. "There ya're, now. Weren't that an interestin' way ta board the big ship? Did ya like our wee adventure?" With deliberate movements, he helped her from the wooden box, half lifting her in order to clear the rim. In the tight quarters there was no place to settle her but on the bed.

He didn't wait for an answer. "I promised ya tea and biscuits, didn't I? We'll have 'em—but—well, I've a job to do first. Is that okay?"

He thought he saw a nod but wasn't sure. "But I do have somethin' here—from a bake shop." He pulled a brown paper bag from one of his deep coat pockets. "Let's see what we've got inside. Well—look at that. Two penny tarts. Look good?"

She nodded cautiously.

"Now, like I say—I need ta go do me job. But I'll come back as soon's I can and we'll have our tea. Fer now tarts'll have ta do. And there's water there in the jug, a cup b'side it." He pointed, and her eyes followed his extended finger.

Passing her the bag of tarts, he wiped his hands on the sides of his trousers. "We do have some rules. Yeah? Ya must ne'er go outside the door—nor open it. Understand?"

She nodded.

"And ya must ne'er answer the door if someone knocks. Just let 'em go away. And—this is a big 'un—ya must always stay very quiet. *Very* quiet." He placed a finger at his lips in emphasis. "Can ya 'member the rules?"

Her large eyes opened even wider. This time she whispered, "Yes." Her voice was so soft it was almost imperceptible.

"Good. Now, I'm goin' ta lock the door when I go out. I'm the only one what has a key, so when ya hear the key again you'll know it's me. Yeah? I'll be back just as soon's I can." And so saying, he turned to retreat, drawing the rattling cart along behind him as he left. He'd try not to keep her waiting long for her tea.

• • • • • • •

"Grace, Grace!" Lillian tried to whisper loudly enough to call the attention of her sister.

At last the brown head turned toward her and Grace took a few steps closer, a puzzled expression on her face. "What is it? Why are you whispering?"

Walter had gone for the car so that they could ride to the diner for their celebration. The twins were playing on the foyer steps, bouncing a small rubber ball repeatedly against the risers and trying to be the first to catch it again.

Lillian had retreated to a corner of the foyer next to the window in order to watch for Walter's return. Keeping her voice low and motioning for her sister to come closer, Lillian asked covertly, "What did you think of their reaction? I expected them to be so happy about going home, and they seemed—almost disappointed."

"Did you think?" Grace tipped her head a little.

"Well, they weren't very excited."

Grace let her gaze linger on the boys' play before she answered. "Well, it's not as if we told them that there was any risk of another outcome. We didn't make them carry that worry, so it's not too surprising that they don't feel very relieved."

"That's true. We did work hard to keep them from understanding the implications of this trip."

Her voice still low, Grace explained further, "So, I doubt they gave it much thought once they settled in and felt comfortable here. It was just a matter of when we'd go home again, and I suppose they've made friends and enjoyed their stay without really catching on too much. It was sort of a vacation for them. Which is exactly what we hoped would happen, the best possible outcome."

Lillian sighed in relief. "Yes, of course. I hadn't thought of that. I was starting to worry that they liked it here better."

"No need to fear that. And as much as we want to celebrate with them, it might be better if they just see it as another normal, happy day rather than any kind of victory."

Lillian sighed. Her closed fist rubbed a circle on the cold windowpane, wiping away the fogginess caused by her whispered words. "You're right, of course. It's so difficult to understand all of this through their eyes, even when I'm really trying, even when I'm constantly attempting to do the best thing for them."

"I agree." Grace nodded. "It's a complex world. And add to it that children don't all respond in the same way. They're twins, but they may have very different reactions to what they face. So there's never going to be a sure way of helping each of them in every situation." Grace shook her head. "We do our best, but it's a humbling process."

Still no car in front of the building. Lillian added another concern, glancing again toward Matty and Milton. "And you can't see their hurts on the outside. Except for Matty's labored speech, they appear to be just like all the other children. But inside, what if they're worried? Or sad? How on earth does a person help them in the best way?"

Grace leaned her shoulder against the door. "Well, I think in my experience that means you have to take them one at a time, and try to earn their trust so they can tell you what they think about. But even with that, a child rarely has the capacity to articulate feelings in that depth. They often don't have the words—nor do they understand how they're *allowed* to react, especially when it's the adults around them—or lack thereof—that create the problem."

Thinking of Hazel, who'd seemed so strong, and then Bryony, who'd withdrawn instead, Lillian wondered what questions she should have asked that might have helped the little girls overcome some of their hidden struggles. And then there were the boys: Lemuel, whose thoughts were always deep and protected. Harrison, who wore his bravado like a mask. And steadfast George, who'd taken the role of his sister's protector upon himself.

"Can I tell you something?" Grace's words interrupted Lillian's brooding.

"Please do."

"If it helps, I think God makes children kind of resilient, gives them a little bit of a protective shell so that they can continue to grow and mature in the face of terrible life experiences." Grace pushed away from the door and turned to face Lillian directly. Her back was to the boys now as her eyes became more intense. "Now, don't get me wrong. I don't mean that children are free from harm like some people claim. But I think sometimes they get a reprieve *for a while* in childhood so they can survive it—in order to keep them from being crushed by things that are far too much for them to comprehend otherwise. I've seen them play and laugh during the worst of times. However—" The word and the way Grace was shaking her head for emphasis made a lump rise in Lillian's throat. "However, the hurts that happen to us when we're young *always* leave a lasting imprint. We don't help by covering up pain or compelling people to pretend as adults that they haven't been deeply affected by their childhood. Dear Mrs. Copsey, who ran this very home when I was just a resident, taught me that. She left such a lasting imprint on my life. She always said that we have to face the hardest truths at some point—even just speak them aloud, share them with someone else—before we can begin to heal. But I'm very, very grateful for the thought that God might often delay the real work of reparation and restoration until a person is an adult and more able to understand that the bad things that happened to them as children were not their fault, and are *not* a judgment about their own value. God help us to intervene, in any way we can, to plant those higher truths while they're still young, eh?"

Lillian's hand reached out to catch Grace's sleeve. "Yes, please, God, help us to do that well."

Suddenly Walter entered the foyer before either of the sisters had noticed his arrival with the car. While stamping the snow from his boots, he was waylaid by the playful duo. He caught Matty up into his arms and let his eyes sweep around him, turning at last to the corner where Grace and Lillian huddled.

Trying to shake off their deep discussion, Lillian faced him with a still-furrowed brow. "Oh, I'm sorry, Walter. We stopped watching. We got to talking instead."

His eyes softened as he studied her expression. "That's important too. Need more time?"

"No, we're ready. It's just going to be a different kind of celebration now."

Looking from Lillian to Grace and back again, he nodded. "Okay. But I hope you'll explain that to me sometime. I'd like to understand it too."

• • • ● • • •

Ben felt impatient through the long procedure of checking in the list of twenty-nine wide-eyed orphans. They were assigned to their quarters, crowded into small spaces, girls in one room housing bunk beds stacked three high, boys in another. There should have been an even thirty, but word had arrived at the last minute that a little boy had been deemed unfit to travel. No one knew the circumstances—but it was accepted as part of the process of moving children from one country to another.

Ben hated this part of the procedure. Checking off each name tag against the list he'd been given meant looking into eyes that were mostly empty—devoid of all hope. He saw they carried no faith in the promises that had been spoken to them. He was certain that these poor children, exhausted after what had likely been days of travel already, had long since learned they were alone—totally alone among the little crowd of others. His only offering was to try to distract them with interesting comments about the ship, trying to persuade them to smile at what he called their upcoming adventure. But their smiles were short-lived within these dank, dark steerage compartments of the hold, whose creaking corridors echoed with so many other occupants.

Inadvertently, that same word, *adventure*, spoken aloud brought Ben's mind back to the little waif in his stateroom waiting for her promised tea. Whatever would become of her? Would he really be able to find her a better life? Or would his own promises fail? "Please, God . . ." he began but stopped as he recalled that he was no longer entitled to pray.

It was her eyes—those big, imploring blue eyes—that had torn away some of the practiced hardness of his soul. Little Janie. And what if it had been *his sister* in such a state? If there were any goodness left in the world, he wanted it for Janie, would sacrifice if need be, to see that she had a chance. In an inexplicable way, the little girl and his praying sister seemed connected by more than just a shared name. As for himself, he'd strayed from the correct path when he'd run away and forsaken his parents, he knew. But he also knew that the shared sibling bond reached out to draw him near again from wherever Jane had gone. And he was certain her warm heart would be just as touched as his own looking into the eyes of that little girl. To demonstrate love to Jane Henry seemed in some way to honor his lost sister.

As soon as the list had been checked and the little herd shepherded by a pair of government caretakers into the confinement of their play area, Ben hurried off to the ship's common galley to gather something for an evening meal. He hoped to do better than tea and biscuits. There was a stew being served. He filled a large bowl, buttered some rolls, and placed it all on a tray. Here he had the makings for a fine tea in his room. As an afterthought he picked up a lemon. Perhaps she wouldn't mind some in her drink. It was important for days at sea that one had the proper nutrition. *I hope the ol' crone at least had the Christian pity ta feed the child.*

Rapping softly on the door, Ben inserted his key. "Janie," he said quietly. "Janie?" There was no response. The room had become dark. The sunlight from the small porthole had faded. He wished he'd shown Janie how to switch on the modern electric light. She'd likely be afraid of the dark. Not a sound answered as he moved to the small table and set down the tray. He hadn't meant that she should be totally silent.

Flipping the switch, he looked about the room. At first he saw no one, and fear prickled along his spine. Then he spied her. She had curled up among the rumpled blankets and pillow on his bunk and was sound asleep. In her present position she looked even smaller, even more vulnerable. A strong urge to protect her surged through his whole being. At that moment, somehow, she became not just a little mite of an orphan, but his own kin, as if she were somehow his Jane's very own child—the little girl of her own that Jane had never achieved.

• • • • • • •

Lillian watched as Walter tapped his fingers on the wooden armrest and shifted in place on the firm cushion of Mrs. O'Shea's settee. There was clearly something on his mind, but he seemed unwilling to speak it aloud. The evening was growing late, and from across the room Grace had already yawned several times as if to prompt his departure. Still, Walter lingered uncharacteristically.

Seated beside him on the settee, Lillian was reluctant to intervene. *Poor Walter, he still hasn't followed Grace's advice to make a new declaration to me. Is that why he's procrastinating now?* A flutter of emotion rippled through Lillian's core. *And what would I have him say? Well, honestly, I think I'd prefer that he say nothing at all tonight. I feel today has been full enough. Don't I?*

Grace yawned again. "Well, it was such a lovely evening. But even with Sid's request that we're present when the new children arrive from the East next month, I don't think we're going to be able to commit to anything for a while."

"I can understand that. It's been a long haul for you, I'm sure," Walter agreed. "Even though you'd no doubt like to help settle them all in their new homes. Do you think you might come back again later?"

"We certainly can't wait another month to head back to Brookfield." Lillian hoped her curt words didn't betray too much of her impatience to be home. She cast a glance around her and hurried to justify her claim. "We also can't impose on dear Mrs. O'Shea for such a long stretch. Matty and Milton should be back in school. Don't you think, Grace? And if there's a chance we might find some way to travel back to Lethbridge again later to be of use to Sid when the new children arrive—well, we'll just have to cross that bridge when we come to it. There's no way to work it all out now. Right?"

Grace untucked her legs from beneath her, stood, and stretched. "You're right, sis. Sid was a little vague about what he wanted us for, anyway. Plus, it doesn't help that Brayton House has lost its driver and can't help us with transportation. Obviously, Walter, we're not going to keep taking advantage of your generosity. You've made too many trips back and forth in your car because of us already. But as for me, I'm with Lillian. I'd rather just go home now and figure out a way back later if we feel we need to come."

Lillian stood and began to gather the empty teacups. It was nice to hear Grace speak of *going home* to Brookfield. Smiling back warmly, Lillian added, "I agree."

At last Walter rose. He cleared his throat. "I have somethin' I wanted to tell you both, but I'm a little reluctant. I'm sorry if it makes anythin' more difficult for you."

"What is it, Walter?"

His eyes lifted to meet Lillian's. His words came more deliberately than ever, brown eyes flickering with gold light reflected from Mrs. O'Shea's fireplace. "I got that job with an oil company. My application was accepted, and I'm supposed to report to a rig up north tomorrow."

Lillian blinked slowly in shock. It seemed to her that time stood still.

Grace answered evenly, "I'm so pleased for you, Walter. I know you hoped you would. Is it the position you wanted?"

He answered Grace's question without turning his eyes away from Lillian. "It is—the overseer's role—once they train me, if I can manage it."

"You will," Lillian whispered. "You've always done anything you set your mind to."

His brows drew tighter. "But I'm afraid I won't be goin' back to Brookfield for a while. They run men pretty hard on the rigs with only a day off here and there. The schedule can be at the mercy of how the rig is runnin'." His voice was growing strained. "I'm sorry, Lillian. I've been tryin' to find a chance to talk with you about it all. It's just been so busy around here."

"Oh. I see."

Grace moved past, taking the stack of teacups from Lillian's hands as she went. "I'll just wash these up in the kitchen."

Still Walter held Lillian's gaze. "I'm sorry I won't be able to help out. I've really enjoyed bein' someone you can count on." He took a step closer. "I'm proud of what you're doin' with the kids, Lillian. I'm proud of the woman you are."

Faltering, Lillian stammered, "I—It's mostly Grace. I just . . ."

"No, please don't sell yourself short. Not to me. You've got such a servant's heart, Lillian. It's always been there—for as long as I've known you—servin' others in ways that I can hardly imagine. Your mum and dad. I think so much of you. And that's why it's just so hard to leave." His voice quieted to almost a whisper. "I'm gonna miss you."

Lillian's cheeks grew warm. She was certain her face was flushed now. She fought the urge to flee to Grace, knowing that later she'd regret having given in to such timidity. Though her mouth had gone dry, she forced her words, hoping she could find a way to embolden him. "I'll miss you too, Walter. I knew you might be going, but I never dreamed it could happen so fast. You're such an important person to me. The most important. It won't be the same without you in Brookfield."

"I only expect to work for them for a couple years. I hope my absence from you will be worth the trouble—that this is the right decision."

A frown. Lillian searched his face and asked meekly, "Won't you even visit?"

"I hope so. At Christmas, maybe—holidays."

"I hope so too." There was a long, strained pause as she felt tears begin to form. Lillian was aware of her own breathing. Her heart raced. *How can Walter be leaving? Shouldn't I say something to make him change his mind? Is he waiting for words that would convince him to stay?* And then she remembered the advice Grace had given to him. *So this is it. He's leaving, but maybe he's going to repeat his declaration now.*

His eyes were filled with emotion, glistening. But instead of speaking, Walter stepped away. And Lillian, as if affixed to her spot on the floor, watched him begin to gather his things. Her mind clouded with confusion.

"I'll see you in the morning, Lillian."

"Oh. Of course."

"Maybe we'll have a chance to speak again. I'm sure I can help you find another ride back to Brookfield. There's gotta be someone who's headin' that way."

"No doubt."

"Well, good night, Lillian." For the first time she noted how pinched his face appeared, a cloud of lament in his eyes.

"Good night."

The front door closed softly just as Grace returned from the kitchen. Walter was gone. Lillian fought the urge to chase after him and call him back. Instead, she turned away and prepared for sleep, too stunned now to even react further.

A large round moon had risen to fill the small window in the shared bedroom, and still Lillian felt she could make no sense of it all. The conversation had raised more questions than it had answered. Why hadn't he declared his intentions again? Why had he given voice to so few of his thoughts—particularly after

Grace had encouraged him to? Was Walter not as interested in marriage as Lillian had understood from their shared moments? Had she misread the words that had passed between them? But what about the conversation Milton had overheard? Had the little boy misrepresented it? Yet, why would he do so?

Despite all the questions, Lillian reminded herself that long ago Walter had asked to call formally. He'd said he was a patient man. Perhaps the patience he'd demonstrated was more about uncertainty than persistence. And yet, that didn't seem to fit the character of Walter that Lillian believed she knew. *Perhaps he's waiting for Father to return from Wales. That makes sense. That's the kind of man that Walter is—doing things properly by first asking Father's permission.*

And then a niggling thought crept in between the trails of logic. *If only Walter had kissed me, then I'd be sure. Why didn't he kiss me? It seemed as if he would, and then he left rather abruptly instead. Was it because Grace was so near? If only he'd kissed me before going away—even if he hadn't found the words to declare his feelings, I wouldn't have to wonder now.*

Tears began to soak Lillian's pillow. She gave in to the sorrow of waiting once more, as her mind filled with worry that it was simply her lot in life—waiting, always waiting, for someone else before her own life could begin.

CHAPTER 7

Jane

The days aboard ship fell into a routine. Ben discovered that Janie was bright. Not only could she read and write very well for her age, but she loved to do so. She spoke casually of a governess, as if she assumed all children had such a benefit. Ben was hard put to supply the little girl with means of filling her silent hours. But she could converse well, and he looked forward to every opportunity to spend time with her. Time together was scarce though. He still had full duties on the ship. In addition, out of a strong sense of propriety, his sleeping hours were spent hidden away elsewhere on the ship again. The child needed his bunk, the narrow straw mattress. So Ben was relegated to dark hallway corners nearby with his kit bag as a pillow once more.

To keep Janie company while he was absent, Ben smuggled up a cat from the hold, a slender gray female whom he'd befriended during the days he'd spent loading cargo. The captain chose to follow the age-old wisdom of keeping several cats among the cargo in order to control the vermin. Ben felt this particular moggy wouldn't be missed and would serve a much better purpose by becoming a companion for the little girl.

Each day it was necessary to pirate food for Janie, to sneak about for fresh water, and to empty her slops. Ben didn't mind the work, but daily his mind was plagued with his dilemma. He'd managed to smuggle her aboard, but how was he ever going to be able to smuggle her off? And to whom would he deliver her?

Janie accepted him now. She even smiled when his key in the door resulted in a few minutes of shared conversation. She was a sensitive little soul. Old for her age. Wise for her years. Kind in nature and quiet in manner, not the least withdrawn, as he'd first feared. He began to enjoy her company beyond what he would have dreamed. She was a child with a wonderful imagination and an undaunted spirit, much like his sister when she was young.

"Did you know that unicorns are just pretend?" Janie asked him one day. Sitting cross-legged on the bed, using the loose sheets of paper Ben had managed to provide, she was drawing her imagined visions of what she'd read about in the discarded children's book he'd brought her to peruse.

"That so?"

She nodded her head. With a flourish she added a crooked tail to her unicorn.

"And how d'ya figure that?"

"'Cause they would have been on the ark with the other animals. Then they wouldn't have got distinct."

Ben raised his eyebrows, answering with a gentle smile. "Extinct?"

"Oh." She froze, aware of her mistake. With an exaggerated blink she admitted, "Oops! Yes, I mean *ex*tinct—distinct is another word, isn't it?"

He ignored the mistake. "Maybe yer right," he agreed. "Makes perfect sense ta me."

"And did you know that the rainbow has all of those special colors because it's like a prison?" She stopped and her hand went to her mouth, though this time she giggled at her own mistake.

"No, not prison," she corrected herself quickly. "That's silly. A *pri-sm*." She exaggerated the last word.

They chuckled together. Then she sobered. "I've read all of the Noah picture book. Seventy times, I think." She sighed.

"I like yer art. Nice to see it all 'round the room."

"Thanks, Mister Waldin."

His mind went to the two volumes in his kit. Shakespeare and Virgil were too much for a child—even this one. Somehow he would find her another suitable book. The seven-day voyage was likely an eternity for this poor little ragamuffin. And yet, he knew the other babes were faring no better. They were almost as tightly constrained in their rooms. *It helps to have companions, I s'pose.* He tossed another bit of dried fish to the cat Janie had dubbed Tumblepuss.

* * *

"Lillian, Lillian! I figured it out. I worked out a ride home for us. And you're never going to believe who volunteered."

Lillian looked up from the simple primer she was helping the twins read aloud. They were huddled together at a table in the group dining room, where it was quiet for the time being now that the evening meal had been cleared away. "Is it someone we know?"

"That we know? I should say so! In fact, someone we all know and admire." She grinned down at Lillian and the boys, who were drawn close to Lillian on either side. In light of the distraction, Matty began to squirm away immediately. Milton's busy hand reached out for the pencil they'd been printing with earlier.

Frustrated now, both that they'd been interrupted and also that Grace was withholding the pertinent information, Lillian sighed and lowered the book in defeat. "Please just tell me who it is, Grace."

"It's Quinley—Quinley Sinclair."

"Quinley? Why would he drive us all the way to Brookfield?"

"It seems he has children in the area he needs to check up on. He'll stay at the hotel for a little while and make his rounds. He needs to be back here in Lethbridge in a month when the new group arrives from England, but until then he plans to make Brookfield his headquarters." Grace smiled as if the news satisfied all of their concerns.

Lillian was losing her grip around Milton's middle. Matty was becoming a noodle on the other side, sliding toward the floor. Still Lillian wondered aloud, "He's going west in the winter? Does he know how bad the roads can be around the mountains? I'm not sure he'll be able to use his time well."

"I don't know about that. But I'm sure Quinley can manage."

"Well, I'm grateful to hear it. When does he plan to leave?"

"Tomorrow. We can pack up first thing in the morning and then we'll be ready to leave by noon."

Milton clapped his hands. "We get ta go home! We get ta go home!"

"We go home," Matty chimed in.

"Home," Grace agreed.

Closing the book, Lillian released the boys, who immediately ran across the room and back again, chasing each other. "I guess we should get started packing. Might as well do the boys' laundry tonight so it's dry and ready to pack tomorrow. I'll see if the laundry room will be available."

• • • • • • •

The ship was halfway through its journey when the dreaded happened. Some type of ailment swept through the crowded rooms in the steerage section. It seemed to have been caused by either tainted food or a quickly spreading stomach flu. The two women shepherding the group of orphans were horrified by the speed at which their children fell ill. Ben, the crew member designated to care for them, listened to their panicked requests as they feared the worst and prayed for the best. Night and day they fought to aid their sick kids with the help of the ship's busy doctor.

But no one was more distraught than Ben. His heart ached for the children who lay curled up in their narrow beds. He made certain to bring a steady supply of fresh water for sipping and cleaning, as well as fresh sheets whenever possible. But that wasn't the worst of his job. He was the one responsible to write the final status report for the captain and, in the stillness of one dark night, to commit to the sea the frail little bodies that had succumbed to the illness. There would be no resources in Canada to bury the children there.

He'd done it before and despised the process, but this time it tore at his very soul. *What if it had been Janie? It easily could'a been Janie. An' is it any less a tragedy that it happened to those what I hardly knew?*

But instead of falling ill with the others, Janie had gained in health. The few days at sea, the simple meals he'd stolen from the crew's dining area, the dead-of-night walks through the fresh, salty air when he sneaked her from the cabin to parts of the ship he knew were unoccupied, all of it worked like an elixir on her. She already seemed to have improved—though perhaps only in appearance. She was still tiny. Fragile. It was in her eyes that he'd seen the most change. The hollowness had slowly faded.

Even so, he was fully aware that if she'd been in the belly of the ship with the others, housed in close quarters when the sickness struck or sharing the same food, her frail little body most likely would not have survived the assault.

Silently, he descended to the private aft deck, where he was to tend to his unwelcome job. The little bodies had been surrendered to the ship's morgue. He would check the name given against the ship manifest, read through any descriptive information given by their guardians, and check the box that there were no next-of-kin on record. Even with all the precautions he'd tried to take not to let himself become too involved, he wondered if he'd recognize any of these specific children—if he had made the offer of a small toy or shared a brief conversation.

After the paperwork had been completed, he would lay aside any unneeded items together with a case of possessions and carefully, so carefully, encase the lifeless bodies in long gunny sacks loaded at the bottom with ballast, tie them securely, and then silently—unceremoniously—move them out to the railing and drop the bundled little forms into the deep sea's darkness.

Why, oh why had he ever accepted this job? In his heart, he'd known this would happen again, just as it had before. Once this journey was over he'd apply for something else, even if it meant a demotion. And then he remembered his vow to find his parents and Jane in Canada. For the first time, the thought came as a relief that he might soon turn his back on the beloved sea altogether.

The first body laid out before him was a boy named John Wall, twelve years old, no known kin and very little other information. Slowly and respectfully, Ben prepared the young man for his sea burial, slipping the sack around the lifeless form as gently as he was able. The lanky frame was difficult to carry toward the ship's rail, particularly in the manner in which Ben was determined to show respect. But there was no solution to the irreverence of allowing the sack to slip from his hands. He winced as he waited for the sound of a splash into the trail of waters churned white by the ship's propellers. "Good-bye, John. May ya go on ta a life much better than the one ya knew here."

The second was another boy. Only seven—and slight for his age. Ben read aloud, "Edgar Keighley. Poor little Eddie. I'm sorry, lad. I'm so sorry." As he straightened the clothing, he felt a strange hard lump inside one of the trouser pockets. "What's this?"

Gingerly reaching inside, he produced a small stone with

cornered edges. Ben froze and studied it carefully. *Not odd fer a young boy to have a rock in his pocket. But this seems diff'rent—outta place. It ain't come from the shore or it woulda been worn smooth.* Three faces of the little pyramid shape had clearly been chiseled smooth—as if it were the corner off a larger structure.

Ben leaned closer and brushed a wisp of hair away from little Edgar's eyes. "Don't know what ya got there, Eddie. But it's yers anyhow." He hid the piece away in the pocket again and wiped at his own forehead with his soiled handkerchief before maneuvering the body slowly into another rough fabric bag.

"God bless ya, son. May ya be reunited with yer loved ones an' be at rest."

After the body slipped from Ben's arms, his tears followed, lost into the dark mist below. *This is a task too much to ask'a any man!* Slowly he returned inside, leaning a hand onto the back of a chair and doubling over, head down low, eyes closed for a few moments in order to regain his composure.

The last was a girl. He turned her name tag and read, with a horrified start, *Jane*. But leaning closer, he was able to look fully into the child's face. *No.* He sighed with relief. *Not me own Jane Henry. This is Jane Grey. Only eight. Only eight!* How on earth could another life be over at only eight? Ben mourned this little girl as he removed her identification to add it to his report and bundled her carefully in the last rough sack, lashing twine around the end as if it were some kind of protection against the elements into which he was delivering her.

Suddenly he stopped. Picked up the tag and looked again at the name. Jane. Certainly not Jane Henry—but he could change that. She was small. There was no listed kin. Very little information at all. Could he really make it work? Certainly not with the two ladies in charge of the orphans on ship—but perhaps with those who'd be checking off the list when they reached port. Dare he report only two deaths aboard ship for this night? Could his Janie take the place of the little girl lost?

He knew it was wrong, even irreverent. He knew it was a tremendous gamble. He also knew it might be the only way to save Janie—to give her a new life. Therefore, it was worth a try. He slipped the identification tag into his shirt pocket, folding up her sheet with the information. He would take it back to his room when his shift was over. There may be some details he would need to change in the report, but he could care for that. Then, with heartfelt apology to the little bundle laid out before him, he lifted the small body, eased her over the side of the ship, and heard the ocean waves welcome her below. He muttered softly, "Rest in peace—wee Janie Grey. Rest in peace."

Gathering a small pile of their discarded possessions onto a table, Ben tried to force the image of their faces from his mind. Someone else would see that the extra clothing was taken care of—given to other needy children. Just before turning off the light, Ben picked up little Jane Grey's battered old suitcase. He'd left the one that had come with Jane Henry in the Liverpool shed. Now the child hidden above would carry on with more than just the lost girl's name.

• • • • • • •

Ben had achieved a name tag and a sheet with information that roughly described a girl like Janie. Yet he would not be able to display the tag openly or make Janie's presence known. She still had to be kept separate from the other youngsters, safe in his room until the voyage was complete. But somehow he had to introduce her to her new identity. How was he going to explain this to Janie?

He broached the subject as they sat having their morning porridge together. "Ya have a name tag now."

She frowned. "A name tag? What does that do?"

"It tells who ya are. You'll need one when we get ta Canada."

"Why?"

"Because that's the way they know if you'll be allowed to stay'r not."

"I read about Canada in the new book you brought me an' looked at the pictures. It's pretty there. I want to stay," she said simply, as if that settled it.

"I know. That's why it's impor'ant to have a name tag."

She nodded. "Okay." She licked the spoon and carefully laid it on the tray beside her empty bowl.

He pulled the slip of thick paper from his pocket and held it out for her to see. She crowded in close beside him and fingered the strange object. Suddenly her big eyes grew even larger. "That's not my name!"

He knew he might have trouble explaining that fact but hoped she'd be reasonable. "Not quite," he began. "But this can be yer new name now."

Her eyes lit with intensity and she began to shake her head. "I can't," she declared firmly. "That would be a lie. My mummy said to never, ever lie. It's bad."

He took a deep breath. He didn't wish to tell the girl that it was okay to lie if it was reasonable, necessary. He knew in his heart he didn't want to destroy the faith—the uprightness—her mother had instilled in her. He struggled to sort out this dilemma in his own thinking, his own head. How could he be truthful yet convince her?

"Many times," he began, "when folks move from one country ta 'nother, they change their names."

"Why?"

"Well, there's many'a reason. Some do it 'cause they want a new name. Some do it 'cause their ol' name, it no longer fits 'em. Might be too hard ta understand or spell."

"My name isn't too hard to spell," she quickly responded. "H-E-N-R-Y. Just like that."

He nodded, refusing to allow himself to be sidetracked. "Some do it 'cause it's the *wise* thing ta do."

She puzzled over that. "Would it be *wise*—for me?" she finally asked.

"I think it would, yeah. Take me, now. Me name is really Ebenezer—but that's a very long name, so I changed it ta Ben. That's easier fer people to 'member—and ta say."

She still frowned. "Eb-en-ez-er. But that's fun to say." She tried it again. "Ebenezer. I like it. Why did your parents call you that?"

"Not sure. I think it comes from the Good Book. Me mum told me once there was a big rock by that name—so I don't think it's too impor'ant."

She sighed. "That's nice to have a Bible name. I always wished mine was too. I'd like to be Esther or Mary or . . . what was Mrs. Noah's name?"

The conversation was slipping far away from Ben's intended target. "I don't know her name. But I still think t'would be wise—aye, wise—if ya change yer name ta Jane Grey."

Her face lit. "Why not Leah, then? Can I be Leah instead? I knew a girl named Leah. She was—"

"No, no." He scratched a hand up under the back of his hair. *How do I get her to see what I'm askin'? Aye, back to the tag.* "We don't get ta pick any ol' name. It's gotta match what we got here."

"Oh." Jane sighed with deep disappointment. "Then I guess I could—if it wouldn't be lying?" She checked the tag once again. Her eyes still held doubt.

"It would be yer new name. A Canada name. Jane Grey. 'Tis a nice name. Jane Grey. Seems I can recall a princess who had it. Lady Jane, she were."

At last Janie seemed to accept it. "All right." She took the paper from him. Studying it for a minute, she looked up and spoke frankly. "But I like my old name better. Jane Henry makes me think of a king. But Jane Grey is just a sad color."

CHAPTER 8

Farewells

Riding with Quinley would not be the same as riding with Walter. Lillian had mixed emotions as they said their goodbyes at Brayton House and set out across the rolling hills, happy to be headed home but sorrowful at Walter's absence. Quinley had an elegant new automobile, streamlined and swift. However, Lillian hadn't realized how much the man talked.

Grace, who was riding in the front passenger seat, was the target of most of his conversation. This left Lillian free to observe and contemplate. The twins, who shared the bench seat on either side of her, were promptly lulled to sleep by the motion of the car over the rough road, jiggling and bouncing in steady rhythm. Quinley's fancy automobile made Walter's rather old model seem rough and rustic.

Lillian watched the side of Grace's face. It was animated and lit up with their conversation. She seemed captivated by the things that Quinley was explaining. In fact, she seemed positively enamored.

Lillian's stomach lurched a little. *Is Grace interested in Quinley?*

Glancing at the back of their driver's head, Lillian felt a little more trepidation. *Does Quinley feel the same?*

The thought came as a shock. Yet the more Lillian pondered the idea, the more she felt it might be the most natural of occurrences. Quinley seemed to be a fine man. Everyone thought highly of him. He was poised and educated and handsome. It seemed that he came from a fine family back East and had been successful in his career. Not only that, he cared for children. And he was equipped to help orphans on a level that few others were able. Could it be a perfect match? *Of course, I was wrong when Roland Scott was visiting with us and I assumed that Grace fancied him. Still . . .*

Lifting a tuft of blond hair away from Matty's eyes and tucking it behind his ear, Lillian considered how she'd felt about Grace intervening with Walter. *As if those efforts helped!* Still, though Lillian had been annoyed by the exerted influence at first, perhaps Grace had been right. Perhaps it was necessary for a man to have encouragement in order to proceed. She felt an ache of regret that she hadn't been more direct with Walter when she'd been able.

Raising her eyes to Grace once again, she listened to her sister's laughter. If there were any chance that Quinley would be a good match for Grace, Lillian made up her mind to do whatever was in her power to help him see it.

Grace's head tossed as she shook it and laughed again. "I've never done any theater. I can't imagine that I'd be able to keep composure and remember all those lines."

"It's not as difficult as you might think at first, Grace. I suppose there are some people who are inclined to enjoy the feeling of all eyes focused on them and others who prefer not to be the center of attention."

"Oh, I don't like to feel all eyes on me at all. It makes my mouth go dry and my mind just stops working well."

This time it was Quinley whose gaze moved sideways and back

again. "Well, I believe you're articulate and winsome enough. I'm certain you'd be talented. But I've always taught my students that it takes all kinds to make the world work smoothly. We can't all be spotlight people—but there are plenty of other ways to matter. And you certainly matter, Grace."

Lillian lowered her eyes. She wondered how much Quinley would be around, if he planned to use this time to call on Grace. If perhaps she was a big part of his reason to travel west just at this time.

• • • ◆ • • •

Ben had one more giant obstacle. He had to get Janie from the ship and mingled among the Home Children slowly making their way toward the check-in station. Fortunately, he was actively involved in the process. In his hand he held the bundle of reports with the information regarding each immigrant child who was seeking residence in Canada. He also had responsibility for reporting the deaths that had occurred while at sea. Guilt about withholding information regarding the real little Jane Grey troubled him, but he knew that to reveal her loss would be to disclose Jane Henry. He couldn't jeopardize Janie's chance for a bright future.

Then suddenly he realized he had not one but *two* huge hurdles facing him. Getting Janie into the new country—and then giving her up. Once she was welcomed to Canada, she would no longer be his to protect. The thought brought him deep pain.

However, it was easier than he had feared to get Janie debarked. The two ladies who had accompanied the orphans from London were only too glad to turn the lot over to him and to the two receiving guardians from the new society just at the top of the gangway. The women were completely spent and seemed pleased to desert their duties for a few restful days in port before beginning their own homeward journey. Ben didn't blame them. He was well aware of how hard they'd worked in caring for sick children during the difficult voyage.

Figuring out ways to stay ahead of the group's schedule, Ben used the confusion of the change of guardians to move Janie to a bench where he knew the Home Children would wait. Once the two British women left, he expected to simply shepherd little Janie into the group. "After all," he reasoned quietly to himself, "nobody watches so close who sneaks *off a ship*, as who sneaks *onto it*."

Now if only Janie won't make a mistake an' give herself away. He'd cued the child one last time as she trailed behind the group down the gangway. "'Member yer new name."

She nodded somberly. "I need to be Jane Grey now."

Ben felt a little more confident.

He saw a few curious stares from other orphans as they noted a new girl tagging along with the group, but thankfully not one commented. The children were far busier taking in the view of the new setting. It seemed that the country to which they'd arrived held their interest more than the appearance of yet another youngster among them. Each waited obediently in the place they were told to stand.

For Ben it was once again their eyes that troubled him, eyes that seemed often vacant and hopeless, some even fearful. He swallowed hard, fighting against his own anxiety. *What've I done? What future am I sendin' Janie to?* Only the threat of a workhouse by the old woman in England kept him from wishing he'd never begun this desperate act of subterfuge. But he'd worked alongside men who'd spent their childhood in a workhouse. He could not imagine such a fate for Janie. If he could just get the child into Canada, he could, Lord willing, at least rescue her from such a grievous fate.

One by one the children's names were called out and arrangements made for the incomers. They were sorted into groups, and new tags were given of various colors indicating what the future held for each as he or she stepped forward. Most of them made no comment and stoically accepted their label—but a few clung to one another. Ben didn't know if they were connected by family or merely acquaintances, but for each tear he saw shed, his own heart ached.

The list appeared to be in order of age. So they were getting toward the end before *Jane Grey* was called. Janie turned to look at Ben. By now she quite understood the process. She was to step forward, claiming the name. But she didn't. Instead, she held out a hand to him, pleading with her eyes. He couldn't forsake her. Yet he couldn't expose her. Battling his own desire to flee with her, he took a step and received the little outstretched hand.

"She's a mite shy, this wee 'un," he said to the attendant. "We've had a long voyage t'gether an' have become . . ." What was a word he could use? He settled on the simplest label he could claim, one he hoped they'd understand. "Friends."

The surprised look still remained, but the new guardian nodded.

He dared go further. "Do ya mind if the wee girl stays with me 'til yer finished?"

The woman simply shrugged and turned back to her list.

Janie let go of his hand but moved halfway behind him, clinging tightly to the back of his jacket. The final names were called and matched with their destinations. He saw the woman sigh as she sensed her duty was now complete. Then she looked up, remembering that she still had Jane Grey to deal with. She walked forward, frowning as she came.

"Jane Grey," she said, as if trying to force a cheerful voice. "I'm sorry, but the family who'd asked for you had a—a circumstance and will not be picking you up."

Ben's arm instinctively drew Janie to him.

The woman hurried on, as if now encouraging them both.

"But don't you worry. We've arranged everything. You'll be traveling by train in just a few days to the prairies with some of the other children—this group over here. You'll like it there, I'm sure. You might even see the big Rocky Mountains. Wouldn't you like that, dear? To see the mountains? The people there will take good care of you—but it will take just a few days before they leave here by train. Don't you worry," she repeated, making Ben's stomach churn even more. "You'll be well looked after."

Ben's heart wanted to protest. To tell them that he'd take care of the little girl instead. But in his head he knew the idea was preposterous. How could he, who had no home of his own—no destination or direction? How would he ever be able to provide for Janie?

The woman continued cheerfully, "Until the lady arrives who will shuttle your little group to the place where you'll stay, we'll all go upstairs to my office. I have cookies—uh, biscuits. Isn't that what you call them? Biscuits? We can have a little snack together. How's that?" She reached out for Janie's hand.

Janie was slow in responding.

"Tell, uh—your *friend* good-bye," the woman instructed firmly. It was obvious that she was weary from the day's activity and anxious to return to the comfort of whatever home she knew.

Ben sucked in his breath. This was it. He had to say good-bye. He didn't know if his voice would work, if he could say the word. He squatted down to Janie's level and inwardly pleaded with himself to be a worthy example—not to cry.

She looked at him. Those big blue eyes open and frank. Then she stepped close and wrapped small arms tightly about his neck, her face pressed against his wavy hair.

"Remember—when you come to find me—my name is Jane Grey now," she whispered into his ear as she hugged him. "Don't forget."

Stepping back and looking directly into his eyes, she lifted one small hand to his whiskered cheek. He knew better than to try to speak, so only nodded.

"Remember," she urged again.

And then she was gone.

CHAPTER 9

Money Troubles

Lillian woke to a familiar bedroom, Mother and Father's room. After so many days away, she was first aware of feeling grateful to be home again at last. Slipping her feet out from beneath the covers, she dropped down onto her knees on the coolness of the knotted wool carpet and prayed, leaning against the bed. "Almighty God, I thank You for bringing all of us back to this house. Thank You for intervening on behalf of our darling little boys and for restoring our good name at Brayton House. I pray that we can go forward again now and finish the work of finding a home for Matty and Milton. But most of all, I just thank You—thank You with all my heart for setting things right again." And then a persistent, nagging thought caused a frown and prompted her to add, "I'm sorry, so sorry once again that I failed—that I lied." Her hands were clasped and resting on Mother's favorite quilt. *How ashamed would Mother have been to know it?*

With a sigh Lillian rose and pulled the blankets back into position, then dressed carefully. She knew she'd already prayed for forgiveness, and yet she didn't really *feel* forgiven yet. She'd hoped the feeling would follow once the whole business was left behind them in Lethbridge, but still the guilty sorrow lingered.

Passing quietly through the hallway and down the stairs, Lillian found Miss Tilly already working in the kitchen. Breakfast smells wafted around the warm room, coffee on the stovetop and biscuits in the oven.

"Good morning, Miss Tilly."

"Mornin', dear, thought ya might sleep in a mite today."

"No, I'm not tired. Just glad to be home and ready to be busy again. I don't suppose you'll let me help out with breakfast."

"Easier ta do it myself, dear."

"I suppose. But I can't tell you how hard it's been to feel so useless while I was away." She spied one of the large tin water pails standing empty beside the woodstove. "I'll fetch water, anyway. A bit of exercise will do me well right now."

A chuckle. "That cold'll wake ya right up, fer certain."

Tossing a scarf around her neck and buttoning her coat over the scarf's tails, Lillian stepped out into the dark winter morning. By the time she returned to the house, hefting the filled pail, her lungs were already complaining. Miss Tilly had been right. It was bitterly cold.

She stamped the snow from her boots as she entered the back porch and called, "Do you need more wood or coal?"

"Heavens, no!" Miss Tilly answered firmly. "Come back in and warm yerself. Lemuel filled 'em both yesterday and left more in the back room. I poured ya a cup. It's on the table. Biscuits'll be out in a minute. Set yerself down. We can chat while I ready the meal."

Gratefully, Lillian sat down at the table and sipped slowly. "How have things been while we were gone?"

Miss Tilly moved in practiced motions, talking as she worked. "Much as always. Though, Sophie McRae has had a baby girl. Named her Ruby."

"Oh, that's nice. Mother and baby are healthy?"

"Yep. Hale and hearty. Doc Shepherd delivered her, happened ta be in town."

"I'm so glad."

"An' a letter come."

"From whom?"

"It's there—beside the bread bin. I jus' save 'em, I don't read 'em."

There were three letters from Father. Lillian wondered if any of them would discuss her trouble with the Szwedas. She sighed. *What will Father say? Will he understand—or reprimand me for my failings?*

Footsteps sounded from above them. Lillian tucked the envelopes into the wide waistband of her skirt. She'd read them later when she had time to be alone.

"Guess Miss Grace's up." Miss Tilly pulled the heavy iron skillet to the center of the stove, then turned on her heel to lay out the sausage patties on a plate. She chatted easily as she worked. "New family moved in—down by Eidersons' place. The Caulfields, I think. Nice man an' his wife. She's Catherine. Don't recall his name."

"Do they have children?"

"Didn't hear that yet. But he's new ta farmin' on his own. Got him a fancy new tractor jest delivered. That was a sight to see comin' down the road on a trailer, let me tell ya. Most folks come out to watch it pass."

More footsteps came from above. It seemed the boys were also awake.

Miss Tilly continued, now cracking eggs into a bowl with a skillful hand. "Had a visit with Roxie Mooreland an' little Bryony. They had me over after Sunday church."

"Oh, that's nice. How's she doing?"

"Growin' up fast as a thistle. Tol' her I'd make her a new sock dolly soon. Old one got left too close ta the fire an' burned on one side."

"Ah, that's too bad. She loved that dolly."

Louder movements sounded from above. Lillian fought the urge to go upstairs to help Grace dress the boys. But she knew they needed supervision more than assistance.

While beating the eggs, Miss Tilly added, without a pause in the rhythm, "Meant ta go up ta the valley fer a visit but didn't wanna brave the weather." She shrugged. "Plans change. Can't stop it though we try."

Lillian frowned down at her drink. "They do. And it's frustrating."

"Is it?" The older woman halted to glance over her shoulder.

"I think so."

"What plans is that?" Her busy hands laid a circle of sausage patties into the ready skillet.

Slowly the patties began to sizzle as Lillian pondered what she really meant. "All of them. Going to Lethbridge all of a sudden. Walter going north for work."

"I heard that—'bout Walt. Talk in town is he'll do well there."

"Oh, I'm sure he will."

Softly Miss Tilly said, "But you'll miss him."

Lillian set her coffee cup on the table, letting her mind wander back over her memories of Walter. Her reply came quietly. "I will." She closed her eyes and tried to put into words what she felt, finding it impossible. "Did you hear how long he expects to be gone?"

Miss Tilly approached, taking a seat beside Lillian. She leaned her elbows on the table, offering her full attention. "Didn't hear that, dear."

"A couple years. Something like that." She tried to keep her voice even and unemotional, but the older woman appeared to know better.

Miss Tilly whistled. "That's a powerful long time when yer young."

"It's just so hard to know what the future holds. I try to picture it, plan for it, and then something changes—or *everything* changes."

"I'm sorry, child. I know it's hard. I been there too." She patted Lillian's arm. "But the good Lord, He knows ahead. He guides and helps us along." She laughed. "S'pose my mother tol' me the same. Hard to grasp it 'til ya face it. Sounds like jest flowery words, but it ain't."

"Grace and I have been talking about ambages—bends in life's path that make it impossible to see the future."

A smile. "Ambages. That's a fine word fer such a worrisome thing. Might hold on ta that one. Sounds French. Ambages." Miss Tilly rose to turn the sausages.

But Lillian pushed back. "It's not so fine when it happens though. I prefer knowing what's ahead."

"Aw, we never know, honey. Jest when we think we got it figured, life takes another turn. Sometimes it's a good surprise, an' sometimes hard. But the Lord is always in't. Can't be no other way, lesten ya don't believe He's strong an' good."

"Hmm."

"I 'member when I was new married. Had high hopes ta be a mum. But we struggled to keep a baby ta its birthin' day."

"Oh, I didn't realize," Lillian stammered, "but you—have *seven* children."

Lifting sputtering sausages from the skillet with a fork, Miss Tilly explained evenly, "Well, that weren't easy. Was a long road—mostly them ambages, that! Then God give us Carl when he was three. An' I finally carried ta deliverin' time. The rest was a mix a' birthin' an' receivin'."

"I didn't know you adopted some of your children, Miss Tilly."

A hiss of steam as Miss Tilly poured the eggs into the skillet. "Guess we didn't think'a it as adoptin'. Weren't no papers writ up back then. Some'a ours just come ta us another way."

Lillian was stunned. "How many? Which ones?"

The woman smiled directly toward Lillian and gave a wink. “Can’t ’member now. Been too long.”

Two little boys came tumbling over each other down the stairs, both talking at once.

• • • • • • •

Waiting in the payroll office, Ben dreaded what must be done. He’d known of many other men who’d quit their ship assignments before the return voyage. They were generally looked down upon, seen as lacking good judgment and loyalty. After so many years with this company he hated to sully his good name.

Will I ne’er return ta sea? The question brought a tightness to his chest.

However, family was most important, finding Jane and his parents wherever they’d gone. Of course, he had no idea how that was to be accomplished. It wasn’t as if he’d never looked at a map. The country of Canada was far vaster than England, and he hadn’t the faintest idea where to begin. His mind had been working on the dilemma for days.

Ben’s father was a tinsmith by trade. For most of his life he’d labored whenever he could in someone else’s workshop, making kitchenware, shiny farm containers of all sizes, and rarely, more decorative items that displayed his underlying artistry. In more recent years the aging man had begun to do some work of his own. He’d even developed his own stamp to imprint on the bottom of his products. But there were too many others with whom to compete and not nearly enough customers to keep him busy.

Ben wondered if Dada might have hoped that Canada could provide increased patronage for his merchandise. On the other hand, perhaps there’d been a complete turnabout. Maybe instead the man had opted for one of the jobs more plentiful in the developing industries of the much younger country. There was really no way to know. He thought about the callused hands and stooped shoulders of his father. The greasy gray hair. The wrinkled skin on his face aged by years spent leaning in too close to hot furnaces, his hearing dulled by the clanging of metal on metal.

"*Eh?*" Dada would always reply first whenever anyone addressed him. "*What's that, eh?*"

Having now worked independently to support himself in life, Ben had gained more respect for this man who'd sacrificed his best years to provide for his family. Still, Ben wondered why, if family was so all-important, the man had been so gruff and unapproachable. He'd seemed to prefer the company of his peers to those in his own home.

A door opened and the paymaster appeared at the desk. Ben rose from his seat and approached, hat in hand. "Mr. Kinsey, sir, I'd like ta ask fer me pay."

"An' ya can have it, soon's we dock at home."

"I'm sorry, sir. Most sorry. But, ya see, me fam'ly come ta Canada an' I feel I have ta follow 'em. So I can't be returnin' this trip." He hurried on to explain, "But, sir, ya see, I was in charge'a them orphans on the way here. An' ya won't be needin' me fer that on the trip back. Won't need ta cover that job at all 'cause they're all stayin' here."

The man's expression was grim. "Ya breakin' yer word, then, are ya, Ben?"

"No, sir. I feel that, rather so, I completed me task."

"Hmm." The man drew a ledger from beneath the desk and flipped through it to find the page with Ben's name listed. "Says here yer ta assist with repairs."

Ben bristled but held himself in check. "Now, sir, ya know ya got more'n enough men fer that."

A wry smile. "Don't say that here. Says ya agreed to it 'fore we left."

"An' I ain't askin' fer me full pay. Just the half I already done."

The man turned away slowly, walking to the back room. Ben was well aware that it was where the company's safe was kept. He heard the tumbling clicks of the lock, the shuffling of paper bills, followed by the hard clank of the door closing again. After several more minutes the man returned, now looking rather pleased with himself.

"That's it, then." He pushed two bills across the desk toward Ben.

Grabbing them up, Ben resisted the urge to explode. He forced his voice to remain even. "That ain't half what I'm owed."

"Well, ya broke yer contract, mate. Ya can't tell me yer breakin' yer word, an' then tell me what I gotta do fer ya. 'Twas you what changed the plan."

"Mr. Kinsey, ya know ya got plenty'a men fer repairs. Ya know I ain't needed fer it."

His eyebrows rose and the smile faded. "Ya comin' back again? I can sign ya up right now. When ya returnin' to work, then?"

Ben looked down at his feet for a moment, found that he couldn't lie even now. "I don't know. I don't expect I will."

"Then we're done here." With that the man closed his book and walked away. He paused for a moment and added over his shoulder, "Ya shoulda got yer pay 'fore ya said ya was quittin'. Ain't ya learned nothin'?" With a chuckle to himself, he left the room.

Ben stared down at the two bills in his hand, shaking with rage. He took a step forward to follow Mr. Kinsey into the back room. Then corrected himself and spun on his heel, slamming the door behind him as he stepped back out onto the street. It wasn't enough to pay for his travels, or room and board, for long at all. How would he ever find his family?

Dejected, he strode forward, lifting his eyes toward the new surroundings as if to feign more confidence than he felt.

• • • • • • •

As the pale morning light filtered through the trees over Brookfield, Lillian walked the boys to school. In their layers of sweaters, jackets, and scarves they looked like two stuffed sausage links waddling upright ahead of her. She was grateful that, mercifully, there wasn't a biting wind.

She found herself once again missing Hazel and Bryony and the other boys, the little crew of children who'd kept one another company on their way to school. It occurred to Lillian far too late that she should have asked Lemuel and Harrison if they would pick up the twins as they passed the house for the remainder of the school year. However, since arrangements hadn't already been made, it was necessary for Matty and Milton to be escorted on one of the coldest days Lillian could remember. Grace was doing the bookkeeping at home instead.

Once the boys were safely delivered, Lillian stopped by the post office. She watched as Sophie McRae collected from the countertop the letter that Lillian was sending. The woman stamped it with a thud. This envelope held Lillian's response to Father's gracious and uplifting words about the trouble. In fact, in his long reply he'd relayed a story of when he'd been a young man and had failed to live up to his own conscience. Lillian felt strongly that she didn't deserve to have gotten off so easily by those around her, but she'd written this letter to thank Father for being so gracious.

"How's yer dad, dear?" Mrs. McRae asked.

"He's well. Thank you. And your new baby? How's little Ruby getting along?"

"Just fine, dear. She don't sleep well at night, but she's real healthy—so I ain't complainin'."

"I'm sorry—and you're working again already?"

Sophie smiled. "We do as we must. My Ernest is gone most days. So, as my mum used ta say, 'It's a good life if ya don't weaken.'"

What a disparaging thought! Lillian wasn't quite certain how to respond. "I hope she sleeps well very soon. At least you know how quickly they grow—that it won't be long 'til she's toddling."

"True enough."

"Well, have a nice day."

"Thank you, Lillian. You too."

Stopping next at the grocery store for a spool of thread for Miss Tilly, Lillian reached the driveway just as the sun lifted its full circle away from the horizon and began its arching journey over their valley. It would be a bright Alberta day, and Lillian hoped to make the best of it, settling back into routine at home.

But that was not to be. When she returned home, Grace met her in the foyer, an ashen look to her face. "I was going through the mail that Otto dropped off earlier when he came to shovel snow for us. There's a letter you should see. I hope you don't mind that I've already opened it, but it was addressed to both of us."

Lillian continued to remove her outerwear, her eyes on Grace. *So that's why Sophie McRae had no letters when I checked.* Words came slowly as she sensed Grace's concern. Lillian's first thought was of the difficulties at Brayton House, but the second possibility was far more unnerving. At last she asked, "What is it, Grace? Is it from Father?"

"No. I would never have opened one of those! It's from that law office. It had a stamp from Mayberry, Parks, and Dorn on the envelope. That's how I knew."

"And it's addressed to both of us?" Lillian dropped her boots onto the mat and slipped on her house shoes, rising to face Grace.

"Yes. It has to do with . . ."

". . . the estate—our parents' estate," finished Lillian. "That's been in the back of my mind for some time."

"Yes. That."

They walked together in silence to the dining room. Lillian sat across from where Grace had been working, her notes and other correspondence still laid out neatly on the table.

Grace said, "They've been communicating with the man in Toronto who had been considered the other possible heir—the one who was responsible for the estate not being settled previously. The letter gives more information about him. Do you want to read it?"

Lillian drew in a long breath, wrestling internally with her feelings. *After Mama and Papa died of tuberculosis when I was so little, and everyone assumed that Grace had also succumbed, where was this man? Did he know about me? Why would he subsequently hamper the settlement of the estate? Or did I misunderstand?* And yet, it was the search for a proper heir that had led to Grace's discovery by the lawyers. "No, thank you. Don't bother reading it aloud. Will you please just summarize it for me?"

"Of course." Grace lifted the pages once more. "The letter tells that the man in Toronto is the stepson of our grandfather. That would make him our uncle by marriage."

"Does it give a name?"

"Yes, sis. But you might think I'm making this up." Grace paused, a tiny smirk lifting the corner of her mouth. "His name is Saul Brazington-Bennett."

"What? I thought our family line came from fairly simple folk. He sounds rather hoity-toity."

"We do. But, well, try to follow along with me. Our grandpapa was Oliver Bennett. His first wife was the mother of three sons: James, George, and Wilbur. So our papa, George Bennett, was the middle son. He came to Alberta with our mama, and later began farming with Uncle James, just as we'd heard before. Apparently Grandpapa was a fairly modest man, a shop owner in a small city. But after Grandmama died, he married a widow who had means. Her name was Serena Brazington."

Lillian's head was spinning. "Then they had a son together too—the man in Toronto?"

"No, Mrs. Brazington already had a son from her first marriage. His name was Saul Brazington until his mother and our grandfather married. That's when she and her son took on the double last name."

Slowly, "Then he's not really our relation at all—not by blood, to be accurate."

"No, he's not related by blood. And he doesn't need Papa's estate settlement, that's for certain."

"What do you mean?"

"Well, Lillian, he's quite a wealthy man." Grace offered the letter so that Lillian could see the disclosures for herself.

Reaching across to receive the pages, Lillian skimmed them quickly, as if she could find some sense in it all by looking on her own. "But I don't understand. Why did he drag out the settlement of the estate? Why didn't he just leave it all uncontested? Surely he can't care a whit about such a small amount of money as our parents must have had." She paused. And then, "Grace, does it say how much money?"

"It does."

"Where? How much?"

"At the bottom there. The entire estate is valued, with interest accrued, at just over two thousand dollars."

Lillian gasped. "That much? Goodness me, we could buy our own automobile and still have some left over. I hadn't imagined it would ever be so much."

"I know. I still can't believe it either. It doesn't seem real."

The motivation of this uncle had quickly become even more important now that Lillian understood the assets that he'd been deferring from them. "Why didn't he just let us have our parents' inheritance? Just think how much help it would have been through the fall season when we had so little to work with."

Grace shrugged and leaned forward on her elbows. "I don't suppose anyone knows. It seems he's been quite evasive throughout the investigation. But Mr. Dorn plans to travel to Toronto to speak with Uncle Saul Brazington-Bennett." She spoke the name with exaggerated flourish. "Mr. Dorn was merely waiting for some of his other cases to be settled before he left." Grace paused, as if allowing Lillian a moment to process what had already been said, before adding more. "Mr. Dorn has invited us to join him."

"To go to Toronto?"

"Yes, to speak with Uncle Saul."

The idea of such a journey was far too much to comprehend.

CHAPTER 10

Unsettled

The first order of business for Ben was to find a room to rent. He didn't want much, as he needed to guard the few dollars still in his possession, the meager pay from this voyage, and the previous coins he'd hidden away in various places among his things. Stopping by a large church closest to the docks, he inquired to see if the custodian there knew of anyone who might be in need of a tenant. He was put in touch with a fishmonger near the docks who rented a room above his shop by the week. Most potential occupants would have been put off by the strong smell of fish, but Ben had long since grown accustomed to anything having to do with the sea. It took most of the afternoon, but he was soon settled in the small room, grateful to have achieved his most pressing need.

The morning after, he began the pursuit of evidence of his family's presence. Here again Ben deemed it best to consult a nearby church, this time searching for those that would have most suited his parents. If they'd been in town for any length of time, he was certain they would have attended services. So there was nothing to do but begin traipsing around the city in search of local Anglican congregations. It was a laborious process spanning three days. And in the end, it provided not a single clue as to their whereabouts.

"They must'a moved on quick," he concluded. "Me mum would ne'er have let 'em miss a Sunday."

Exhausted upon returning to his room on the third evening, Ben spied a used bookstore. He'd begun to contemplate his meager funds and what might be done about them. The only items he owned worth selling were the two books he carried in his kit. He decided to inquire about their value to the shop owner before retiring for the night.

The very smell of the bookstore brought a sense of comfort. Old books, though often dusty and worn, had been his best and longest-lasting companionship through his years of sailing. If it were necessary to give up his volume of Shakespeare, it consoled Ben to remember that another might be purchased again at a later time. The stories, the words, the themes would never be lost to him entirely, fixed as they were in his memory, his very being.

"Good evening. May I help you, sir?"

"Aye, sir. I've a single-volume Globe Shakespeare. The one by Clark an' Wright in 1867. It's in good condition, though it's been well read. I'd like ta get a reckonin' on what ya might give me fer it."

The man eyed Ben warily. "Do you have a receipt for its purchase, sir?"

The question was one Ben had been asked often before. He'd made his peace about presumptions others might make based on his less-than-cultivated appearance. "Aye, sir. I use the bill o' sale fer a bookmark. I can show it t'ya if we can strike a deal."

"How long have you had the volume?"

Ben scratched the hair at the back of his head roughly. "Nigh unto three years now. But I read it through many a'time."

"Bravo," the shopkeeper answered, his attitude shifting rather unexpectedly. "Well done, you. How is it you're ready to give up such a treasure now?"

"Well, I haven't made up me mind just yet. But if ya will give me a fair price, I might." He paused before confiding, "I need money more 'an inspiration just now."

As he wrote a number on a slip of paper and passed it across to Ben, the man's interest seemed to increase. He had a strange expression in his eyes, one that could only be read as *hope*. "You're not a sailor, are you, sir?"

"Well, yes. Just up from the docks."

A broad grin. "Is your name Ebenezer by any chance? Ebenezer Waldin?"

Ben stumbled back a step, suspicious now. "Who's askin'?"

"Mr. Waldin, I'm so pleased to meet you." A hand stretched across the desk, reaching for Ben's own, shaking it heartily. "The good Lord in heaven must be smiling on you today. I have a letter for you, sir. From a woman claiming to be your sister."

"From Jane?"

"Yes, I believe so, the very same."

The man turned away and rummaged through the cubbyhole shelves behind him. Ben stood in utter shock. *Jane? A letter? After three days wearin' out the soles of me shoes in the search, how's it possible?*

Sliding the envelope across the counter toward him, the shopkeeper chuckled aloud. "Well, to be entirely honest, it's not quite as shocking as it first appears. It seems your sister was very busy while here in our city. I hear tell that every bookshop within a mile of the docks received the same letter, held by its owner just in case you might walk in through its door."

Of course Jane knew his custom of buying and selling books. She'd chosen the one place other than church that might have caused him to cross paths with her correspondence. He found himself laughing aloud, this being the first good news he'd received in quite some time. "I can't tell ya how much I'm in yer debt, sir. Thank ya. I'm flabbergasted, that I am."

"My wife," the man added sincerely, "will be very pleased to hear it. She's been praying for you, young man. Hoping you'd find each other again."

Shaking his head, Ben added once more, "Thank you. Thank ya so much, sir!"

Hurrying the last few blocks to his rented room, Ben rushed inside and lit the oil lamp on the table, his hand trembling with eagerness. Were they close? Could he find them quickly?

Dropping onto the bed without even removing his heavy coat, he tore open the letter and fed on Jane's words as if they were fine delicacies.

My beloved Ben,

It is with many prayers and great desperation that I write this letter to you. Dada has decided we must travel west in order to begin our new life. May our Heavenly Father grant that you will read these words and follow shortly. I can't tell you precisely where we'll come to rest, but the province where we're to settle is known as Alberta. Today we purchased train tickets to a city called Winnipeg and have no definite plans as to our route thereafter. Follow us, please, dear brother. But also take care to look out for yourself as well. You're so very important to me. I cannot bear the thought of something untoward happening to you, nor of never seeing you again.

God bless you in every way,
Jane

With his free hand Ben clutched at the coverlet beneath him, twisting it cruelly as his fingers clenched into a fist.

They're gone! I missed 'em.

The single page fluttered to the floor as he covered his eyes with his empty hand. Far from bringing him closer, the letter had driven them farther away. Grateful as he was for the information, Ben felt like a fisherman in a small boat on a vast sea, helplessly seeking where he might cast his tiny net. If only Jane could find another way to make their new location known.

• • • ● • • •

"I can't go, Grace. I just can't." Lillian's evening cup of tea had grown cold while the sisters discussed the possibility of traveling to Toronto to meet with Uncle Saul. "We've only been home for a few days, and there are the twins to think about."

"I'm not pushing, sis. I just wanted to think it through from all angles." Grace's tone remained patient, though she continued to express her honest thoughts. "I don't imagine we have much to lose by not going along. Mr. Dorn can represent us well. It's just the very idea of meeting a relative that's so hard for me to let go."

"And don't forget, there's the possibility of more children being billeted to us. Have we had any correspondence from Brayton House? They think the new children should arrive by the middle of February. The last I heard, there should be homes for all of them already, but I'd like to be prepared just in case something unexpected happens and they need us to take in another child. February *is not* far away." Lillian could feel her toes curling tightly inside her house shoes. She was trying not to let her tension show to Grace.

"No, I haven't received any letters from them, but I can ask Quinley. He might have been in touch with Sid by telephone."

"*If* he's in town." They both knew that it was the man's intention to travel throughout the area evaluating adoptive families. Lillian wasn't sure if he'd already gone off on a business trip. He'd spoken frequently of the heavy workload of his occupation, so it seemed likely.

"True. Yes, that seems wise. We can speak with Quinley about it, provided he's still in the area. Should we walk in together tomorrow? I think the weather's warming again."

"I'd like that. Miss Tilly has a short list of things we need, and I'd like to be out in the sunshine rather than cooped up all day."

It was at least a direction in which to proceed. Lillian breathed a sigh of relief and headed back to the kitchen for a fresh cup of tea. She disliked the tensions of such big decisions. If only it were possible to live a quiet life without disruptions and strife.

I don't know anything about this Saul Brazington, Lillian thought to herself, *and I don't know that I need to. It's not as if he's close family at all. He's just the man who caused our inheritance to be delayed.* Even before she returned to the parlor she found herself regretting the sour attitude, her thoughts pivoting in a new direction. *He may be a very nice man, someone my papa and mama would've been glad for me to know. I suppose they would have been acquainted with him—had dinners and shared special occasions. He might even be able to tell us more about their story. And of course, we don't have many members anymore in our little family. Perhaps we have none to spare.*

As an afterthought she realized, *And maybe he'd be pleased to know us too.*

In the morning Lillian and Grace joined the four boys on the way to school, particularly glad to have a chance to catch up with Harrison and Lemuel again.

"How's arithmetic going, Harrison? Have you mastered the rest of those times tables?"

"Miss Grace," the boy muttered, "I could figure with numbers long before now. 'Ad to in the street, lest someone cheat ya."

Tossing an arm around his shoulder, Grace refused to back down. "Yes, but *figuring* and mathematics aren't quite the same thing. Don't skip any steps now or you'll regret it later."

Harrison shook his head, but Grace squeezed tighter, her voice still cheerful. "I'm serious, son. Just ask Lemuel, he'll tell you."

Lemuel smiled, a twinkle in his eye. "Feels as if I skipped plenty'a steps, Miss Grace. Not sure if you counted up all my days at school how many you'd come up with. Good thing the *skipping* way can work out too, or I'd be in trouble."

"Well, we're all very proud of you, for sure—both of you." Lillian, who was walking closest to Lemuel, pushed a mittened hand under his arm. "In fact, we couldn't be prouder. But I'm not sure that's a good argument for allowing Harrison off the hook."

"No, miss. Prob'ly not."

"What's happening with the horses now? Any new developments?"

It was a pleasant conversation and not a long walk from the edge of Brookfield, where Father's house stood, into the heart of town. But despite it all, Lillian found herself wrestling again with the worrisome idea of a trip across the country. This very moment was what she wanted most, to be here, as near to all the children she loved as she could be. Her heart reached out tendrils to Hope Valley, where George and Hazel had been taken.

The town of Brookfield, for all its quiet style of life, was a pleasant place to live. Now that she'd spent time in both Calgary and Lethbridge, it was easier for Lillian to understand how suitable this situation was for her. She thought again of Walter so far away, learning a new vocation, making his way among strangers. *How's he settling in? Is he glad for the choice he made? Does he miss me at all?*

The sisters parted ways with the boys as they reached the center of town. Waving them off and wishing them a good day, they turned toward the hotel where Quinley Sinclair had taken a room. Once more Lillian's thoughts turned back to Walter. The hotel lobby, a glance toward the dining room—it all reminded her of their time together.

"Sis, why don't you wait here? I'll ask at the desk to see if they'll send a page boy up to Quinley's room. It wouldn't be proper to go up to knock by ourselves."

"That seems best." But rather than taking a seat in the

chair Grace had suggested, Lillian chose to stand in the front window, looking out over the movements of townsfolk in the morning.

"Lillian!" a voice called to her from somewhere above.

Startled, she spun toward the sound to find Quinley striding down the broad staircase.

"Well, what a surprise! Lillian Walsh, what brings you to my home away from home?"

"Quinley? Grace was just trying to have you paged. We weren't certain if you'd be here today or if you'd be on the road."

He flashed a winning smile. "I'm glad I didn't miss you two, my favorite pair of sisters."

Seeing his cheerful face brought an instant lift to Lillian's spirits. "Have you settled in? What do you think of our little town?"

"It's charming. I could live here forever. So much more pleasant and picturesque than the city."

"And less exciting." Lillian laughed. She couldn't imagine that Quinley would be satisfied with Brookfield for long. "How's your work coming?"

"Oh, well, very well. Though I've discovered that most of the families this far west don't have telephones in their homes. So I'm afraid I'll have to do some surprise visits. That always sets people on edge—as if you're trying to catch them doing something wrong."

Grace broke into their conversation, approaching with a quick, light step. "Hello, Quinley. Has Lillian told you that you're precisely who we've come looking for?"

"Yes, she hinted at it. Is there something I can do to assist you ladies?" His eyes lifted to the room behind him. "Why don't we take a table in the dining room? We can have something to drink, a bite to eat, while we catch up again."

The idea sounded lovely to Lillian. She followed behind Quinley and Grace as they moved into the dining room and settled themselves at a table. He seemed to pay special attention to Grace, drawing out her chair and saying things that made her laugh. *He's so thoughtful with her. If only he and Grace would have reason to get to know one another better—time to spend together. I wouldn't be surprised at all if they would make a good match.*

Once their order had been placed, Quinley took charge. "How can I help you today, ladies? Up to half my kingdom, it will be yours."

Smiling at his theatrics, Lillian responded more directly. "We've been wondering how soon the new children will arrive in Lethbridge. And the status of the families waiting for them. Does it all seem to be working out?"

"I haven't heard the latest, but I believe they'll arrive by train in about three weeks. Sid already knew that one little girl was not on their original list. She was supposed to stay in the East, but that family fell through. I'm not sure if she'll be assigned by then or if they'll want you to house her for a while. There might be another boy as well. An older boy. He's causing some concern for the caretakers, not very cooperative, rather disruptive—and he's fourteen—old enough to cause serious issues if he won't settle down. We'll have to wait and see."

Lillian drew in a slow breath. She wasn't certain what they'd do with a boy quite so old who was difficult to manage. And yet, her heart went out to him too. By now she'd learned enough about the children's stories to expect that his had been a troubled life.

Their conversation quickly turned to other things, to the town and its inhabitants, its businesses and surrounding agriculture. Quinley seemed interested in it all.

At last the bill arrived, and Lillian reached for her purse.

"No need. I'll take care of it." Grace started to protest, but Quinley insisted. "I have a travel allowance. I'm pleased to have a chance to treat." And with a flourish to his penmanship, he signed the bill over to his room.

Making his way through the crowded railway station, Ben watched carefully between the shoulders of strangers for the schedule board. He reached the purchasing area and spied the wide sign across the room. Weaving among the passengers, he found a patch of floor near enough to read the board easily. He'd come first thing in the morning supposing that there would be thinner crowds. In fact, the opposite was true. It seemed that the entire city had turned out to catch a train. It was an effort just to hold his position while the streams of people moved past him, hurrying along on their own business, jostling against him from time to time.

He scanned down the list until he found Winnipeg. As he estimated the number of location names between here and there, it appeared to be quite a number of stops away. With a sigh, he hoped the fare for the lengthy ride wouldn't eat up too much of his precious funds. Just as he joined the back of the line at the ticket counter to make his purchase, he felt a hand on his shoulder.

"Excuse me, sir. I believe we've met?"

Ben took a step sideways, shaking his head quickly. "I'm sorry, ma'am. I don't live here. I . . ."

"Yes—yes, we have. You helped the children from the ship a few days ago."

This time Ben allowed his eyes to focus on the middle-aged woman before him, his hand reaching up quickly to draw the wool flat cap from his head. She did seem familiar. In fact, she was the one who'd led little Janie away. *What's she doin' here?*

"May I ask, if it's not too presumptuous, sir, where it is you plan to travel?"

"I . . . I . . ." Words were difficult to conjure while she stared at him. "I'm headin' west—ta Winnipeg there." He pointed up at the board as if she'd be able to follow his gesture.

"You are? Oh, that's good to hear. You see, I've come to purchase our tickets too. Not for today. We plan to leave on Tuesday now. We make a stop in Winnipeg to place some of the children before going on to Alberta with the last few."

Does she mean wee Janie's group? Ben's mind felt numbed by the unexpected encounter. He remembered that the woman had spoken about mountains but had no idea how far west one needed to go before encountering them.

She chatted on. "I don't want to bother you, but . . ." Then she took hold of the sleeve of his coat as if to keep him from getting away. Her smile grew wider, with an expression like the face of an experienced salesman. "What was your name again, sir?"

"Waldin. Ben Waldin."

"And you work for the ship."

"I do—no, no, I *did*, miss. I'm done with it fer now."

"Oh, are you currently employed otherwise?"

It was a strange series of questions, and Ben wasn't sure where the woman was guiding this conversation. He glanced over his shoulder and noticed the line he'd been in had shuffled forward several paces. Hesitating, he allowed those behind him to move past. "I ain't workin' now. I hope ta be soon."

"Why, this could be an unexpected blessing, Mr. Waldin. It's just that we're in need of one more supervisor. And since you're already familiar with these children, and you happen to be traveling in the same direction too . . . Well, wouldn't it be just a godsend if we could hire you to replace the other man who can't come?"

"I'm sorry, what now?" The voices of a hundred conversations around them made Ben doubt the reliability of what he'd just heard. He hunched his head lower to ask, "Ya say yer takin' the kids ta Winnipeg?"

"Yes. And I'd be so grateful if we could hire you to assist us. We're in quite a pickle without one more chaperone. And, as I said, you already know them—have already been in a position of responsibility over them. I'm certain I could make arrangements for—well, the society would buy your ticket and your food for the journey, and you'd receive a little remuneration for your troubles. I'm afraid we can't afford much, but . . ."

Ben needed to hear no more. "I'm very int'rested. What was yer name, ma'am?"

"Miss Davis. Miss Mary Davis."

For a moment they stood in awkward silence. Then Ben roused himself enough to know what to do. He stepped aside to motion her into line ahead of him. "You'll be needin' tickets, then? Can I help ya in any way, Miss Davis?"

"Thank you. Yes, I think this is a very fortunate meeting. I believe I'm ready to proceed."

CHAPTER 11

Boys

Ben waited on the bench outside Miss Davis's office, his knee bouncing up and down as if it were a piston thrusting inside a steamship, chugging away on its own. He could rarely remember having been so impatient. Then the door opened and he was invited to follow. He swallowed hard and rose, staying close behind.

A long hallway. A door into another section of the building. But the next threshold opened to reveal a room with children dispersed around it, playing with a few scant toys or reading. Ben's eyes swept the room, his heart now racing.

There she is! "Janie," he whispered.

Though his voice was not loud enough to summon her attention, the large eyes turned toward him. A joyful smile broke across her face. Janie ran across the room and stood before him as he dropped to one knee.

With the gentle confidence that he'd come to expect from her, she simply stated, "I knew you'd come for me." Then her arms went around Ben's neck, and he held her for as long as he dared with so many eyes upon them, one of his hands reaching up to his own eyes to pinch away the tears that had gathered.

"It's good ta see ya again, child."

"I missed you." And with a happy whisper directed into his ear, she added, "I 'membered, Mister Waldin. I'm still Jane Grey for you."

Giving him little time to recover, Miss Davis beckoned Ben to follow her to the paperwork waiting on a desk on the far side of the room. Ben righted himself and crossed after her, smiling and nodding at the children he passed whose eyes followed the oddly familiar man reappearing unexpectedly.

Through the days at sea Ben had come to know some of the names of the other children, though, in truth, he'd rarely spoken to any of them. He could best recall who among them had been terribly sick and how long they'd remained so. The faces of the three who'd been lost were imprinted on his mind most clearly. He shook his head, as if doing so could dispel the memories.

"Now, sir, we'd like your duties to be supportive. We'll lead the children and provide all instruction to them. We'd like you to follow at the back whenever we're moving as a group, constantly watching for dawdlers and making sure we haven't left anyone behind. Believe me, it's not so difficult to lose someone while traveling with such a large group."

Ben understood perfectly. He'd spent enough time observing how hard the guardians of such groups worked to maintain order.

Miss Davis's voice quieted, and she turned her back toward the main part of the room. "While we're on the train we will likely have you bunk with the boys. Are you a heavy sleeper, Mr. Waldin?"

"No, miss. I wake easy."

"That'll be helpful. We don't know most of these boys well. It's best to watch them closely."

Ben eyed the woman. He wasn't certain if the warning came from the common prejudice that lawlessness was simply in the blood of street children and orphans, or if the woman was actually compassionate yet experienced with the harsh consequences of losing one's place in life.

He'd seen it often enough himself—but he rarely held it against the poor folk around him. Those down and out, young and old, who found themselves alone were at times required to break laws if they were to survive at all. *Goodness knows*, he pondered as Miss Davis continued speaking, *they've no reason to look fer much from the world 'round 'em. An' it don't matter rich nor poor, hard times can make sinners of us all. Even wee Janie, God love her, with nowt but cruelty could grow dark an' hard.*

His mind flashed a memory of the two old women back in the eatery. He resolved to do whatever was in his power to see that Janie arrived somewhere that she'd be loved and cared for. But, at any rate, he knew it would be best to be vigilant in watching the boys during his time as their overseer.

"Do you have any questions, Mr. Waldin?"

Ben startled back into focus. "No, miss. I believe I got it."

"Good. I'll show you where you can put your things."

• • • • •

"Miss Grace! Miss Grace! Look outside! Is it 'nough? Can we go t'day?"

Overnight the yard had become a fresh winter wonderland, silky snow laying thick on every level surface. For some time, the twins had begged to go sledding with Lemuel and Harrison at the big hill on the other side of town—the place where their friends often gathered. And since this gift from the heavens had happened on a Saturday morning, they were anxious to see their idea come to fruition.

"We'll ask the Thompsons. I expect we can work something

out." Grace tried to pat Milton on the head, but he hopped away too quickly, dancing around the kitchen table. She laughed and added, "I'll walk down and see if that works for them."

But Lillian countered, "No, I'll go. I'd like a good walk, and Lemuel had asked me to come see the bicycle he found in Mr. Thompson's shed. He was going to show me the parts he needs to fix it up. I thought Father might have something in the barn that would work."

"All right. I'll get the boys ready." Then Grace added more quietly, "I think at this point we'll have to take them whether the others can go or not. We'll leave chores for later, and our correspondence too."

Lillian nodded. The cold snap had broken and the sky was clear, a rather nice day for the end of January. It would be good to spend time outdoors and to visit with other families from town. *Perhaps we can even invite Bryony to join us.*

Cutting a fresh path through the drifts in the yard, Lillian labored toward the road. Already vehicles had left long, criss-crossing lines of narrow tire tracks. There were two trails of horse prints, one on either side of the road. She wondered if it were one horse going to town and returning, or two horses who'd already braved the day. *Lemuel would know. Arthur Thompson is teaching him how to read tracks like that.*

Though the sun had not yet fully risen and gray shadows still slept in large patches across the ground, Lillian could already see the sparkle of diamonds wakening where the light reached the pristine snow. She was grateful to be outdoors and glad to have a reason to drop in on June Thompson. Lillian knew that their neighboring household would be busy already so early in the morning. Farmers in the area rose long before the late-winter sun. And Mr. Thompson worked especially hard, with his additional occupation as school principal.

After making arrangements with June, Lillian walked to the barn with Harrison and Lemuel, chatting happily. They saddled the pair of pinto mares in order to help the group cross town more easily. Lillian watched the deft movements of the boys and marveled at how fully they'd adapted to their role as country boys. She waited nearby, breathing in the moist smells of hay and horses.

"Miss Lillian, you can ride behind me," offered Harrison. "An' when we get Miss Grace and the twins, Lemmie an' me can just lead 'em from there. The four of you can get on. We don't mind walkin'."

"That's kind of you. I know Milton and Matty will be thrilled to go for a ride."

Soon they were on their way through town, dragging the sled that Lemuel had tied behind his horse. They stopped at the Moorelands' to inquire about Bryony and found her father and brothers had already taken her to the hill. Lillian's excitement grew a little more.

The long slope was covered with a blanket of crystal-white snow peppered by the dark shapes of bundled children, most of them making their slow trek back to the top of the hill. At first it was almost impossible to recognize anyone, but slowly they were able to make out familiar individuals. Lemuel and Harrison walked the horses up the steep road next to the sledding activities.

"Hey, Orville!" Lemuel called out to his best friend as a sled flashed past near the road. Just then the party of three riders launched over an unseen mound and were thrown from the sled in various directions. Their screams made the horses shift a few steps farther away. Lemuel and Harrison howled in laughter.

Pointing a mittened hand, Harrison asked, "Did ya see 'em, Lemmie?"

"I did!" Lemuel let the reins slip from his hand and hurried to the edge of the road, laughing loudly. "Hey, Orville! Hey!"

For a moment the three riders lay dormant where they'd fallen.

Then one by one they rose, laughing and brushing away the soft snow.

Lemuel called again, "Orville!"

A bright pink face turned toward them, half hidden by a green scarf and snow-covered cap. Even from her seat on the pinto Lillian could recognize Orville, as well as the girls, Emily and Lorraine.

"Lemmie!" came the answering shout. "Thought ya'd never get here."

They hustled the rest of the way up the hill. At the top was a cluster of adults talking together. Grace and Lillian unloaded the smaller boys, and Harrison loosened the sled. They tied the horses to nearby trees beside three other mounts: a small black pony, a chestnut, and an old gray donkey. Lemuel produced a small amount of grain from a burlap bag tied to one of the saddles and placed it in front of their pintos, a token payment for their service.

Then the group struck out for the launching area on the hill, their sled bobbling along behind them in the churned-up snow. Grace and Lillian trudged toward the small group of adults who stood supervising at the top.

"Ya ain't comin'?" Harrison called over his shoulder to them.

Grace waved a hand toward him. "Later. We'll try it in a little bit. Promise."

Though it felt as if the sledding activities included every student from the school, there were few adults who were brave enough, or available enough, to join them. Pastor Bukowski's dark brown beard and hearty laugh prompted Lillian's attention first as the sisters approached. Then she noticed Kenneth Mooreland, Bryony's new father, calling out encouragement as his boys helped Bryony back up the hill. There were five other adults standing together. She recognized Verna MacCodrum, who was a mother of eight; big Charlie Jensen, who'd been George's teacher; and Hannah Orlinger, the town's part-time librarian. This left one couple Lillian didn't recognize.

"Good morning," Verna greeted as they approached.

Grace's answer was confident. "It certainly is. Were your children all begging you to be let off chores this morning too?"

"Oh yes, never did their work faster."

Friendly laughter followed, coming in bursts of breath visible in the cold air.

"Have you met the Caulfields, girls?" As always, Pastor Bucky was ready to make introductions.

Lillian glanced at Grace. "We haven't. Miss Tilly—or rather, Mrs. Tillendynd—told us we have new neighbors, but we haven't had the pleasure." She smiled and stepped closer.

It was the woman who answered first, shuffling a few steps forward in the snow. "It's so good ta meet you. I'm Catherine. An' this is my husband, Sam."

Lillian reached for her hand. She was unexpectedly tall for a woman. The hand that met Lillian's had a strong, firm grasp. Catherine's thick wool coat seemed to cloak broad shoulders above a slender form. On first impression she appeared to Lillian to be a workhorse of a woman.

"How have you been settling in, Catherine?" Grace asked while taking her turn at accepting the woman's offered hand.

"Well as can be. We got much ta do in the new house. But we're readying it now to farm in the spring."

"Have you farmed before?"

"Yeah, in Saskatchewan. My Sam's family was one of the first to their area. His brothers took over his father's land, but we wanted to—find a place of our own."

"Do you have a family? Children?"

A strange pause, a deep breath, but she recovered quickly with her answer. "Our son, Francis, is sledding there with the other children. He's the one with the gray scarf and brown cap. He's twelve."

At last Mr. Caulfield spoke, his voice much softer than his wife's. "Most call 'im Frank. He already made friends. He's the main reason we feel so good hereabouts. Frank's doing well—enjoyin' school. He left a whole slew of cousins, so we were kinda worried." He looked up toward Mr. Jensen. "The teachers are 'specially fine."

Charlie Jensen laughed. "Sure! On good days, even the students like us."

Conversation moved along, interrupted frequently by children needing help finding a lost mitten, settling a dispute, or just procuring a handkerchief to wipe a cold, drippy nose.

True to their word, Grace and Lillian took their turns on the long sled. They sat in line with the others, tucking in their feet around the rider in front of them and sailing down the long hill, tears streaming from their eyes as the wind whipped across their faces. But as they shook off the snow and joined the trail of others trudging back up the long hill, Lillian felt her joy kindled again. It was good to be home, good to be among people she knew and loved, good to have a shelter from the strange ambages of life she'd been struggling against.

All too soon it was time to strike out for home and lunch in a warm kitchen.

• • • ● • • •

Now that Ben was to be an official assistant, the boys eyed him with greater interest. He could perceive already that they'd sorted themselves into a functioning unit, each with a role. The self-appointed leader was clearly one of the older boys named Alfred Jones. He seemed to have been ruling the younger lads with rather an iron fist. Ben watched closely, gathering as much information as he could while the other guardians were nearby and responsible. He would wait to draw conclusions about how to best handle Alfred. Ben reasoned that there was no sense taking a stand and making an enemy of the youth. He'd wait to engage until he knew much more than he did at present. As he understood the arrangement, only he and Miss Davis were to travel on the train with the children. The other supervisors would remain to disperse children in the eastern areas.

There were nine boys. It would be a great responsibility.

The boys closed in around him following supper as the other adults worked among the younger children. Alfred Jones came first, his hands tucked deep inside his pockets, his eyes peering up from his tilted-sideways face, a cocky grin almost concealed. He was likely full grown, almost as tall as Ben, hair cropped close to his scalp in the fashionless style of a Home Child. Two others were close behind.

"What's yer name, Mister?" Alfred addressed Ben first.

Before responding, Ben set his face, unwilling to demonstrate a reaction of any kind. Still, he looked directly into Alfred's eyes as he spoke, keeping his voice even and unaffected. "Waldin," he answered.

"Saw ya on ship. Ya was a deckhand then."

"Yes."

"Now yer here. With us. How come?"

Ben shrugged a little. "New job."

Alfred walked past, turning as he went so that Ben was always before him. "An' that girl. She yers, then?" The boy lifted his chin toward where Janie sat at a far table.

"No."

"Then how'd she come when you did?"

"She was always on ship."

"But not with us. With us there were another one called Jane Grey. 'Cept she died. Funny how they're both that same name." The eyes narrowed to slits.

"Nope. She wasn't with you."

"Then where'd she come from?"

Ben crossed his arms and leaned back against the table that stood behind him. "Ain't me business. Ain't yers neither."

"I think it be."

The first trace of a smile cracked a little across Ben's face. "Ya can think as ya like. Ain't no law." But he hoped to quickly direct the conversation away from Janie. "Where ya from, lads?"

Alfred refused to forsake the lead. "An' that's another thing. Ya ain't from here, from Canada."

"True."

"Why ya here?"

Ben hesitated, then considered that it might be best to offer some of his own true story to the boys as a way of opening a door to friendship should they choose to cooperate. "I'm lookin' fer me fam'ly."

"They dead too?" a second boy asked quickly.

Alfred immediately scoffed. "No, idiot! If they was dead, he wouldn't be lookin', would he?"

"Lookin' fer a new 'un, like us, in'it?" the embarrassed boy answered under his breath.

Ben's heart went out to the second lad. "What's yer name, boy?"

The second boy was easily subdued. His eyes already refused to meet Ben's. "Malcolm, sir."

"Where ya from, Malcolm?"

"Cheshire, sir."

"I'm from Liverpool." Ben reached out a hand, holding it low where Malcolm couldn't help but see it. It was received dutifully with a glance toward Alfred.

"An' ya others?"

One by one the boys introduced themselves. In truth, Ben had already figured out all of their names during the afternoon among them. He merely used the opportunity to study their reactions, paying close attention to whether or not they were willing to look him in the eye. *Poor lads. I know ya don't want me pity, but ya got me sympathy just the same.*

Miss Davis called the boys away, seemingly pleased as she noticed that Ben had been conversing with them. It was a beginning. He hoped to establish good rapport with them, for as long as they traveled together—just an ordinary man along the way who had shown them some respect.

Gathering the remaining dishes from the boys' table, Ben carried them to the kitchen sink. Then he returned with a damp cloth in order to wipe the surface down. All the time he was watching, keeping one eye on Janie and the other eye on the boys who'd soon be his responsibility.

Alfred Jones and four of the others were to remain in Winnipeg, although for some reason there seemed to be an undercurrent of doubt that Alfred's particular situation would be suitable. Malcolm and three younger boys were set to continue on to Alberta from there. In addition there were two girls staying at their first destination and another three, including little Janie, who would travel farther.

It'd be easy as fallin' flat ta stay on with 'em past me stop—these lads what just need folk ta tell 'em they matter. If I don't watch meself, I'm afraid I'll forgo finding me own Jane, and that cannot happen. It cannot. In his heart, Ben began to steel himself against surrendering to such an outcome. *One payin' job. Free trip ta Winnipeg. After that, lookin' fer me own fam'ly.*

Chapter 12

Discussions

Miss Tilly had been very stern in her insistence. Grace and Lillian were instructed to invite the Caulfields to supper on Monday evening. The busy woman hadn't had a chance to spend much time with Brookfield's newest family yet, and Miss Tilly seemed to think that perhaps they might know some of the same people. She explained to Lillian that she had family who farmed in the same region of Saskatchewan.

In order to make the arrangements, Lillian planned to walk the boys to school again, hoping to catch sight of Mrs. Caulfield dropping off her son, Frank.

"We gonna talk to Frank's mum?" Milton trotted along beside her, skipping and dodging from one distraction to another as he went. Lillian was certain he covered twice the distance that she did on the way to school with all his wanderings. This morning Matty, on the other side, held Lillian's hand quietly as they walked along.

"Yes, dear. Harrison said he thinks she still brings Frank in for school. We're going to invite them all to supper."

Making a trail through a deep drift, Milton circled back

around. "Can we play in the barn, Miss Lillian? He can help us build our fort. Harr'son's too busy now."

"Maybe. But you might want to play indoors instead. You could set up your train tracks in the attic if you like. There's lots of room there to spread out."

He frowned in Lillian's direction, stopping midstride. "Yeah, but it's too cold up there."

"I suppose, but it's colder in the barn, isn't it?"

From her other side, Matty giggled.

Milton's response was to fashion a quick snowball. But Lillian's words came faster than his small hands could move. "No sir, no throwing snowballs at each other on the way to school. You know the rule."

"Yes, Miss Lillian." Instead, the boy let the white sphere fly at a tree, chasing away a blue jay that perched above, scolding at them to go away.

There were few parents who accompanied their children to school, so it was easy for Lillian to watch for Catherine Caulfield's tall form above the students who gathered in front of the building, chatting and shouting to one another as they came. Matty and Milton hurried inside to join the others in their primary class. Lillian's eyes were on the road as people arrived. She greeted some of the children she knew from church, spoke with Orville Hafner and his sister Elsie for a few minutes regarding the upcoming science fair that Lemuel was enthusiastic to participate in. At last she spotted Catherine Caulfield and hurried to catch her before she kissed her protesting twelve-year-old good-bye and left again for home.

"Mrs. Caulfield, may I speak with you?" Lillian called as she moved toward the road.

Face tucked beneath the edges of a woolen plaid headscarf, the woman's expression was puzzled for a moment. "Of course. I remember your face, dear. Would ya please repeat your name though?"

"Lillian. Lillian Walsh. My sister, Grace, and I met you at the sledding hill on Saturday."

"Oh yeah, you've got the place for orphans."

"Yes, the children's home. Yes." Lillian smiled up at the woman.

"An' you've got just the two little ones still?"

"Yes, ma'am. Milton and Matty Baines—they're six. But I wanted to ask if your family might come for supper tonight. Miriam Tillendynd, who cooks for us, has family in Saskatchewan and she's anxious to meet you."

"Oh, that'd be a treat. Someone to share talk about home. Yes, that's kind of ya. What time d'ya want us?"

"Any time after school. The boys can play together. I know Frank is a good bit older than our twins, but I'm sure they'll find something they all enjoy. And then we can have a good chat until supper."

"I'll tell Sam. I know he'll be tickled to come."

Lillian, having met Sam Caulfield, could not picture him being tickled about much. He'd been quiet and reserved, almost reclusive, at the hillside gathering. But she enjoyed his more spirited wife's assurance of his interest. "Tonight, then. Whenever you're able to come."

"Yes, see you then. An' I thank ya for the invitation, Lillian."

As she worked her way across town toward home, Lillian made a mental note of what needed to be done still before they might accept new children shortly. She was so completely lost in her own thoughts that she failed to notice a man approach quietly from behind, striding up close, reaching out two leather-gloved hands to cover her eyes.

"What? Stop!" She spun quickly, ducking aside so that the hands released. Her scarf was stripped away by the motion, falling lifelessly to the snow at her feet.

Hearty rolls of laughter followed.

At last Lillian realized who the perpetrator had been. "Quinley?"

She snatched up the scarf, shook it to remove the snow, and wrapped it back into place, a hot blush burning her cheeks.

"Oh, Lillian, if you could have seen your face!" Dressed impeccably in a full-length navy coat and gray fedora, Quinley stood before her, unmoved by her obvious annoyance.

Her heart was still drumming with adrenaline. Lillian struggled to speak evenly. "I thought—you were away—from town. What are you doing here?"

"Well, that's an unfriendly welcome, I must say. I'm back. I thought I'd see if my two favorite young ladies would like to join me for dinner."

"I'm sorry, we can't." She knew her voice was still snappish. But Lillian's mind struggled to make sense of the moment, wondering why she was the one apologizing while he seemed merely amused at having upset her. "We have dinner guests tonight." She added with a poor attempt at sounding cordial, "The Caulfields. Have you met them?"

"Oh, that's a shame. I'd been looking forward to your company." Then he smiled broadly. "I don't suppose there's any chance I could coerce you for an invitation? Any chance at all?"

Knowing what Grace would say, Lillian pushed aside her irritation with effort. "Yes, of course. We'd like to spend some time with you. And, no doubt, the new family would enjoy meeting you too."

He seemed to have presumed that she'd acquiesce to his request. "What time, then?"

"Well, as soon as . . ." For some reason Lillian felt reluctant to extend the same openhanded offer to Quinley as she'd given to Catherine Caulfield. "Why don't we say at six? That's normally when Miss Tilly serves."

"Six it is." Quinley doffed his hat and winked. "And I promise to be on my best behavior."

Walking away, Lillian still found herself feeling cross. *Why can't I shake this feeling? It's not as if he did anything sordid, just irksome*. And then she realized that in the fleeting moment of confusion, her mind had immediately gone to Walter. Though the teasing encounter was not something she could imagine the gentle, considerate man would ever do, she knew that her first reaction after the initial shock was to hope that it was Walter's hands, his laughter, coming unseen from behind her. She wondered, with a sigh, how long it might be until she saw him again.

• • • • • • •

Ben stood toward the back of the room, distancing himself a little from the conversation the other workers were having. These were not the things that would be said openly when others were listening. This was the way people really thought, the way they really spoke when unguarded. And it was unsettling to him.

"We've got to make adjustments. I understand the issues, but we can't just deliver the children as planned."

"What do you suggest, then? We've been over this before."

"Well, Malcolm is a fairly compliant boy. If we want to make a swap, I still think he'd be a good replacement for Alfred. I'm sure the pastor and his wife would be able to manage Malcolm."

"But he's been promised to the farm family. They've already been given his name. No doubt they'd object to our substituting one boy for another. It would certainly leave us open to questions. And how do we know they'd be any better able to deal with the problem?"

"So you want to just leave Alfred with Pastor Miller? That's a recipe for disaster. He and his wife are in their sixties. He'll run them ragged and leave them in despair. We'd, in fact, just be postponing the issue rather than addressing it, because Alfred would come right back to us in a few months. I tell you, I've met them. They're not equipped to discipline him. They're far too trusting and inexperienced."

Ben shifted in place where he leaned against the back wall,

then rubbed at his temples. He wasn't surprised. Already he'd learned that Alfred was deceptive and manipulative. That much couldn't be denied. Ben doubted, too, that any unsuspecting parent would be prepared. Yet the lad deserved a chance to be loved and accepted. Was there no one equipped to care for such a troubled boy? Maybe a man of the cloth and his wife . . . But no, not if they were older, and inexperienced with difficult children. So why set up a situation that would ultimately fail? Maybe the others were right in their seemingly dispassionate assessment.

"If we leave Malcolm at the first stop instead, we've got just three boys rather than four to go farther on to Lethbridge. Stanley goes to the baker, there's the Kennards who are expecting Malcolm, and we still need two boys for that other farmer. What's his name again?"

"Szweda. Jack and Katrin Szweda."

"Can we give them one boy, instead of two? Just Vaughan and not Michael?"

"No, sir. That new guy who just started working in the West promised them two. Two boys to replace the ones they gave up."

"I heard it wasn't quite so simple. The first boys were twins. They only wanted to give up one. But somebody refused to take just one of the brothers."

"Well, I'm glad they stopped them from splitting them up."

"Doesn't matter. Szweda pitched a fit, and even though he's just a farmer, he knows influential people. Now we've got to bring them two more boys. And we only have four for Lethbridge. How're we going to do that if we place Malcolm Hedley early?"

"It's a nightmare."

"Well . . . would any of them take a girl instead? We don't have a place for Jane Grey yet."

Ben felt his neck bristle. He pushed away from the wall and turned an ear toward the group discussion.

"The Szwedas specifically want boys. They want them for chores. And we can't take a chance of upsetting them again.

He's loud and not afraid to raise a riot, I assure you. He and his wife both. That man, Sinclair, just wants to appease him and make the problem go away."

But Janie? What happens to Janie?

"The Brayton House manager, Sid Brown, he thinks he can easily place the little girl. And can house her for as long as it takes to make a match. They have some Good Samaritans in their area who'll keep a kid for as long as necessary. So we don't need to worry about the girl. Plus, she's younger and appears to be well raised. She'll be easy."

"And you don't think she can go to Szweda? A boy and a girl to them?"

"We can talk more later, but I don't think that'll work. That man Sinclair would never agree. He can be pretty hard-nosed about things."

Ben was relieved. If all the family wanted was farm help, little Janie should not be given to them. He determined quickly that he'd do what was needed to stop such an outcome.

"Okay, how about this? We keep Alfred for out West. Give Pastor Miller a girl. Then we give Alfred to the Behrends in place of a girl. Their paperwork says that they already have a son. Surely they can manage him. Give the nine-year-old girl, Millie, to the pastor and his wife instead. She's old enough to be useful. Surely that would appease them."

Miss Davis sounded incredulous. "You want to make her *Millie Miller?*"

"Oh dear, we probably can't do that. Can't they just change her name?"

Ben edged away from the meeting. He'd had enough. No one noticed as he opened the door quietly and slipped down the hallway. He realized with a heavy heart that there were likely more children who needed their own personal defender than just Janie. *How on earth do these people make such decisions? It's a foul business, this! 'Cause it should ne'er be a business at all.* And yet, was it better to leave children in their original dilemmas? What person with a Christian heart could merely ignore them? The conundrum perplexed Ben.

• • • ● • • •

Lillian and Grace had a successful and pleasant evening with the Caulfields. Miss Tilly was able to trace Sam and Catherine's associations to several of her own family members. In some way it made them instantly feel like old friends. Even quiet Sam Caulfield seemed comfortable joining the discussion as they talked about people from home.

After he arrived, Quinley offered a great deal to the night as well. Though he knew nothing about the area, he had no fewer comments to make than the rest. Between the boisterous Catherine and the self-assured Quinley, Lillian spent the evening enjoying the role of observer, smiling and laughing until her face felt weakened with the effort.

Toward the end of the visit, Quinley took up even more of their attention, explaining his job and the Home Children system to the new family.

Catherine seemed entranced. "What will ya do after these kids are settled? Are ya gonna keep bringin' more? From overseas?"

"Yes, these children come from all across the British Isles. The orphanages there don't have room to accommodate them all. And they're not just sent to Canada. Other British areas of the world have receiving programs. Many in Australia, in fact."

"How can it be that so many kids need a home?"

Quinley sighed and shook his head. His forehead puckered in concern that, oddly, felt just a little too practiced for Lillian. "Poverty. Sometimes families are lost to disease. It's a great tragedy of our time. The greatest empire on earth unable to care for its own destitute."

"Who do they pick? I mean, how's a body get their name on such a list?"

"It isn't easy, actually. There are many families applying. But that just means we can be quite selective about the kind of homes we send children to. We can be more certain that they'll be taken care of and loved. Because, of course, that's our first priority. The children."

"O'course."

And Sam added quietly, "It's a terrible thing ta give up a child."

His eyes held a sadness that struck to the core of Lillian's heart. She wondered if he'd known of such a family situation.

Catherine's quick words brushed her husband's comment aside, though there was a twinge of sorrow in her own voice as well. "Needs must when the devil drives, I s'pose." She continued, "We do what's gotta be done. We don't always like it, but sometimes there ain't no choice." Her expression changed and she added rather hopefully, "Has nobody claimed your boys—those sweet little pups?"

"Not so far," Grace said, smiling as she shook her head. "But we just trust God that He'll bring the right family when it best suits them. And we're grateful to go about that process slowly, carefully, for the sake of the children—giving them time to adjust emotionally. We know God has a plan for their good."

Catherine looked at Sam. Their expressions seemed heavy with meaning. It sent a rush of hope through Lillian. They seemed openhearted and kind. Even young Frank seemed to enjoy the boys' company and might make a good big brother.

• • • • •

When the house had quieted and the sisters were alone in the parlor with their evening tea, Lillian broached the subject of the Caulfields with Grace.

"Did you notice that Sam and Catherine both seemed particularly interested in discussing adoption and the twins?"

Grace blew on her tea for a moment before answering. "I did. I certainly did."

"Wouldn't that be lovely? To see the boys go to a family so near us that has lots of room in their new house and, it seems, plenty of money to support them? I sure hope it works out."

"Why? Because they're loving, or because they're well-to-do?"

"Both." Lillian was surprised that Grace's words seemed rather curt. "Can't I be happy about both?"

Setting down her cup, Grace smoothed out her dress before answering carefully. "I've seen lots of children placed in homes. I can assure you that money is rarely an important factor. It's sometimes even a hindrance."

"You think so?"

"Please don't misunderstand. I'm not saying that poorer families are better suited to adopting. It's important that there's enough income to provide for all of the children in any home. After that, the pocketbook of the parents is likely the least important factor. Lillian, can I tell you what I figured out even before I became an adult?"

"Please do." But something within Lillian was guarded now. She wasn't certain she was prepared for a lecture and hoped that Grace's words would be encouraging instead.

"When I was young I often wondered what it would be like to be wealthy. I thought a great deal about it for a while. Then I realized that what I would call *rich* can be broken down into two things: having someplace warm and safe to call home, and not having to worry about getting enough to eat."

Lillian chuckled to herself. "So you think *we're* rich? I mean, we have to manage our food carefully sometimes, but there's always *something* to put on the table. Would we fit your definition too?"

"Yes. I would say we're rich." Grace seemed confident.

Uncertain how to answer her sister, Lillian remained still. It would do them no good to begin an argument over semantics. There was simply no point in pressing an explanation for something that, to be certain, life had made necessary for Grace to contemplate—given her more opportunities to observe than Lillian. Surely her sister was just expressing sincere gratitude.

The room became very quiet. Grace stood and walked to the fireplace, laying a hand on the mantel in front of Lillian's family photograph, Father and Mother and a teenage Lillian, before continuing. "It's easy to believe that being rich is a matter of comparing how many possessions each of us has. If I see people around me who seem to have more, by comparison, I feel less well off. But that only happens as we compare ourselves within the community where we live. If we open our minds to people elsewhere, we begin to understand the scope of the real truth. Do you realize that most people don't have *both* a warm place to call home and enough food for their table? Most people go hungry some of the time. Maybe not here in Canada as often, but certainly back in Europe and Africa and the Far East." Grace made her eyes sweep through the parlor, glancing from the blazing fire to the plush seating, across at the grand piano. Her voice became softer still. "Everything else is extra. It's just *stuff* that makes us more comfortable. But it's extra, in a sense. Don't you see? It's not necessary to be content."

Lillian's gaze fell to her lap. She'd had no inkling that Grace had been thinking such heady thoughts after the Caulfields' visit.

"*Stuff*," Grace continued, "always needs to be taken care of, guarded. It's a responsibility, not just a blessing. And sometimes it even distracts us from things that are truly important—like love and service and God. Even generosity can actually be stifled by it. I've observed that people with little are often some of the most generous people you'll meet. Sometimes, wealth just gets in the way. I've seen people choose the care of their earthly belongings over the child standing in front of them who needs a home."

Lillian's gaze rose to meet Grace's impassioned eyes.

"Oh, sis," Grace went on, "I don't pray that any of the children get lots of possessions. I pray they get things that are far more important than that."

Lillian wasn't sure how to respond. She tried not to feel chided, reminding herself that Grace wouldn't want to make her feel ignorant of such lofty ideals. Yet it was a puzzling way to express her view of the world. Father had always worked to provide for his family. Lillian wished the same love and care from a father for their small charges. Then she thought about Father's openhanded response to Grace and the children. This was not a man who hoarded wealth. This was a kind and generous man. It made her gratitude for him grow a little more.

At last she answered, "You're right, of course. I wish for the twins nothing less than parents who demonstrate how to be loving servants and trustworthy providers. I'll pray that God gives them nothing less than that."

Chapter 13

Division

Mr. Waldin? How many?" It seemed that for the hundredth time, Miss Davis's rather shrill voice called back to Ben.

He faithfully counted the heads of the children walking before him, announcing again, "Fourteen, Miss Davis. All here."

The days of travel by train from Toronto to Winnipeg had been a blur. Now the group of Home Children waited at the curbside of the train station in Winnipeg for a vehicle that was to be sent to pick them up. Miss Davis was in constant motion, reminding Ben of a sheepdog circling her flock. She checked the watch on a chain around her neck, pressed herself through the crowd and toward the station again, moved farther down the busy sidewalk, then scurried back to join the group once more.

"I can't imagine what's keeping them. They should know we can't be expected to wait here long."

At last a long, horse-drawn bus, a lumbering extended coach, pulled up beside them. "You must be Miss Davis."

"Where've you been? We arrived half an hour ago."

The driver in his perch far above them seemed rather unaffected, only nodding. "Did my best, ma'am. Can't hurry the horses too much in this traffic. Seems ta get worse by the day."

Soon they were squeezed together on two long benches inside the narrow coach, all facing toward the center. With a lurch they set off toward Main Street and the hotel in which they'd stay. With Janie on the bench nearest him, Ben stood at the front instead, balancing carefully as they swayed along, amazed at the city. Here he was halfway across Canada, miles and miles of open country behind them, and suddenly there were so many people all in one place again.

Almost unconsciously he searched faces among the crowds on either side of the road. Would he see Jane among them? Dada? Was his family nearby, or had they already continued farther?

Ben had checked the train map as they'd waited in the station. Winnipeg appeared to be a hub, gathering trains from places east and even south, distributing them once more to points west. If his family had traveled beyond, there was almost no way to know which of the routes they'd continued along. *I'll look fer another bookstore. If Jane found one, she surely left another note.*

Miss Davis was chattering at the children even while seated in the bus, giving instructions to them regarding the hotel lobby. She kept them informed, always one step ahead for their benefit. In Ben's mind, it was good to keep the children aware of what they'd face next, step by step.

Their hotel was not a luxurious one, but after spending time rollicking along by train, it was a relief to have quiet and stillness. The boys were assigned two rooms with a door between them. It made Ben nervous to know he couldn't watch both doors to the hallway at once during the night. If one of the boys, Alfred in particular, were to decide to sneak away while everyone was sleeping, it would be almost impossible to catch him. All during their supper meal Ben pondered the dilemma. At last he felt he had a plan.

There followed the long process of supervising baths in the

public washroom down the hall. One after another, each boy trudged along the worn green carpet in his street clothes and trudged back in his long nightshirt. Ben worked between the rooms, gathering the discarded clothing from the washroom and leaving behind both a fresh towel and each boy's sleepwear on the chair beside the tub.

When baths had been accomplished, Ben had nine neatly folded piles of clothing on his bed nearest the door and nine pairs of shoes tucked away beneath. Only Alfred had grown suspicious of his methods as Ben began to stack all the clothes into one tall pile.

"Ya gonna give us back our togs?"

"Nah. Ya don't need 'em fer sleepin'." Ben kept his voice matter-of-fact.

"We got cases. We can pack 'em away now ourselves."

"Ya got cases? Where's that, then?"

The boys looked around, only at that moment realizing that the cases were no longer next to their beds.

Ben assured them cheerfully, "Don't worry none, lads. I packed 'em up fer ya. By mornin' yer clothes'll be ready and returned."

Alfred cast a scowl around the room. "What if we gotta use the privy 'fore then?"

"Nightshirt'll cover ya walkin' down the hall."

"An' shoes?"

"No need 'til mornin'. There's carpet."

Another scowl, this time directly toward Ben. The angry eyes said, *Ya think yer smart, eh? But ya ain't so grand as ya think.*

Ben stepped forward, returning the direct gaze. He placed a hand on Alfred's rigid shoulder. "Lad, I just wanna keep ya safe, that's all. We all need a good night's sleep. Big day tomorra. Folks ta meet."

From the corner of his eye, Ben noticed that Cecil, the tall boy with a crooked nose, sank down onto his bed as if his legs had suddenly turned limp at the reminder. Timothy, who was seated on the cot next to him, tucked his knees up to his chest, arms hugging them tightly.

"Lads?" Ben offered guarded words, not entirely certain what he might have to say that would be of any help to the boys. "I know it ain't what ya wanted from yer life. An' I don't *know* ya, not really. I wish there was time fer such. Ya each got a story'a hurt an' trouble. I ache fer ya, I do. And I know it ain't easy ta think'a joinin' a fam'ly that ya don't know in the mornin'. It ain't easy. Can't be."

Nine-year-old Percy began to sniffle, hiding his face in the folds of his nightshirt. Ben wondered if it had been wise to address the subject at all. He pulled a clean handkerchief from inside his own bag, crossed the room to Percy's cot, and offered it to the boy. Then he dropped down onto the chair between the beds.

"Will ya gather 'round, lads? Can ya all come nigh?"

Reluctantly, the group moved nearer, sitting on beds or standing beside them, arms crossed over slender bodies in long nightshirts.

"I can't tell ya much ya don't already know, lads. It's a mean, hard life. An' it's easy ta get bitter an' empty. I don't see that in ya. Least, not yet."

"Easy fer you, ya got fam'ly."

"Yeah, I got fam'ly. I got a dada and a mum. An' a sister too. But it were me what threw 'em away. I run from me home when I was just fourteen." He looked up at Alfred. "Same age as you, lad."

Ben's words were met with a lopsided smile. "An' you was okay. Yeah?"

"Yeah, I kep' alive. I worked. I worked hard, no bones 'bout it. Earned not just me own food, but ta help me fam'ly too. Went home just ta share me wages."

The boys were attentive now. These were words they could comprehend.

"Mister Waldin, d'ya miss 'em when ya was gone away? Were ya sad, sir?"

How could he answer honestly? "I weren't sad, not fer a long while. Was too full'a meself ta be sad. I went ta sea. I loved ta work on ship and I loved ta travel. It felt a charmed life fer a time. But a man gets lonely. He wants ta belong. We need fam'ly. So I'm lookin' fer mine. Don't know where they be, but I'm gonna find 'em." He paused, scanning from one boyish face to the next. "It's worth the search, lads. It's worth lettin' the good Lord give ya a home. It's worth lettin' somebody love ya, as oft ya can."

With all his heart Ben wanted to gather the boys into his arms in hopes of comforting them, but he knew them enough, knew their kind. Such a gesture wouldn't be well received nor trusted. So with faltering words he offered the only other thing he could think of. "Let's pray, lads. Let's pray one time while we're all still t'gether, fer Percy an' Tim, fer Howard an' Cecil an' Alfred. All you lads stayin' here in this city." *If there's a God watchin' from heav'n a'tall, His heart's gotta be carin' fer the orphans.*

Their solicitor, Mr. Dorn, sent a telegram. It was delivered early in the morning while Lillian was baking the week's bread with Miss Tilly and Grace was doing the mending at the kitchen table, taking a break from the paperwork she'd begun earlier. The telegram stated that he planned to leave for Toronto to meet with Saul Brazington-Bennett and his solicitor on the following Friday. It was his last offer for one or both of the sisters to travel along.

They retreated to the privacy of the dining room so that Grace could read the telegram aloud. Lillian had already determined that she would not go. But Grace was wrestling with indecision.

Standing in the doorway to the dining room, Lillian saw the confusion written across Grace's face and heard the strain in her voice. "It's just that we might never have another chance to meet Uncle Saul—to meet anyone from our family. It's so hard to let myself decide that I'll never even talk to him."

Wiping her hands on a kitchen towel, Lillian eased down onto the chair next to Grace. "I understand how hard this is for you." She bit her lip before offering, "I think that I can take care of things here if you decide to go. You should do whatever your heart tells you. Don't make a decision for the short term that you might regret later."

Grace's shoulders straightened. "You're right." She laid the piece of paper on top of the other correspondence spread out on the table in front of her with an air of newly gained confidence. "And when I think about the decision that way, then I know just what to do. I simply have to stay here with you. I'd regret it so much more if I felt I'd failed the children."

"That's not what I meant. I was saying—"

"I know what you were saying, sis. But my commitments matter most. So, if God wants me to meet our extended family, then God will make that work out at another time. I can rest in this decision. I'm sure that I can."

It was Lillian's turn to sigh. "Maybe we can go together another time. Maybe when Father comes home he'd be willing to take us east by train."

"Um-hmm." Grace refused to commit.

But what will our arrangement become once my father arrives home? Will we still care for children then? Will we all live together here in this house? I can't stay in Mother and Father's bedroom then. I'll have to move back to my smaller room—the one we've used to house the little girls. And there'll be so many other things needing adaptation. The future seemed to be such a fluid concept, impossible to envision. Summer and Father's expected return seemed a lifetime away.

Lillian reached across the table and drew the telegram and envelope toward her. She read it through once more before planning to hand the page back to Grace. Then she noticed that there was a letter under the telegram. By accident she'd gathered them up together. "What's this?"

"Oh, well . . ." Grace's face flushed. "I was just answering correspondence here earlier. It's something else I'd written this morning."

Lillian stiffened. "But it's written to Walter."

"Yes."

"You're *answering* a letter—from Walter?"

"Yes." All the confidence had drained from Grace's tone. Her face paled. "We've been writing. Just a few times. Just keeping in touch to see how he's doing with his new job." Her voice trailed away.

"Well then, what did he say to you?" Lillian's mind was working hard to process the strange turn of events. She'd exchanged letters with Walter also. But why was Grace writing to him? Were they closer than Lillian had presumed? Was there something more to their relationship than Lillian had perceived?

Her voice scarcely a whisper, Grace answered, "It's been difficult for him. He's quite homesick."

"I see. Well, I guess he hasn't been so honest with me, then. He told me he's doing very well." Gathering the towel on which she'd wiped her hands, Lillian retreated quickly from the room. Suddenly, Uncle Saul hardly mattered. *What's going on with Grace? Why hasn't Walter written so candidly to me? Have I been a fool to let myself believe I'll still matter the same way to him now that we're so far apart?*

Stoically, Lillian returned to the mound of dough she'd been kneading at the kitchen worktable. Forcing the tears away, she pressed and pushed and pounded the dough. The knot that had tightened in her throat, however, refused to loosen its hold.

Miss Tilly said nothing, made no attempt at small talk. Lillian wondered if perhaps she had overheard.

• • • ● • • •

Alfred Jones was not given to Pastor Miller and his wife. Nor was Millie Cook. As it turned out, the family who had agreed to take in Lizzie Payne was unable to follow through with their agreement. Ben never overheard their reasons. He learned only that the Millers were just as pleased to accept the thirteen-year-old girl into their home instead of the expected boy. It had been unnecessary to explain anything further to them regarding the reasons.

Lizzie and little seven-year-old Pearl stood nearest to Ben as they waited for families to arrive in the hotel lobby. They watched together as each adoptive couple met at a table with Miss Davis, then crossed the wide room in order to be introduced to their waiting child. Ben was unable to keep from smiling to himself as he overheard the girls' conversation.

"That them, Lizzie?" Pearl twisted a small handkerchief in her hands.

"I think so. Must be."

A horrified whisper. "But he ain't got no hair!"

The teenager responded with equal sincerity. "I'm so sorry, Pearl. That'll be hard ta bear. But maybe he's a good daddy anyhow."

Clearly disappointed, Pearl seemed unconvinced.

When at last Mr. and Mrs. Falkenrath stooped low to introduce themselves to Pearl, it was clear that they were fully attuned to winning over their new daughter. By the time they departed, Pearl walked between them holding on to her new mummy's hand, and with Mr. Falkenrath now clad in a soft black bowler hat, the little girl seemed quite at peace with the outcome.

"Lord bless ya, child," Ben murmured as each one was led away.

When the process was over, he returned upstairs to where the five boys bound for Lethbridge, which now included Alfred, were waiting. There were no questions. Hardly an eye lifted at Ben's return. They were playing a game of jacks in a corner of the room, clearly intent on conveying to him that it made no difference to them that four of their number were not returning to their group. Four of them would never be seen again.

He thought sadly, *Ya got no grievin' left in ya, do ya, lads?* Aloud, he forced his voice to be cheerful. "Can I join ya? I was pretty good, long ago."

The boys parted and allowed Ben into their circle. He laid a hand on Vaughan's shoulder and took up cheering instead. His thoughts were much darker than his face alleged. *This is all there is, then? Makin' do, gettin' along as best ya can?*

Miss Davis had not approached him yet regarding his further plans. With almost half of the children now settled in homes, she might manage the last eight alone. But as they were mostly boys, Ben wondered if she had hoped he might be willing to travel on from there with them. He'd promised only to go as far as Winnipeg, but the truth was, he hadn't worked out additional plans at all.

The next morning when delivering the boys to the breakfast room, Ben requested to be excused for much of the morning. Though he didn't explain his reasons to Miss Davis, he planned to find as many bookstores as possible and ask if they were holding a letter from his sister, Jane. If only she'd been able to leave information as to the family's progress. He considered, too, that it was possible his dada had decided to remain in the area.

Walking quickly around the downtown streets near the hotel, Ben refused to use his precious money on something as superfluous as a cab ride. The day was cold but clear. It wasn't unpleasant. His body quickly warmed with his efforts to hurry.

Periodically he asked for help and advice locating shops, finding three used bookstores. Unfortunately, none of them had heard of Jane Waldin. His heart sank. With only a little time left before he was needed to watch the boys, he worked his way to the streets nearest the train station. This was as close as he could get to crossing the path where his family must have journeyed. There was only one store in the area, and he was disappointed once more. No letter. It was a crushing blow.

Tired and discouraged, Ben walked back to the hotel again

the way he'd come. But he found it too difficult at the moment even to contemplate his next decision. He focused his attention on taking in the city of Winnipeg instead, trying to make himself believe that his heart wasn't racing, his mind humming with worry.

Upon his arrival at the hotel, Miss Davis immediately cornered him. She motioned him nearer and smiled winsomely. "Mr. Waldin, I had planned to speak with you. I suppose you can already guess at what I'm going to ask." She tipped her head, squeezed one eye into almost a wink. "I could certainly use your help with taking the children through to our last stop. Is there any way I could coax you to continue with us for one more leg of the journey?"

Ben sighed. There were a number of options for which route he could choose next. It mattered little which one, he guessed—and if there'd be payment, well, that would certainly help him along. On top of that, there was Janie to see settled with a good family, and the welfare of the remaining boys to consider.

"I'll come with ya. I'm willin' ta help ya long's I can."

"Oh, Mr. Waldin, that certainly puts my mind at ease. I was concerned about watching over the boys. But you do so well with them."

Her flattery made no difference to Ben, but the boys—it was true they would likely be better off if he were around.

• • • • •

"Lillian?"

Grace's voice brought Lillian's hands to a stop, fingertips resting now on the piano keys as the strings reverberated with the sound of her last notes. For a moment she refused to lift her eyes.

Grace spoke again. "Sis, I've been thinking. If we can't go to Uncle Saul, we might still be able to communicate with him.

There are things I'd like a chance to ask. Do you think Mr. Dorn would be willing to take along a list of our questions? And would you be willing to work with me to write it up?"

Days had passed. It was the first of February already. Lillian still felt the sting of betrayal regarding the letters Grace had exchanged with Walter. But rather than posing more questions directly, she let the ill feelings simmer inside her. It had become somewhat difficult to interact with Grace, to answer her questions even now.

"That's fine. I'll help," she said, repositioning her hands to begin the stanza again.

"Tonight? After baths?"

"Yes, that's fine." Offering no warning, Lillian struck the keys with her curled fingers and her song continued, just a little louder than it had been.

Grace turned without further comment and walked away. A pulse of guilt shot through Lillian's body. It was dreadful to feel alienated from Grace. But why had she written to Walter? And why had he chosen to share his deepest thoughts with Grace? It was a matter of trust on both parts.

Fingers tangling as Lillian played a difficult section in the song, her troubled mood spoiled even the music. With a sigh she lowered the lid back over the keys. There was no point in playing now. Her heart wasn't in it.

Feeling far more self-controlled later in the evening, Lillian sat across the parlor from Grace as they drafted their list of questions for Uncle Saul. *Did you know our parents? And if you did, when were you able to spend time with them? Can you describe them at all? What was Grandpapa Oliver like? Do you have family pictures? Would you be willing to make copies for us?*

By the time they'd finished, the list had grown quite long.

"Now," Grace said, "we won't have time to send this list to the law office by mail courier. Will you call Mr. Dorn in the morning with our questions?"

Lillian was relieved at the thought of leaving the house. "Yes, I'll walk into town and use the telephone in the drugstore."

"Thank you. I'll help with the laundry, then."

"Fine."

Hesitating, Grace added, "Sis, you're not angry with me, are you? For writing to Walter?"

How on earth can the tumult of emotions be put into words? "I'm not angry." A deep breath drawn slowly. "I suppose I'm confused. I just don't understand it."

Grace expended a few moments in silence, folding up the page of questions she'd written. "I'm sorry. I'm just not sure what to say."

Lillian frowned. "May I read the letters?"

It was Grace's turn to withdraw. "I'm sorry, no."

Standing quickly, Lillian excused herself and went straight up to bed. Her hands trembled as she worked at the shell buttons on her nightgown. *What is happening? Why is Grace being secretive about Walter? How much have I misunderstood?*

Chapter 14

Tentative Plans

Miss Tilly sent Grace along with Lillian to make the telephone call. She refused to hear any reasons or excuses why not. Lillian wondered if the older woman had an inkling of the conflict between them. She explained, "These questions mean a lot ta both of ya. So ya should both have an ear ta the telephone in case ya think'a more ta say."

The sisters spoke very little on the way into town. A strong wind and heavy clouds meant that another winter storm was on its way. So they hurried along, felt hats pulled down snugly, thick scarves tight over their faces, as the cold wind searched for exposed skin.

"I'm going into the grocery first. You set up the call." Lillian's words were statements.

"All right." Grace opened the door to the drugstore, where a telephone was available to customers for a small fee. "Please don't be long."

"Of course."

Crossing the street instead, Lillian stopped at the post office and asked Sophie McRae for the mail. She flipped through it stealthily, her eyes watching the window too. She wanted to know if there was a letter for Grace—if Walter had written to her again. No letters. Not even from Father. She rushed back to the grocery, knowing her time was almost spent, that Grace would be on the telephone call very soon.

But before Lillian had an opportunity to shop for the two items she needed, she looked across the store and spotted Quinley Sinclair. He was chatting with a small group of men by the checkout counter. For a moment Lillian fought the urge to duck away down the nearest aisle. But it was already too late. She'd been spotted.

"Lillian? Lillian Walsh. How is my favorite young philanthropist? Everything going well at your little home?"

His usual nonsense, despite Lillian's sour mood, prompted a smile. "We're well. We're just in town to place a telephone call. I actually don't have more than a minute to buy what I need and get back to Grace next door."

"Well, please don't let me stop you. May I help?"

This time she laughed aloud. "Certainly. I need black tea and seven white buttons."

"I would never presume to be able to choose something as important as buttons, so I'll find the tea. I'll meet you back here in thirty seconds."

"How will you know what we like to drink?"

"My dear"—he grinned—"I do know tea. So I know just what type you should buy. Trust me."

In very little time Lillian was leaving the grocery store, accompanied now by Quinley. He walked her to the nearby drugstore and also entered in order to speak with Grace.

Already holding the telephone handset, Grace was still waiting for the call to go through. She smiled as Lillian arrived with company. But then she straightened, turned away, and began to speak to Mr. Dorn. Quinley dropped onto a stool at the nearby food counter as Lillian hurried to take her place beside Grace.

They delivered all their questions and ended the call. Turning away from each other quickly, the sisters chose instead to take available seats on either side of Quinley and have a few moments of pleasant conversation.

"I would never mean to pry, ladies, but may I ask to whom you were speaking?"

Grace answered, "To Mr. William Dorn, the solicitor who represents us. He's planning a trip to Toronto soon in order to track down a missing family member. He had invited us to come along, but we felt it would be best to stay put for now."

"You have a missing family member?" There was a twinkle in Quinley's eye. "How enticing."

"Well, he's not *missing.* He's just a family member that we didn't know existed," Lillian explained.

"And he lives in Toronto?"

"Yes, it seems."

"I'm from Ontario. What's his name?" He turned again toward Grace with his question.

"Oh, I doubt you'd know him. His name is Saul Brazington-Bennett. His mother was—"

But Quinley finished Grace's sentence. "Was Serena Brazington-Bennett. I had no idea you were from such affluent stock." He added with a wink, "If I had known, I'd have snatched up one of you eligible young ladies right away—the first time we met and I saw that you're both beautiful." A laugh. "And I might pursue you still. Marrying into status would be so much easier than all the schmoozing of the elite I've done."

Grace brushed aside his nonsense. "Well, we're not from affluent stock at all. His mother was the second wife of our grandpapa. She was never our relative."

But Lillian was far more interested in Quinley's knowledge. "You know about them? What do you know?"

Quinley swiveled on his seat to face Lillian more directly, turning at even intervals to emphasize his answer to Grace as well. "I know a little about your . . . step . . . grandmother, is that right? I attended a gala given by Mrs. Viney Boggs—the benefactor of our society, long before I came to be employed there. It was quite a high-society event. So I had a chance to meet Mrs. Brazington-Bennett before she passed away. She was a very important person back East, a very wealthy woman. She started with family money and then later turned it into an even larger fortune. I heard she was shrewd and quick-witted and . . . well, ugly as a toad, if you don't mind me just relaying what people said."

Lillian blinked hard. Few people were as honest and direct as Quinley Sinclair dared to be. "She was . . . she was rich?"

"She was what one might comfortably call *excessively rich*."

From the other side of Quinley, Grace was frowning but kept silent.

This was all too baffling for Lillian not to explore further. "But our Uncle Saul, he's supposed to be the other heir to my parents' estate—after the two of us. Why would he . . . ? I mean, it feels as if he chose to slow down the execution of the legal process. Why would he do that, if he's already rich?"

"I don't know, Lillian. There could be any number of reasons. But . . ." His eyebrows rose, his eyes widened in mock fear. "The first thing that comes to mind for me is that he worried you might want an equal share in *his parents'* estate."

"But we're not even descended from his mother. And our grandpapa wasn't a particularly wealthy man when they married."

"Sure, but when a couple marries, everything becomes communal property—according to law in some places, the man is considered to own it all. I wouldn't be at all surprised if your dear old Uncle Saul were looking out for his own interests by stalling." Almost to himself he added, "And that's why it would be a brilliant decision on my part to marry one of the two of you."

Lillian's face paled. She wasn't sure how to respond to such a bold statement or to such an accusation against her uncle, feeling a little indignant that Quinley might suggest such a thing about the only living relative she had besides Grace.

Grace spoke at last. "Mr. Dorn will know more soon. I doubt they'd be able to misrepresent our interests in any way. I trust him. I do trust Mr. Dorn." Then she rushed to change the subject. "How has your work been going, Quinley? Have you been away much?"

A slight shrug of disappointment. Quinley's playful tone shifted obediently. "It's going well. I should be done in this area by the middle of next week, in time to return to Lethbridge. I'd share more with you about it all if I could, but of course I'm sworn to privacy." Then he added quickly, "Actually, I was secretly hoping you ladies might ride out with me. Sid said the other group will arrive on Friday next, and that they expect to have two children without assigned homes."

"Two? I wonder what happened." Grace was fully engaged again.

"I don't know the stories. I should find out more soon. I plan to check in with Sid by telephone tomorrow."

By the time they were walking home, Lillian had all but forgotten about her reservations regarding her relationship with Grace. Their words flowed freely again. "Grace, do you think they'll expect to send both children to us?"

"Maybe. It would feel good to have a few more in the house again. I find that I miss the noise and busyness."

Lillian wasn't certain she felt as strongly as Grace. But as she allowed her mind to recall happy dinners and watching children playing in the yard, she was able to honestly say, "I miss the bustle too. The house feels so quiet now."

They walked along for several moments before Lillian posed another question. "What do you think about Quinley's ideas? Do you think there might be some unpleasant reason that Saul Brazington-Bennett didn't want to settle the estate?"

"I don't know. I hope not. But I do think that Mr. Dorn will put things right." Then Grace added, "I hope Quin is wrong. I'd like to think that there was some other reason. I hope Uncle Saul turns out to be kind. But at any rate, I'm not the least bit interested in his fortune anyway. I'm perfectly content the way I am."

When did Grace begin to refer to Quinley as Quin? Lillian wondered about their relationship in silence as she entered her home's front gate. Were Quinley's words spoken only in jest, or did he have an interest in pursuing Grace, masking it behind his silly comments?

• • • • • • •

"Mister Waldin?" Janie had crossed the room to take a seat next to Ben.

"Aye, bunny. What is it ya need?"

"Do we have to go on another train soon?" Her eyes were large, imploring him to deny the rumor.

"I guess we do. Don't ya want ta have another little ride?"

She shook her head with great solemnity. "I don't know where we're going."

Taking her hand, he smoothed out her fingers over his large palm, then pointed toward her outstretched thumb. "We started here, on this side'a Canada. Then we traveled here to the middle, where we are now. Next we're goin' farther on—to a place called Lethbridge. It's not so far as the other ocean but almost acrost, as I'm told." Then he added, swiping a finger along her pinkie, "An' here, all along this far side, rise them great big Rocky Mountains. Maybe ya can see 'em sometime."

Janie's mind was set on far too practical matters to be distracted by his playful explanation. "Why am I going there? Is that where I have a family?"

"What makes ya think that?"

"That's what the boys said. That we're going there to find our families—all 'cept Alfred. He doesn't got one yet."

Ben sighed. How could he explain? He wanted to be truthful so that she'd continue to trust him, but how might the small child respond? "Do you know what happened ta Lizzie an' Pearl?"

"Yes. They got new mums and dads."

"That's right. And because children need people ta love 'em an' take care of 'em, Miss Davis and the people she works with found 'em new families ta care fer 'em."

"'Cause their first ones died? Like mine?"

He unconsciously closed his hand around Janie's before he could answer. "Aye, that's right. That's what happened to some of 'em."

"Am I . . . am I gonna get a new family too?"

Her voice seemed so sorrowful, as if to accept that it was true would be giving up her first parents completely.

It was difficult for Ben to keep his voice controlled. "Would that be all right? To have a new fam'ly?"

She pondered her answer for some time before asking, "Can't I just stay with you? I like to be with you." Eyes turned upward plaintively, she said, "You love me, don't ya, Mister Waldin?"

One arm slipped around Janie, hugging her close against his side. His throat tightened. "I do love ya, bunny. I don't have ta be yer dad ta love ya. I think Miss Davis'll find ya a good fam'ly. But I'll love ya always. You can count on it, Janie."

Rather abruptly, she pressed a little kiss against his rough hand. "I love you too, Mister Waldin." Then she gathered herself up and trotted away to play dolls with Millie Cook.

Ben felt stunned. Even now, having lost so much, Janie was trusting and candid. He wished there were some way that he really could take her to his sister, Jane. Between the two of them, could they give this child a good home? Probably not. She deserved all the advantages of two real parents.

• • • ● • • •

There came a knock on the door. Milton sprang up first to answer, but Grace urged him back to his supper. "Miss Lillian will get the door. She's closest."

Shooting a puzzled expression to her sister, Lillian rose quickly. It was always an event to have a surprise visitor. Sometimes they were bearers of good news, sometimes trouble. So it always made her heart skip a beat as she drew open the front door.

"There she is!" Quinley's bright face greeted Lillian with confidence. "My favorite red-headed sister."

"Oh, hello. Please come in, Quinley. What a surprise!"

He stepped inside, shrugging out of his long wool coat and sliding it over a hook without a pause in his flow of conversation. "I spoke to Sid and I wanted to come right out to see you and Grace." He dropped his gray fedora onto the same hook. "There are plans afoot. I knew you'd want to know what's happening in Lethbridge, and I had some time this evening for a quick visit."

"I'm glad you came." Lillian led Quinley through to the kitchen.

"Mr. Sinclair, how nice ta see ya." Miss Tilly rose to fetch another plate.

"As much as I'd like another taste of your fine cooking, I can't stay long. I've made dinner plans with the mayor."

"The mayor?"

His only acknowledgment of their surprise was a lopsided grin. "What brings me to you tonight is my conversation with Sid Brown. It seems he's heard from the crew coming on the next train. He wants to know if you'll be available, officially, to take in two more children, just as I'd previously said."

Questions filled Lillian's mind. "When do they arrive? What do you know about them?"

Miss Tilly placed a fresh cup of coffee on the table in front of Quinley. He stirred two heaping teaspoons of sugar into it, then turned to Grace, who was seated next to him, as he explained, "The train is set to arrive on Friday. They have eight kids coming. Six of them have families already. But arrangements for one little girl fell through even before she arrived in Canada. Her name is Jane Grey. Funny thing, she was listed on our forms as being eight years old but turned out to be only six. That's unusual. I have no idea how that kind of an error happened."

A little girl. It would be so nice to have another little girl.

"The other is a boy. He's fourteen." A weighty pause.

Lillian noticed a frown cross Quinley's face. She'd rarely seen him with a shadowed expression.

"The boy was intended to go to a minister and his wife. But he seems to be a handful. So other arrangements were made. I'm afraid I can't share all of the particulars with you. Suffice it to say that Alfred Jones is now without an assigned home."

Grace leaned closer, placed her hand gently on Quinley's arm. "Why does he trouble you? Surely you can at least tell us that much."

Their eyes met and Grace seemed to study his face for a moment, then shyly withdrew her hand.

Quinley set his cup on the table, shifting on his chair. "I can tell you that it won't be the same as taking in Lemuel. This boy is as hardened as they come. I want to be sure that you have people around—men, in particular—who can intercede with him if need be. I just don't want to see you working with him alone."

Grace's eyes held steady. "Do you know his story? Anything about where he comes from?"

Shaking his head, Quinley looked around the table. "I don't know much about him, but I have a feeling that all of you will figure him out. I think this might be the very best place for the boy just now—so long as he doesn't push you beyond what you can manage."

Miss Tilly rose, two hands resting on the table before her. "Don't ya fret. We ain't been bested yet. S'pose we'll float 'til we sink—but we won't go down easy." She turned away to refill the bowl of potatoes.

Quinley answered her with a wink toward Grace. "I wouldn't want to cross you, Miss Tilly. I think the boy will have met his match."

But the no-nonsense woman was unmoved by his intended charms. "The good Lord'll ne'er give us more 'an we can do. So we'll serve any He brings us, eh?"

"That's right," Grace answered with equal confidence.

"Well, we'll all find out soon enough. Will you be able to head back to Lethbridge in just a few days? Sid will be ready for us soon. He hoped we could come Thursday to help prepare for the children's arrival on Friday."

"Of course. We'll come whenever you need us there."

In her mind, Lillian began immediately to make a list of things to do. There were clothes to wash at the start of the week, and a trip to town for groceries. She wanted to be certain Miss Tilly would not need to go out into the cold while they were gone.

After a bit more conversation, Grace walked Quinley to the door. Lillian waited in the kitchen, clearing the table and trying not to let her face betray the questions her mind was exploring.

Chapter 15

Junction

"Someone has broken a window at the back of the hotel, Mr. Waldin. The manager suggests that it was one of our boys!" Miss Davis seemed quite upset by the accusation. "I don't know what to say to him. He has no proof, and the children have been thoroughly supervised. How on earth are we to answer him?"

Ben stood in the long hallway, silent for a moment, scratching a finger behind his ear as he considered the problem. "Ya spoken ta the boys?"

"Not yet. I wanted to speak with you first."

"I can ask 'em. Want me ta call 'em together?"

Her distress was obvious. "Would you please? I don't suppose they'd confess to you, but I think it wise to confront them."

Ben peeked inside the boys' room, finding Malcolm and Stanley doodling on scrap paper. Michael and Vaughan were playing with Millie and Janie where he could see them at the far end of the hall. He motioned them over and they rose obediently. "Lads, do ya know where Alfred be?"

"No, sir."

"Hmm."

One hand on Michael's shoulder, he followed the two younger boys into their shared room and closed the door behind him. Then he asked the two older boys the same question.

"We don't know where he is, sir. He was gone after mornin' lessons."

Ben frowned. "I'm gonna ask ya another question too. I need the gospel truth. Understand, Vaughan? Mickey?"

"Yes, sir."

"What d'ya know 'bout a broken window?"

Four pairs of eyes grew large, staring back at him.

"Nothin'." Stanley was first to rebut the charge.

Ben studied the boy's expression, kept his gaze fixed and stern. There seemed to be a ring of truth in Stanley's alarm.

"Malcolm? What d'ya know 'bout it?"

The lanky boy shook his head too, desperate to be believed. "Honest, Mister Waldin. We been here t'gether."

Ben relaxed his gaze. "I believe ya. Lads, ya need to stay put. I'll be back soon's I can."

"Yes, sir."

There weren't many places to which Alfred could steal away. Miss Davis guarded one end of the hallway and Ben the other. His only idea was to check the bathroom. Knocking before opening the thin door, he noticed with a grimace that the window across from him stood open.

"Miss Davis, would ya come, please?"

Her expression matched his own as she realized the concern. "Who's missing?"

"Alfred. I'll go an' look. I don't think he's gone far. Talked this mornin' 'bout goin' on the train with us again—like he was plannin' it still."

"Merciful heavens, how will we find him?"

"I'll go have a look."

Having spent some time wandering through the downtown area, Ben felt it would be solitude that Alfred sought. Collar turned upward, he headed away from the busy streets and toward a nearby park. The winter weather had caused most to forsake the open area surrounded by tall trees and shrubbery. It would do little to deter a teenage boy.

Hurrying forward as stealthily as possible, Ben scanned around him. He made a circle of the open area to get his bearings and then worked his way toward the densest of the undergrowth, his best guess as to where Alfred might take refuge. He found a small stream encrusted by ice hidden there. Beside it on a fallen tree trunk sat Alfred. Ben breathed a sigh of relief before approaching him from behind.

"Alfred Jones. Where ya been, lad?"

There was no jolt of realization. It seemed, rather, that the boy had been waiting to be discovered. His words came slowly, confidently. "Been here, Mister Waldin."

Feeling it wise to match the boy's demeanor, Ben dropped down to a seat on the log beside him. "An' how'd ya get here?"

A sly grin. "Privy window. But ya know it already, yeah?"

"Yeah, I do."

They sat in silence for a moment. Ben looked toward Alfred. His coat was insufficient for such a cold climate. His shoes were wet through from walking in the snow. "Ya look cold."

"Yeah."

"Let's get ya back."

"I'm waitin'."

"Fer what?" Ben kept his voice matter-of-fact.

"Fer *that*." Alfred motioned toward a low-hanging bush across the little stream.

Ben could just make out a string carefully stretched between branches, ending in a small loop. "Ya trappin' somethin'?"

"Yeah. That squirrel."

Ben waited in silence a moment again, carefully considering his best response. "We're goin' back, lad. Can't wait so long, but I'd like ta see yer work first, if ya'd show me."

The waryness in the boy's eyes faded a little. "I'll show ya."

Stepping carefully, they crossed the stream on exposed rocks. Alfred crouched down and traced the trapline with his pointer finger.

It was well designed and well placed. No doubt it would have been a successful contrivance if given enough time. "It's good, Alfred. Ya must'a trapped b'fore. Let's take it down. Ya won't be back."

The eyes flashed for a moment and then deferred, feigning indifference.

Ben added, "Maybe you'll do more trappin' in yer new home."

"Ain't got no home," Alfred countered. "Ain't no one wants me."

"Lots'a folks want lads. We'll find ya a home."

"Not me."

It was a vain argument, better left without further comment. Ben tried a different approach. "What ya hopin' fer, lad? Ya'd rather go back again?"

Clearly it was a question few had posed. Alfred recoiled in surprise. "Nah. Ain't no reason. Got no home back there, neither."

"Then ya might give this a try. Come along with us an' just see."

Winding up the line of string, Alfred shrugged. "Might do so. Too cold ta stay here."

Ben laughed. "Can't argue with that." He unhooked the low-hanging loop and placed it in Alfred's open palm. A shudder stopped him. There were ugly scars etched into the boy's hands. Ben's eyes lifted to meet Alfred's. "What happened to yer hands?"

Immediately, the boy stood and strode away, thrusting his hands firmly into his coat pockets. No explanation. No further conversation.

Ben walked back behind Alfred, his mind grappling with what might have left such sickening scars. The story, no doubt, would be dreadful.

Just before they arrived at the hotel, Ben stopped Alfred with a hand on his shoulder. "Somethin' I gotta ask ya, lad."

"What?"

"Manager says there's a broken window. Ya know 'bout that?"

Alfred's eyes clouded. "No, sir. Not me."

"That the truth?"

"On me mum's grave." There was a hardness in the set of the boy's jaw. Yet Ben judged it to be more likely defensive rather than deceptive.

"All right. I'll tell Miss Davis." As far as Ben was concerned, that would be the end of the questioning. He was prepared to stand up for Alfred and, if push came to shove, to pay for and repair the window himself with his own preciously guarded funds.

• • • • • • •

Thursday arrived and the house was turned upside down preparing for another trip out across the prairie. Quinley was expected at nine o'clock in the morning, and Lillian feared they wouldn't be ready for him. Originally they had planned to leave Milton and Matty with Miss Tilly. Then a telegram came from Hope Valley that Miss Tilly's friend Gerta had fallen ill. With little notice the short trip became far more complicated. Grace and Lillian stayed up late packing clothing for the boys, schoolbooks, and precious toys—all while trying to keep the luggage to a minimum. In addition, there were the two bedrooms to prepare for the little girl named Jane and the boy named Alfred.

"Girls," Miss Tilly called, "yer ride's here."

"Oh, sis, can you get the bag I left in the boys' room? I couldn't carry it on this trip down."

Lillian hurried up the stairs again. She stopped at the door to her childhood bedroom. The linens were fresh and the room neat as a pin, ready for Jane. Miss Tilly had stitched up a new rag doll, which was sitting on the bed, resting against the fluffed-up pillow. On impulse, Lillian lifted it and set it inside the bag Grace had asked her to fetch. Then she did a last inspection of the room that would be given to Alfred—the small room that had been Lemuel's.

A new quilt was stretched across the bed. Grace had felt it important to send the previous one along with Lemuel, even though she knew the Thompsons would have provided well for him. It was her attempt to be certain each of the children had a reasonable amount of their own possessions to take to their new homes. "*Ownership*," she'd explained, "*is important when one has so little continuity in life. And it makes a person feel a little more in control, a little less like their world is chopped into bits of time here and bits there.*"

So Alfred would have a quilt that Miss Tilly and some of her Hope Valley friends had assembled. Green prints and brown prints with some accents of navy, scraps from clothing that someone in Hope Valley was still wearing. The ladies had prayed for it, too, as they gathered together to do the stitching, prayed for the child God would bring to sleep under this blanket's protection and comfort. Lillian spoke a short prayer over the room now, thinking of the boy who had already been described as difficult.

"God, help us to know him—to see him for who he really is—not just his reputation or the behaviors that come from his hurts. And yet, help us to know how to discipline him in a way that would benefit him most. Help us to love him the way You love him. Amen."

With a last-minute rush, they had all the bags waiting on the back porch for Quinley and his long, sleek automobile before he'd finished speaking with Otto in the driveway. Quinley, it seemed, was very fond of talking.

Once again, Lillian took the back seat with the little boys while Grace sat up front with Quinley. They pulled away from Father's home and headed out of the familiar valley where Brookfield was nestled. Another turn in a long series of ambages. Another fork in the road where the path forward was unseen. But Lillian's heart was stirring already with love for the children they'd soon meet.

• • • • • • •

Janie slid the now-familiar children's storybook onto Ben's lap, then climbed up beside him onto the train's leather-covered seat. Without even making the request, she seemed certain that he'd understand and yield to her appeal. It was the story of Jack and the Beanstalk from a book of English fairy tales that she enjoyed most. He was happy to pacify her, keeping an eye on the boys who were scattered around him. Soon Michael joined them on the bench, listening to the rise and fall of Ben's voice as he narrated the familiar story above the rattle of the train's thrumming wheels.

Though Ben's attention was focused on the children surrounding him, his mind was never far from its familiar questions. *Where's me fam'ly gone? What'll I do once me time with Janie's done? And what'll happen to Janie when we get there?*

He knew about the two sisters who had opened a small orphanage. He knew it was far from the city, toward the mountains, in an area that seemed to him remote and obscure. Were the people in such a place living in log cabins still? Did they have grocery stores and schools so far from civilization? Would there be a permanent family who would see the delightful child he'd come to know and give her a good home?

And what about Alfred? Would the sisters be up to the challenge of such a headstrong boy? He hoped they would. With greater affection than he'd expected to feel, he wished that the boy would be given a good chance to succeed.

The train clattered along its tracks. Ben read and played and slept. Tomorrow, they would arrive at their last stop. And everything would change once more.

It was a strange landscape they traveled through. Scattered

trees and farms gave way to undulating white hills—snow-covered plains as barren as the ocean and as rolling as the waves. The tracks of the train cut through them like the prow of a ship. He thought once more of the life he'd given up and pictured in his mind the view from high up on a balcony of the great ocean steamer.

Night closed in around him and the children stretched out on the benches, falling asleep where they had spent their day. He tucked an arm around Janie to keep her from slipping off the slick bench seat during the sharpest of the turns and the infrequent stops. Then the moon rose round and bright, filling the window beside him.

It's the same moon. The very same I've long knowed. For some reason, the thought brought Ben a measure of peace. *Jane is out there, too, under that great dark sky. She may be lookin' up at that same glowin' face and the stars shinin' 'round about it. An' maybe she's thinkin'a me.*

He wasn't aware of feeling tired, or of the moment when he fell asleep at last, head coming to rest against the cold metal of the window's frame. But the sun was rising pink against a cold gray sky by the time Ben opened his eyes. He rubbed at his neck to work out a sore spot. The view hadn't changed. It was as if they were lost forever on this ocean of snow.

The children woke one by one, and there was no longer time to muse. They'd arrive at their final stop shortly after supper. There was a long day of care and a list of tasks to accomplish before then.

At the station as the day was already almost spent, Ben was alert again to the movements of the little group. Miss Davis, out front, searched for their next contact. A man with a broad forehead greeted them.

"You must be Miss Davis. I'm Sidney Brown from Brayton House, the local children's home here. Welcome to Lethbridge. We'll be your hosts until you place the children tomorrow. I've brought two vehicles to transport your group." And then, "May I introduce Mr. Sinclair? Quinley is the representative out West for the Mercy Society."

Miss Davis extended her hand to each man by turn. Adding, "Yes, I've met Mr. Sinclair previously."

"Oh, of course. You work for the same society. How silly of me."

Ben observed their conversation from a distance but felt no need to join in the introductions. He noticed that Miss Davis had not lit up at the sight of a familiar face. *'Course, she's sure ta be tired an' cranky, like the rest'a us, by now.*

"We have a cart here to help with the luggage. Are you waiting for more bags?"

Miss Davis smiled then, as if taking pride in her efficiency. "No, we have everything here with us. The children are carrying their own cases. We're ready to follow where you lead."

The younger man stepped forward with a flash of white teeth. "Let's have you load your bags on the cart, children. No sense working any harder than we need." He dropped a hand gently onto Vaughan's head, then tugged at one of Millie's braids affectionately as he spoke. "You must all be tired after such a long journey. I think we can get you settled and comfortable very soon."

Sidney Brown agreed. "Mr. Sinclair is right. We're all ready for you at Brayton House. I'm sure you'd like a break from all the travel."

Following in step, Ben placed his own bag and Janie's onto the cart.

• • • ● • • •

A quiet day spent in the familiar rooms of Brayton House transformed in a moment. Children who'd been clearing the tables after supper hastened to the bottom of the stairs before Grace could even attempt to call them back, though Lillian was certain her sister's efforts were rather halfhearted. She knew that Grace was as excited as anyone to meet the new children. They gathered, curious and watchful, gazing up the half set of stairs to the landing where Sid and Quinley had just arrived, a ruckus of footsteps following in their wake, new faces crowding in together on the landing.

"This is our children's home, Miss Davis. We've been here since—" Sid was midway through his words of welcome when he noticed the second group had convened nearby. "And these are the children who live here. Children, could you please say hello to welcome our new friends?"

A faint chorus of greetings answered him obediently. "Hi, hello, hi."

Lillian felt like she was snooping where she didn't belong. One hand on Matty's shoulder, she smiled rather shyly at the overwhelmed strangers. Only one set of eyes met her own. She drew herself up into another smile toward tempestuous dark blue eyes. The boy's brows only lowered in response, but he refused to look away. Scanning around the group and seeing just two full-grown boys, she wondered if the turbulent eyes might belong to the boy named Alfred. She attempted a welcoming expression in his direction.

"We're going to get everyone settled into their rooms for the night and then have hot chocolate and cookies in the dining room," Sid instructed. "In order to do that, we need to go upstairs first. The rooms down there on the lower floor include our dining room, kitchen, and classrooms. Up here, on the main floor, we have offices, the playroom, and the sitting room. All the way upstairs are the bedrooms. Grace, would you please show Miss Davis and the girls where they can settle themselves and wash up after their long journey? Quinley and I will go along with the boys."

More shuffling feet. Lillian stood in place and watched as the large landing gradually cleared. Grace had moved past them to climb the stairs, and the children around Lillian returned slowly to their chores. Alone, hat in hand, stood a last man, seemingly forgotten.

"Hello," Lillian offered in surprise, stumbling over her words. "Welcome. I'm sorry I didn't catch your name. I'm Lillian Walsh." She wondered if she should reach out a hand to shake his, but she faltered because of the distance and short flight of stairs still between them.

"Me name's Waldin. Ben Waldin."

Lillian was uncertain what to make of this strange man who'd been left alone. His clothes were very simple and quite worn. He seemed badly in need of a haircut, though he'd clearly made an attempt to slick back his sable brown waves. Now, however, they'd broken away into loose spirals falling onto his forehead, until he looked rather wild and unkempt.

"Well, Mr. Waldin, if you'd like, you're welcome to join us in the dining room. We have hot coffee and cookies. If you're hungry, I'm sure we can make you a sandwich with some of the leftover roast beef."

"Thank ya, Miss . . . Miss Walsh. Coffee sounds good just now." Slipping out of his heavy greatcoat, he hung it on a hook, placed his flat cap over it, and followed Lillian toward the kitchen.

She found a clean coffee cup on the drain board and poured the steaming liquid for him from the pot on the stove, setting the cup on the counter close to him. Then she asked, "Cream or sugar?"

"Just cream, if ya please."

She retrieved the small pitcher of cream from the icebox and handed it to the man. His large hands were tanned and callused, making her even more puzzled about how he fit in with the people supporting these traveling children. Still, she preferred not to ask.

"Thank ya, miss."

"Won't you join me in the dining room, Mr. Waldin?"

"Please, miss, just Ben's fine."

"All right, Ben." Lillian chose a table far away from those that the children worked to clear and wipe down after their supper.

Ben reached to draw out her chair. She dropped onto it quickly and tried not to appear as uncomfortable as she felt. *What on earth will we find to talk about?*

But Ben was quick to fill the awkwardness. "It's a fine home ya got here, miss. D'ya work as a teacher, then?"

She shook her head, trying to meet his gaze. "No, my sister and I don't actually live here at all. Well, that is, my sister, Grace, lived here long ago—well, and worked here, too, I guess." Her words trailed off.

Expressive brows dropped low as he seemed to puzzle over her response.

Lillian tried again, looking up into his gray eyes purposefully. "It's a long story. My sister was a resident here during her youth. You see, our parents passed away and we were separated. Grace was raised in orphanages. As she grew older, she volunteered here with the children."

Ben leaned forward, his gaze intense now. He set his cup on the table in front of him as if he'd already lost interest in it. "You and yer sister? Are ya . . . d'ya have a home fer orphans of yer own? I heard there was sisters here described as such."

"Yes, that's right. Grace and I have a small children's home in a town west of here."

"I wonder, miss—if ya don't mind me askin', do ya plan on takin' in any of those we brung ya?"

Lillian studied him for a moment. *Can I trust this man with such information? What's his purpose in asking?* Still, he'd come with the others. Surely he was considered respectable.

The gray eyes had brightened somehow. They were softer now, giving him a gentler appearance. He continued hastily, "Miss, I don't mean ta pry. It's just that there's a child among 'em. She's only six—an' she don't have a fam'ly takin' her in. She's like . . .

like a niece ta me by now—like me own fam'ly. An' I hoped ta see her settled 'fore I have ta move on."

Lillian relaxed a little. "What's her name, Ben?"

"Janie. Jane Grey, 'tis."

"Why, yes. She was one of the two we expect to bring home with us. How do you know her better than the others? Did you know her back in England?"

The eyes clouded slightly. "We met aboard me ship."

"*Your* ship?"

"Aye, miss. Ya see, I was a sailor on her ship. Me job was ta care fer the young'uns on their crossin'—not to watch o'er 'em, but ta provide fer their needs where the ship's passage was concerned. But Janie, she's special. We grew ta be good friends. An' after we docked, I was hired ta join 'em crossin' the country by train."

The hardened hands, the unkempt hair, the worn clothing. Now Lillian understood better. "I'm sure they were grateful to have you, Ben. Do you have plans now? Will you travel back to the East? Will you go back to sea?"

He lifted his cup, sipped before answering. "Not jus' yet. I've an errand first."

The answer was rather vague, but already Lillian was warming to this stranger. He seemed to be truly concerned about the children.

Grace appeared and joined them at the table. She had the glow of gratification on her face. "They all seem to be settling well, though I know they're tired out from their journey. I met little Jane Grey. She's just delightful."

From the corner of her eye, Lillian could see Ben's face light into a wide smile. "Grace, I'd like to introduce you to Ben Waldin. He traveled with the children all the way from England and is particularly fond of Jane."

Grace answered with an easy smile. "Oh, well, I'm very aware of that. Little Miss Jane told me so herself. She was quite concerned that you hadn't left yet."

"We're great friends, she an' I."

"I suppose Lillian has already told you we're to have Jane stay with us for a little while?"

"She has, yeah. I'm glad to hear of it."

"We have two other little boys right now," Lillian added. "Do you see those twins sitting across the room at the farthest table? They're six, too—so I'm sure they'll be good little playmates for Jane. And we're also to take in a boy, an older boy."

"Yeah, so I'm told."

Lillian watched him closely. His eyes had changed again. The bright gray had turned ashen. She wondered if the change was an effect of his animated brows. At any rate, it seemed possible to read his mood by the color of those gray eyes. "Ben," she prompted him, "is there something you can tell us about the boy?"

He dropped his gaze to his cup before answering, "Aye, miss. The boy, Alfred, he's a good lad. A tad spirited, ya might say. Needs a firm hand too." Then he hurried on. "But he's a good lad still. Needs ta know he matters, that he's wanted."

Grace's eyes filled with emotion. She leaned her elbows on the table. "We'll tell him that, Ben. I assure you, we'll do our very best to make certain he knows."

CHAPTER 16

Bereft

Ben tried to fade into the background. He wanted to stay nearby, yet there was really no need for his services any longer. Janie had been delivered safely to where she'd be cared for by the two compassionate sisters. They seemed capable and kind enough. And there was nothing further required of him.

Yet he found it impossible to extract himself from the busy children's home. If he could just go unnoticed, perhaps he could find a quiet corner to rest for the night. Miss Davis was far too busy confirming plans for the morning to notice his movements, to remember his existence at all. And Sid Brown, who was in charge, seemed to take Ben's presence for granted.

So Ben slipped into one of the empty basement classrooms, dropped his old kit bag next to a wall, and stretched out on the cold linoleum floor. His body reminded him at once that he was getting too old to be comfortable with such arrangements. Still, it would be only one night.

Mentally, he counted the money left in his possession once again. Miss Davis owed him a few dollars more. How long would the meager funds last in his search for his family? Would it be necessary for him to settle somewhere temporarily and find a job? What should he do next?

Then he let his thoughts turn to the sisters. They almost seemed too kind to be real. Of course, he'd met people who were generous and good, but he wondered how these young ladies had come to have an orphanage of their own. Then he recalled how the taller one, the auburn-haired Lillian, had stumbled through an explanation of their past. They were both orphaned. So they understood the plight of these children better than most. Surely that was the reason they'd taken on such labors.

I'd like ta help 'em, if I could. But how?

Ben fell asleep pondering ways he might prove useful and woke early in darkness, his mind still wrestling with the same troubling thoughts. *If only I could figure a way ta work fer 'em—get me feet under me better. I could help with Alfred. Could watch over Janie. If only . . .*

During breakfast Ben sat with a table of anxious boys. They hung closer to him now. He was suddenly the familiar one, a safe retreat in the unfamiliar surroundings. All about them were strangers and newness. And four of the boys faced the prospect of meeting new families soon. Their anxiety was demonstrated by their silence at breakfast.

He tried to break through the gloom. "Malcolm, ya get 'nough? Food's good here, eh?"

"Yeah, Mister Waldin."

"Ya sleep well, lads?"

Slow nods. "Yeah. All right."

Alfred stood suddenly, plate in hand, rejecting Ben's efforts at beginning a conversation. "I'm goin' back fer more." He strode away to the kitchen.

Ten-year-old Stanley blurted, "Okay fer 'im. Ya can eat when ya don't got no new folk waitin' ta meet ya."

Ben shook his head. "Lads, sometimes we put on courage ta cover up worry. Feels easier, I 'spect. Just 'cause Alfred don't show it, don't mean he ain't worried 'bout his unknowns too. But I want ya ta know, I don't doubt Miss Davis has found ya good folks. I hope ya soon feel safe an' cared fer with 'em."

"They just want us fer workin'," Malcolm muttered. "That's what I heard."

"Where d'ya hear that?"

Malcolm dropped his head, silenced once more.

Ben shuddered. "I can't promise that ain't true. I don't know these folk. I can't speak fer 'em. But whether they see ya fer the men ya are or not, ya need to know ya matter—much as any other boy. You ain't less. In fact, the hard life ya have now'll make ya strong, if ya let it." He swept his gaze around the table. "What ya might hear from ign'rant folk, don't ya believe it. What happened to ya, it ain't yer fault. All ya can do is not listen to such words. Keep tellin' yerself, 'I'm no diff'rent from 'em.' An' ne'er stop lookin' fer folk what know better—who'll see ya fer what ya are and love ya."

He willed them to hear him, wished with all his being that the words might convince them and plant a seed of willfulness in them to stand up to the often-cruel world. He knew they'd need that along the way.

In a flash Ben's own story flooded his mind. The sense of rejection, a perception of failure, escape from a dogmatic father. Certainly, such ideas as he'd tried to implant in the boys had never been explained to him. He'd figured it all out on his own while watching the moon arch across the night sky as a youth. And yet, it was never quite enough. *Fight or perish. Can't there be better ways to encourage these lads? More hope to offer 'em?*

True, in the course of time, Ben had also discovered the beauty of words printed on a page—the exhilaration of a vast, untamable ocean—the satisfaction of work well done. And there was his sister, Jane—and now, wee Janie. Still, a niggling yearning made him always hope to uncover more beauty in the world. *If*

I'da e'er figured it all out fer meself, maybe I could'a offered something better to these lads.

· · · ◆ · · ·

There was a palpable tension in the air. Lillian watched from a corner of the dining room as the boys who'd been sitting in a circle around Ben Waldin rose and dutifully departed together. Hers weren't the only eyes that followed them away. All of the children who lived in Brayton House were turned toward them as they exited. Then one boy returned from the kitchen with a fresh plate of food. He set it down on the table and drew up the chair beneath him, fully aware that he was being scrutinized.

Grace stood. She motioned Lillian to follow. *It's time to introduce ourselves to Alfred Jones. I hope we're ready.*

"May we sit with you?" Grace was already slipping onto a chair across from the boy before awaiting his answer.

"Do's ya like."

"My name is Miss Grace Bennett. This is my sister, Miss Lillian Walsh. Has anyone told you about us?"

"Yeah." A careless shrug. His fork lifted food to his mouth rather indelicately.

Grace was undeterred. "Well, that's good. We won't have to introduce ourselves further, then. But please feel free to ask any questions that you have, at any time."

No response from Alfred, though his eyes were fixed on Grace as he continued to eat his breakfast.

"We look forward to getting to know you, Alfred. You've had a long journey. I'm sure it's been strange and unsettling at times."

Lillian watched her sister in awe, so confident, so at ease despite the boy's intentional indifference. She prayed silently that Grace would be given the best words to say, that he'd hear her honest concern for him.

"Is it all right to ask you a few questions?"

For the first time the boy looked away, allowing his gaze to drop to his oatmeal. "If ya like."

Grace leaned closer, crossing her arms and resting them on the table amiably. Her head tipped to one side, her voice softened further. "Thank you, Alfred. I guess I'd like to know where you come from—a little about your home. Can you tell me something about what England is like?"

"It's cold. An' it rains a lot."

"I see. Did you come from a city, a town, or a farm?"

"Town. Small 'un."

"Who took care of you?"

He set his spoon down, rose onto his own elbows. He was clearly indicating he was ready to do battle now. "Nobody. Me dad liked the drink. Me mum, she was sick. Least, that's what she liked ta call it. Weren't nobody takin' care'a us, an' then we lost our house."

"You had siblings? Brothers and sisters?"

"Nine, younger 'an me. I liked it better just ta sleep outdoors—liked ta catch me own dinner in the woods. Easy. Got so good I could oft feed me sisters too."

Lillian tried to listen closely enough to catch the implications behind his words. She was quite certain she wasn't detecting all of his insinuations, but she was convinced that Grace was deciphering his meaning well. This would not be the first time that Grace read between the lines as she conversed with a wounded child. And yet, Lillian was surprised to see that her sister held steady, met his eyes evenly. And, oddly, offered very little visible empathy.

"Did they pass away? Your parents?"

"Yuletide last. Mum died, and then later me dad."

"Where'd you go? And your siblings?"

"Weren't none left then. Just me."

"Oh dear. Illness?"

"No, miss. I tol' ya. The house burned up—with 'em all."

Quietly but evenly, "I'm sorry, Alfred. I'm so very sorry."

Did he weaken? Just a little?

"Guess t'were good I didn't sleep there too, eh, miss?"

"I'm sorry you lost your family, son." A pause as Grace collected her thoughts, and then, "Well, we look forward to having you stay with us for a while. But for now, I think I have just one more question—and it's an important one."

"Miss?"

"What do you prefer to be called? I want to be sure we use a name you prefer."

His dark blue eyes searched her face, the light in them fading a little as he hesitated. And then quietly he said, "Freddie. Me name's Freddie, miss."

• • • • • • •

Ben hung his head, exhausted. He lowered himself onto the cold foyer steps. Watching these boys distributed among strangers had cost him even more than he'd imagined. Their pale faces were fixed in his mind, impossible to forget. Malcolm, eyes down, had obediently fallen in step behind the farmer and his wife. Stanley's fearful expression had warned that he was far more likely to flee. Ben had placed a gentle hand on Stanley's trembling shoulder to steady him, silently wishing him well with the baker's family in Lethbridge.

It seemed a benefit that Michael and Vaughan were staying together, made brothers now by the peculiar forces of fate. Though the farmer and his wife who claimed them were surly and gruff, the boys thankfully would have a chum to mitigate the experience, to be a safeguard against the loneliness of their new farming home.

Miss Davis had stood with the girls as Sylvia and Millie were received by strangers. By the look on Miss Davis's face, it seemed she found the experience to be invigorating. She actually looked pleased to have accomplished such a morning.

Ben shared none of her enthusiasm. Instead, there was a physical sense of emptiness he felt even in his hands. The boys were gone now. He could never reach out to steady them again, would likely never know what became of them. His stomach turned at the thought, so he'd retreated to the quiet of the foyer.

Janie slid down to the step beside him quietly. She placed a hand on his knee and waited. At last she whispered, "Are you all right, Mr. Waldin?"

Instead of answering, Ben pulled her close against his side. Words were impossible.

Her small voice explained sweetly, "God'll take care of them. God is good. And He's strong. We can trust Him."

Oh, child! It ain't God what worries me. It's men! I seen too much'a 'em. He blinked hard to keep his eyes from filling. He dared not allow his own weakness to cause little Janie to lose confidence.

"Mr. Waldin, I think we should go see Miss Grace and Miss Lillian. They asked me where you were. I think they'd like to talk to you."

Ben rose. There was someone he needed to speak with. It was not the sisters. "I'll be back in a little while, bunny. Why don't ya go on up to the playroom? I think them boys, Matty an' Milt, are there. Most'a the others'll start lessons soon, but the wee boys can maybe play with ya."

"All right."

Ben headed up the stairs beside Janie, walked her to the doorway into the designated play area. Next he went toward the offices, looking for Sid Brown.

"Excuse me, Mr. Brown. Don't mean ta interrupt ya, sir."

"Come in, Ben. Please."

He took the chair across the desk from Sid. "I'll get to the point. I know yer busy." He cleared his throat. "Mr. Brown, I find meself in a tricky place. To be blunt, sir, I need a job." He hurried on before Sid could respond. "Don't know what ya might know 'bout jobs in yer town, but I wondered, would ya vouch fer me? Now, we ain't known one 'nother long, but I don't know none other here an'—"

Sid interrupted, "I'd be glad to give you a reference, Mr. Waldin. I know enough about you to know what a hard worker you are—that you're diligent and conscientious. Miss Davis has spoken very well of you."

"Thank ya, sir."

"If I could hire you myself, I certainly would. We lost our driver not too many months ago. If we do need to hire someone and you're available still, I'd like to bring you on. But we don't travel much in the winter, and I'm sure you can't wait until spring for work. Sometimes warm weather is rather tardy on the prairie."

"Thanks." Ben rose to leave.

Sid held out a hand to deter him. "One more thought. I suspect there's work at the train depot. I happen to know that a couple of the fellas there are out sick this week. It's worth speaking with Rudy Skeates about it. He's the foreman there."

"Thank ya, Mr. Brown. Rudy Skeates. That's a good start."

There was no time to waste. Every day without pay was a burden. Ben wrapped his heavy coat around himself and strode away from Brayton House, grateful that the cold wind was coming from behind him.

• • • • • • •

The playroom walls were already closing in around Lillian. Having spent time so recently in limbo at Brayton House, she wanted nothing more than to return home to Brookfield with the four children now in their care. Lifting the edge of a long yellow curtain, she peered outdoors into the bright sunshine reflecting off the snow. Immediately she noted the form of a man striding away. *Who is that? Is it Quinley?* But no, Lillian couldn't recognize the man from this distance, nor the dark coat he pulled tight around him. It was certainly not Quinley's fine navy overcoat, however.

Next her gaze traveled to the parking lot. Few vehicles remained of those that had gathered earlier in the morning. Her eyes were drawn to movement. Two dark figures were motioning toward a car that approached from down the street. They seemed oddly familiar.

And then it came to Lillian in a wave of realization. The tall man with hunched shoulders. The short, thin form beside him. It was Mr. and Mrs. Szweda gesturing for a vehicle to attend to them.

Lillian felt the blood drain from her face. *Why are they here? What are they doing?*

More figures came into view, two boys huddling nearby between parked cars. Jack Szweda motioned them over with a wave of his arm. Lillian saw an obvious hesitation from the children. Then Jack's arm shot out, rising as if he might strike. The boy dodged before the blow could land, and the pair hurried forward obediently toward the waiting vehicle.

Though Lillian had been supervising Matty and Milton all morning, her eyes instantly swept the room once more to assure herself that the twins were still building with blocks in a nearby corner. *Then who are those boys?*

"I have to find Grace." She spoke the words aloud fiercely, drawing the eyes of the children around her. "Excuse me. I'll be back soon. Please stay here. I'll be right back."

Rushing from the room, Lillian faltered in the hallway. The last she'd seen Grace was in the dining room, but that was just after breakfast. Where would she be by now?

Heading instead toward the office wing, Lillian pushed open the door to the sitting room. It was empty. From there she hurried to Sid's office and heard voices from within. She knocked loudly.

Sid's voice called, "Yes, come in."

Trying not to appear as frantic as she felt, Lillian opened the door and scanned the room. "I'm looking for Grace. Do you know where she is?"

"I believe she's in the kitchen."

"Thank you." For a moment Lillian floundered. Should she question Sid directly? *No, I want to talk to Grace first.* Without further comment she pulled the door shut again behind her.

Flying down the stairs toward the dining hall, Lillian was out of breath by the time she spotted Grace in the kitchen and hurtled toward her.

"What on earth? Sis, you look like you've seen a ghost."

"I wish I had!"

"What's happened?" Grace reached a hand to grasp at Lillian's arm.

"I saw the Szwedas. They're in the parking lot. And they have two boys. I don't know which ones. Grace, they've got two more boys!"

Grace's mouth fell open. "Sid. We need to talk to Sid."

Rushing back up the stairs, Lillian followed Grace to the office hallway once more. But her sister wasted no time with knocking.

Grace burst into the room. "Sid, was that the Szwedas in the parking lot?"

Silence. He closed a notebook that sat on the desk in front of him and then said, "I'm sorry, Rolly. It seems something has come up."

Again Grace demanded, "Sid?"

Roland stood, but rather than moving out of the way, he stepped forward toward Grace, reaching out to catch her gently by a forearm. His voice was pleading, his blue eyes intense. "We didn't want to do it, Grace. We didn't have a choice."

Grace pushed him aside. "Sid? What on earth?"

The man's voice remained controlled. "Take a seat, please, ladies."

"No. You can't let them leave. Bring those boys back here, Sid!"

"Rolly, please give us some time. Close the door on your way out."

Lillian wilted onto the closest chair. *This was not a mistake. This was a deliberate choice.*

Grace stood firm. "You should have told us this was your intention, Sid. You knew how we'd feel. You knew I'd never allow it to happen."

"Grace, please." He motioned to the chair, but Grace paced to the window instead.

She looked outside, though Sid's window faced the back of the property. Still, she spun around as if she'd just confirmed her suspicions and commanded, "Stop them, Sid."

"I can't. Don't you think I would if I could? But it's out of my hands. They're Mercy Society kids."

For a moment Grace's face fell into her cupped palms. Then her shoulders straightened again. Her eyes rose, her look even more determined. "Where's Quinley? This is under his authority. Right? Where's Quin?"

"This was *his* decision, Grace. Please try to understand. The Szwedas were approved by the Mercy Society. They signed a contract with the society to receive two boys—not with us. That first contract was still in effect after you . . . you . . . they came to your house."

"They're not a suitable home, Sid. You know that."

"It wasn't our decision, Grace. We have no authority over those boys."

Lillian's lip began to quiver as she thought of her own encounter with the Szwedas, her mind picturing again the swing of Jack Szweda's dark arm silhouetted against the snowy parking lot as he attempted to strike at the young boy. "What were their names?" she murmured. "I want to know the boys' names."

Sid's face drained of color. "Why?"

"I want to remember them. I want to hear you say their names. And I want you to remember that they're people—just children."

He cleared his throat. "Michael Allard and Vaughan Mynatt." Then his eyes lifted to meet Lillian's, his brow crumpled with emotion. "And please don't think I'll ever forget them. These children have been my work for decades—my ministry. This is not something I'll ever forget. But the society has made it very clear we can't treat these children as *ours* anymore. We're allowed to house them as a temporary safe place, but we don't get to make any decisions regarding their care—their placements."

Grace shook her head, spoke again with resolution. "I want to talk to Quinley. Where is he?"

"He's out. He had a meeting with a local businessman. He's trying to garner more funding."

"When is he expected?"

"After lunch."

"We'll wait for him."

Lillian stepped forward, grabbing at Grace's arm before posing her own question. "Sid, what about the children for whom *we* found homes? What about Bryony and the others? Does this have any impact on them? Surely they won't second-guess those placements!"

Grace gasped aloud as if she'd been struck.

"No." Sid shook his head, swung his hands as if he were an umpire declaring a runner safe. "We fought hard for that—so I can absolutely assure you that they cannot. They won't go back now and undo any of the work that we did before they sent Quin—not for your placements or for ours either. Don't forget, we have other children who'll be affected by what they authorize here too—others that came to us for shelter during the year, kids we were able to place in homes here in Lethbridge."

Lillian softened, overcome with sudden compassion by the stress on Sid's face.

"And the twins?" Grace demanded.

Lillian's empathy for Sid instantly dissolved. "Yes, Matty and Milton. What about them?"

"They're still registered with the Mercy Society, but . . . but . . ." He held back their response with a swift hand gesture. "But they've agreed to work with us concerning the boys. They'll need to approve their placement, but they're willing to let us be the ones who recommend the home."

Grace retorted, "Well, that's a relief, because I think there's a family in Brookfield already interested."

"You didn't tell me that."

"Well, they haven't said anything for sure. It's been evolving slowly, at a pace that benefits the boys."

"Yes," Lillian agreed. "But I think the Caulfields are definitely interested. It's just been such an overwhelming time. . . ."

"You should have told me about all this, Sid." Grace's tone had begun to frighten Lillian. She'd never heard her speak so harshly before, especially to someone in authority over her.

"The truth is," he countered, sighing, "I shouldn't be telling you now. You're not an employee, Grace. It's become far more complicated than it used to be. I wish we'd never . . . No, I don't wish that. But it's *far more* complicated than it used to be." And then Sid shook his head and his voice slowed. "We all knew it was out of control when children showed up on our doorstep needing shelter and the society who brought them here was way on the other side of Canada. We *need* Quinley to get this all under control. We *need* them to take responsibility for their placements—and this is what taking responsibility looks like. They're not the enemy here. Can't you see that? Can't you concede that much to me?"

Grace had wilted. Even the energy from her eyes had visibly faded. "I just don't know what to think. I can't even . . . I just need some time to understand it all."

"Yes, that's a feeling I'm well acquainted with, believe me."

As they left Sid's office, Lillian fought the urge to rush out into the parking lot, to somehow chase after the Szwedas. It would be useless and desperate, she knew, and yet, wasn't it justified to try something wild? Instead, she stumbled along numbly, following Grace.

O God, Lillian begged internally, *what now? The boys, Michael and Vaughan. What about them? I promised not to lie again. I promised not to take matters into my own hands. I said I would trust You instead. But, what's happening? Why aren't You stopping this? O God, can't You make it all stop?*

• • • • • • •

Grace paced back and forth across the foyer. Lillian attempted to entertain the children in the playroom but found herself frequently hearing sounds that brought her dashing out to where she could see Grace and keep track of who'd arrived. Each time she was disappointed to discover that Quinley had not returned. At last she was rewarded.

Grace's voice was rather high-pitched as, without a greeting, she demanded of him, "Why were the Szwedas given more children? I thought we'd agreed that they were unsuitable parents."

"Grace, Grace . . . please let me hang up my coat. It's cold outdoors. Let's find a warm place to have a good conversation. I'll be more than happy to explain everything to you." Lillian's movement from the landing above caught Quinley's eye. "Lillian? I see I'm to have the full attention of both of you. Lucky me." His smile never subsided, but it seemed to be stretched out somewhat thinner than usual over his white teeth.

As Quinley climbed the stairs with Grace close behind, he said, "I hope you haven't waited long for me. You'll be pleased to know that I had a good meeting with a member of the town council. They're favorably inclined toward some very good advantages for Brayton House."

"That's nice." Lillian's mind clouded as she struggled to remain polite.

He motioned them to the left. "Let's go here, into the parlor.

We'll have our privacy with some comfort." Pushing the door open, he stepped back to allow Grace and Lillian to enter first.

Lillian took a seat in the nearest chair, but Grace passed by toward the large window, turning and crossing her arms in front of her body. Without speaking she announced that she was ready for a fight about the matter.

Quinley stepped up close to the ornate parlor stove and held out his hands to its warmth. "I'm sorry if there's been some kind of misunderstanding. You must believe me. I thought you always knew that Jack and Katrin Szweda would be receiving two more boys." He hurried on before Grace had a chance for a rebuttal. His gaze moved from one sister to the other, eyes soft, expression confident in its empathy. "Our committee discussed the case carefully, and we did come to the agreement that the twins were too young to be given back to this couple. But denying them any children at all was never something we considered. They'd been approved and had followed all of our procedures—"

Grace broke into his explanation. "But you went to their place. They're dreadful. How can you see that this placement will be anything but a disaster for the boys?"

"And that's exactly what we worked with them to find out." Leaving the warmth, Quinley reached out for Grace's arm, drew her toward a seat on the sofa, and sat on the footstool in front of it as if he were trying to stay as close, as intimate, as possible with Grace. "I shouldn't be telling you this. It's really confidential information . . . but the Szwedas were thoroughly vetted. We spoke with them at length, talked to other family members, to their local pastor—even asked for information from their bank to be certain they had means to provide for the boys. We did everything to be sure it was an appropriate home. There is no legal reason to deny them."

Lillian broke in. "I saw him! That man took a swing at one of the boys!"

Quinley's tone changed slightly. "Where were they?"

"In the parking lot."

"Where were you?"

"Upstairs. I saw them from the playroom window."

Hesitating, he puckered his mouth to one side. "I'm not sure that's going to stand up legally. It could be argued that you didn't know who they were."

"It was the Szwedas. I'm sure of it. I'd testify to it in any court."

"Oh dear, that's not quite the way these things work."

"Fine, then," Grace pressed. "What did the house look like? Their farm?" Her voice sounded flat and combative, even to Lillian's ears.

"No, there wasn't time to—"

"What? You didn't go to their place? Then how can you know anything if you didn't even do an inspection? Milton mentioned once that it was very unclean, poorly kept."

"Ladies, please hear me. We followed all of the procedures about—"

Lillian had heard enough. "Excuse me, I have to see to the children." She exited abruptly, slipping out the nearby door, refusing to be drawn back by his persuasive words. *I don't have it in me to argue in vain with him. I'm too spent!*

Instead, she went directly to the playroom and drew Matty up onto her knee just to feel the comforting weight of him in her arms. She choked back her emotions and offered aloud, "Let's read another chapter in our book."

Milton and Jane crawled up beside her on the sofa, ready to hear more about *Alice's Adventures in Wonderland.*

CHAPTER 17

Consultation

Just after noon on Saturday, Grace canceled their ride back to Brookfield for Monday. Though Lillian heartily agreed that there was a far more pressing need for their influence where they were for the time being, she wished she'd been consulted. And it was difficult for Lillian to keep her mind focused on the children around her, difficult to think of lunch and washing up and supervising chores. But as she tucked blankets under the chins of the three youngest and bid them to have a good nap in the afternoon, it became impossible for Lillian not to let the persistent machinations play freely in her mind.

How can Quinley claim that he thought we always knew? It's so obvious that he kept this as a big secret. He went to great lengths to be sure we didn't know about the Szwedas. Oh, I want to go home! But there's got to be something we can do about this if we stay here. I wish I could ask Miss Tilly what she would do. I wish I could get our children safely home just as soon as possible. And yet, Lillian hated the idea of conceding defeat—of giving in to the terrible decision that had been made. Was that what was expected? Even planned? That their journey home would put an abrupt end to any protests they'd wish to make?

I don't know those two boys, but that doesn't matter. It's not enough to fight only for the children I'm personally acquainted with. What difference should that make? That's exactly why Quinley and people like him will expect us to walk away from this. So then, that's exactly why we should stay. Who else will stand up for poor little Michael and little Vaughan?

All at once Lillian realized who it was that wore the long dark coat, whose broad shoulders hunched as he strode away from Brayton House in the morning, flat cap pulled down low over his head. *Ben Waldin! He knows these boys. He traveled with them on the train and on the ship before that. He'll care enough to stand up for them. I think he will.*

But Ben was gone. Maybe he'd already caught a train back East.

Lillian rose quietly from the stuffed chair in the corner of the dormitory room. She peeked over at the three little faces with closed eyes before moving as silently as possible out into the hallway. Grace might know more. In fact, even Freddie might know about Ben's plans too. The boy had traveled with Ben.

Once again hurrying through the corridors, Lillian descended to the classrooms where the older children were studying their Saturday lessons. She peeked through the glass window set inside the door and noted the new boy at a desk far in the back. She told herself that the interruption was warranted. It was a matter of acting quickly.

The moment Lillian knocked and opened the door, all eyes turned up from their desks. Roland, who sat at the large desk in the front of the classroom, rose to his feet.

"I'm so sorry, Mr. Scott. May I please speak with Freddie—that is, with Alfred Jones—for a moment?"

"As you wish." There was a quizzical expression on Roland's face.

Freddie followed Lillian out the door, clearly as pleased as he could be that she had called him away from the classroom.

"I'm so sorry to bother you."

"Ya ain't. I ain't doin' nothin'. They jus' put me in here 'cause they wanna watch me 'til we leave. When is that?"

"Well, I didn't want to disturb your lessons."

He shook his head, amused. "Ya didn't. He give me a book ta read, but I ain't."

Lillian got straight to the point. "I just wanted to know if Mr. Waldin has told you any of his plans. Do you know if he's gone back East already? Do you know if he's planning to stay in the area for any length of time?"

A crooked grin spread across the boy's face. He seemed positively delighted to be a source of information. "He weren't goin' east. Tol' us his folks're out here somewhere. Was goin' ta find 'em."

"His folks? Do you mean he has family here? In Alberta?"

"Yeah, miss. They up an' left England without 'im. So he's gonna track 'em down here."

"I see." It was a puzzling revelation. "Do you . . . Does he know where they might be?"

"No, miss. That's just the problem, in'it? Mister Waldin, he don't know where."

Lillian exhaled as the realization sunk in. "So there's no way to know how to follow him."

"Could be. He talked ta Mister Brown. I saw 'em."

Lillian patted his arm as if he were a child, though the boy was taller than she was. "Thanks, Freddie. You've been very helpful."

"I could come 'long, miss. I'm happy ta help ya look fer 'im."

"Thank you. No. I can't keep you from your studies any longer."

"Aw, miss, I said I ain't studyin'. Just draw'ring me next trap on a page'a that book."

She wanted to scold him at first, but his eyes were too lit up with mirth. "You should go back. But I'm grateful for your help, Freddie. Truly." She started to turn away.

"Miss?" the boy asked.

"Yes?"

"When do we leave? Ta go to the country place?"

"I'm not sure, Freddie. We were supposed to go back on Monday. But there's been a . . . a delay. It should be soon. As soon as possible. There's just something we need to take care of first."

"Is it Mickey and Vaughan?"

Lillian stared back at him. *How could he possibly have known?*

"I'm a kid, but I ain't dumb, miss. I got ears."

"What do you know?" She watched his face closely.

"I saw 'em. Them folk what took 'em. Even Mister Waldin tol' us some folk just want kids ta work fer 'em. An' we all saw it. They just want Mickey and Vaughan ta do their chores."

Lillian froze in place. Tears began to well in her eyes. "You all knew?"

"Yeah, miss. It ain't no secret."

Her hand grasped at his fingers lightly. "I'm sorry, Freddie. That's not what we want for any of you. It's not right, and we'll do everything we can to correct this."

He shook his head, tipped it to one side. "Why?"

Again Lillian felt stunned. "Because you matter to us, son. You all matter to us."

It was the boy's turn to be speechless in surprise. He moved away on his own accord, returning to his seat in the classroom as Lillian rushed back up the stairs once more in search of Grace.

• • • • • • •

Ben hopped from the back of the stranger's truck while it was still moving slowly. The courteous man had seen him walking along in the cold and had offered him a ride through the city, back to his destination. He saluted the driver as the truck pulled away and Ben headed toward the looming orphanage building once more. There was really no reason to assume that he'd be welcome again. He no longer had a role to play. But there was simply nowhere else for him to go. So it worked in his favor to try to blend in for as long as he could, hoping to be seen as necessary and useful. Miss Davis was traveling east by train again in the morning. Ben's only hope for shelter was that Sid Brown and the sisters would accept his presence for a while longer.

He'd been offered a short-term job loading and unloading boxcars at the train depot. He'd also inquired at several of the local businesses that sold goods such as lumber and coal. Beyond such manual labor, he wasn't certain what type of work would suit him.

As an afterthought he'd walked into a small bookstore, asking if they'd received any letters to hold. The woman behind the counter had laughed and then shook her head. She did, however, advise him to try the post office. Though he doubted that Jane would have deviated from her previous actions, he asked there too. There was no letter waiting. He supposed that the defeated slump in his shoulders was what had prompted the stranger to offer him a ride.

Entering the foyer of Brayton House rather stealthily, he descended to the basement and crossed the dining room area. He'd noticed earlier that there was a dripping pipe in the boiler room. This was something he knew about. He'd get busy making the repair just as if someone had directed him to do so.

Finding the supply closet and gathering the necessary tools and materials, he spread himself out on the floor and assumed the uncomfortable posture of lying on his back, head tucked under the lowest-hanging pipes so that he could work to release the appropriate fitting. Just as he was about to twist shut the feed valve that regulated water flowing into the boiler, he heard a woman's timid voice murmuring above him in the tiny room.

"Mr. Waldin. I'm so glad I found you. I hate to bother you, but could we speak for a moment?"

Setting down the heavy wrench on the floor with a clank, he shuffled himself out from under the cast-iron pipes. "Aye, miss, o'course. What is it ya need?" He rose quickly and dusted off his trousers, trying to make himself presentable enough to speak with Lillian, who'd appeared unexpectedly behind him. She was clearly from a higher place in society than he, her store-bought dress fashionable, her words articulate. Yet she seemed just as anxious as he felt, wringing her hands and shifting in the doorway. He wondered why, relieved that it didn't appear she'd come to scold him for returning unannounced.

"Again, I'm so sorry to bother you, Ben. Um, it's about the boys, Vaughan and Michael. I wondered, did you happen to meet the couple who adopted them?"

"I saw 'em, yeah. But I didn't speak with 'em." *What do ya know 'bout Mickey an' Vaughan? What's happened to 'em?* Unconsciously he ran a hand through his hair, realizing as he did that it was no longer combed down neatly. He feared it was standing on end, giving him a rather wild appearance.

"I see." Lillian looked away, biting her lip. And then, "Ben, may I confide in you? I don't want to trespass on your good standing here in any way, but I'm afraid I find myself at odds with decisions that have been made regarding the Szwedas. And I'm looking for . . . well, for support in my objections."

What on earth's she askin' me fer? What could I e'er do fer someone like her? Swallowing hard, he answered humbly, "Aye, miss."

Lillian searched his face for a moment, a pained expression in her eyes. "Oh, Ben, I'm afraid there's been a terrible action taken. I fear that this couple will not treat the boys as sons, the way they should be treated. I'm afraid they're seen as little more than farmhands."

So that's it. She's worried fer Mickey an' Vaughan, fer their welfare. "I had the same feelin', miss."

"You did? Oh, that's a relief. I'm just afraid I don't know what to do about it."

Ben stepped forward away from the hiss of the pipes, motioned with an open hand for her to exit the room before him. He followed her out into the empty dining area. "Would ya like ta take a seat, miss?"

Her hands went up to her temples, pressing against them. "I don't think I could, Ben. I'm too upset."

"Let me pour ya a cuppa, miss."

Lillian followed meekly into the kitchen, accepting the coffee he placed in her hands.

"I'm tryin' ta figure how ta help ya. I haven't worked long fer 'em. But, Miss Davis, she's goin' home in the mornin'. Might speak ta her tonight, then, if ya can."

"I don't think she objects to this placement. After all, she was the one who arranged it." Lillian took a sip of the hot liquid. "But I'm not certain she realizes what kind of people the Szwedas are."

As they walked back out to the dining room, Ben noticed a stain of grease on the side of his hand. He attempted to wipe it discreetly on a rag from his pocket. "I'm fair certain what it is she'd wanna know. Will they feed 'em? Will they keep 'em healthy? Then, it's a decent enough home. Better 'an they had b'fore."

"Oh dear, that's not enough. That's not nearly enough."

"Please, miss. Won't ya sit?"

Lillian slid down onto the offered chair as if defeated.

Stuffing the rag back into his deep pocket, Ben took a seat across the table from her. "Where's yer sister? Miss Grace, is't?"

"I'm not sure. She was arguing . . . speaking with Sid Brown again the last time I saw her. She was also quite upset."

"I'm sorry." Frowning, he tried to work through the difficulties she'd presented. "If Mr. Sinclair an' Mr. Brown don't say it's wrong, an' Miss Davis don't say it's wrong, then I'm not sure where ya might appeal ta fer help."

"I can't think of anyone else either."

Ben hoped she wouldn't begin to cry. He struggled to spark an inkling of hope. "D'ya know anyone else from that society? Surely there's someone else ya met."

"No. There's a board of directors for Brayton House who made all the arrangements with them. But the children themselves were never truly our responsibility. We were just a temporary host—a gathering point for the Mercy Society children and the families they'd assigned."

"Oh, I see." He thought for a moment. "What kinda checkin' up on 'em do they have? Fer the kiddos?"

"Quinley does that. Mr. Sinclair. He visits the homes. It's supposed to happen every year. By contract, the children are supposed to be provided with adequate food and clothing and appropriate lodging. They're supposed to receive a suitable education—though that's difficult in many areas of our province. Some rural areas don't even have a school yet."

"An' who visits ta check the houses b'fore they give 'em kids?"

"Well, *Quinley* is supposed to do that too. It's all on him. And I don't think it was done much at all before he came. I know he's very busy with it all. I've been told that it's almost an impossible task, and more children are placed each year."

"Huh." Ben mulled it over again, scratching behind one ear. "If only ya had a solicitor, miss. Someone ta appeal ta the law fer ya."

Lillian's eyes widened. "We do. We have legal counsel who works for us already—and he's in the East just now researching a case for us."

"Could ya telephone him?"

"Yes! Yes, we can. We could place a call to Mr. Dorn. It's possible that he could find someone out East to speak with about the boys while he's still there. I wouldn't have thought of that. Thank you, Ben. I'm so glad I was able to get your advice." She rose quickly. "I need to find Grace. We should call him right away."

Ben smiled in relief. "Glad I could help in any way." He watched her hesitate. Her hand began to reach out toward the table. "I'll take yer cup back, miss. Go find yer sister."

"Oh, thank you for all your help, Ben."

Chapter 18

Frantic

Lillian found Grace in the children's dressing room, laying out clothing and possessions that belonged to Matty and Milton, Jane and Freddie, packing all of it into their cases. While the twins stayed at Brayton House, it had been agreed that it was easiest to include them in the normal functions of the house. Jane and Freddie, too, had unpacked as if they intended to remain. All of their clothing had been stored alongside the other children's in the upper-floor dressing room filled with little shelves and hooks. None of the children was allowed to have possessions that weren't supervised by the dorm mother, old Mrs. Rickard, who sat reading in the hallway between the bedrooms during the night.

At first glance Grace seemed calm. She moved through the small room purposefully. However, as Lillian moved closer, she could see that there were tears streaming down Grace's face.

Without comment, Lillian came closer to offer a hug of empathy.

Grace turned away. "Oh, sis, I'm almost done. I was hoping that we'd be able to go home in the morning."

Softly, "Grace, we don't have a new ride yet. And it's Sunday tomorrow."

"God will provide."

"But we had a ride already—on Monday morning. And you canceled it." Lillian had never seen Grace so frantic, her judgment compromised by raw emotion.

"That was before I spoke again to Sid. I can't stay here. We can't stay here. We need to get the kids home as soon as possible. So I'm packing."

Rather than argue, Lillian stooped down to collect Matty and Milton's good pairs of shoes from their designated spots. She added them to each case, then turned to collect those of Freddie and Jane. "I spoke with Ben."

"You did?"

"He had an idea."

"What was that?"

"He thought legal counsel might help. I wondered if Mr. Dorn would be able to contact the society while he's still in the East in order to make an appeal to their board of directors."

Grace froze in place. Lillian could hear her slow, heavy breathing as she processed the idea. "What do you suppose he could do?"

"Well, he could warn them that the placement is wrong. He could have someone look into it, someone of a higher position. They might find that the Szwedas are unfit as a placement family."

Hands moving once again, Grace muttered, "They'd probably just come to the same decision."

"They might not, Grace. I think it's worth trying."

They finished the packing together without further comment. Lillian wondered what Grace intended to do with the suitcases once they'd been packed. But that seemed inconsequential. Instead, she simply allowed her sister to feel as though she'd accomplished something in the moment.

With four little cases in a row, it seemed that Grace was at last prepared to give her opinion on the matter. "All right, I agree. We should confer with Mr. Dorn. If nothing else, he might be able to advise us. And if we wait any longer he may have already left for home."

Lillian uttered carefully, "Where will we stay, then? If not here?"

"All right. I can see your point, sis."

Lillian stifled a laugh. "So, we'll stay on for a few more days, and try to find some way to change the decision about the boys? Are you sure?"

"Yes. I think I am."

In silence, they began to unpack.

• • • ● • • •

Ben lingered in the basement of the children's home even after he'd completed the repair in the boiler room. He wasn't certain where to go next. If he hoped to spend another night on the floor in the empty classroom, it was important that he wasn't noticed enough to be questioned about his presence. He ate supper with Janie, cleared tables and wiped them down with Freddie. Then he offered to help by carrying hot water into the laundry room next to the kitchen for bath night. The next day was Sunday. It was time to see that everyone was clean and ready for morning church.

Children were escorted down to the dining room in groups. First came the youngest, which now included Janie, Matty, and Milton. One at a time they were sent into the laundry room for their evening bath. As needed, Ben added buckets of steaming water to reheat what remained in the washtub. After scrubbing away the residue of the week, each child then returned to the dining room in a fresh nightshirt, bare feet padding across the linoleum floor. They were allowed to play quietly at a designated table until everyone in their group was finished and it was time to be led back up to the bedrooms to be tucked in for the night.

Freddie came down last with the oldest group. Most of these were considered permanent residents at Brayton House. Ben had been told that, for one reason or another, they'd spent the bulk of their teen years following the strict routines. They were being prepared for a life beyond these walls through school lessons and vocational training. The thought of it troubled Ben's heart, though the residents themselves appeared to take it all in stride, conforming to what was expected of them.

By contrast, Freddie was restless. He sat alone where he could stare out a narrow window, his foot audibly tapping against the leg of his chair. No one else seemed to notice his state. But Ben had come to realize how important it was for the boy to be out in the open, to be free to roam. It was clearly an effort for him to submit to having his movements constricted, to be led along in step with a group of others—even to sit in the classroom for much of his day. Remembering that Freddie had escaped from an upper-floor hotel room, Ben hoped that Mrs. Rickard would be able to stay awake all night on guard. She seemed rather frail for such a task.

"Mr. Waldin? Ben?"

His attention spun toward the young woman who now approached him. "Aye, Miss Grace?"

"I wanted to speak with you privately, if I may."

Ben glanced back at Freddie, who was watching them. "O'course," he answered.

Grace led him into the kitchen, where the used towels were piled in a tub, ready for Monday's washing. "Lillian has told me about your suggestion to seek legal counsel."

"Now, miss, I don't know much 'bout—"

"I understand, Ben. I just wanted to thank you for—not just for your *willingness* to help—but rather for your genuine concern for these children." Her voice sounded quiet and contemplative.

"I've seen so many people who are willing to help. Unfortunately, I've seen fewer who understand what it's like. . . ." Her voice trailed off.

Ben stood in silence, uncertain how to respond. He remembered that Grace's sister had said they'd both been orphaned as children, that Grace had once been a resident here. He pushed his hands into his pockets in an attempt to keep them from scratching at the long, itchy hair against his neck. How must he appear to her?

"I've spoken to Sid about you today, Ben."

"Ya have?"

"Yes. I've explained to him that we're in need of a handyman. In Brookfield, where we live."

Ben's brows dropped low. "Thought that were far from here, miss."

"It's—well, it's not too far, really. Not by automobile."

"I've a job at the train depot. I start Monday morn."

Grace's head tipped to one side. "Oh, I didn't realize you were planning to stay in Lethbridge."

"No," he hurried to explain, "the job ain't fer long. Only whilst others're out sick. But . . ." Should he explain to this woman about his plans to find his family? After all, earnings were what he needed most in order to accomplish that very goal. If he were working for these women in some capacity, surely they'd also allow him room and board, plus a wage.

Grace turned away. Her shoulders were drawn up tightly as she seemed to consider his response.

Unwilling to let the offer pass, Ben brought up his hand to rub at his neck. "I could . . . I could help ya fer a while." His hand dropped quickly again as she turned back to face him.

"That's good. I'm glad. Lillian and I have decided now to stay in town for just a bit. So we're kind of stuck here for the moment." And then she followed with, "What do you need? How can we make this work well for you?"

It was a bewildering question for him.

"I'm afraid we can't pay much. But you'll have a room while we're here—Sid was agreeable to that—and all the food you can eat. You should have time to fulfill your obligations at the job you've lined up for yourself if it doesn't last too long—maybe a week? Then, when we do move back to Brookfield, we'll find a room for you there too. That'll take a little more doing." She frowned as if to herself.

Her plan seemed desperate, like she'd spoken before she'd worked out all the details. He tried to keep his eyes from clouding, but certainly his doubt must be showing on his face. "I don't need much, miss. I do need ta earn some kinda wage."

"Yes, well, Brayton House has agreed to cover your services in either location. Sid is in a rather generous mood at the moment."

Though she was petite, she seemed to Ben a rather formidable woman. "Thank ya, miss. Then I agree."

"That's good. Thank you so much, Ben. I'm very pleased. Now, while we're here, the only room that Sid can offer you is in the building out back. Rolly lives there too. Lillian was going to fetch a key." Grace paused. "Is there anything else you need, Ben? Anything you've been doing without that we might supply?"

At first he fully intended to dismiss the question, but with uncharacteristic honesty he lifted his hand again to rub at his neck. "I could use a haircut. 'Fraid I look a sight."

Grace smiled back warmly. "I think that can be easily accomplished, Ben."

True to her word, she rummaged through a kitchen drawer. "No time like the present, eh?"

Feeling rather numbed with the abruptness of it all, Ben did as he was instructed, using the hot water he'd been hauling to wash his hair. He was thoroughly embarrassed that somehow he'd enlisted such a fine young lady to serve in such a menial role. He hadn't expected Grace to fulfill his request herself, had thought she'd find someone else more suitable. But she appeared to be fired with energy at the moment.

After rubbing his hair mostly dry using a towel that was now draped around his shoulders, he took a seat on a dining room chair as he was directed so that Grace could begin. From across the room, he could see Freddie watching intently, a sneer of amusement on his face. Perhaps these Canadians couldn't see the social mismatch of this unassuming event, but Ben knew Freddie understood it all too well.

Just then Lillian returned to the dining room. She seemed startled at first, approaching with a hand over her mouth that half concealed a look of amusement.

A girl named Ruth called out, "Miss Lillian, can you believe it? Mister Waldin's letting Miss Grace cut his hair!"

Grace's confident words greeted her sister. "You see? I don't just cut hair for children. I told you I could be trusted."

Stilted snickers all around them. Grace seemed unaffected.

"Mr. Waldin has no idea what he's agreed to," said Lillian with a smirk. "I'll withhold my compliments until I've seen the finished product."

A tingle of nerves prickled down Ben's neck. *What've I got meself inta?*

Sable brown curls began to drop onto his shoulders and lap. Whatever she was doing, it felt she was removing far more than he'd expected. Too ashamed to object, Ben held his tongue, watching the wide eyes all around him. Then Grace began combing his hair straight up as she cut directly above his head. Did she expect him to wear it in such a way? Was that how she planned he'd style it? Or did she plan to cut it all off?

By the time the scissors slowed to making smaller snips around the edges, Lillian was back from the laundry with a hand mirror. She held it out now so that Ben could see the finished product. For a moment he closed his eyes tightly, then braved a peek.

All around the sides of his head she'd cut the hair close to his scalp. It was neat and clean, even fashionable. Then toward the top she'd blended his hair into longer strands so that tidy, damp coils dropped onto his forehead lightly. He was surprised to feel immense relief.

When he pushed the mirror farther away, his own reflection shocked him. The sailor was almost gone. He appeared far more genteel now. The transformation felt strange and extraordinary.

Ruth blurted, "You look real nice, Mister Waldin."

"Yeah," agreed a nearby boy with a laugh.

He cleared his throat, aware of all the eyes still upon him. His own voice sounded tight and unfamiliar. "Miss Grace has done a fine, fine job. Thank ya, miss. That's jus' the ticket."

Her eyes were soft. She seemed pleased with her own efforts. "You're very welcome, Ben."

"And this is your key," Lillian added. "For your room out back. I'm glad you've agreed to stay with us for now at least."

Soon the children were escorted upstairs and Ben had made his way out into the cold night, crossing the backyard to the old carriage house that stood behind it. A set of stairs perched against the exterior wall rose to a single door above. He climbed them and tried his key in the lock. It opened smoothly.

Inside was a small sitting room with a potbellied stove sending out fingers of warmth from a coal fire, a table with two wooden chairs, and an old sofa. There were two doors leading beyond. Opening the nearest one, Ben found a bedroom clearly already occupied. The bed was unmade, Rolly's possessions were spread across the dresser, and his spare clothing hung on hooks against the wall.

Ben closed the door and tried the second room. Though the bed was neatly made, the rest of the room appeared empty. He dropped his kit bag onto the floor, then removed his coat and hung it on a hook. Turning in a circle, he wondered when he'd last had a bedroom all to himself.

This woulda been me first voyage with me own berth, 'ceptin' fer Janie's needs. He chuckled. *Well, the world has paid me back. Guess it's me turn at last.*

Easing himself down onto the comfortable feather mattress, the soft pillow cradling his head, Ben closed his eyes in wonder. *Such an unferseen change'a fortune, this! Who woulda thought it?*

For a moment he pictured himself simply falling asleep where he lay. But habit brought him back to his feet. He unpacked his kit, hung his spare set of clothing where it could air out on the hooks, placed his toiletries on the dresser in a straight row, and, on a last impulse, set his two precious books upright against the vanity mirror. Then he dressed for bed.

Just before retiring, a glint coming in through the bedroom window caught his eye, caused him to stop and gaze out into the night. His room faced back out toward the great house. Ben was quite certain that he could see the pale light of an oil lamp shining from a second-story window. *Must be Missus Rickard, readin' whilst she watches the kiddos as they sleep.* He thought of Freddie and hoped the boy would remain where he'd been assigned. There was little Ben could do to guard him from here. He turned away and drew back the covers, anticipating a sound and glorious sleep.

• • • • • • •

Lillian's nerves were on fire. The idea that she and Grace were stirring a controversy that might well end their good relations with Brayton House had increasingly filled her with panic. But the telephone call had already been placed. She and Grace were waiting now in the spare office for the operator to inform them that their party was on the line.

At last, "Good morning. Grand Hotel. How may I help you?"

Grace's voice sounded far more composed than Lillian felt she herself could have managed. "I'd like to speak with a guest. His name is William Dorn of Mayberry, Parks, and Dorn. Could you contact him, please?"

"Who may I say is calling?"

"Miss Grace Bennett and Miss Lillian Walsh. Thank you."

"Hold, please."

Lillian's eyes darted to the door of the room. *What if someone comes in? What if we're discovered? We didn't ask for permission to use this office or make this call.*

It was a painfully long wait. At last Grace snapped to attention. "Mr. Dorn? Thank you for taking my call, sir. This is Grace Bennett, calling from Lethbridge."

She tipped the round receiver piece out a little from her ear so that Lillian could lean in close enough to hear too as they huddled together. She positioned the shaft that held the mouthpiece for the candlestick telephone in front of them both. But the sound crackled badly, distorting and fragmenting Mr. Dorn's reply. "I'm pleased to hear . . . you, Grace. You've caught . . . finishing a late Sunday brunch at . . . hotel."

"Oh, I'm sorry to interrupt, sir. I thought that perhaps you were more likely to be at the hotel on a Sunday than any other day."

"I'm sure that's . . . What can . . . do for you, Miss Bennett?"

Grace adjusted the way her fingers wrapped around the small receiver. "If you don't mind, sir, Lillian and I would like to ask if you could give us some advice." As succinctly as possible, Grace laid out their difficulties. Often she was stopped short, needing to repeat words so that Mr. Dorn could understand her over the poor telephone connection.

Finally he answered, "I see. Well, there's . . . one tack you could . . . challenge their decision. It would be to prove . . . these people are unfit. When I return, I'd . . . willing to look . . . contract for you—to see . . . are any justifiable . . . to remove the boys . . . the home."

"Is there nothing that could be filed now? A temporary order or something?"

"I'm afraid . . . Miss Bennett. The law . . . prescribed solutions and . . . you have evidence . . . abuse or neglect . . . don't suppose it's likely . . . the outcome you'd hoped. I will, however . . . to contact the Viney . . . Society . . . your behalf."

"I see. Well, thank you for being willing to address this with them. Please don't forget to tell them that Lillian observed the man take a swing at one of the boys on the very first day they were placed. And please let us know if you need more information. I wish there were something further that could be done."

"I shall attempt . . . the society tomorrow . . . and will telephone you . . . Tuesday morning before . . . train for home."

"We would appreciate that, sir. So much."

Lillian's hands rose up to her chin palm-to-palm as if she were praying; her fingers then bent and intertwined, locked tightly with the stress she felt. *Nothing? There's nothing else that can be done?*

"Miss Bennett? While I've . . . on the telephone. May I speak with . . . regarding the inheritance?"

"Our case?"

"Yes."

"Of course, Mr. Dorn. What is it?"

". . . met with Mr. Braz . . . yesterday . . . unexpected answers . . . inquiries regarding . . . period when your parents . . . possible that he . . . of your existence and situation."

"I'm sorry, Mr. Dorn. It's such a poor connection. I'm afraid I don't understand what you said."

". . . already sent you . . . by post. It should . . . next day or two."

"You've sent a letter to explain?"

"Yes, Miss Bennett and . . . If you'd like . . . a telephone call . . . Brazington, we could . . . before I depart on . . . my office so we can . . . if you like."

"Can you repeat that, please? I didn't understand."

His words came more slowly. "Yes, if . . . speak to Mr. Braz . . . arrange a call before . . . depart on Friday, please contact . . . arrange it . . ."

"Yes, I have that telephone number. I'll try to contact you at your office when we receive your letter."

"That's fine. . . . Good day, Miss . . . look forward . . . soon."

"Good-bye, Mr. Dorn. And thank you."

Grace dropped the handset back onto its cradle. "Did you get any of that?"

Lillian's head was swimming with the effort. "I think he said something about Saul Brazington—that he might have known something about our parents—that we can arrange a call with him if we'd like."

"That's what I think I heard too." Grace moved away from the desk, abandoning the upright telephone where it stood silently now. "He said we should expect a letter in a day or two." She let out a slow breath. "What on earth do you think the letter contains, Lillian?"

"I have no idea."

Chapter 19

Inducements

Ben returned to his private room after a hearty Sunday dinner. It had been the path of least resistance for him just to follow along after Rolly during the morning and attend church services with the others. He doubted that anyone else had paused to consider any other option for him. Yet, fearing the gaze of the crucified Jesus after so many years had lapsed, he was surprised that this building had replaced the crucifixes with empty wooden crosses instead.

He'd wondered as he entered, *What would me mum say? Is it worse ta just not go or worse ta go where it's diff'rent?* He wasn't certain what instruction she'd have offered.

As the line of children and adults from Brayton House had streamed up the main aisle of the sanctuary moments before the service was to begin, Ben had dropped out from among them and slipped onto a pew at the very back, hoping that his movements would go unnoticed. To his surprise, Freddie had appeared next to him, grinning broadly as he settled himself on the pew.

Ben had frowned back at the boy. However, how could he tell Freddie to follow the others to a proper place if he wasn't willing to proceed so far himself? He looked away from the smirking teen. Instead, his eyes scanned the room for more insights about the unfamiliar building.

Once the service had begun, Ben watched with concern. It was quite different. Far less structured—even notably less eloquent. And yet, also perhaps it felt more real, more aligned with ordinary people. *Well, that's me, then. Ord'nary ta the marrow.*

Long after they'd returned to Brayton House, had eaten their Sunday dinner together and all of the children were sent to a rest period in the two large rooms, Ben mulled over the event. He wasn't certain if he'd appreciated their rituals at all. In his heart, he didn't truly feel as if he'd been to church. It had seemed more of a gathering, albeit one that was centered around the Christ.

There was no work on Sunday at Brayton House. Most of the other adults disappeared to parts unknown. It seemed to Ben the perfect time to hide away as well, to read the next play in his tome of Shakespeare's works. With a belly full of roast chicken, a bedroom all to himself for privacy, and ample time on his hands, the decision to retreat had been clear.

Just as he was settling in, there came a persistent knock on the outside door. He preferred to ignore it. But at last, he rose from his bed to answer. It was Freddie who'd broken into Ben's attempt at solitude.

"Yer s'posed ta be sleepin', lad."

"Yeah. So?"

Ben didn't bother asking the obvious questions that didn't matter. "Ya could be anywhere. Why're ya here?"

Freddie sauntered past him into the small sitting room as if he'd been invited. "Weren't gonna sleep, then, were I? I ain't no baby."

Ben closed the door again. "If yer here, yer gonna be quiet. I'm readin'."

"Got a book fer me?"

Ben raised an eyebrow.

"What? Ya think I can't read?" Clear blue eyes remained fixed on Ben, daring him to begin an argument. Finding no spark, Freddie merely laughed and made his way around the room. One of Freddie's hands reached out toward the warmth of the blackened stove, his fingers wiggling in the air as if measuring the heat.

Ben answered at last, "I think ya *don't* read. That much I can claim ta see."

Freddie snorted scornfully. "Yer right, then. I'm not stayin'. I'm goin' ta the woods. There's a creek where I sit an' think."

Ben circled around, keeping a few steps away. "What d'ya think 'bout?"

"'Bout life . . . me own life. That's right ta do, in'it?"

"O'course. Yer of an age when ya should figure what ya want next."

Pulling a kitchen chair along behind him, Freddie walked to the sofa and sat down. He leaned back, raising his arms and interlocking his fingers behind his head. Boldly, he set one booted foot onto the chair, then crossed over it with the other. Once he was completely settled, he lifted his gaze toward Ben. "Yeah, a man should think 'bout things—like jobs, an' haircuts, an' where he stays." Amusement danced in Freddie's eyes.

"Thought ya was goin' ta the woods. What's stoppin' ya, then? Go on." Ben reached for the doorknob.

"No, no, no. I got a question fer ya, Mister Waldin." The boy's arms dropped. He laced his fingers over his stomach instead. A look almost like sincerity shadowed his eyes.

"Yeah?"

"Ya goin' ta the farm place or not?"

"Why?"

"If ya go, then I might too. That's all."

"What's it matter?"

Freddie removed his feet from the chair and pushed it away. He sat forward on the sofa, chewed his lip for a moment. "I almost trust ya," he confessed candidly, as if he were endowing a favor. "I might wanna work fer ya, if it comes ta that."

Ben held his breath, grappling for a proper answer among the complications tumbling over one another in his mind. "I don't know what me future holds, Freddie. But were ya in it"—he nodded slowly for emphasis—"I'd be chuffed ta have ya."

The boy stood. "All right. I'll come."

"Where?"

"Ta that farm place. I was gonna leave, gonna go off on me own—ya know, like ya did when you was fourteen—but I'll come with ya, then." With a last grin, but no further comment, he exited, closing the door quietly behind him.

Ben stood in shock. He hadn't intended to make any commitment to the boy.

• • • • • • •

Lillian paced across the bedroom at Mrs. O'Shea's. Grace was stitching in the parlor and chatting with their hostess, but Lillian had claimed to prefer a rest during the Sunday afternoon instead. However, *rest* was not something she was able to accomplish at the moment. Her mind was too stirred up by its own controversies.

It's hard, so hard to think of working now to save Michael and Vaughan from a desperate situation and yet to still repent of doing the same with Milton and Matty not long ago. What is it God wants from us? How can I obey Him? I know—I know. It was our lie that crossed the line. Still, in the end, is it just inevitable that the Szwedas will receive children? Is this the way God works? If He saves one person, does that mean someone else falls prey to the same calamity? How is that better? Have we effectively caused harm to come to these two new boys by rescuing the twins?

She was well aware of the unbridled feelings that were driving her muddied thoughts. And yet Lillian seemed powerless to control or correct her racing emotions.

Work. I need to work. That's the only thing that can quiet my anxious heart.

But it was Sunday, and no work was allowed. On impulse, she reached for her open suitcase and dumped its contents across the bedspread. Slowing down, she shook out and folded each item neatly, arranging them back in the case with exaggerated care. After a few moments she began to feel the desired effect. But there were simply not enough clothes to fold.

She caught hold of Grace's suitcase, not giving a second thought to what might be considered a breach of privacy, folding and sorting and placing each piece of Grace's apparel with care. Then her eyes fell on the letters.

Tucked between layers of Grace's handkerchiefs was a small collection of letters. Lillian averted her face as she lifted the paper bundle gently and hid it back within the stack of hankies that she'd already folded and placed in the case.

For a moment she stood and contemplated the discovery. The letters were obviously from Walter. Lillian recognized his heavy lettering. With effort, she moved a step away, reached for the last two lace squares that needed her attention, and set them aside on the corner of the bed, not even daring to come near the case while the temptation was so strong in her heart. When all of the items of apparel had been faithfully returned, Lillian lifted the neglected hankies and returned them with great care. She shut the top of the suitcase firmly and stepped away.

If I read them, Grace will never know. With great effort, Lillian bent over the bed to slide her hands back and forth across the bedspread, straightening the quilt just how Mrs. O'Shea liked it. She fluffed the pillows and set them back in place too. Still, it was difficult to keep her eyes from constantly returning to Grace's suitcase.

Spying her Bible, Lillian lifted it instead, sinking down onto the rocking chair. *I'll read. That's what I need right now.*

And yet her mind refused to focus on the words. With a sigh,

Lillian rose and crossed the room. She paused for a moment of soul-searching. Then, slowly, she reached out a hand and grasped the doorknob. Bible in hand, she strode out to the parlor and sat down on the sofa next to Mrs. O'Shea. But she avoided Grace's eyes, fearful that her sister would somehow be able to read her guilty conscience from across the room.

• • • • • • •

The sound of a train whistle split the air. Following it almost immediately came an earthquake that shook the ground, then a rush of steam spraying across the platform. Four men rose to their feet in unison. Ben stood among them, ready to unload the boxcars from the train that was just arriving. They'd been given an hour. It seemed an impossible assignment.

Though the winter air was far below freezing, Ben was soon drenched in sweat beneath his heavy wool sweater. Cartload after cartload rolled down the ramp and into the adjoining warehouse. Though he'd cast aside his overcoat, he ignored the cold. He was moving too quickly to feel it. Only his fingertips and ears burned in the frigid temperatures.

Without a pause, they switched to loading instead. Now each loaded cart had to be forced up the ramp with greater effort. His lungs began to tingle, and breathing took more effort.

Once the pace slowed, Ben reached quickly for his coat again. He knew too well, from his years at sea, the danger of allowing his body to cool in such a state.

"Good work," the foreman said. It was the only encouragement he'd received. But it was enough.

Now the task of sorting began. Every item must be arranged so that delivery trucks could complete the journey without fail. Most items would be received by the stores. Some of the crates were destined for homes in the area. Last of all, Ben hefted the heavy sacks of mail and piled them in one place.

He was shocked to hear another whistle. It was already time to begin again.

When Ben was dismissed on Monday afternoon, he was worn out. Climbing the stairs that clung to the side of the carriage house seemed an insurmountable task. He collapsed across the sofa, promising himself that he wouldn't sleep—would just rest a few moments before changing clothes and fixing himself some supper.

It was dark when he opened his eyes. A firm knock at the door had awakened him. Every muscle ached as he rose to answer. "Who's there?"

"It's Sid. Can I come in?"

Ben unlocked the door and stood aside so that the man could enter.

"I know it's late. I was hoping you wouldn't already be in bed. But I wondered if you might help us, Ben. We have a delivery that needs to go out tonight. I think I mentioned that we don't have a driver right now. Do you think you could get this letter to an office across town? Quin needs to have it signed and back out in the morning post."

"O'course. I can do it." Ben's head was only just beginning to clear from his unexpected awakening.

"Great. Thanks. The car is parked below in the carriage house. I drew a map for you on this paper, guiding you to the office where you'll find Quin, and here's the envelope you'll need to give him. Do you have any questions?"

"No, it's fine. I'll change me clothes 'fore I go."

Sid closed the door. Ben could hear his footsteps descending. It was only then that he realized what he'd just agreed to do. *I ne'er drove no car. How'm I ta do it?*

While changing his clothes, he made a plan. Once out in the cold again, he went first to the back of the house with a lantern in one hand. Using the other, he picked up a pebble from the ground and flung it with precision at a certain window on the second floor. Then he repeated the task. After a third attempt, a ghostly face appeared in the darkness.

It was Freddie. Ben raked the air with large arm movements to indicate that the boy should come down. He'd never asked how it was that Freddie had been escaping the bedroom, but he was convinced it could be done again despite the presence of Mrs. Rickard.

After a few moments of waiting, a familiar form rounded the corner. It was too dark to see Freddie's eyes, but the flashing smile was easy to recognize.

"Mister Waldin? Why'd ya call me? It's bally late!" But far from being perturbed, clearly Freddie was pleased to have been summoned.

"I gotta drive the car. Need yer help."

The flicker of the lamp glowed in the boy's eyes. "Then here I am."

Together they pulled open the large carriage house doors and entered. Ben hung the lantern on a hook and climbed into the automobile. "Ya have ta crank her up. I'll give her gas. I seen it done, but ne'er from the driver's seat."

The boy laughed. "Well, good luck ta us, eh!" He unfolded the crank and began to turn it, slowly at first and then faster as he became comfortable with the motion. After a few moments the car sputtered and stopped.

"Try her again!"

Freddie spit into his hands and resumed. This time the car fired into ignition, trembling in place like a bulldog at the end of its chain.

"Get in!"

Ben had a great deal of experience with engines. He knew the mechanics of how they were started. Unfortunately, he knew little about what to do next with an automobile.

Freddie was on his knees now on the bench seat next to Ben, leaning forward eagerly and pointing toward Ben's feet. Over the sound of the engine he shouted, "D'ya got yer foot on the clutch? Ya gotta keep it down."

"Yeah! That pedal there? I got that."

"Now ya have ta give 'er gas, all while ya let the clutch out—but slow! Real slow."

The automobile jerked severely and shuddered to a stop. Freddie laughed. "I said slow. Ya gotta do both at the same time, but slower."

They started over, this time edging forward from the carriage house with only minor jolts. Anxious not to let the car stall, Ben careened around the first corner. Freddie howled into the night with glee. Soon Ben had better control. He pressed the map into the boy's hands and ordered him to direct them. Ben was grateful it was late and there were no other cars on the roads. However, the dim headlamps made the journey far more difficult, and he found himself frequently retracing his path, each time getting a better feel for how to slow and regain speed.

If he hadn't been so focused on making the vehicle perform properly, Ben was sure he'd have enjoyed the drive just as much as Freddie so obviously did. Soon they arrived at the office building and Ben instructed the boy to remain where he was. At the last moment he changed his mind and motioned Freddie to follow. *No sense leavin' the fox ta guard the henhouse!*

Finding the correctly numbered door, Ben knocked.

Faintly, "Come in."

He opened the door slowly. The waiting area was empty and dark. A light shone from beyond. Freddie followed close on Ben's heels.

"Mr. Sinclair?"

"I'm here."

They approached shyly along the short hallway. Ben held out the large envelope. "Sid said ta bring it t'ya."

Without rising, Quinley muttered, "You're late. I thought you'd be here an hour ago."

"We come pretty fast," Ben stated quietly. After his words came the sound of Freddie's snicker. Ben poked an elbow behind him without turning toward the boy.

"It required both of you to come?" With an impatient flick of his fingers, Quinley motioned for the envelope to be passed forward.

Ben reached far across the desk in order to place it in the man's grasp. "Needed help ta crank her up."

No reply. The seated man was already reading through the document he'd slipped out of the envelope. Ben dared not look back at Freddie. Mr. Sinclair was no one to trifle with. He hoped the boy would have the good sense to behave now.

After a few awkward moments, Quinley picked up his pen and signed at the bottom of the page. He blotted the signature dry and slipped the page back into the envelope. At last he stood and moved out from behind the desk.

There was a strange look on his face, amusement mixed with guile. "I wonder, Ben . . . did Miss Grace approve of the boy helping you?"

Ben's eyes widened. "No, sir. She don't know."

"Sid Brown?"

"No, sir." Quickly Ben tried to think of an acceptable excuse, but nothing came to mind.

Quinley shook his head. "Well, don't worry. I won't tell. I think driving's a good skill for a boy like him to learn. Might come in handy soon when he needs employment. He may be out on his own before we all anticipated—since we can't seem to place him."

"Thank ya, sir." Ben was already backing out of the room, nudging Freddie along behind him, hoping the boy would refrain from speaking.

"Not a bad skill for you either, Waldin. At any rate, it's one step up from *warehouseman*." The door closed.

They were back out in the hallway before either spoke. "Let's go," Ben urged.

He'd hoped Freddie wouldn't comment, but the boy muttered, "Weren't like we was killin' the canary or nothin'. We was helpin' Sid an' him. Guess he don't think us fit fer more 'an servin' the upper crust."

"Don't matter." Pushing the boy along, Ben moved them back out into the night. Then suddenly he found the unnecessary offense to be more than he could tolerate too. He grabbed hold of Freddie's jacket sleeve and drew him back so they could look each other square in the eye. "Don't matter, lad . . . so long's *we know* what we're worth. Ya hear me? So long's ya always 'member it's we, the workin' men, what keep it all runnin', eh? The rich can strut an' flaunt all they want, but ya can always know, they'd come ta nothin' without us. All the grandness ya see 'round ya rests on the shoulders'a the workers what built it."

CHAPTER 20

The Letter

The telephone call from Mr. Dorn on Tuesday had revealed no encouraging news. The society claimed to have an extensive file on the Szwedas. They appeared unlikely to revisit the placement. It was a discouraging result. So there was nothing left to do but begin plans for heading home. However, few hired drivers headed out toward the mountains midweek. It seemed likely that the first available taxicab would be arranged for Friday.

Grace and Lillian turned their attention to the expected letter instead. Grace had gone to the post office early on Monday and written an order so that their mail would be forwarded to Brayton House until further notice. Brookfield's post office was served from Lethbridge via a delivery man in a truck. All of the town's mail originating in the East came first to this much larger station.

They were pleased when Sid was able to deliver the letter to Grace just before supper was served on Tuesday evening. From the doorway to the kitchen, Lillian could tell by the expression on her sister's face what the envelope contained even though they stood across the dining room from one another. She hurried to join her sister.

"Let's go," Grace urged. "I think we can read this in the hallway. The children will be fine."

"I just want to fix plates for the littles," Lillian answered. "I'll get them settled and join you in a minute."

Lillian slipped behind the counter where the older children were waiting in line to receive their dinner. She hurried to dish up a bowl of stewed chicken for the three young children in their charge and balanced a slice of buttered bread across each. Then she carried the bowls to the table where Matty, Milton, and Janie waited together.

She called across the room to summon help. "Freddie, Miss Grace and I will be gone for just a moment. Will you please see that the younger children have what they need?"

"Yes, miss."

"Thank you, Freddie. I appreciate your help." Speaking to the three sets of upturned eyes in front of her, she added more quietly, "Now, you need to stay here until Freddie has his food and comes to sit with you. Miss Grace and I will be back shortly."

Out in the hallway, Grace was seated on the lowest stairstep. She looked up with wide eyes as Lillian approached. "You won't believe it, sis."

"What? What is it?"

"There's a bank check."

Lillian dropped down onto the step beside her sister. "What do you mean?"

"It's the inheritance. There's a check written out to the two of us." She held it out to Lillian. "It's more than we'd expected. Much more."

Almost too frightened now to look at the amount, Lillian received the offered paper from Grace. Neatly printed across it was *Twenty-five thousand dollars*. She read it again, unable to comprehend exactly what it meant.

"I can't believe it," Grace gushed. "How could they have had so much? Mama and Papa? They were just farmers, weren't they? And didn't the papers originally say it would be around two thousand?"

Lillian shook her head in an attempt to clear her confusion. "Papa was a tradesman. I don't know much more than that. But he was the one who built our house in Brookfield. So they had to have been somewhat well off."

Grace's voice came again, this time choked up with unshed tears. "We won't have to worry about money now. God provided everything we need—and more."

Still, Lillian found it difficult to convince herself the check was real. "What does the letter say? How does Mr. Dorn explain it?"

"Here. You look. I can't see well enough to read."

Lillian took the pages, skimmed through them. "The first sheet is just a letter of explanation from Mr. Dorn. After that it looks like some kind of settlement document. It's from a solicitor's office. We should probably show that to Mr. Wattley before we sign anything. Father would insist upon his own solicitor taking a look."

"We'll cash the check though."

Shaking her head, Lillian warned, "If Father taught me anything, it's not to act rashly where money is concerned."

"But, Lillian, just think what we could *do* with it! We could buy our own automobile. Imagine! We wouldn't have to depend on others to get around. We could even get something large so we'd all fit in it well."

Grace, your imagination is running away with you. "Stop, please. We won't know anything until we've read through the document. For all we know, there's a downside to cashing this check. We just have to slow down and be careful."

There was an audible grumble. "I suppose. But, sis, you're taking all the fun out of it."

Lillian's eyes shot up to meet Grace's gaze. There was just a hint of good humor showing itself at the corners of Grace's mouth. It was a strange expression, pouting in the center and yet breaking slowly into a rather pained smile.

Lillian laughed aloud, rolling her eyes. "Yes, I'm the wet blanket. I know it. You can be happy if you wish, I suppose. After all, if it's true, then it really is wonderful."

"You see! We can be excited. It's not a crime to be pleased to receive a small fortune in the mail." Grace leaned hard against Lillian's shoulder, pushing her off balance. "It's loads more than I ever made at Murray's diner."

"I'm glad you're happy, Grace. Of course you can be grateful for this. But let's save the letter to read later. I want to go through it carefully after supper."

Grace rose, offering an outstretched hand to pull Lillian up after her.

"Just don't tell anyone," insisted Lillian. "Until the cash is received by the bank, don't tell anyone. Not Sid. Not Quinley. Not the kids. Nobody."

"All right. I agree." As they walked back toward the dining room, Lillian heard Grace mutter under her breath, "But you *are* kind of a wet blanket."

• • • • • • •

Twisting the knob on the oil lamp so that the flame pushed the darkness farther away into the corners of the room, Lillian drew her chair closer to the sofa in the Brayton House parlor, where Grace was seated, her feet tucked up under her.

"Okay, let's see what Mr. Dorn says in the letter."

"You read aloud, Lillian. I'll listen."

"All right. Let's see."

There was a short introduction before, with his familiar efficiency, Mr. Dorn got to the point.

"Regarding the estate of George and Suzanne Bennett, formerly of Enchant, Alberta, through investigation as outlined below, the sole beneficiaries shall be as follows: Miss Lillian (Bennett) Walsh, residing in Brookfield, Alberta, and Miss Grace Bennett, also of Brookfield, Alberta. It has been determined by the law offices of Mayberry, Parks, and Dorn of Calgary, Alberta, that there are no other legal claims against this estate."

More legal explanation followed, until

"Regarding additional relatives, there was found to be one living uncle related by marriage only: namely, Mr. Saul Brazington-Bennett of Toronto, Ontario. The following signed document shall be considered the legal relinquishment of any claim upon the estate of the deceased, George and Suzanne Bennett, by Mr. Saul Brazington-Bennett, including all assets, property, investments, or royalties belonging to said estate. Furthermore, in exchange for remuneration such that the total inheritance of said estate shall be set at the amount of twenty-five thousand dollars, there shall be a reciprocated legal agreement that no claim shall be made by either or both of the sisters, Miss Lillian (Bennett) Walsh and Miss Grace Bennett, in regard to any assets, property, investments, or royalties belonging to the estate of Mr. Saul Brazington-Bennett, whether such assets were bequeathed to him through the estate and effects of his late father, Mr. Jasper Brazington, formerly of Toronto, Ontario; or through the estate and effects of his late mother, Mrs. Serena Brazington-Bennett, formerly of Toronto, Ontario; or through the estate and effects of his late adoptive father, Mr. Oliver Bennett, of Toronto, Ontario."

Lillian struggled to make sense of the stream of words and names. She had deciphered that Uncle Saul would not claim any of Mama and Papa's inheritance but also that, similarly, she and Grace would not be allowed to make a claim on their grandparents' estates. She'd heard enough already from Quinley to know that these were far wealthier folk than her parents had been.

She paused. "Did you understand that, Grace?"

"I'm not sure."

Lillian lowered the document and simplified the words as best she could. "We get nothing from any relatives back East."

"Well, that's not exactly true, is it? What was that part in the middle—about the twenty-five thousand dollars?"

Lillian read through the long paragraph again. "You're right. It seems that Uncle Saul has increased the inheritance we got from our parents from what it would have been to a much larger amount." Her eyes lifted to Grace, brows drawn tightly in concern. "Why would he do that?"

"I don't think I care about that. Should I?"

Lillian looked back down at the page. She hesitated. "Do you think we should have expected something? I'd never given it a thought before. It seems—I don't know, maybe underhanded, somehow."

"If the money belonged to Saul's mother—not to our grandpapa—then I don't see why any of it matters."

"But this document also includes Oliver Bennett. And he was Papa's own father. Surely his own estate amounted to something—and wouldn't our papa have a stake in that?"

"That's true."

Grace lowered her feet to the floor. Her toes inside her wool stockings wiggled above the carpet for a moment as she seemed to contemplate the issue. "Well, Mr. Dorn would have warned us if there'd been a reason for us to stake a claim. I'm sure we can trust him to represent our interests."

"I suppose that's true too."

"Keep reading, sis. Maybe it gives some sort of reason."

Lillian struggled through the remainder of the page, trying

hard to concentrate on what the legal phrases and run-on sentences conveyed. Some of it escaped her in the ponderous specifics. "I still want to take it to Mr. Wattley. We should leave as soon as we can now. Mr. Dorn can't help. We've exhausted our efforts here. I want to have Father's solicitor explain the letter to us so that we know what we're signing."

"I agree. But how do we go home without a car? And we can't buy one if you don't want to cash the check."

"Oh, Grace, we don't *need to* buy a car." Lillian tried to keep the frustration she felt about the difficult document from venting toward her sister, but she could feel her muscles tightening all up and down her neck. She drew a long breath and slowed her words, rising from her chair and pushing it back into its proper position in the parlor. "We didn't even consider such a thing yesterday. We'll just use some of Father's money to hire a driver to take us home. It shouldn't cost too much."

"But we have Ben to drive us. He agreed to come back to Brookfield with us too."

"Fine, then. All we need is a borrowed car." Lillian shuffled the papers once more, planning to push them back into the envelope. For the first time she noticed a handwritten paragraph included on the back of the first page. It was signed by Mr. Dorn. "What's this?"

Grace stood and crossed the room in order to see the note. "Read it to me."

> *"Dear Miss Walsh and Miss Bennett, I shall return on Friday next to Calgary. Would you please call my office regarding the contents of this document? I have had the opportunity to speak at length with Mr. Brazington-Bennett and would like to convey to you some of the troubling comments he made in my presence. It seems, I fear, that he was fully aware of your situation upon the sudden death of both your parents and that he chose not to involve himself in any way that would have*

benefited the two of you as children. It seems clear that he even understood you had been separated from each other inadvertently, but that he made no attempt to rectify the situation. Furthermore, I believe that the reason he didn't come to your aid was that he feared one or both of you would eventually make a claim against his mother's large estate."

Silence. Lillian became aware, for the first time, of the sound of children moving loudly in the nearby stairwell. Then she realized that her eyes had closed. She forced them open enough to see that tears had filled Grace's eyes.

Lillian's lips moved but no sound came.

Grace affirmed the mouthed words with difficulty, "You're right, sis. *He knew.* He knew all about us."

•••••••

On Wednesday morning Lillian rose with one thought in mind. *I want to go home.* She'd had enough of living in someone else's home, of caring for their small group of children among so many others, of trying to fight through dilemmas that felt far too large for her to carry. She was ready to leave immediately, even if it amounted to running away.

But there was still the difficulty of arranging for a car. If Ben were their driver, then somehow the borrowed automobile must be returned. And if he drove it back to Lethbridge, how would he then manage a return trip to Brookfield again without a car?

Grace went to speak with Sid first thing in the morning. Lillian chose to remain at Mrs. O'Shea's home instead. Her energy had been drained by the letter. She had no interest in breakfast, no desire to speak with anyone. She stayed in the small bedroom instead, thinking about the recent disclosure and crying sporadically. *How could anyone be so cruel? How could anyone who could call himself an uncle desert defenseless little girls? Even if we weren't blood relatives, we were humans! We deserved better.*

She thought about what might have been. Saul had apparently known about both of them, about their separation. He'd knowingly allowed Grace to grow up without a family. Allowed them to live in ignorance of the other's existence. *He's a beast! He's an abomination!*

And then her tears began again.

Grace returned following breakfast at Brayton House. There was a fierceness to her demeanor that unsettled Lillian. She seemed so resolute in her plans, ready to move forward without hesitation. Lillian wiped her face on her wadded handkerchief and rose up from the bed. Her head hurt from crying, and her eyes felt swollen.

Grace gave no indication that she noticed. Instead, she began packing, explaining as she did, "I've hired a car. It means we'll pay for a driver too, but it's the quickest way home. I spoke with Quinley one last time about the boys. He finally promised to do what he can about them, though exactly what he'd do was very difficult to pin down. Then I placed a call to Pastor Bucky, and he's going to let Ben stay with them at the parsonage until we figure out better arrangements. I know we have one last empty bedroom, but we don't know when other children might be assigned to us and I don't want that to inhibit us in any way. I wish I could have spoken with Miss Tilly, to let her know when we'll be back, but we don't have a telephone at home." Then she muttered, "Well then, that's another thing I plan to purchase."

"What do you mean?"

"Oh, you can show those documents to Mr. Wattley. That's fine. Take as long as you need to make up your mind. But make no mistake, I will be using some of my share of that money—and very soon."

It was rather frightening for Lillian, seeing Grace in such a state. "Your share?"

Finally Grace faced Lillian fully. "I don't care about him—about that—that man. He could have helped us. He could have saved us both from being alone. It seems he was the only person alive who knew about our plight. But he chose not to involve himself. Fine. I can't change the past—what he did. The judgment for that I leave in the hands of Almighty God alone. But I can assure you of two things, sister dear. I will never chase after him for more money. Not a penny of it. Even if all the legal counsel in the world advised me to! And I will use my share of what we've just received to help as many children as I can, Lord willing."

Lillian reached out to Grace. At first she felt rigid in Lillian's arms and turned her face away, but then Grace's body slowly relaxed. Her embrace warmed and reciprocated the comfort of closeness.

Grace whispered, "I didn't see this coming, sis. I never would have imagined such a thing."

"It's the worst of all the hidden corners we've turned," Lillian agreed.

"Loathsome ambages!" But despite her inflamed exclamation, Grace seemed far more composed now that she'd softened than when she'd seemed so strong and forceful.

Lillian's words came as a plea. "I want to go home."

"Yes. Yes, let's. It's time."

CHAPTER 21

Striking Out

Ben hated the idea of leaving Brayton House. After weeks of wondering from one day to the next where he'd sleep and how he'd find employment, he had finally arrived in a place of relative stability. The accommodations here for just a few days were the best he'd known. Perhaps for his entire life. He even enjoyed the company of many of those around him, found great value in their endeavors on behalf of the children. *Life's strange, in'it? An' madly fickle.*

And yet, he felt as if his sister were fading into mist beyond his reach. Little Janie had somehow displaced her. His concerns for the child's welfare had consumed his thoughts more and more until she'd begun to overtake Ben's determination to follow after his own family. Even Freddie had managed to crowd his way into a position of importance in Ben's attentions.

If I'da been able, I'da followed me Jane long ago. Not like I di'nt try. But without knowin' where she's gone, it ain't worked out. And now, when I'm prob'ly closest of all, I've gone an' made a pledge ta Miss Grace an' Miss Lillian.

He contemplated the sisters. They were an unexpected pair.

On one hand, they seemed to come from a station far above his own, out of reach. He wondered that they spoke to him with such familiarity and, yes, with actual respect. However, on the other hand, they seemed so needy, without strong support in a particularly daunting situation. They'd taken on such lofty work. Work that he'd be proud to participate in for the sake of these children, work that he saw as superior to the likes of that performed by Miss Davis and Mr. Sinclair. *That pair* had conspired to send Mickey and Vaughan to live with tyrants. It was wrong. So much so, in fact, that he was certain his sister, Jane, would fully understand his current decisions.

Regardless, he couldn't allow himself to concede defeat. He needed to know where his family had resettled. He needed to know that Jane was cared for and well. Somehow he'd need to accept this next stage in his life without ceasing to pursue the goal of getting those answers. How that might be accomplished eluded him. This farming community of Brookfield seemed like the ends of the earth.

Arriving back at the children's home on Wednesday after his last long day of difficult labor at the train depot, Ben was ready to eat and then retire for the night. Instead, Grace met him in the foyer.

"We've been waiting for you, Ben. May we speak with you?"

"O'course," he answered, unable to keep himself from glancing toward the dining room.

Lillian spoke up on his behalf. "He needs to eat, Grace. He's just come home from work. We can talk to him after supper."

But her sister countered, "It'll only take a minute. Do you mind, Ben?"

"That's fine, miss." *If only I could sip a little water first.*

"Let's go to this classroom. I know it's empty." Grace led the way down a short hallway toward one of the stark rooms.

She lost no time explaining. "We're ready to leave in the morning, Ben."

"Aye, miss. I could do that. McGillis 'as recovered. So he comes back ta work tomorra. An' I'm done there now."

"That's good. I'm glad that worked out for you." Grace hurried on. "It's not that we're giving up on fighting for Vaughan and Michael. But we don't need to stay here in order to do that. There are telephones. And Quinley has promised to do what he can."

"Quinley, miss?"

"Yes. Mr. Sinclair. I thought you knew him."

"O'course. But—it's just—did he offer ta help ya? With Mickey an' Vaughan?"

Lillian was watching him intently. She seemed to register his doubt. "What is it, Ben?"

"Ain't me place ta say, Miss Lillian."

"No. Please, if you can tell us anything that can help, we'd appreciate your candor."

Ben cleared his throat. "I'm sure he's good at his job, miss. But with the kiddos, he don't see 'em quite the same's you an' me. He looks down on 'em a mite."

Lillian frowned. Grace drew a breath as if to argue but stopped as her sister grasped her elbow firmly. "Don't stop him, Grace, please. Just listen." Their faces turned back toward Ben expectantly.

He tried to express his opinion carefully. "I seen lots'a folk. Most'a 'em poor, like me. Mr. Sinclair, he puts on airs, miss. He thinks he's 'bove it all—like he don't have ta answer ta the rest. His money gives him power over most. Now, I know his work is fer the kiddos, but he don't seem ta me ta pay 'em no mind. I'm sorry, miss, but it's like Virgil says, 'I fear the Greeks, e'en when they bear gifts.' Mr. Sinclair, he looks ta be helpin', but I don't trust him quite."

"You've observed this in him?" Grace asked, her voice strained.

Lillian queried, just as surprised, "You've read Virgil, Ben?"

He nodded, uncertain which sister to answer first. "Yes, miss, 'bout Mr. Sinclair. An' . . . well, I got a copy'a *The Aeneid* in me room. One'a me fav'rites."

Her eyes bulging, Lillian whispered aloud, "*Longa est injuria, longae ambages.*"

Trying not to appear startled by the young woman's knowledge, Ben calmly repeated the line as he'd seen it translated into English. "Great the injury an' long the tale."

Lillian fell silent. Grace seemed worried about far more pressing matters.

"Regardless, we need to be ready to leave in the morning. I'm sorry you're tired. But would you be able to help us gather the children's things tonight so we can leave in the morning?" And then Grace added, "We can wait until after supper. It'll be dark by then, but there should—"

"D'ya need me now, miss? I can come now, if ya like."

Grace paused for a moment as if weighing the importance of her tasks and then turned back to face him fully. Her brown eyes peering up toward him were now bright with renewed conviction. For a moment he felt her hand rest gently on his arm. "No. No, please go and eat. We don't want to trespass on your kindness further. Ben, I'm sorry I bothered you with this before you could have your supper. It was selfish of me. I hope you can forgive me."

He felt himself blinking down toward the brown eyes in surprise. "Aye, miss. O'course." He was certain he'd never met anyone else with such penetrating eyes. Except perhaps his little Janie.

• • • • • • •

The evening was a blur. Grace directed the production of packing and stacking crates in the wide foyer while Lillian followed the children up to their rooms. To some extent, Ben's physical energy was renewed by the very tension he felt, though his spirits were low. *What kinda place're we goin' ta? What'll this wilderness town be like? How much can I count on these sisters,*

Grace an' Lillian? There was little time for him to ponder such questions.

Then he came to discover that the sisters had made several large purchases while in the city—many supplies and a surprising number of books for the children. A place for all of this needed to be found in the car they'd hired. One corner of the foyer was filled. Without luggage and bodies yet accounted for, it seemed an insurmountable task.

"It won't all fit," Sid commented as he descended the stairs toward Grace. "It's not possible. You'll have to leave some of it here and have it delivered later."

"We can't." Her words sounded rather clipped. "We need it right away."

Ben watched them both from across the landing. How would Sid—this man who was the woman's authority, her superior—respond to her?

"Grace. Grace, please stop for a moment."

Reluctantly, she set down the towels she was packing. "Yes?"

"I don't understand fully—I know we've disagreed about the boys. But clearly something has you quite upset." Sid approached her, lowered himself to sit on one of the crates that had already been nailed shut. "Is it the boys? Or is it me? Have we done something you haven't said?" His eyebrows drew tighter, wrinkling lines of genuine concern across his forehead.

Suddenly Grace grew more tender, more childlike, as if the gentleness of his words had cracked through the shell of protection she'd encased herself in. Her hand rose to cross over her eyes for a moment, then closed into a fist next to her face. "I'm sorry, Sid. There's so much you don't know—what I'm struggling with. But I can't talk about it right now." She shook her head, lowered her hands, and turned her freckled face toward him like a girl turning toward her father. "But it wasn't fair for me to make you feel as if you've done something wrong. I'm afraid I've let my emotions get the better of me again."

Her hand gestured toward Ben. She added, "I had to apologize to Ben earlier. I don't know what's come over me." And then she corrected her answer. "Well, I do know, actually. But I'm not sure why it's making me behave so disagreeably toward people I trust. I'm sorry, Sid."

"It's okay. We're on the same team. Please remember that. We've known one another for such a long time and we've always worked together well. You're like family to me. If I've done something to offend you, I truly want you to tell me so that I can make it right."

"No, Sid." Grace shook her head again. "Yes, we disagreed about the Szwedas, but this isn't about you."

"Well then, will you allow me to send some of these things along later?"

Her eyes pleaded with him silently, wordlessly.

"All right then, you'll have to take our car. Ben can drive it to carry the extra baggage. I'm glad he's going. I've always thought he'd be a great help with Alfred Jones. But he'll have to bring the car back promptly. I'm not quite certain how to work out all the implications of that."

"Oh no, it's too much trouble. It's too far for him to come back."

Both sets of eyes turned toward Ben in unison. Roused from his role as observer, he hurried to say, "Whate'er ya need. I don't mind helpin' ya how I can."

They both seemed appeased. But Ben's thoughts began to churn immediately. With a car all to himself on the drive back to Lethbridge, he'd have some freedom. With a car he could possibly make an excursion of his own. The speculation began to lift his spirits. A plan began to form.

• • • • • • •

Lillian felt numb. She was tired of it all. Tired of traveling, tired of thinking, tired of worrying. She wanted to retreat into her own little world once more, where life had been predictable and safe. But how long ago had that been? Her mind pushed back through the memories.

Before Father had gone to Wales? No, because they'd lost Mother so recently. When Mother had been alive? No, because she'd been sick for so long. Maybe there'd been such security before Mother had fallen ill? Well, not really. It had honestly taken many years for Lillian to feel self-assured in their home, despite her adoptive parents' tender affection. Perhaps, if she were honest, life hadn't really felt so safe and predictable at all. Perhaps it was an illusion that her heart was seeking after now.

Grace had chosen to stay at Brayton House, working with Ben to load the two vehicles long after Lillian had retired to Mrs. O'Shea's home. They'd planned an early start in the morning. Once they unloaded in Brookfield, Ben would bring the automobile back again, then make the trip for the third time two days later with the driver who delivered Brookfield's mail on Saturday.

Rather than help Grace with the children's packing, Lillian had chosen to see that all of their things at their temporary residence were gathered into one place. She worked alone, once more setting their cases on the bed and packing clothing into them. She remembered the packet of letters, had not forgotten their presence for a moment. *No, I'm not going to read them. They're private. Whatever it is she's communicating to Walter, it's none of my business.* But Lillian's heart argued back, *Of course it's my business! If there's more to it than friendship, it's certainly my right to know.*

At last her fingers slipped between the layers of Grace's handkerchiefs and drew out the small bundle. Even as she held it in her hands, Lillian tried to resist. She counted the letters. There were four. *Four!* She tried to recall if he had written so many letters to her. She couldn't remember ever observing four prolonged conversations between Grace and Walter in all the time they'd known each other. Was it possible she'd misinterpreted the correspondence entirely? It would be such a relief to know for sure.

Lillian drew one envelope from the center of the stack. She pulled the letter out and unfolded it, holding it out just too far away to read. It was written with Walter's heavy script and, yes, it was signed with Walter's name. Lillian felt guilty tears begin to form already.

As her eyes attempted to focus on the words, her hand brought his letter close enough to read. Lillian began at the top of the last page, where she'd checked for his signature.

> *. . . don't know how I can stay away, Grace. I'm so lonely I can hardly get up in the morning and force myself to start another day. My heart is there with you. Even my boss has noticed . . .*

The tears shook loose. This was a love letter to Grace! This was a betrayal of everything—by everyone she held dearest. Lillian sank onto her knees beside the bed, lowered her face to the tiny sprays of printed flowers, and wept.

She had no idea how much time had passed until she heard a soft knock on the door. It came again.

A quivery voice asked, "Lillian? Are you all right, dear?"

She forced her answer to sound composed. "Yes, I'm okay. I was just packing."

"Have you hurt yourself, dear?"

"No, Mrs. O'Shea. I'm just about finished."

"That's good. You need your rest." And then the older woman prodded once more, "Are you sure you don't want a chat? I can put on the teakettle, honey."

"Thank you so much. No. I'm almost ready for bed."

"Well then, have a good sleep. I'll see you in the morning."

"Thank you."

Lillian wiped her eyes on the first hankie within reach. She didn't care at all that it belonged to Grace. Now able to see clearly again, she returned to the letter, reasoning that she might as well know the extent of their infidelity. She perched on the edge of the rocking chair and drew a long breath.

Then she began again at the top of the page.

> *. . . don't know how I can stay away, Grace. I'm so lonely I can hardly get up in the morning and force myself to start another day. My heart is there with you. Even my boss has noticed my dragging spirits. He questioned me about it on more than one occasion. But how can I admit to him that I long for the woman I left behind? This was my plan, the path toward my goal of preparing for marriage. Surely I can't give up before I've achieved what I set out to do! Oh, Grace, I'm not sure I'm strong enough for this.*

Lillian sank back in the chair, her head spinning. She forced herself to continue.

> *Christmas cannot come soon enough. I want to see her. I want to tell her so many things that I was too cowardly to speak about before I left. And yet, I'm still convinced it wouldn't have been a kindness. It would have drawn her into my own heartache with the distance between us. It would have forced Lillian to carry the same burden of feelings that I . . .*

What? What had she just read? Realization swept over her like a gust of wind forcing its way inside a half-opened door. *It isn't about Grace at all! It's about me.* Suddenly Lillian didn't care if Mrs. O'Shea could hear the sound of her sobbing. She wanted Walter to come home. She needed to see him. Now she didn't have to wonder any longer if she'd correctly interpreted his commitment to her. It was there in print.

She read the words again, more slowly this time.

• • • • •

Watching the prairie miles stretching out in every direction from the driver's seat of the second automobile, Ben thought again of the sea. However, now that much of the snow was melting, a warm chinook breeze having provided an unseasonably mild day midwinter, the brown grasses were exposed, giving the prairie a barren look. For much of the journey there was nothing in sight, rarely even a farmhouse or barn on the horizon. Gradually, though, the dark hills to the west grew larger, the white peaks of mountains loomed closer, increasingly spectacular. There were more patches of trees in the valleys, covering the rising hills. It felt wilder and yet somehow more sheltered than the prairie had been.

He smiled as he remembered a similar feeling of watching for land to rise up out of the ocean swells on the horizon. The call of the sailors echoing around him that the shore had been sighted at last.

Deep within one of a series of valleys he saw a clearing, a small town. By no means large, but far more settled than what he'd pictured Brookfield to be. As the car slowed, Freddie stirred on the seat beside him.

The boy had slept for most of their journey. He asked in confusion, "What's that, then?"

"It's a town. I think we're almost there."

"No, not that. That!" He pointed at the mountains beyond.

"Oh, yeah. I figure it's the Rockies folk talk so much 'bout."

"Wow!"

They slowed even more as both cars approached a large row of shrubbery. The vehicle in front of them turned onto a hidden lane. Ben heaved on the steering wheel, and their automobile rattled in behind.

The house was large. He wasn't certain if he'd expected a log cabin or a shack of some kind. He knew, however, that this was not what he'd envisioned. It looked impressive. It looked grand—like an estate house rather than a mere home, not built with stone as they were back home, but clad with New World wood instead.

Freddie's hand reached to grasp at the dash. "Blast! That it?"

"I think so."

The boy let fly with an expletive that brought a scowl from Ben. "Ya can't use such language here, lad. Ya just can't."

"Sorry, sir."

Ben let the engine die. They watched the twin boys tumble from the first car and scamper around the yard. Snow still lay in the shadowed places. Mud was thick in the driveway. Little Janie emerged more slowly, holding on to Grace's hand. Then Milton lifted a dark speckled cat that coiled around his legs, carrying it for Janie to see. She began to smile, reached to pet its head. Ben's heart warmed. If Janie would be happy here, he was satisfied with it.

CHAPTER 22

Scrutiny

Miss Tilly was clearly taken aback by the quiet man who followed Lillian, Grace, and the children into the kitchen. She'd been told to expect two additional youngsters but was not warned of another adult. Lillian attempted an affirming nod after introducing Ben.

For the moment, Miss Tilly seemed to purposely switch her focus toward their new charges. "Well, yer a gem, ain't ya? What's yer name, dearie?"

Setting down a case, Lillian smiled toward the little girl standing next to her. "Her name is Jane Grey. She's six."

"Oh, so young," whispered Miss Tilly. Then softly brushing the back of a finger against Jane's cheek, Miss Tilly added, "Glad ta have ya, Jane. Got yer room all ready fer ya."

Jane smiled timidly. "Thank you, ma'am."

Grace was standing next to Freddie. She put a hand behind the boy's shoulder. "And this is Alfred Jones. We call him Freddie. He's been such a big help to us. We're just getting to know them both, but we're so glad to have them with us for a while."

Freddie's hands slid into his pockets. The shadowed look that crossed his face caused Grace to lower her hand again.

Lillian spoke up quickly. "I think we'll unload onto the front porch. The boys can work outdoors, and we girls will unpack things inside the house. Does that work for everyone?"

Miss Tilly added with authority, "Go out through the back door. You'll find boots ta save yer good shoes from the mud in the yard. Boys, be sure ya put yer boots on, now. You too, Freddie. An' Ben, there's a pair large enough fer ya too."

With nods and shrugs, Ben led the small crew back out to the yard, stopping in the porch to change footwear. Lillian hoped the twins would be more useful than distracting for him.

As soon as they were gone, Miss Tilly raised an eyebrow. "Tell me 'bout that man."

Words poured out quickly as Grace tried to explain, occasionally glancing toward Jane. "He's Ben Waldin. He came with the children on the train. But he was a sailor on their ship first. That's how he met them."

"A sailor, huh? Pretty far from the ocean. What's he doin' here?" And then she interjected, "Jane, dear, why don'tcha go an' see that the front door's open fer them boys?"

As soon as the child had sauntered out of the room, Grace tried again, whispering, "No, you don't understand, Miss Tilly. He's been such a help. And he deeply cares for these children—particularly Jane. She dotes on him. You should just see them together."

"Hmm." Her eyes swept from Lillian to Grace. "He stickin' around? Where's he gonna live?"

Lillian took a turn explaining. "With the Bukowskis. We've already made arrangements. Sid and the people at Brayton House are paying him to serve as our handyman here as long as we need him."

Miss Tilly wiped her hands across her apron and seemed to ponder further. "Ain't ne'er met a sailor. Heard my fill'a stories though. Don't know what's truth, er what's make-believe. But ya mark my words, we got a sailor so far from the sea—there's a tale ta be told, fer certain." And then her hands rose. "Well, it's yer house. But I d'know it's wise—bringin' in a strange man with yer own daddy away. No way ta know what he's leavin' b'hind 'im—or runnin' from. Might bring ya more trouble than the kids." Without waiting for a reply, Miss Tilly picked up Lillian's suitcase and headed toward her own bedroom door just off the kitchen. "May as well git started. No sense carryin' up what needs washin'. Make a pile of the dirty clothes in my room an' I'll git to it real soon."

• • • • • • •

Miss Tilly was pleased to have the additional supplies that Lillian and Grace had brought back from Lethbridge. It seemed to Lillian that the woman's mood lifted with each crate they unpacked. There was fabric that could be sewn into necessary garments, and sacks of flour and cornmeal and sugar that were cheaper to purchase in the city. In addition to ordinary foodstuffs, there were eight tin plates for the children so that Lillian no longer needed to fear that Mother's everyday dishes would be broken during a meal.

Matty and Milton returned indoors before long, and Grace put them to work helping her carry things up the stairs to the rooms above. Soon Freddie and Ben stepped across the threshold, having finished unloading the cars. They stood awkwardly in the front entryway as if they'd prefer an excuse to be sent back out again.

Rounding the corner from the kitchen, Miss Tilly seemed to take pity, though she maintained her characteristic brevity. "Leave them muddy boots on the porch an' come ta the kitchen, gents. Kids, ya come too. I've somethin' ta show ya, Freddie. An', Ben, ya help yerself to a cup'a coffee an' a fresh bun."

When they'd all followed obediently, Miss Tilly motioned Freddie and the younger children to come through to the workroom that served as both her bedroom and storage. Lillian fell into step behind them.

"Now, young'uns, look here. See thet box in the corner there, where it's warm? Lift the corner'a that towel an' look 'neath it."

Matty and Milton moved to obey at once. Jane stood just behind them, watching carefully. She seemed poised to run should something frightening escape from under the towel.

"Eggs!" Milton exclaimed.

"Oh my," whispered Jane, causing Lillian to smile.

"They've a day or two more 'fore they hatch. Then we'll have chicks ta tend. 'Tis earlier than I woulda liked ta have 'em. So we'll all have ta keep an eye on 'em. Can ya help me?"

"Yes," the children answered together.

"Now, who wants a cookie an' milk with their lunch?"

• • • • • • •

Shortly after lunch the children went out to play in the yard until nap time, taking full advantage of the unseasonably warm weather. Still finishing off their coffee, the adults remained at the table with a fidgety Freddie. It was then that Miss Tilly chose to address Ben directly. Lillian held her breath.

"I'm told yer a sailor, Ben."

"I was, ma'am."

She brushed the crumbs on her plate to one side using a pinky finger, the knuckles thickened with arthritis. Rarely had Miss Tilly rested at the table following a meal. She fussed with her water glass a moment more. Then her eyes lifted toward him sideways. "So, Ben, ya have kin, do ya?"

"Aye, ma'am." Ben cleared his throat, shifted in his chair.

Lillian wasn't certain if he intended to add more information. He seemed reluctant to respond too readily.

But then he said, "I've a sister, ma'am. Her name's Jane. Me parents're with her—here in Alberta, but I don't know where."

Miss Tilly pressed further. "How come ya ain't with 'em?"

"When I come home from a voyage at the end of the year, I found 'em gone. They'd moved ta Canada b'fore me. So I set out after 'em."

"I see. And how'd ya come ta know the little girl?"

They seemed evenly matched in stubbornness—the old prairie woman and the weathered young sailor. Even with the tidy haircut that Grace had given him, Ben's worn clothing and humble bearing revealed his life had obviously been a hard one. But he met Miss Tilly's gaze evenly, seeming to answer honestly the questions that Lillian and Grace had not dared to ask.

"I—I met her by the ship. Her parents was dead. I come ta be her friend and grew ta see her as—as—well, as somewhat a niece, best I can describe it. Though, in truth, I ain't really got one, miss. Me sister's husband died b'fore they was blessed with such."

Miss Tilly folded her hands across her belly. "You a Christian man, Ben?"

His eyes fell to the table and then slowly rose to meet her gaze as he answered. "Were baptized so. But I ain't certain, ma'am."

"Ya moral though? Ya keep God's laws? 'Cause if yer gonna be 'round our young'uns, we gotta know." She leaned forward, refusing to look away from him as she pressed for an answer.

"On me mum's Good Book, ma'am, I am that." Then he added grimly, "It's right that ya ask, though, ma'am. I'da done so meself where them kids're concerned."

"All right then, Ben. We'll hold ya to it." At last Miss Tilly stood and began to clear the table, as if the matter were settled. Her voice took on a conversational tone. "So yer goin' back, Ben. Ta return their automobile. Ya headin' out today?"

"Aye, ma'am. Soon's I can."

Lillian looked up in surprise. She hadn't expected for Ben to depart so quickly.

Miss Tilly nodded. "No time like the present, I'm prone ta say."

* * *

There was a particular reason that Ben wanted to leave as soon as possible. He figured that the simplest way not to be missed was to return before he was expected back. And there was one expedition he was determined to take.

Two days ago he'd been waiting in Sid's office when his eyes had fallen on a piece of paper he most certainly should not have been shown. It contained a location that piqued his interest based on the whispered conversations around him, the things he'd overheard. And since it would also be a benefit to Grace and Lillian, he felt it worth borrowing a pen and inscribing the address directly onto his arm, where it would be covered safely by his sleeve. Later, he'd found a map in the carriage house and searched for the precise location. He was ready now to start out, heading from Brookfield first toward the north instead of east.

He knew there was one last task to accomplish first. So he walked out to the yard to bid Janie good-bye. Freddie followed on his heels.

"I'm goin' with ya," the boy insisted.

"No, lad. Ya need ta settle in here."

"I won't. Said I'd stay with you. Ne'er said I'd stay here."

Ben stopped in his tracks across the driveway so that he could face Freddie. "I'm comin' back, lad. I won't be long. Give ya me word."

Freddie shook his head. "I'm comin' too."

"But Miss Grace an' Miss—"

"They don't care 'bout the likes'a me. An' they got them other kids ta fuss o'er. So, as I say, I'm comin'."

It was futile. "Do's ya like." Ben continued on to where Janie was playing among the evergreen trees, trampling the remaining snow beneath her to outline a playhouse with Milton and Matty. "Janie, I need ta talk ta ya."

"Hi, Mister Waldin."

"I'm drivin' the car back ta Mr. Brown now. But I'll be back again on Saturday."

She jutted out her chin. "Do you promise? Do you promise to come back right away?"

Ben lowered himself to a squatting position so that she could wrap her small hands around the whiskers on his face. She repeated, "You will come back? For certain?"

Smiling, Ben answered with mock solemnity, "Haven't I always kep' me word? Always?"

"You have." She laughed.

"Then play with yer friends an' have a good look 'round. I want ya to show me what ya've discovered when I come back."

"Like the chicks! They might have hatched by then."

"Aye, bunny. Ya take good care'a them eggs in the house 'til I'm here 'gain."

"I will."

He patted her shoulder. "I'll see ya soon."

He rose again, strode toward the waiting automobile and the boy who leaned back against it, stubbornness etched on his face. "Go tell the women yer goin' along. Guess I need ya fer crankin' her up anyway, lad. I shoulda 'membered I couldn't go without ya."

They were back on the road again soon after. Freddie stretched out in the empty back seat this time. He chatted for a while before falling back into the easy slumber of a growing youth. Ben felt an odd disappointment at emerging from the trees again and making his way back out to the open prairie. Still, it was much easier to navigate when one could see so far across the rolling hills.

• • • ● • • •

It was time to confront Grace. Or, more accurately, for Lillian to confess her own actions to her sister. She wasn't certain how Grace would respond, but while the children were napping and Miss Tilly was wringing out laundry and hanging it on lines strung across the basement, Lillian knew there would not be a more appropriate time.

"Grace? May I speak with you for a moment?"

Grace was just spreading out her papers across the dining room table, ready to calculate the expenses they'd incurred while they were gone. "You're so serious, sis. What's wrong?"

Lillian wished she'd spent more time deciding how to phrase her confession. "When I was at Mrs. O'Shea's last night . . . well, I read one of your letters from Walter."

For a moment Grace sat like a statue, her face impossible to read. But Lillian could think of nothing else to add until she heard how Grace would respond. She waited, biting her lip.

At last Grace broke the silence. "I wish you hadn't."

"So do I." Then Lillian asked, "Are you angry?"

Grace slowly shook her head. "Not angry. Just disappointed. I feel as if you've caused *me* to betray a confidence."

The comment seared Lillian's conscience. "I'm sorry, Grace. I misunderstood what the letters were about. I thought you and Walter . . . that you were . . . I mean . . ." It was impossible to complete the thought.

Grace's eyes squinted back at her, hardened. "You didn't! How could you think that?"

"It's been so awful." Lillian hung her head in shame. "I was so worn out by Mr. Dorn's letter. I just wanted to be home. But I let myself give in to feelings of, well, selfishness and mistrust."

Patting the table to her left, Grace summoned Lillian to take a seat. Her voice had lost its edge. "I know how hard it's been. We didn't see this coming at all." Grace sighed and set down her pen. "Do you feel any better—having read the letter? I don't even know which one you read or what you've learned."

"To be honest, yes. I feel somewhat better about my worst fears. But I've never missed Walter more." Lillian sighed. "He never wrote anything of the kind to me. I'm not sure why." Her tears had all been spent at Mrs. O'Shea's house. There was nothing left but an emptiness in her chest.

"I'm sorry. I don't really understand it either. But, even now, I'm reluctant to discuss it with you. It still feels like betraying Walter's trust." Grace wiped a hand across her forehead. "And there are more imposing things to fret about right now. What are we going to do about the check, sis? Do we have a plan?"

"I guess, first, we need to pay a visit to Mr. Wattley. I still want him to look over the document. But I don't suppose it'll take him long. Should we go now?"

Grace pushed back her chair. "I think we should. And we may as well go now while Jane is napping and the boys are at school." She tossed an arm around Lillian's shoulder as they entered the foyer. "I love you, sis. I forgive you too. In fact, I even understand quite easily how awful you've been feeling and why that would make it harder, so much harder. But I assume you know by now that, where Walter's concerned, you have nothing to fear."

Lillian choked a little. "I believe I do know that. I'd just rather hear it from him directly."

"Oh, you will. When he's ready." Grace's words were filled with sweet confidence.

• • • • • • •

Hoping he'd found the correct lane at last, Ben aimed the car up the muddy ruts in the driveway and let it coast to a stop in front of a ramshackle house in the middle of nowhere. Chickens skittered away from the wheels and a dog came out from beneath the porch, huffing with age rather than truly achieving a bark.

A door in the barn opened and a farmer with hunched shoulders sauntered out in their direction. Ben's eyes searched further, at last finding the two figures he'd expected, a boy chopping wood near the house and another forking hay down from a loft.

"Mr. Szweda," Ben called, "I come ta talk t'ya."

"Who is it?" the gruff voice demanded as the man approached warily.

"I'm Waldin—from the Mercy S'ciety. Come ta check on the lads."

The back door of the car opened and Freddie crawled out. He rubbed at his eyes with one hand, having a difficult time understanding where they'd just arrived.

"Katrin, come on out here," Jack hollered toward the house. "Katrin!"

Soon his petite wife had joined them, glowering up at Ben. "Whatcha come fer? What business we got with you?"

"Just a 'spection, ma'am. Nowt to concern ya. Gotta see how the lads're settlin'."

Vaughan had set down his ax. Ben motioned him forward with a nod. Michael descended from the hay loft by rope, hand over hand. Spying Freddie beside the car, they hurried forward at a quicker pace. Ben could only imagine what they thought his presence meant.

"Hello, Mickey! Hi'ya, Vaughan!" he called cheerfully. "We come ta visit ya."

Chapter 23

Declarations

Mr. Wattley slowly examined the document. Lillian and Grace waited across from him, trying not to glance at each other. Lillian could hear the muffled pop of her sister's fingers as Grace twisted her gloved hands together anxiously.

At last Mr. Wattley raised his eyes. "Do you understand the intention of this document, ladies?"

"I think we do," said Lillian. "We can't ever make a claim on Uncle Saul's money, or even Grandpapa's estate."

"That's correct. You'd be effectively cut off from those inheritances."

"But why is the amount greater than expected? We thought that maybe Saul Brazington-Bennett added money as some kind of—kind of a payoff, to keep us from seeking anything more."

"Money has been added to your inheritance, certainly. A large sum, in fact. I can't speak to the intentions of the other party."

Grace chewed on her lip for a moment before addressing him boldly, shrugging as she insisted, "I don't care. I don't want his money. But I would like to know whether *you* think we're being wise or foolish if we sign it."

"Have you spoken to Mr. Dorn?"

Lillian answered for them both. "Not yet. He asked us to call him tomorrow when he's back in Calgary. I believe he's on the train today."

"I see." Mr. Wattley made a note on a page in front of him. "I want to speak with Mr. Dorn myself, if I may. There's really no rush to sign this. It doesn't give a deadline to meet."

Grace swallowed. "But the money. When can we deposit the check? Lillian thought that if we did so we'd effectively be agreeing to the terms of the contract."

"Not necessarily. I'd say it's the very least that you can expect as a settlement. Certainly, the fact that Mr. Dorn sent it to you without a warning regarding its use would indicate to me that he's not concerned on that count. I think it's fair to say you're free to use it as you wish."

His eyes moved from Grace to Lillian. "I do hope, however, that you'll be cautious with the funds, ladies. It's obviously a considerable amount, and I know your father, Lillian. I'm quite certain that Elliott would appreciate a chance to advise you on how it's allocated. He's always taken the greatest of care with your family's finances."

"Thank you, Mr. Wattley. I do agree. Father would definitely want to help me with my share. And I fully intend to wait for him to return from Wales."

A quizzical expression crossed his face. "And you, Miss Bennett?"

Grace paused. Her back straightened. She looked at Lillian with rising consternation. "Mr. Wattley," she finally replied, "I want to use some of mine to purchase a car." Her hands fluttered in front of her for a moment. Then she blurted out, "And a telephone. A telephone for Lillian's father's house." Her eyes flashed with a passionate intensity.

Lillian reached across for Grace's hand and squeezed it hard. "No, sis. For *our* house. And I agree completely that it's something we should do. It's something I'm certain Father would agree to. I don't know if it's possible to put a line out to our property yet, but I think we should try. Maybe if we asked the Thompsons if they'd like a line at their farm, too, the telephone company would agree to string the wires." Lillian's mind was already tumbling with plans.

• • • ● • • •

Katrin Szweda stamped her foot in the dirt. "Ya got no right ta be here! Yer not in charge."

Ben held his ground. He placed an arm loosely around Vaughan's shoulders and ruffled Michael's hair, refusing to let anyone see evidence of the doubt that churned his stomach. "Not claimin' ta be in charge, Missus. As I said, I'm just checkin' in on the lads." He turned his attention away from the frustrated woman. "How's it goin' here, Mickey? Ya eatin' well?"

Michael's eyes grew round and dropped to the ground as he refused to answer Ben's question. But Vaughan spoke up. "Not what we're use'ta. But we get 'nough."

"Good, good. Glad ta hear it. An' beds? Where's that, then?"

Almost inaudibly Michael answered, "The barn."

Ben's head came up. "The barn? That a temp'ry thing?"

The Szwedas exchanged glances. "Why d'ya care?"

"There's laws, sir. Ya signed a paper. Says the lads gotta have a proper place ta lay their heads. If they was ta get sick now, that'd be an offense. I ain't from here, but I think ya got a good bit'a winter left."

"Harrumph."

"Ya got books?"

Two bewildered old faces stared at Ben in surprise.

"Now, looky here." Mrs. Szweda wagged a finger. "There's no school in these parts. Can't give 'em educatin' if there ain't no school."

Ben stood a little straighter. "Now, Mr. Szweda, sir, ya know that ain't what yer contract says. The one what ya signed with the Mercy Society while you was at Brayton House. I seen it. Schoolin's a promise, sir. Ya gotta give 'em time ta learn. It ain't like these lads're just hired help. An' since they can both read, they can keep learnin' without no teacher."

His eyebrows lowered. He let the Szwedas contemplate his words for a moment before adding, "An' I mean ta see the law's enforced here. A'that ya can be sure."

Ben patted Vaughan on the back. "I'm gonna walk out ta see where the lads're sleepin'. Better if ya don't follow—'course, I can't stop ya." Ben moved decisively toward the barn, nudging the boys along in front of him.

Jack Szweda rocked back on his heels and let them pass, as if confused as to how to respond.

But Ben chatted amiably, the three youths surrounding him. "How'd ya like the prairie? Don't know 'bout you, lads, but I ain't ne'er seen the like. Was thinkin' on the train it looks a bit like the sea. 'Cept with no water. Just waves'a land far as the eye can see."

Even Katrin remained where she stood in the yard, startled into silence.

As soon as they were out of earshot, Ben's tone changed. "Tell me quick, lads. Don't know how long they'll hold off. Ya all right?"

Vaughan cast a glance over his shoulder. "They're mean, Mister Waldin. But not jus' ta us—ta each other too."

"He e'er hit ya?"

"Naw. Raises a hand now an' again, but he's ne'er brought it down. Ta be honest, I don't know's he still got the strength. He's pretty old, sir. Guess that's what he got us fer. All the work he can't do no more."

They approached the barn. Michael led the way. "It's here. Vaughan an' me, we set it up kinda nice. Piled up bales'a hay ta make a little room 'round the stove what's in there."

From where Ben stood, it seemed to be just a stack of bales that pressed upward to the low ceiling.

Vaughan added, "Bet it's warmer in there 'an in their ol' house. Anyways, we like it better out here."

"Yeah, it ain't bad—'cept fer the mice at night. They come lookin' fer a warm bed, too, I s'pose."

Ben stifled a chuckle, not doubting that the thick bales provided a warmer bedroom than the thin walls of the old farmhouse. He put out a hand to push the bangs of Vaughan's hair away from his eyes. "Ya lads lackin' fer anythin'?"

Michael nodded. "Books. If we had somethin' ta read . . ."

"Yeah, an' time to read it!"

"Can't promise ya, but I'll do what I can." They turned quickly back to the yard. Ben added, "Barn'll do fer a while. Can't stay in there though. I'll try an' press 'em to see yer indoors a'fore too long."

"No thanks, Mister Waldin. We like it here. Fer sure."

Vaughan nodded a vigorous agreement.

It was all Ben could do to pull himself away. "I got more business, lads. But I promise ta come ag'in. Not sure when."

"Thanks, Mister Waldin. Helps ta know yer comin' back." Vaughan smiled up at him bravely, making Ben's heart ache all the more.

As the little crew trudged back across the yard and passed by Jack Szweda, he muttered something under his breath. Ben preferred not to allow an argument to begin.

"I'm sorry, lads, that I can't stay on longer. Gotta get back ta Brayton House." He repeated his promise loud enough for the nearby couple to hear. "But I'll come back ag'in. Soon. I'm gonna keep checkin' on yer progress, see that yer eatin' an' learnin'. See that yer kep' warm an' safe." He drew Vaughan just a little closer against his side, cupped a large hand around the back of Michael's head affectionately. "I'll come back, soon's I can."

The visit had gone as well as could be expected, but Ben

wiped clammy hands on his trousers as he drove from the yard. He contemplated the boys' situation while his fingers drummed on the steering wheel in frustration. *I'll be back*, he repeated as a promise to himself. *Can't do much more'n report what I see, but I'm gonna keep checkin' on 'em regular.*

• • • • •

After their meeting with Mr. Wattley, Grace went immediately home, but Lillian stayed in town in order to walk home with the boys after school. Not many parents bothered to meet their children in front of the small school building today. There was only one other woman, a tall form silhouetted against the bricks.

"Mrs. Caulfield," Lillian called across the yard. "Catherine, so nice to see you."

"Is that you, Lillian? How come you're here?"

"I'm walking the twins home." Lillian hugged her newest friend. "We were in town anyway—Grace and I."

"Oh, those boys. We've missed 'em so! I used to chat with 'em when I'd pick up my Frank. They oft came out together."

"That's lovely. It's kind of Frank to pay attention to them. He's twice their age. I'm glad the boys get along so well."

"Well, I'm not gonna lie, I've encouraged it. I don't know as we've said as much aloud, but we kinda hope to be considered for adoptin' the twins. They're 'bout as cute as a bow on a mouse."

Lillian smiled at the mental image. "We think so too."

The school door opened, but only a solitary man walked out. It closed again with a thud.

When Lillian glanced back again, there was a look of distress crowding out Catherine's smile. "I'm not sure if you wanna know this, Lillian, but I just can't stop myself from speakin' up."

"What does it concern?"

"That man we met at your place. That Mr. Sinclair."

A wave of fatigue shuddered through Lillian. She wasn't certain she was equipped to handle any additional revelations. "I'm sorry, I don't like to . . ."

"Oh, this isn't gossip, honey. I think it's important you should know what I've seen."

"Yes?"

"He didn't go anywhere."

"What?"

"Mr. Sinclair, he didn't go anywhere while he was in our town. Just stayed in the hotel an' ordered food an' had meetings with important people from around here."

"What?"

"He didn't go see the families he was supposed to check on. He never did."

Gradually the accusation began to register. "He didn't do the work for the society while he was here? Quinley?" Then she recalled what he had explained. "Oh, Catherine, it's because he made telephone calls instead. He told me that." *Or was it the other way around? Had he said he was unable to place the calls?* Now Lillian couldn't remember for sure.

"No, honey. He was working for himself the whole time instead. Lots'a people noticed it."

The door burst open and the sound of children's voices filled the air. Lillian squeezed her eyes shut. *Quinley? How is it possible?*

Clutching at Lillian's arm as if to keep her close, Catherine continued. "I wasn't sure, but I feel I need to tell you something else. You'll wanna know it. But not here." She drew Lillian aside to a shadowed corner of the building.

Stunned into silence, Lillian followed.

"That's not all of it," Catherine whispered tersely. "I talked to my folks back home. They remembered him." After a glance in all directions, the woman hurried on. "I haven't said anything to anyone since we come to Brookfield. But my Sam, he had a son before we were married. His name's August—Gus, we call him. He's sixteen now."

Lillian remembered the sorrowful expression on Sam Caulfield's face as he talked about giving up a child.

"The mother fought to take him when she left my Sam an' moved back East. Sam, he fought back too. But she got herself help from a big-city law firm. Hired a solicitor. An' *his* name was Sinclair. We didn't remember—never did meet him—but my sister did—she's from the East. So I checked on our papers. It's the same name. *Quinley Sinclair.*" She exaggerated the pronunciation.

Lillian stood in stupefied silence. *It's not possible.* And yet, once she began to review her moments with the man, she wondered that she hadn't suspected his character long before. He had refused to protect Michael and Vaughan—had kept their placement a secret until there was nothing to be done. He always took the best for himself, shared only when he could build advantageous friendships—even with Grace and herself. From the moment of their first meeting, when Quinley had so clearly noticed Grace was young and beautiful, he had seemed to change his attitude toward them immediately—suddenly posing as someone coming to their aid. And he'd even been bold enough to suggest he might marry one of them, announcing aloud that it would be an advantage to marry a wealthy, socially connected bride.

Of all the gall! This will be more than Grace can stand. Then Lillian groaned aloud. "Ben knew. Somehow Ben judged him much better than we did."

Catherine spat out, "It makes me sick. I'm glad he's gone. I'd have given him a piece'a my mind—aiding a woman to steal a man's son away. Shameful!"

• • • • • • •

Ben arrived back at Brayton House late on Thursday evening, amazed at the number of miles they'd traveled in a day. He knew that Freddie wouldn't be expected, but they clumped up the steps together in the dark and Ben knocked on the door to the second floor of the carriage house. Rolly promptly opened it to them.

"Welcome back, Ben," he said cheerfully. "Come on in."

"Brought Freddie with me." He motioned back toward the boy with a thumb thrown over his shoulder.

"I can see that."

"All right if he sleeps on the sofa?"

"That's fine with me." Then Rolly asked, "Have you eaten?"

"No, we missed supper."

"I don't have much to offer you, but there's half a cake left on the counter and hot coffee on the stove."

Freddie moved toward it quickly, picking up the knife to cut himself a large piece.

Ben cleared his throat to get Freddie's attention, raised an eyebrow toward the questioning look the boy shot back.

"Yeah, then, thanks, Mr. Scott."

"Glad I had something to share," Rolly said with a laugh. He turned. "Hey, Ben, looks like you don't have to ride back with the mail truck. Have ya heard that?"

"No?"

"Yeah, it just seemed to fall right into place. Grace called to say she planned to look for a car to buy for their place—and asked if we'd watch for something around here with extra seats, if possible. Sid knew of someone right off the top of his head who was anxious to sell a car that fit the bill—one the man had altered so that it's longer than most. It has an extra row of seats, room for loads of kids. Now, mind you, it's not new. But it should be reliable enough. So they're gonna have you drive it back for Grace and Lillian to take a look at it. If they like it, they'll send a bank draft by mail."

I only left today! What a hurricane these sisters are fer gettin' stuff done! He contemplated the news as he watched Freddie scoop up his large piece of cake, forgoing a plate and dropping it directly onto his unwashed hands. At last Ben answered Rolly. "Guess it'll be good fer 'em to have a car. But why didn't they jus' get it while they was here?"

"Oh, they didn't have the money then. Didn't you hear about that either? The girls just inherited from an old uncle."

Ben's mind clouded further. "Thought they was orphans?"

His comment caused Rolly's head to tip in confusion. His lips puckered from side to side. "I didn't think'a that. Yeah, I'm not sure how that worked. Huh!" He shrugged. "Though, nobody here thought Grace'd have a sister show up all of a sudden either. Her kin just keep comin' outta the woodwork." Laughing, he said, "At any rate, they're buyin' a car with the inheritance money."

• • • • • • •

Friday morning was the time set for the telephone conversation with Mr. Dorn in the comfort of Mr. Wattley's law office. Lillian hoped his travel plans hadn't been delayed. She wasn't sure her nerves could take much more waiting, worrying.

Grace seemed to be bearing up much better under the pressure. *Perhaps that's because I haven't told her anything I've learned about Quinley yet. I'm not even sure how Grace will react to such a disappointment—such a jolt to the senses.*

This time the telephone connection with Mr. Dorn was strong. The sisters could easily understand all that he explained.

He wasted no time on small talk. "I'm terribly sorry we couldn't communicate better, ladies. I'd hoped to share the information about Saul Brazington-Bennett in a much more sensitive way. I hope the strain of it all wasn't too much for you both."

"We've managed," Grace assured him, leaning in close to the mouthpiece on the telephone.

Lillian was well aware that she hadn't really grappled with the impact of knowing about Uncle Saul yet. It was still too much to comprehend that any relative would have merely ignored two little nieces in such a state. However, she kept her thoughts to herself.

"Well, I don't have much more to explain to you—no more shocking disclosures. I'd like to answer any questions that you might have. And I think we should discuss the document I sent. Have you signed it yet?"

"No, we wanted to speak with you about it first."

"That's fine. You really have two options. You can agree to this settlement, or you can file an appeal in hopes of receiving more."

Lillian swallowed hard, trying to imagine what Father would advise. "I don't think I want to fight with him."

"Nor do I," Grace added with far more conviction.

"Just so that you understand, if you sign this it will mean that you can't change your mind later—even if more of the story comes out. It will mean turning your back on any further financial resources from family back East."

Sweeping her eyes along the edge of the desk and shifting in her chair, Lillian cleared her throat. "Do you feel it would be foolish for us to sign this and be done with it? Or do you think we wouldn't likely gain more than we'd lose if we were to choose to appeal?"

She could hear him sigh through the wires. "If I could judge those difficult questions before I even filed a case, I'd be a very wealthy man. One never knows. It comes down to a personal decision about how you might find peace. Will you be plagued with regret should you allow the matter to end? Or would the stresses of suing a relative be more than you can manage?"

"I know what I'll say," Grace assured him. "I'm done with it. I want to walk away."

Lillian's thoughts whirled. *Yes, wouldn't it be better just to put it behind us? But what if Father would have said otherwise? Still, I have to consider that Grace's mind is made up.* And suddenly Lillian knew exactly how to respond. "Mr. Dorn, I need to defer to my sister on this matter. After all, I'm the one who was adopted.

Sadly, Grace was not. Apparently, Saul Brazington-Bennett is the reason we didn't stay together. So I'm confident that this is a decision Grace can make for both of us. I want her preference to stand."

She felt a hand catch her by the elbow. Grace leaned her head closer to Lillian's and sniffed quietly.

"I'm certain," Lillian affirmed.

After the call ended, Mr. Wattley helped them to sign the paperwork and encouraged the sisters not to second-guess their decision.

Then he added, tugging at his shirt collar just a little, "I should tell you, Lillian, that I've taken it upon myself to send a brief telegram to your father. Though he's not legally involved, I know that he'd want to know. And as his legal counsel for many years, I don't want him to be caught off guard."

"Oh, I want Father to know," she assured him. "Thank you. I wish he were here right now."

"I thought you might. I'll let you know as soon as he responds."

"Thanks, Mr. Wattley." Lillian recalled the help the man had given her when Lemuel had been taken to jail, and the way he'd aided with her finances. She added earnestly, "I appreciate the way you've served our family, sir. I know that Father rests easier knowing you're here as an advisor to us."

His smile revealed his appreciation for her words and, perhaps, a little relief.

CHAPTER 24

Janie

Lillian was pleased when little Jane Grey fit into their home like a hand in a glove. She played well with the twins, was mild-mannered and friendly, and even offered frequently to help in the kitchen. Though the little boys had already returned to their school classes, it had been decided that Jane should have time to adjust first. Miss Tilly wasn't able to hide her own immediate affinity for the child, inviting Jane to sit on a stool close by, chattering away happily as the girl attempted to peel a potato.

"I think the chickies are gonna hatch today," Jane informed their busy cook, sitting next to her as she rolled out biscuits for supper. "I keep telling the boys to be quiet in your room. But they make too much noise. An' they might scare 'em."

"The *chicks*? They ain't hatched yet, dear." Miss Tilly chuckled. "Maybe tomorra."

"Will the hens be girls or boys?"

Miss Tilly wiped her chin on her shoulder in order to hide her amusement.

Lillian, from where she stood setting glasses on the kitchen table, was grateful their housekeeper wasn't the type of adult who would openly tease a child for her innocent questions.

Miss Tilly's answer was matter-of-fact and instructive. "A growed-up girl is called a hen. When it's still young we call it a pullet. But we won't know 'til they hatch if they're boys or girls. Then ya can tell by the color'a the downy little feathers on their heads and backs. Don't work fer all chicken types, but it's fair certain in ours."

"What'll we do with the boys? 'Cause boy chickens don't lay eggs, do they?"

Lillian cringed at the way the facts of life came up so quickly for children on a farm.

"Well, we'll let 'em grow fer a while. Then we'll cook 'em up an' eat 'em while they're still young and tender."

Jane pulled a face. "You're gonna cook them?"

"Yes. You see, God give us some kinds'a animals fer our food. An' I guess God knows best, don't you?"

There was only a mild hesitation before the child conceded the point with a little nod of her head. She added, "I guess I won't play so much with the boy chickens."

Lillian smiled with encouragement from where she now stood counting silverware from the drawer, relieved at an accepted resolution to Jane's questions. Miss Tilly had instructed that an extra place be set at the table that evening, promising that there'd be an unnamed guest—and assuring Lillian that it would not be Quinley Sinclair.

The conversation continued as Miss Tilly asked, "Have ya seen real chickens b'fore?"

"Why, yes. Where I lived in England we had stables behind the house. An' the chickens were all across the yard, pecking up bugs and worms and such."

"Ya had a grand house, did ya?"

Jane paused over the potato she was still attempting to peel. She'd been sculpting it mercilessly with clumsy hands into smaller and smaller shapes. "I guess so. I had a room to myself, and Margaret—she's my sister—she had a room beside me. I liked it b'cause there was a door in between us and she let me sleep in her bed sometimes when I was scared at night. Margaret is twelve. So she's not scared of the dark anymore."

Lillian's face fell. It was an effort to govern the emotion in her voice for the sake of the child. "You have a sister, Jane? We didn't know that. What happened to your sister?"

"Oh, she had ta go away to school after my mummy and daddy died. But I was too young. So Aunt M'tilda sent me on the big ship." Her eyes remained fixed on the scrap of white potato. "They didn't wanna take me, but Mister Waldin helped. He put me inside a great big box, and then he kep' me in his room. It was too quiet there and sometimes I was scared, but he brought me food and books—oh, and even a cat to play with for my very own. I named her Tumblepuss." She added sorrowfully, "'Cept I had to leave her behind."

Lillian held her breath as she caught Miss Tilly's eye. She wondered if her own face had drained to the pale color of the older woman's. "You didn't come aboard the ship with all the other children?"

"Oh no. Mister Waldin, he said it was a 'dventure. I stayed in his room. An' he said it was okay to change my name to Jane Grey, 'stead of Jane Henry, because that was better for me in Canada. He said it would be *wise*." Her eyes swept around her for affirmation.

Lillian nodded, eyes round and unblinking. "It's a lovely name. Was that your name—Jane Henry? Before your parents died?"

"Yes." Her voice slowed. She pronounced the familiar words carefully, lovingly. "My parents are Lawrence and Agnes Henry."

Miss Tilly shook the flour from her fingers and, stepping behind the child's stool, tugged at Lillian's sleeve, leaving a splotch of white dust. Her eyes were wide but her voice held steady. "Thet's all right, dearie. We're gonna finish up them taters now and talk so' more 'bout it when Miss Grace comes down. Miss Lillian now, she's gonna go see what's keepin' Miss Grace upstairs. Ain't ya, Miss Lillian?"

Lillian nodded and rushed across the room toward the stairs. By the time she reached Grace's bedroom she could hardly see or breathe. "Grace, come quick."

"What's happened?"

"Janie—she was *smuggled* out of England by Ben Waldin. He hid her in his room on the ship. Her name was really Jane Henry until he changed it to Jane Grey. Oh dear, that's probably why her age was different than the one listed originally! Do you remember that Quinley commented about that?"

Grace abandoned the small trousers she'd been mending. "What happened to the real Jane Grey?"

"I have no idea. Oh dear, I hadn't even thought of that!"

Grace held out her hands, splaying the fingers as she swept them slowly in front of Lillian. "We've got to remain calm, Lillian. Do you understand? We'll find out what her story is—and we will *certainly* address this in whatever manner is appropriate, but we've got to stay calm or we'll upset the one person who matters more than any of the rest of us. I don't know much, but I do know that Janie feels safe with Ben. I don't understand how this can be—oh dear, how *can* this be? But we're going to do everything in our power to keep from confusing or frightening Jane's tender little heart."

"Yes," Lillian whispered. "I won't scare her, I promise."

"If you feel you have to cry, then you'll need to leave the room."

Immediately Lillian's lip began to quiver. She pulled it in and bit down. "Yes, I'll control myself."

"All right." And then, "Sis, did she have any family? Did she mention if there were people who looked after her in England?"

Lillian nodded her head. "She said that when her parents died an aunt sent her sister away to school, but that Jane was too young so her aunt tried to foist her off with the other orphan children on a ship. She said that Ben *helped* them."

"Oh dear. Surely he's not one of those . . ." Slowly, Grace led the way back downstairs.

Lillian's thoughts careened off course. It was impossible to remain calm. *This isn't happening!*

The potatoes were ready. Miss Tilly had directed Jane to finish setting the table.

The little girl's eyes lit up to see the sisters return. "Look, Miss Grace. I'm helping set."

"You're doing a good job." Grace drew closer, gathered her skirt, and dropped down onto one knee. "Let's see what else is needed. We have forks but we don't have spoons. And we'll need spoons to eat our applesauce. Let's find the spoons in the drawer. Can you count out six spoons?"

"Uh-uh, Miss Grace, we have to have seven. Somebody's comin' to dinner."

"That's right. I forgot about that. Seven it is."

Lillian waited at the foot of the stairs, too worried about her composure to risk moving farther into the room.

"Jane, Miss Lillian told me what you said, about the way you came to us from England. How did the boat trip make you feel?"

"Hmm." The girl's voice rose and fell in childlike fashion as she did her best to answer the question. "At first I didn't like to feel the boat rocking. It made my tummy tickle. But pretty soon I liked it. When I was all alone in bed, it kinda felt like I was on a great big swing." Jane set another spoon carefully in place. "I didn't like to be alone so much. But whenever he could, Mister Waldin took me for walks in the dark—so I could see the big ocean. I liked that. It was my fav'rite." She paused to think. "An' he read me books, an' he said he liked the pi'tures I drew. He said he was sorry I had to be alone so much, but I tol' him, 'I'm a big girl.' And—did they tell you? I had a cat. Her name's Tumblepuss. My mummy had a cat called that when she was a little girl."

"That's nice. What color was Tumblepuss?"

"Gray, mostly. But she had some white on her belly. That's where she was softest."

"That's nice. Look, Jane, we're all done. Will you sit down with us for a moment, please?"

"Yes, Miss Grace." She scooted up onto a chair.

Lillian slipped onto the nearest seat. The child's descriptions had helped a little to calm the palpitations of her heart.

Grace became more direct. "Where did Mr. Waldin sleep, Jane? Did he stay in the bedroom with you?"

Jane's voice saddened as she answered, "No. He never did. I don't know where he slep'. He said he couldn't stay there, 'cause I was using his bed. Silly Mister Waldin."

Grace smiled. "Aw, that *is* silly. Maybe he slept in a shoebox."

Laughing, Jane suggested more seriously, "Or on the deck. It was very cold on the deck."

"I'll bet that's just where he slept."

The little face tipped up toward Grace. Suddenly Jane frowned. "Miss Grace, I wasn't s'pose to tell you 'bout being Jane Henry now, was I? Do you think Mister Waldin will be mad at me?"

"Oh no, dear. He won't be angry. I promise."

A knock at the front door gave Lillian such a jolt that she caught herself just before slipping off her chair. She rose quickly instead and headed to answer, her hands still trembling. *It won't be Quinley. Miss Tilly promised it wouldn't be him.*

When she drew the door open, a gasp escaped from Lillian's gaping mouth.

Walter stepped quickly inside, his brown eyes sparkling with joy. "Lillian, I've missed you so much."

Instantly her lip began to tremble again. *How can it be Walter? He's working up north.* She took a half step closer, dropping her face against his shoulder.

Walter's arms folded around her. "Oh, Lillian, I came as soon as I heard about your uncle."

• • • ● • • •

Over supper it was explained to Lillian that Grace had sent a telegram to Walter after they spoke to Mr. Wattley. Walter still had the paper in his pocket. Grace had written, *UNCLE SAUL KNEW WE BOTH SURVIVED—STOP—HE TOLD NO ONE—STOP—LILLIAN NEEDS YOU—STOP—CAN YOU COME—STOP.*

At first Lillian was annoyed that her sister had taken it upon herself to interfere with Walter again. *Hasn't she already inserted herself enough?* But since she was now sitting beside the very person she'd been longing to see, Lillian quickly set aside her feelings of irritation.

"What happened then? Did you sign the papers?" Walter asked in wonder.

"We did."

His eyes were filled with concern. "How do you feel about that, Lillian? Did it feel strange to sign away that part of your family?"

Lillian smiled toward Grace. "I'm happy with the family I have. I don't want to chase after someone who so clearly isn't interested in us."

"But," Grace added with emphasis, "the money doesn't hurt."

"There's money?"

As she caught Walter's eye, a slow smile spread across Lillian's lips.

Grace answered on her behalf. "A good amount. We already ordered a telephone to be wired all the way from town to this house. And I bought a car with my share, big enough for all of us to ride in comfortably. Ben's going to . . ." She grimaced at the mention of Ben's name.

Walter's eyes came back to Lillian. His brow furrowed.

She merely shook her head in reply and changed the subject back to what was pleasant in the moment. "I need to speak with Father before I do anything with my share of our inheritance."

Is it poor manners to say the amount aloud? Lillian decided she didn't care. She was dreadfully tired of secrets. "It was a bank draft for twenty-five thousand dollars. We chose to divide it in half."

Walter reached quickly for his water glass, took a sip, and cleared his throat. "That's a considerable amount. I've been workin' hard and thought I was doin' quite well with accumulating a little stash of my own. But, no, that's—that's a great deal of money."

Lillian looked away. She couldn't allow him to see the hopes that were rising in her eyes.

Miss Tilly intervened. "Got a Saskatoon pie fer dessert with fresh whipped cream."

Jane piped up brightly, "I helped make it. Do you like saspatoon pie, Mr. Norberg?"

"I like *any kind* of pie. Pretty much any kind of pie at all. Right, boys?"

The twins giggled in agreement.

• • • ● • • •

The group gathered in the parlor and sang several songs together while Lillian accompanied them on the piano. At last Grace volunteered to manage the bedtime rituals, and the pandemonium of children followed after her up the stairs. The parlor grew suddenly still. Walter pulled the doors closed behind them and took a seat beside Lillian at the piano.

"I enjoy listenin' to you play. I forgot how much I enjoy it." He lifted his hand to the keyboard, his fingers brushing over the keys gently as if too afraid to strike a sound of his own. Lillian noticed several new scabs and scars on the skin of his hands. It seemed his hard work had taken a toll.

"Thank you," she whispered, fidgeting with the folds of her apron. And then, "Oh, Walter, I can't tell you how grateful I am that you came back. I know it hasn't been that long, but it seems like the world has tipped upside down since you left."

"I want to hear all about it." His voice sounded strained. "But if I may, I'd like to apologize to you first."

She dared a glance up at his face. "What for?"

"For the way I left. I should have . . . Well, believe it or not, Grace warned me that I should have a serious talk with you first. But I convinced myself that if I let you know what my intentions were for choosing to work—that is, if I repeated my hope that I could make enough to purchase a home—for us—it would just hurt both of us more when I left—would make the wait seem even longer. But, Lillian, I was very wrong. I understand now that I should have left things settled between us that night at Mrs. O'Shea's—or at least given you a chance to speak your mind too."

Lillian leaned against his side, felt his arm go around her, and listened to the pounding of his heart where her ear was pressed.

"I wanted to make somethin' out of myself, Lillian. I wanted to be able to provide for you in the way you're accustomed."

Squeezing her eyes tightly shut, Lillian whispered, "I never asked for that."

"I know. But I wanted it for you. And you know I wanted to get started ranchin'."

Her mind went to the sum of money she now controlled. She held her breath. *Will it make a difference? Might he stay home now?*

Walter continued, "What I didn't understand is that, without you, I'm pretty empty—empty in a way I've never felt without anybody else before. Bein' with you and talkin' to you—that's what gives me the focus to work hard. I don't think I can do it without you."

She closed her eyes. At last he was saying aloud what she'd longed to hear.

"Do you remember when I told you—standin' right outside here on your front porch—that I wanted to court you, to marry you?"

She nodded, still silent.

"You weren't certain at the time. You said there was too much goin' on, and your father was away." A chuckle. She could feel that he was shaking his head. "Good night, Lillian! It seems like you're always in the middle of some kind of crisis. All these kids sure keep you busy." But he grew quiet. "Will you look at me, please?"

With effort, she lifted her gaze to the beautiful brown eyes she'd longed to see for so long. She told him, "I'm sorry that I'm so much trouble. I know I—"

His large hand brushed back her hair. "I love you and I want to marry you, Lillian. I'm patient, but I'm pretty persistent too. I hope I don't have to wait too much longer. You don't have to tell me *when*. But can you let me know if you're ready to admit you're willin'?"

It was impossible now to look away from his exquisite eyes. "Yes, I'm willing, Walter. I want to marry you too."

A long exhale. "I'm so glad. Can I . . . Is it okay if I kiss you now?"

"I wish you would."

Chapter 25

White Water

The vehicle that Ben was bringing back to Grace was not exactly new. It was a lumbering beast of a machine, extended by its previous owner using the frame of a delivery truck. But there was ample seating inside the leather-roofed automobile. And on a sunny day, the roof could be folded all the way back in stages to expose the sky. Ben found it difficult to drive, far more temperamental than the car belonging to Brayton House. But he was certain that, if he could just open up the engine to look at it closely, he could soon have it humming nicely.

Early Saturday morning he and Freddie set off again. The road was easier to travel for the second trip and the warm weather had held. Freddie stayed awake, chatting uncharacteristically about animals he'd trapped in the past and the ones he hoped to soon discover. "Was talkin' ta the lads at Brayton. They said I gotta try trappin' gophers. That's what they got a million'a here. 'Cept they weren't sure if there's any where we're goin'. Ya e'er seen a gopher, Mister Waldin?"

"Yer gonna go ta school, though, ain't ya?"

"Only if I gotta."

"Well . . . ya gotta." Shaking his head, Ben offered with a smile, "No, lad. I ne'er seen a gopher. Maybe we can catch one t'gether."

The wide valley cradling the little town came into view. Ben smiled. Janie waited below. And as much as he wished he were already searching for his sister, he was glad that he could anticipate more stability for Janie and himself, at least for now.

The car rattled down the long hill. He pushed down hard on the brake pedal, shifted to low gear, and hefted the steering wheel around to make the automobile turn off the road, between the bushes. Janie and the boys were playing on the porch with the cat. She waved enthusiastically when she saw him.

Freddie rolled out from the far door. Ben eased his feet to the ground, stretched his tired legs, then stood to full height stiffly. He was glad the days of driving were over.

Grace appeared in the doorway. She waved toward Ben. *No, it ain't a wave. She's summonin' me in.* Freddie shot him a puzzled look. Ben shrugged. Janie seemed fine, so he wasn't worried.

The youngsters beat a path toward the car but Grace shooed them away, calling, "Don't play in the automobile, please. We'll let you know when your lunch is ready. You can play outside until then."

Janie skipped closer to show Ben the cat that she was finally able to befriend. "Her name's Miss Puss," she explained. "But I'm going to call her Tumplepuss too." Then she scurried off to rejoin the little boys.

Ben and Freddie strolled to the house together.

"Think I'm gonna find me some line fer traps," Freddie said. "An' set 'em in the trees out back."

"I s'pose that's all right."

But the air in the house felt oppressive as soon as they entered. Grace and Lillian stood guard in the foyer, staring across at them like sentinels at their posts.

Ben tried to break through the tension with easy words. "Well, we brought 'er. Seems ta be a sturdy ol' thing. But she runs a wee bit rough. I think I can—"

"We'd like to speak with you, Ben. In the kitchen, if you'd come, please."

"O'course."

Freddie reached for the door handle. "I'm gonna go look fer some line in the barn."

"That's fine," Grace said.

Ben followed the sisters away as Freddie closed the door behind him.

"What is't ya need?"

"Please sit down," Lillian told him.

That's ne'er a good beginnin'. Don't bode well. "Aye, miss."

"I'm going to get right to the point, Ben," Grace announced, bracing herself behind a kitchen chair. "We've heard some things that have made us very concerned."

"What kinda things?"

"Jane referred to an aunt in England."

"Yes, miss, I spoke with her."

"What arrangement did you have with this woman?"

He rubbed a hand across his face, allowed his eyes to sweep the room. Miss Lillian stood beside the stove, seemingly unable to lift her eyes from the floor. Miss Tilly was planted near her worktable, wiping her hands on her apron the way his mother often did when she'd been very cross. And Grace seemed more severe than Ben would have thought possible for such a kind-hearted woman.

He cleared his throat. "She were gonna send the girl to a workhouse. I had a job aboard ship, helpin' ta get them orphans safely 'cross the sea. They call 'em *bone shops*, miss—the work-houses, that is. They're bad, miss. Folk what come outta 'em are skin an' bones, is all. I worked with some men from there. They was ne'er ag'in right in the head, if ya ask me. Didn't want that fer Janie. Couldn't abide it."

"Why? Why this child? How did you know her?"

"I didn't." He rubbed at the skin on the back of his hand nervously. "Can't e'en answer that, 'cause I ain't certain. 'Cept, Jane's me sister's name." He paused. "An' it were her eyes—big as saucers an'—so innocent. She didn't deserve ta be jus' throwed away."

Grace's hands slackened their fierce grip on the back of the chair. "How did you get her aboard?"

He watched her stance begin to soften too. "She weren't on the list, miss. So I'd no way ta put her in with the others. I kep' her in me berth instead. Just waitin' 'til I could find the right time."

Miss Tilly marched a couple steps forward, a rolling pin clutched in her hand. "Look me in the eye, Ben Waldin," she demanded. "Did ya touch her? Did ya lay a hand on this child?"

"No—no, ma'am," he sputtered, searching each woman's face by turn, searching for one that might believe him. "I'd ne'er . . . I wouldn't . . . *She's a baby*. She needed help. An' that's all."

Miss Tilly retreated back again.

She must'a b'lieved me, that woman, or she'da done me in jus' then.

Lillian's voice broke in quietly. "Ben, who's Jane Henry?"

The question pierced Ben's heart, bringing the eerie white face of death to his mind. "Jane Henry's our Janie. It's her real name." He dreaded the explanation he knew he'd be required to give. "Aboard me ship, some'a 'em got sick. Happens oft on a voyage. Three of 'em died. I'll ne'er forget their faces." His eyes closed as he recited their names. "Little Edgar, a young boy named John Wall, and last was Jane, the true Jane Grey." His shoulders slumped, his face hung low. "God help me, but I knew at last I'd found a way ta get Janie inta Canada. I tol' her we'd change her name ta Janie Grey. Tol' her it were needed fer entry. Said that though me name's Ebenezer, I tell folk I'm Ben. It's jus' like that, said I."

Grace eased herself down onto her chair. Her voice had grown softer. "Who did you tell about this?"

Slowly, firmly, he shook his head, his words grave. "Ta tell'd be ta ruin it fer Janie. She d'serves a fam'ly. She needs a chance ta be loved. I couldn't tell. I wish I weren't tellin' it now. But ta do nothin' woulda been ta leave her there fer the workhouse. I couldn't do it. Maybe ya could'a, miss, but not I."

The back door was flung open. Freddie burst into the room. "Leave him be!" he shouted. "Why do ya have ta pick on him, then? Mister Waldin, he ain't hurt nobody!"

Grace was on her feet before the door recoiled and shut again. "Freddie," she pleaded with him, "you can't be here. This is a conversation for the adults."

"Adults? Adults! What gives *you* th'right ta judge?"

"Freddie, please." But Ben had no energy left to send Freddie away.

"Mister Waldin, he's a good man. Helps us all, he does. Both'a ya too. An' none more 'an Jane. Adults? They get ta pick an' choose what 'uns they wanna care 'bout an' what 'uns they wanna throw away. I hate 'em! Everyone'a 'em what won't help a kid. I hate 'em all!"

Freddie crossed the room and stood before Ben's chair. "If ya go, Mister Waldin, I'm goin' too. An' if they think they can make me stay, I'll show 'em. I'm going with ya."

Ben wasn't certain how to respond. He knew that Freddie's outburst hadn't helped his cause.

And then, "Adults!" the boy spit out again. "Adults like them Szwedas, ya mean? Men what make boys sleep in barns an' work from dawn ta dark. Men like that, ya mean? You can keep 'em. I got no use fer adults like that."

Grace's voice asked evenly, "How do you know about the Szwedas, Freddie?"

"Ya wanna know? *Ya wanna know?*" Freddie's voice broke in anger. "'Cause Mister Waldin here, he drove out ta see 'em. Jus' ta see Mickey an' Vaughan. Ta make sure they was all right—an' had food ta eat. He tol' them old coots he was gonna check up on 'em again, ta make sure they was gettin' schoolin' an' not workin' too hard. That's him! That's Ben Waldin. An' ya wanna judge him? Well, you can go right ahead an'—"

"Freddie!" Ben stopped the boy, a hand now clutching at his shirt. "That's 'nough. We're gonna go. Come on." He pushed himself up from his chair.

Grace rose before him, standing between them and the door. "Wait. Please wait. We don't want to persecute you, Ben. That's not our intention. Surely you understand that we have to ask. It's our responsibility to ask the difficult questions. And this situation—it's very, very . . . difficult." Her eyes implored him to understand.

"I understand ya gotta ask."

"Please don't go far. Please give us some time to process all of this. Please."

He nodded his head, took Freddie by the arm, and pushed him between the women to exit the room.

They stepped out into the warm breeze. "Let's go, Mister Waldin," Freddie pleaded. "Let's jus' take the car an' leave."

"I ain't no thief, lad." Ben sighed. "I gotta do the right thing."

"But what they said 'bout ya. That ain't right."

Ben stopped in place and let his head hang low for a moment. Then with effort he raised it again to address the boy. "Lad, it weren't right what I done. Might be some wiser 'an me what could'a done better. But not I. Still, that don't mean I could set by an' do nothin'. Sometimes a man don't get a *good* choice—a *right* choice. Just one what ain't the worst." He looked toward where Janie was playing. "I ain't sorry. I'd do it ag'in today jus' ta see her there—safe an' happy."

• • • ● • • •

O Father, what have we done? What have we gotten ourselves into the middle of now?

Grace's lips were moving in silent prayer. Lillian had seen it before. Miss Tilly had turned back to her worktable. She was wiping it off with a wet rag, the same spot over and over.

At last Grace spoke. "I don't know what to do. I'm in utter shock."

"Well, we have to tell Sid. We should go right away to see Mr. Wattley." Lillian felt herself babbling. "Should we call the police? Is this kidnapping?" Her head was spinning.

Miss Tilly drew back a chair. "Sit, girls. We gotta talk this one out now."

Grace followed the woman's instructions, but Lillian found it too difficult not to pace, remaining on her feet. "What do you propose we do? We're not equipped to handle this."

"If we was ta send her back, where'd she go?" Miss Tilly asked.

Only Grace articulated an answer. "There's probably no one. Clearly her aunt doesn't want her. Ben is probably correct. She'd go to a workhouse or an orphanage there."

"An' would that be good fer the child?"

"No," Grace was quick to assert.

"But, Grace"—Lillian begged her sister to listen—"laws have been broken. We can't be party to this."

"Lillian, please. We've got to ask ourselves, what would be best for Jane?"

Throwing her hands into the air, Lillian raised her voice at Grace for the first time. "It's the law, Grace. We'd be just as guilty as Ben if we didn't report it. We'd be complicit. How can you possibly consider any other course of action? My father would . . . oh my goodness, what will my father say?"

"Sit down, dearie. Ya won't calm yer mind 'til your body can rest." Miss Tilly patted the chair beside her. "Sit down. Please."

Lillian obeyed at last.

The woman spoke softly, deliberately. "Now's I see it, we got only two choices. If we tell 'bout Janie, she's liable ta be sent back. There ain't nobody fer her there. That ain't no better. We keep her here, she'll get a good fam'ly. She'll have a chance fer a future. She'll be loved." Her eyes moved from Grace to Lillian. "Am I gettin' that right?"

Grace twisted at a clump of her hair that had come loose and fallen against her neck. "She can't go back. But I think I should confide in Sid."

"That's a pretty big risk, don'tcha think?"

"I trust Sid. More than most."

Lillian pushed her chair back. "Sid was the one who sent more children to the Szwedas after we rescued Matty and Milton."

"That's not true, sis. Remember? Sid Brown had no control over where the Mercy Society sent those kids. He had no control over that. But we do. Whether we like it or not, this little girl is here now. And we have to make a sound decision for her future." The little clump of hair was spinning tighter and tighter. "Well, what if I don't tell him which child I'm referring to? What if I just say I've learned that one of the children in this group was not originally with them?"

"He'll know," Lillian said. "Lots of people commented on how strange it was to see Jane with Ben. She'll be the first one he thinks of. He'll know."

"You're right. He'll know."

Miss Tilly's palm came down with a thump on the table. "All right then, we'll tell. Let's call fer the Mounties and have 'em write up a report. But let's not stop there while we're at it. If we're gonna do it right, we'll have 'em write one fer little Bryony too. 'Cause we all know't ta be true, that little girl *really was* kidnapped. So let's send 'er back ta England where she come from, so the letter o' the law can be kept."

Lillian groaned.

Grace shook her head, her voice sounding tired and frustrated. "We're not going to call the police for Bryony, Miss Tilly. That's ridiculous."

"Why not, Miss Grace? We don't got legal right to put her in a family neither. Same's this little Jane."

"Oh, you don't even mean that! You're just making a point. But the thing is, we know about Jane. We didn't know about Bryony."

"Ya did too. Ya tol' me yerself she got stole from her home."

"But we didn't know *where*. If we could have found her family, we certainly would have tried to send her back."

"True, an' mercifully, that child woulda gone back ta folk who love 'er. Jane, she's got nobody back there a'tall."

There was a strange logic to what Miss Tilly argued. Lillian watched Grace closely. How would she respond?

And then it didn't matter. "Do you know what, I'm tired of it all!" Lillian blurted. "I'm tired of men keeping secrets—of crimes and lies and scheming. Isn't Ben just as bad as Quinley? They both kept secrets. I'm too tired of it all to be part of it anymore."

Grace was twisting her hair again. "It's not the same," she countered. "Ben is nothing like Quin."

"How so, dearie?" By the way Miss Tilly asked the question, Lillian suspected she already knew the answer, was leading them along in a Socratic way.

"Quinley Sinclair was out for his own gain. He lied and flattered to get what he wanted. It had nothing to do with helping the children. He was just helping himself."

Lillian hadn't heard Grace judge Quinley so harshly aloud. It felt satisfying to hear her sister speak the words.

"Oh, do ya think so?"

"Yes, I do."

"An' Ben Waldin? Is he cut from the same cloth?" Miss Tilly pushed further.

Rather than answering Miss Tilly, Grace directed her words toward Lillian. "It's not the same. Ben lied *to save Janie*. He risked his own welfare in order to help her. Just like he did when he drove our car to visit Vaughan and Michael without asking." Tears were forming in her sister's eyes. "Lillian, Freddie was right. Ben only did what he thought was best. And I have no idea what

I would have done in his place, but I'm sure it wouldn't have been *nothing.* I couldn't have walked away either. Could you?"

It was quiet for several minutes. At last Miss Tilly's voice broke the stillness. "Now, I've been around a long while. I seen some things. The way I see it is, it's like paddlin' a canoe."

Lillian and Grace's bewildered faces lifted to stare at her. *Has she lost her mind?*

"Just hang with me. You'll see. As I say, it's like paddlin' a canoe. When yer comin' to some white water, yer first urge is ta try an' back up. But ya can't. The current's far too strong fer that. When my Joe took me out on the river, he first explained it all ta me. Ya gotta fight that urge and paddle straight on in, 'stead. It don't feel right. Yer scared ta do it. But it's the only way not ta get pushed along willy-nilly. If ya bend yer back inta it, ya find ya can direct where ya wanna go an' miss the sharp rocks." A deep sigh. "Well, girls, this is a time yer gonna need ta bend yer back inta the tumult in order to have any say at all. Ya can't go back. Yer gettin' carried along in this white water patch. So ya better be ready ta paddle with all ya got. Forward. It's the only way."

She rose to her feet as if the matter had been settled. Without further comment, she went right back to their lunch preparations.

CHAPTER 26

The Long Afternoon

Ben and Freddie pushed the car into the barn. The boy had discovered tools inside when he'd been looking for the line that he wanted to use to set his traps. Ben thought that perhaps with a little effort they could get the automobile working more smoothly before he was sent away. He hoped that the sisters would find it in their hearts to have mercy on Jane. She'd done nothing wrong. She was an innocent victim of it all. Surely they wouldn't really send her back to a life of imprisonment because of anything he'd done.

With the hood of the car folded back, Ben reached deep inside, oil oozing between his fingers. Freddie was lying on his back beneath, working from a different angle, when a man's voice invaded their focused efforts.

"Hello? I heard there was a new car. I came to see it before I go inside."

Freddie scooted out quickly from beneath, a look on his face as if he was ready to bolt from the barn. Ben wiped his hands on a rag before approaching. "Hello, sir."

The stranger was tall, wore a cowboy hat and leather boots

with pointed toes. He seemed to Ben to have stepped out of a picture book of the West. His hand was extended congenially. "I hoped to take a minute to introduce myself to you too. You must be Ben. Can I help you at all? My name's Walter. I'm a—close friend of the family. I've been away for work."

"Yes, sir. I'm Ben. An' this is Freddie."

"Sure! It's nice to meet you both. I was here yesterday. Lillian told me all about how helpful you've been."

"Might not say so now," Ben muttered under his breath, so that only Freddie could hear him. Louder he answered, "The car needs ta be tuned. I thought I'd do it b'fore I went away."

The smile on Walter's face faded. "You're goin' away? I'm sorry to hear it. The way Lillian spoke of you, I thought you might be around for a while. I've recently taken a job on the oil rigs, but . . ." Walter chuckled. "I've been the one who served as their driver for some time. I was glad to hear someone else had stepped in to help."

"Yeah, I'm leavin'. Most likely. But the car, it runs kinda rough. I didn't wanna leave 'em with a vehicle what's hard ta drive."

Walter slipped his coat from his shoulders. "Can I help? I don't have too much experience, but I've learned a lot by workin' on my own car and my brother-in-law's tractor."

• • • • • • •

The children finished their lunch, a quiet and dismal affair. Even the small ones could feel the sense of trouble that hung thick in the air.

Lillian ushered them upstairs to take their Saturday nap. She lay down among them on the full-sized bed where the boys slept together and read the next story from their favorite book of fairy tales. She knew that her voice was far less dramatic in her reading than normal. Far less emotional energy animated her words. Her mind was churning beneath the surface, working away at the problem of Ben and what his actions may have caused.

Soon she was tucking Janie into her own bed and saying the usual words of prayer aloud over her. "God, bless this child whom You love. Please give her a peaceful rest, a loving spirit, and a heart that bends to You. In Jesus' name, amen."

"Miss Lillian, I left the kitty outside with Mister Waldin," Janie rushed to explain, delaying the last moment of naptime ritual. "He's fixing the new car. Freddie is helping him."

Lillian closed her eyes. *So here's Ben, shamed and shunned and still serving wherever he finds work to do.* She settled Jane's new rag doll down beside her. "He's a kind man, isn't he?"

The little girl nodded. "He *is* kind—just like my daddy. Mister Waldin, he doesn't talk loud to me. Just quiet and close. He looks at my eyes. My daddy did that too."

The comment pierced Lillian's heart, but after turning away she managed to choke out, "Have a good rest, Jane. I'll see you when you wake up."

Softly, Lillian pulled the door closed behind her. She didn't really want to go downstairs. If there were any way to retreat to her private place in her parents' bedroom and avoid all further conversations today, she was certain it would have been her preference. But Miss Tilly's words echoed in her mind. Against her will she pictured a canoe shared by Grace and herself.

Father had once taken Lillian on such a ride. It was a sunny fall day when she was young, only ten or eleven. He'd sat at the back of the strange, narrow boat that he'd borrowed from neighbors. Lillian sat in front, her rather useless paddle dipping and dragging in the water. Though they hadn't come anywhere near the rapids, she could imagine just what Miss Tilly had described.

Oh, I do know precisely what she accused me of. Whenever trouble comes, I recoil from it like I've just touched fire. But what if I didn't think of things that way? What if I looked at life the way Miss Tilly does? And pressed forward instead? It's certainly never done me a bit of good to try to run and hide, to resist changes and drag my feet—or better yet, my poor little paddle.

She considered her sister. *Grace is so much braver than I've ever been. I suppose it's because she's always had to be. She could never escape the sense of abandonment that was thrust on her when Mama and Papa died. I had my new father and mother to take care of me. She gave herself to others. She had no safe shelter for herself, nor for the children she cares so much about.*

Silently, Lillian touched the surface of the bedroom door next to her, thinking of the small girl resting beyond it. *Well, this work is what I've chosen to do—or rather, have been called to do, sometimes kicking and screaming on the inside. But why should God make it easy for me when it's so very hard for Jane—for any of them?* So what mattered most? And who among the host of authorities was thinking first of the child?

Lillian contemplated Quinley. He was easy to like. He was smooth and sophisticated. She shuddered as she remembered that she'd once hoped Grace would find a match with him. He had turned out to be selfish and greedy, a slick schemer who took advantage of those with fewer advantages in life, in a system that rewarded the very ones who abused it.

In contrast there was Ben. Rough and uneducated. *No, that isn't true. He knows Virgil!* Lillian admitted to herself that there was far more to him than she'd seen. In truth, she'd hardly begun to get to know him at all. *And where is he now? Where he always is. Working hard for someone else. He's actually putting off his mission of finding his own family in order to serve us here—to protect Janie—to take Freddie under his wing.*

Then she thought about Ben's visit to the Szwedas. Of all the people involved with the Mercy Society—or even Brayton House—Ben had been the only one to check up on Michael and Vaughan. Didn't that count for something? Didn't it speak loudly of his character? His commitment to the children?

But hadn't he made the same mistake that she and Grace had

made? Hadn't he also been deceitful? *God, I know You forgave me. Even though I knowingly trespassed on Your law. So can't I forgive Ben—who doesn't even claim to know You personally? After all, he did much the same thing. For the very same reasons.*

She pictured the moment again when the Szwedas arrived at the door unannounced. For the thousandth time she tried to imagine what she should have said. *God, I think I understand better now. You love those boys so much more than Grace and I ever could. You know them—everything about them. Even to numbering each hair on their heads. Bringing them to us was a call on our lives. But You would have kept them regardless, even if we hadn't sinned against You. We needed to trust You. It wasn't our burden to save them. It was You who did it. It was just our job to serve in the circumstances You led us into. And Your strength to save is so, so much greater than ours. I think I'm beginning to understand a little better now.*

Stiffening her back, Lillian took a step forward. *I'm going to try to be brave like Grace. I can paddle forward, too, into unforeseen waters.* The visual image of the two of them in a canoe together made Lillian laugh aloud despite her anxious heart. *How much of my time have I spent ducking down in the front of this boat, making Grace do all the hard paddling? Well, no longer. I'm ready now. I understand better than I ever have before.*

Returning to the kitchen, Lillian joined in the silent contemplation and work. Together the three women washed dishes and swept, cleaned ashes from the stove and stocked it with fresh coal in order to begin supper preparations. All the while Lillian's eyes lifted repeatedly in the direction of the barn. She wondered how Ben and Freddie were managing. She wondered if they had already disappeared. *Should I slip out to the barn to see for myself? No, it's best to give Ben some time, I think. To come to his own conclusions. To make up his own mind. After all, Grace already asked him to stay. What more could I say to him?*

When the sound of little feet on the stairs announced that

naps were finished, Grace was the first to attend to the children. She helped them bundle up snugly and shepherded them outdoors to play, making the most of this sunny respite in the middle of their long winter.

Lillian sighed. What had seemed at first like the pinnacle moment for a swift decision had devolved into a laborious meditation upon what to do next. *God, I'm going to trust You*, she stated once more within her own mind.

• • • • • • •

Walter pushed hard against the wrench as Ben directed him.

If the casing for this part of the motor were ever to be removed in order to grease the moving parts inside, the nut would have to give. "Want a hammer fer that?" Ben suggested. "Sometimes it's all ya can do."

"Yes, please." Walter accepted the tool. The barn filled with the sound of his blows, growing increasingly louder. At last the wrench lurched downward. The rest came easily. "Thanks, Ben. That was just what it needed."

As they twisted and pulled parts off the engine, Ben decided to make use of the time. "So, ya say ya went ta school with 'er? With Miss Lillian, that is."

"Yes, I've known Lillian and her family since first grade."

"But Miss Grace, she weren't here then?"

"No, no. Haven't you heard that story?"

"Well, I heard Miss Grace lived back at the orph'nage. I jus' couldn't figure why. Made no sense ta me, and that's fer certain."

"I'm not surprised. It's quite a strange story." As each part was removed, Walter took them from Ben's hands and laid them carefully on a cloth he'd spread on the ground. With slow and deliberate words the man explained the sisters' background. "Lillian and Grace lived here in this house with their parents when they were very small. That was the Bennetts, George and Suzanne

Bennett. Then they sold the house to a new family—Elliott and Mae Walsh. The girls' parents moved the family to a farm, but they soon contracted tuberculosis and died a year or so later. The girls were separated right away."

"Why's that, then?" Freddie's blunt question interrupted Walter's tale.

"Apparently, it was thought that Grace had also contracted the disease. So Lillian was adopted by the Walshes, and Grace was placed in a sanatorium for the sick. But after they discovered she wasn't ill, she grew up in a series of orphanages, and ended up in Lethbridge." Walter slowed his recitation further. "But Lillian's new mother, Mae Walsh, got some kind of disease. I don't think they ever figured out what it was. Lillian took care of her for a long time, but Mrs. Walsh died a little over a year ago."

Ben watched the man's face. It was clear how deeply Walter felt the woman's loss.

"However, Lillian and her father had no idea that her sister, Grace, was still alive until last summer, just before they were supposed to go away to Wales together. Her father ended up goin' on without her. Lillian stayed here to find Grace instead. Lethbridge is where Lillian eventually tracked her down." Walter smiled with pride. "She seems very quiet and cautious, but she can be a real bulldog when she needs to be."

Ben cleared his throat, hesitated. "Can I ask ya, how d'ya fit in, then, Walter? Are ya . . . ?"

A smile broke out across Walter's face. "Well, I can finally say that I'm Lillian's fiancé. We came to an agreement just last night."

"I see." Ben rose so he could face the man fully. He hesitated. *What do I got ta lose?* "Well, Walter, ya might's well know that I'm leavin' today."

"Oh? How come?"

Ben forced himself not to look away in shame. "Yer gonna get an earful when ya do go inside. They'll tell ya fer sure. An'

I ain't proud'a what I done. 'Fraid the sisters're fair shook up. I don't blame 'em. It ain't a pretty tale."

Leaning back against the car and wiping his hands on a rag, Walter eyed Ben carefully. "What do you mean?"

Recounting the story from the beginning, Ben confessed the long episode to Walter. He gave no excuses. Just a recitation of the problematic details.

The man's eyes grew larger as he listened. At last he commented, "I'm not sure what to say, Ben. Did Grace and Lillian *ask* you to go? That doesn't sound like them at all."

"No, but I can read the writin' on the wall. Better jus' ta take me leave."

"Well, don't go yet," Walter challenged him. "Let them figure out what they'd like to do first. They won't be unfair to you. I'm certain of that."

A sound from Freddie drew their attention. "Didn't sound fair ta me."

Walter shook his head. "This is a tough situation, son. Ben, it's too bad that you didn't have somethin' in writin' to give you the authority to care for the little girl."

Ben stuttered, "I—well, I—I do. I mean, I may. 'Twas an envelope 'mong Janie's things. Looked official ta me. At the time I were so put off with the ol' woman, ne'er paid it no mind—but I kep' it safe. D'ya think . . . ?" Moving toward the trunk of the automobile, where his possessions remained next to Freddie's, Ben dug into his kit bag and produced the envelope that had been pressed inside his book of Shakespeare all this time. The elderly woman had included it among Janie's possessions, and Ben had hidden it away in order to guard the secret. Already he'd smudged it with engine oil. He passed it quickly to Walter, whose hands were cleaner.

With a rustle of paper, the Western man read through the document. A smile quickly broke across his face. His voice rose in pitch. "Are you Ebenezer?"

"Yeah."

"Then this is exactly what you need, Ben! This changes everythin'. And it's got the seal of a law office. The way it's written, I think it was intended more for the woman's benefit than Jane's. But the woman carefully excludes herself from any further responsibility for the child—she gives it all to you. Your name is on it. Right here." He nudged closer to Ben, his finger marking the spot.

Then Walter laughed aloud, snatching up his cowboy hat and tipping it onto his head. "It's legally bindin'. Come on!"

But Ben's feet refused to move. He stood fixed, a stunned expression on his face. Even another nudge from Walter still left him glued to the spot. "What do ya mean?" he finally managed.

"Janie—she's yours—legally."

"Mine?"

"You have full guardianship. That's what this paper gives you."

"Ya ain't lyin'?"

Freddie sprang up on the far side of the car. "Ya mean, you can keep her, Mister Waldin?"

Walter was confident. "We can take it to a solicitor, but that's exactly what it says here."

Ben was ready to move now, Freddie hot on his heels. But rather than heading toward the house, they raced across the yard to the area where the children were playing. Walter followed, still grasping the paper in his hand.

"Janie, Janie!" Ben called as he ran. She turned to look at him, an expression of bewilderment on her face.

When he reached her, he fell on his knees and swept her into his arms. Tears were running down his cheeks even though he knew his face glowed with excitement rather than sorrow. She looked surprised but offered no resistance to his embrace.

"Yer mine, bunny. Got a legal note ta prove it. Yer mine fer good. We're fam'ly. You'll ne'er need ta live in a orph'nage ag'in. Not ever!"

His words seemed to become clear to the young girl. She drew her head back enough to look up into Ben's face, her fingers touching his wet cheeks. "For real?"

He nodded vigorously. "Fer real. Fer good. That note there says it."

Janie looked up quickly at Walter and the paper he was still holding high, then turned back to Ben. Her arms went around his neck. The happy tears on her cheeks mixed with his. "We're family." She turned and loudly announced to the twins, who pushed their way in closer to discover the cause of her excitement, "I have a real family again now."

Freddie let loose a whoop of satisfaction.

• • • • • • •

Miss Tilly had started a pot roast slow-cooking in the oven. Grace sat at the table, peeling parsnips and carrots to add to the heavy Dutch oven. Lillian rose to her feet, planning on carrying the clothing she'd just folded up the stairs to the children's rooms. She paused as she looked out the window. The barn door was wide open. She could see the long end of the new vehicle emerging from it. "Jane told me that Ben is fixing the car. I guess he's still working on it."

"I saw that." Grace rubbed at the loose strands of hair across the back of her neck.

Lillian's eyes traveled to where Walter's car stood in the driveway. "Did you know that Walter's here?"

"I knew he was planning to come by again today. I didn't know he'd already arrived. He must be visiting with Ben outside."

Lillian took a deep breath. "I've been thinking. We've got to face this, Grace. I know that we didn't want to be the ones responsible for cleaning up this mess, but I'm afraid we are. And it's incumbent upon us to see that it's done properly, but with great mercy and love."

Grace lifted her eyes. She seemed surprised to hear such words from her more timid sister.

"I want to share with you what Jane said to me before she went to sleep. She said that Ben is kind, like her father. It made me think of something I hadn't considered yet. What is it that Jane's parents would have us do—if they were here? Wouldn't they just want her to be given to the people who'll keep her safest—love her the most? Don't you think their wishes should matter more than anyone else's? I'm sure they wouldn't have wanted her to be sent to some dark workhouse in England. They would have wanted her to have her best chance to find a new family. And that's just what Ben's given her."

Miss Tilly nodded brusquely. "Amen."

Without speaking, Grace rose from her chair, reached out to wrap her arms around her sister. "You're so right. That's such a good way to look at it all."

The back door opened. Walter entered. Lillian's spirits began to lift until she noticed that Ben, leading Janie, followed him inside—and then the twins and Freddie poured in after them. Something was different. Was it agitation—or excitement? *Oh dear, here we go again.*

Walter motioned everyone toward the table. "Could we sit down? Please?" Even his voice sounded different.

None of the women moved.

Walter said, "I know I haven't been part of these negotiations yet, but I promise you that I have new information to add. Will you let me join you all now? Won't you sit down together?"

The women finally drew back chairs and sat down. Lillian kept her eyes on Walter, surprised at his confidence. *What on earth could he have to add? He's never met Ben before today!*

"All right. Ben told me all about the conflict you're goin' through. He was very forthcoming. Laid it out with great regret, I assure you." Walter's eyes swept around the room. "But then he showed me this." The rather serious expression changed as his eyes lit with an excitement he couldn't hide. He slid an envelope across the table to where Grace and Lillian could read it.

"Doesn't that satisfy what we need to put this all behind us?"

"Just a minute, just a minute." Lillian crowded closer to Grace.

It was difficult for Lillian to focus on yet another legal document. She noticed the signature, read Jane Henry's name in the body of the text. It seemed to have been prepared by the little girl's aunt—*Matilda Henry* was signed in clear script across the bottom of the page. *But who is Ebenezer Waldin? Oh, yes. That's Ben.*

"What is this, Walter?"

"It gives Ben legal custody of Jane. Don't you see? Legally, he could have done anythin' he liked. Kept her with him or placed her with the society. He could even change her name if he chose—which, apparently, he did." Walter shrugged and chuckled a little. "Of course, it would have to be registered. But, anyway, it was all legal. All of it." Walter's voice had risen with his enthusiasm, his words coming uncharacteristically fast.

By now the men's faces were beaming. Ben, who had remained standing next to Janie, seemed about to explode.

"We're family," piped up an excited child's voice as she bounced on the spot. "Mister Waldin an' me. He's going to be my—my—well, I don't really know what he'll be. But he's my family now, for certain."

Lillian searched the document again.

Miss Tilly was the first to lift her voice. "Praise the Lord, He made a way!"

Walter moved before Lillian could speak. He came close to her chair, lowered to a crouching position so that he could look directly into her eyes. "It's all right, Lillian. You don't have to worry about this anymore. God took care of it already, long before you asked Him for an answer."

Leaning forward, Lillian wilted into his arms. She'd forgotten everyone else in the room.

Chapter 27

Growth

The engine shuddered again as Freddie cranked it into motion. But the hum that followed gave clear indication that they'd finally tamed the beast. Ben reached for the hood and pulled it down into place.

"Well, we done it, Freddie. Thanks fer yer help, lad."

He received an answering nod. Then, "What are we goin' ta do, Mister Waldin? Are we stayin'?"

Ben had needed to vacate the house after their discussion with the sisters. He needed time to process everything that had been said. And the repair he'd begun in the barn had once more given him the perfect excuse. He slapped Freddie on the back. "She's mine, ya know. Me little Jane Henry. An' none can take 'er away. That's what the note said."

The boy was less than enthusiastic.

"What's wrong with ya?" Ben prodded.

Silence.

He considered the significance of the recent disclosure to Freddie's situation. "It don't change things fer us, lad. D'ya un'erstand?"

With the toe of his worn boot, Freddie pushed at the straw that was strewn across the floor. "Guess I'll find somewhere ta go."

"Why?"

"If yer not gonna stay, I don't wanna be here. I ain't gonna let 'em stick me with no fam'ly. Said I'd run away an' I meant it."

"Now, lad, I'm not sendin' ya away. Ya got ta go ta school. Ya got ta lift yerself outta the life ya've knowed."

"It ain't like that, sir. I ain't like you."

Ben rubbed his hands on a rag. "Lad, sit down." He motioned to a bale of hay that rested nearby.

"Have I ne'er tol' ya 'bout how dim-witted I was at yer age? How I run away from a home where I was loved jus' 'cause I got so full'a meself I couldn't make room fer others ta see life in any way other 'an me own?"

Freddie nodded his head, regarding Ben intently.

"I shouldn'ta left me home, lad. Was pride what caused it—me own stubborn pride."

"But ya went ta sea. An' ya loved the sea, didn't ya say?"

"I said it. It's true. But what I didn't tell ya is this . . . the sea don't love ya back, lad. It can't. Can only bear ya ta excitin' new worlds and bring ya back—or it can swallow ya up in a watery grave. I seen both. An' it'll break ya as easy as carryin' ya on. But it'll ne'er love ya back, lad."

Freddie's voice had weakened. "But ya had yer freedom, yeah?"

"Yeah. But I give up all that." Ben lifted his chin toward the house. "Just like them folk what care an' worry an' strive. I give up me own sister who'da laid down her soul ta save mine. That ain't no trade ta make. I were a stupid fool, lad."

"No, sir." Freddie was beginning to draw himself away. "That ain't what fam'ly does. It takes an' it takes. An' ya can't save 'em, even when ya want'a."

Unable to restrain himself, Ben knelt in the straw beside Freddie. "What happened, son? Ta yer fam'ly? What'd ya see?"

The young face contorted as at last the boy spat out the words.

"He burned 'em! That's what he did! Not on purpose, maybe so. But he did it jus' the same. 'Cause it was his own liquor what started the fire. Kicked it o'er as he left, he did. I saw it! Then he stood in the yard an' watched the house go up in flames."

"So then, yer hands, lad? That's how ya got them burns?"

Freddie dropped his chin against his heaving chest, the ruined palms he'd kept so well hidden now spread open in his lap. "I couldn't do it, Mister Waldin. I tried ta heave open the door. But he hadn't fixed it. It always stuck. 'Cause he ne'er fixed nothin'!"

Anger and agony were filling Ben's chest. "Well, I ain't leavin'," Ben assured the weeping boy, suddenly certain the words were true. "Stay with me. We can help one another. Don't matter if we three live here, or if we go ta find me sister t'gether. I love ya, Freddie. An' I ain't gonna leave ya. I'm goin' ta take ya with me." He put a hand on the boy's leg. "Ya see, I know it don't matter to ya what them soci'ty folk tell ya ta do. 'Cause you'll just run after me anyhow." His hand squeezed tighter on the boy's knee as he tried to make him see the humor of it all. "I may as well jus' plan fer ya ta come along."

"Yes, sir," Freddie finally admitted. "I'd do it like that. I wouldn't stay without ya."

Ben slapped the side of the boy's leg. "Go set yer traps now, lad. Ya got time 'nough fer that."

"Yes, sir," he answered, wiping a sleeve across his eyes.

After watching the boy walk away, Ben began the less desirable task of putting away the tools, setting the workspace back into order, even sweeping out the trampled straw.

The sound of someone clearing her throat spun him toward the front of the building.

A petite form stood in the barn doorway, dwarfed by the size of the opening. "I'm sorry. I didn't mean to startle you, Ben."

Even though the bright light surrounding her filled his eyes, he recognized Grace at once.

"I'm done, miss. I was jus' cleanin' up. I can be on me way soon."

"Oh no." She hurried forward. "Surely you don't think we'd let you get away from us now. It's all over, Ben. There's no reason for you to leave." She was oddly insistent.

"But ya wouldn't want me ta stay, miss. Not after all this terr'ble mess."

"Listen, please. I'll tell you why I've come. I'd like to invite you to live here. But I wanted to say that I do understand if you *choose* to leave—if you choose to pursue your family instead. It's so important to have a family. I'd have gone to the ends of the earth if I'd known I could see my parents again." She blushed, as if her frank words had left her feeling exposed. "Ben, what I came to say is that I want to help you. You've done so much for all of us. And—and I'd like to feel as if we hadn't left our end of things so deeply in your debt."

"You ain't in me debt, Miss Grace. I'm priv'leged ta know ya."

She stepped closer, forced a slip of paper into his hand.

Ben looked down in surprise. It was cash. A bill with a dollar amount larger than he'd ever seen. "No, miss. I can't take it."

"You can. You should. It'll help you find your sister—your parents."

Ben pushed it back toward her. "It's diff'rent now. I gotta think'a Freddie an' little Janie. I can't be runnin' no more. I ne'er wanted roots, but they grew up under me jus' the same."

"I'm glad, Ben." Grace's eyes misted. "I'm so glad." She folded the money back into her sleeve. "Then, you'll stay with us? I'm sure we can find a way."

"Can't make no promises. But . . . I got no other plan."

"That's good." She sighed. "We'll—I don't know what to offer you—we'll make you a room in the attic or the basement. We'll figure it out somehow."

Ben's eyes lifted to the nearby room in the corner of the barn. It had a small stove that long ago had been used to heat the workspace. With a little weatherproofing he wondered if it wouldn't be enough. He chose to hold his tongue.

"We'll find *some way* to fit you in. And if we do, perhaps we'll be able to keep Freddie too. He needs some stability in these difficult years. He needs to go to school."

"I tol' him just that, miss. Not ten minutes past."

Reaching a soft hand to close over his wrist, she added, "Thank you, Ben. I'm so relieved to hear you'll stay. But we won't forget about your family. None of us. Surely we'll be able to help you in your search somehow."

"Thank ya, miss."

Turning to leave, Grace called over her shoulder, "Supper won't be long. Miss Tilly just took the pot roast out to rest it. She's making gravy. I'll send Janie to fetch you soon."

"Thank ya, miss."

Ben went directly to the trunk of the car. Lifting the lid, he removed his kit bag and then the boy's case. He carried them across the barn to the room he'd discovered before. He'd already swept it out, set aside discarded items to tidy it as he returned the tools to the shelf in order to leave it in better order than he'd found it. Now he nodded to himself. *This'll do. With the boards out back, I can fix it up right. Me an' the boy'll be jus' fine in here. Might shore it up with some'a them bales out back too.* He smiled. *An' maybe, maybe sometime soon, Freddie'll figure it wouldn't hurt him ta move into the house. Think I'd like that fer him.*

• • • ● • • •

Supper now involved the use of two tables. Miss Tilly insisted that the adults and Freddie would use the formal dining room, determined that she'd supervise the three small children in the kitchen. It was no use arguing. She'd already made up her mind. She even asserted that it made her job of cooking and serving easier with fewer bodies crowding around the kitchen table as she worked.

Lillian sat beside Walter at Mother's table, looked across at Grace and Freddie. Ben sat at the head. Still, he chose to serve, making several trips back and forth to the kitchen.

Their conversation came easily. Walter was the key to it all. Without his presence Lillian knew the difficulties that had so recently ambushed them would be nothing less than impossible to set aside. She was grateful for his presence, hoping against hope that he'd remain in Brookfield. *Should I mention the large sum of money again? What would he say? Would he be offended? Would he accept my portion of the inheritance in order to help us set up a home together sooner? Oh, I hope so!*

Just as Ben returned from the kitchen with a platter of bowls for dessert, a knock came at the door.

"What on earth is it now?" Immediately, Lillian wished she hadn't made such a statement aloud. It had sounded terribly impolite. She followed with, "Excuse me, please. I'll just get the door."

It was Byron McRae, Ernest and Sophie's oldest son, with a telegram. "An' I brung yer mail, too, miss. Mama said to."

"Thank you, Byron. Please tell your parents thank you from us."

"Night, Miss Walsh."

Lillian carried the telegram back to the table. Every instinct she felt at first told her not to open it. It couldn't be anything good. But she met Walter's eyes and said as confidently as she was able, "It's a telegram. I suppose it's good news."

Grace laughed aloud. "Well said, sis! Why don't you open it now?"

Lillian drew the slip of paper from its envelope, encouraged immediately as she announced, "It's from Father! And it's so long!" Then she boldly read it aloud. "*DO AS YOU WISH WITH YOUR MONEY—STOP—TRUST YOU AND WATTLEY—*

STOP—DELYTH AND I COMING HOME NEXT MONTH—STOP—WILL STAY IN TOWN—STOP—LOVE FATHER."

Lillian lowered the paper. "What a strange thing to say. He's bringing Delyth with him?"

"Who's Delyth?" asked Walter.

Lillian shook her head. "Father has mentioned him in his letters. They've become good friends. They've been hiking together. And he went along with Father to the lectures in Scotland."

As Lillian lowered herself into her chair next to Walter again, he suggested softly, hesitantly, "Are you entirely certain that Delyth is a man? I mean, did your father actually say so?"

"What do you mean? He's a cousin. Father said he's a distant cousin."

Walter seemed to be stifling a smile. "Well, look, is it possible . . . I mean, is there any chance at all that you misunderstood? That Delyth is a—woman?"

Grace muttered, "A woman? Why would Lillian's father bring a . . . Oh dear."

"What? What do you mean? Father wouldn't travel with a woman unless they were . . ." Lillian flashed the paper back up where she could read it aloud again. "'Will stay in town'? What? No. He must mean that his cousin Delyth will stay there—in town. That's how I understood it the first time. That's what he means. Don't you think?"

Grace's eyes grew large. "I think you should read through those old letters again, sis. I'd watch pretty carefully what pronoun your father uses to refer to his friend."

"Stop it. I don't appreciate you teasing me like this. My father would never . . . He wouldn't!"

Against her will, a voice within Lillian's head began to chide her, the echo of her own words reciting themselves back to her. *I'm going to be brave like Grace. I can paddle forward, too, into unforeseen waters. I trust Father—with whatever—even if—*

And suddenly, from somewhere deep inside, laughter bubbled up. The sensation of humor greeting such surprising news instead of fear came as a tremendous relief. She began to laugh. Her amusement spread around the table as each person joined in her mirth. Even Freddie smiled, his eyes moving around the table with a mixture of surprise and enjoyment.

Epilogue

"Father will arrive tomorrow. And everything will change." Lillian whispered the words aloud as she dressed in preparation for supper guests, shivering in the second-floor bedroom. An early summer storm was descending from over the mountains.

Lifting her customary gray wool skirt from its hook behind the door, she stepped into it carefully, drew it upward, and fastened it around her waist. Then, pushing her arms into her best printed blouse, which was clearly showing signs of wear, Lillian tucked and smoothed the garments properly, tossing a warm sweater over all.

"Father will bring back the rest of my clothing with him. That'll be a relief." She still wondered why he hadn't agreed just to ship the crate back home after it had become clear that Lillian would not follow him to Wales at all. Was it a practical decision as he'd claimed, concern that her wardrobe would be lost in transit? Or merely stubbornness? In truth, Father could be rather set in his decisions. *Never mind, I've been fine without all those clothes.*

With a sigh, she let her eyes move around the room. Father had written that "for the time being" Lillian should remain in the master bedroom. His final telegram had asserted that he would keep his reservations at the hotel in town until the path forward had been considered carefully.

Lillian's mind tumbled. She wished again that she could have spoken to him. It seemed that Father was reluctant to place a telephone call now that he was back in Canada. *I know him. I know he wants to wait to discuss all the changes in person. He wouldn't want to risk an upsetting conversation when he is still so many miles away. He means it as a kindness.*

There was a commotion in the foyer below. A last quick twist of her auburn hair, a couple of pins, and Lillian was ready to join the rest for dinner. Walter was expected, as well as Lemuel and Harrison. She wondered which of them had just arrived.

But as Lillian descended the stairs, she realized the sounds were not a joyful welcoming of guests. Her pace quickened.

"I don't know. That's all they said." The voice was Harrison's, and he was breathing hard.

And then Miss Tilly's answer came more calmly. "Where'd ya see 'em, son? How far down the road?"

Lillian rounded the corner to the landing, eyes sweeping the foyer. Grace was already throwing a coat around her shoulders, and Ben and Walter were pushing their feet into boots.

"What's happened?"

"Oh, sis, they've gone. The pair of them. It seems they've run away."

Instantly, Lillian knew without asking which of the society children would attempt such a desperate act.

"They went together?"

"Yes, yes," Grace answered. "Stay here. We'll get the car started and search for them." She paused at the door, turning back to instruct, "Pray for us, please. Pray for them! It's so dark out with the storm moving in. It'll take an act of God to find them tonight."

Silence fell as the door closed. For the first time Lillian noticed the youngsters crowded together in the parlor doorway.

"Come along, Jane, boys." She drew them forward with gentle hands. "I expect Miss Grace and the men will find them. Let's go eat our dinner and we'll pray that God will keep them safe."

However, even after dinner had been accomplished there was no word. The wind had become shrill before Lillian tucked the children into bed and returned to the kitchen, where Miss Tilly was seated at the table, hands folded in prayer. Her eyes opened when Lillian took the chair beside her.

Lillian found herself articulating aloud the one question that could not be stilled inside of her. "Why, Miss Tilly? Why do these dreadful things keep happening?"

Two workworn hands moved to cover her own, squeezing tightly. "Why'd we have ta go through them things in the past, dear? I guess 'cause now we know what we learnt then. If we hadn'ta learnt it, we wouldn't be set fer this. God leads us forward one step at a time, readyin' an' growin' us for what comes next."

Bestselling author **Janette Oke** is celebrated for her significant contribution to the Christian book industry. Her novels have sold more than thirty million copies, and she is the recipient of the ECPA President's Award, the CBA Life Impact Award, the Gold Medallion, and the Christy Award. Janette and her husband, Edward, live in Alberta, Canada.

Laurel Oke Logan, daughter of Edward and Janette Oke, is the author of several books, including *Janette Oke: A Heart for the Prairie*, *Dana's Valley*, and the RETURN TO THE CANADIAN WEST series, cowritten with her mom. Laurel has six children and several grandchildren and lives in Illinois.

More from Janette Oke and Laurel Oke Logan

In this sweeping companion to the Hallmark TV series *When Hope Calls*, Lillian Walsh rushes to a reunion after discovering the sister she believed dead is likely alive. But Grace has big dreams beyond anything Lillian is prepared for. Can Lillian set aside her own plans and join her sister in an adventure that will surely change them both?

Unyielding Hope by Janette Oke and Laurel Oke Logan
WHEN HOPE CALLS #1

When new schoolteacher Beth Thatcher is assigned a post in a remote mining community, her courage—and her heart—will be tested in ways she never expected. Based on the Hallmark Channel Original Series *When Calls the Heart.*

Where Courage Calls by Janette Oke and Laurel Oke Logan
RETURN TO THE CANADIAN WEST #1

You May Also Like . . .

After turning the tables on a crooked gambler, Larkspur Nielsen flees her home with her sisters on a wagon train bound for Oregon. Knowing four women will draw unwanted attention, she dons a disguise as a man. But maintaining the ruse is harder than she imagined, as is protecting her sisters from difficult circumstances and eligible young men.

The Seeds of Change by Lauraine Snelling
Leah's Garden #1
laurainesnelling.com

After smallpox kills her mother and siblings, Gloriana Womack is dedicated to holding together what's left of her fractured family. Luke Carson arrives in Duluth to shepherd the arrival of the railroad and reunite with his brother. When tragedy strikes, Gloriana and Luke must help each other through their grief and soon find their lives inextricably linked.

Destined for You by Tracie Peterson
Ladies of the Lake #1
traciepeterson.com

BethanyHouse